SOREN'S LEGACY

Painted Wings Publishing

Soren's Legacy

Copyright © 2022 by J. Houser.

This book is a work of fiction. Names, characters, businesses, organizations, places, events and incidents either are the product of the author's imagination or are used fictitiously. Any resemblance to actual persons, living or dead, events, or locales is entirely coincidental.

For more information, visit: JHouserWrites.com

Cover design by Jervy Bonifacio

ISBN:

978-1-957334-00-4 (ebook)

978-1-957334-03-5 (paperback)

978-1-957334-04-2 (hardback)

First Edition: September 2022

10 9 8 7 6 5 4 3 2

Note from the Author

Some of us don't get happy endings, because life doesn't always work that way. But … when possible, I *do* like my characters to have a little more resolution than Leah got in her debut, *The Heir of Exile*.

Will she have a rough go of it? Would it be Leah if she didn't?

This one's for all of us who sometimes get in our own way, who fortune oft forgets to smile on, and for the people in our lives who keep loving us, who don't give up on us.

~J. Houser

Don't forget to sign up for my newsletter to get updates on future publications, promotions, and bonus content! (Including a FREE download of "Son & Soldier: A Seeder Short Story" at JHouserWrites.com)

Book-related merch can also be purchased on my author website!

Content Warning

Select topics in this novel may be more difficult for some readers. These topics include: grief/loss, violence/murder, suicide, ableism, racism, and sexual assault.

Other than grief/loss and mild ableism, the others are only discussed in passing; they are not portrayed on page.

Pronunciation Guide:

<u>People</u>

Acacia: uh-KAY-shuh

Beata: bay-AH-tuh

Boman/Bomen: BOW-man

Camry: CAM-ree

Eleana: el-ee-AH-nuh

    (**Leah:** LEE-uh)

Elanna: ee-LAWN-nuh

Elonta: ee-LAWN-tuh

Elonto: ee-LAWN-toe

Grayas: GRAY-us

Guillen: GUY-en

Kaylah: KAY-luh

Lycha: LIE-kuh

Murialsdotter:

    MYUR-ee-ulz-daughter

Piot: PEA-oat

Scanlon: SCAN-lun

Tain: TAYn

Tobias: toe-BYE-us

    (**Toby:** TOE-bee)

<u>Places & Things</u>

Sanath: SAN-uth

Selen: SELL-en

SOREN'S LEGACY

J. HOUSER

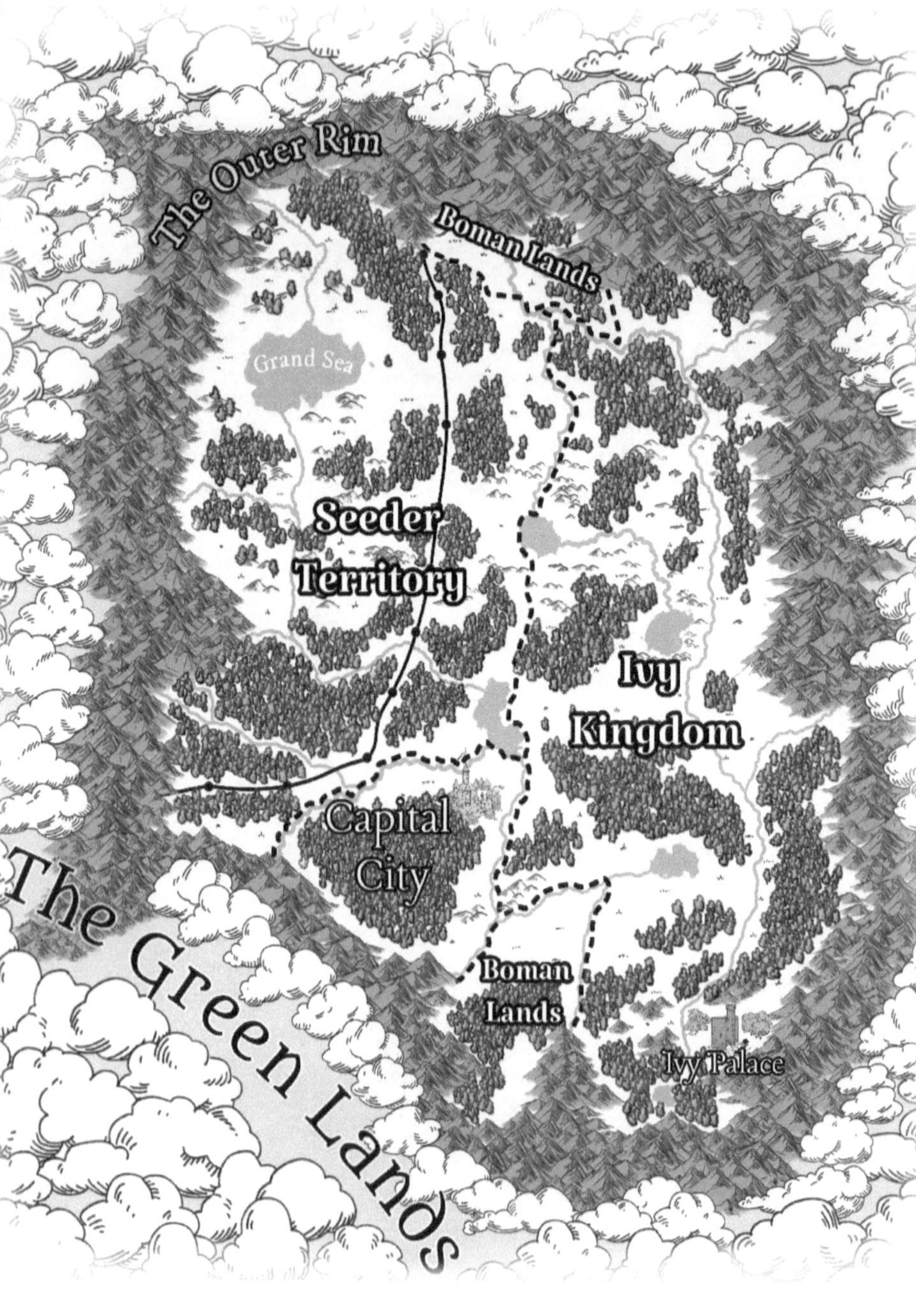

The Outer Rim
Boman Lands
Grand Sea
Seeder Territory
Ivy Kingdom
Capital City
Boman Lands
Ivy Palace
The Green Lands

Prologue

LEAH STOOD OUTSIDE THE IVY PRISON, trying to keep herself together. It was supposed to have been a normal visit with her mom. A run-of-the-mill regular visit.

And now, she was sweating and trying to breathe as she pieced together what her mom had just said, what she'd let slip, and the implications it held for Leah.

Leah wasn't going to cry. She didn't like crying. She was simply overthinking things…

But even her mother had realized the truth had hurt her, and that was before Leah had really let it sink in, before she'd cut their visit short, before she'd left the building to stand here trying not to spiral.

She hugged herself, leaning against the stone building.

I'm fine. It's fine. It's not a big deal.

She could bury those feelings, that secret, bury them so hard she could pretend she'd never felt them, had never heard it.

How many other feelings had she buried in the past?

Her mother had asked her not to share it with anyone else, anyway.

Jamming her eyelids closed, Leah thought of other things. Marcus… Sunshine… Lightning bugs… She breathed slowly in and out. It wasn't that big of a deal, really.

"Are you alright, miss?" her escort, Wren, asked from around the corner where she'd asked him to stay.

"I'm fine."

Drawing a deep breath, she forced a smile on her face.

I'll be fine. It meant nothing.

Secrets couldn't hurt anyone if no one knew them.

Chapter 1

Weeks Later

LEAH HAD ROYALLY SCREWED THINGS UP. Two years ago, that is. But she'd come a long way since then. Lots of learning, and no new assassination attempts on the Ivy queen or anyone else.

She now wore more 'appropriate' clothing for someone of her station. And her station? The ward of Queen Catrina and King Stephan.

She'd learned how to don a polite smile through almost any situation (including the lesson she was currently zoning out in), how to pretend to be interested in politicians' conversations, and how to give the rote responses people expected from her on any given occasion.

That was the thing—she'd screwed up by trying to kill Queen Kaylah, and despite her attempts to better herself, it seemed the realm would never let Leah forget that mistake. Or her parentage.

'Soren's heir,' someone had snidely called her once. Her dad had been a prince. He would have become an earl, had he not been executed for stealing the throne and naming himself king. Had he not had his title stripped from him at the time of his execution. It had all happened while Leah's mom had been pregnant with her. Many people assumed Leah had taken after her parents, and that her sad attempt at killing Kaylah had meant she'd been trying to take the throne.

"Miss Elonto?"

Leah looked up, her heart skipping a beat. She'd definitely zoned out again, but her gentle perma-smile was still there.

The instructor must have noticed she'd checked out. "What did you think of the performance, Miss Elonto?"

She cleared her throat, her palms sweaty. "It was beautiful." It truly had been. Leah only attended the local academy part time, while the rest of her education was carried out by private tutors, usually at the palace. Today at the academy, a troupe of cultural dancers had come to perform. The performance, complete with Ivy vines and acrobatics, had been elegant, but nothing she hadn't seen at the palace before.

"It was, wasn't it?" Skye said, giving Leah a reassuring smile.

Skye was there to save Leah again. But a true friend? Probably not. Leah now had a few 'friends' here in the Ivy Kingdom, in the Green Lands realm. They were really more of acquaintances, and Leah was pretty sure they were there for her only as a personal favor to her instructors or the queen.

Obligatory pals were not the kind of friends anyone really wanted.

After a while longer discussing the performance, the topic returned to women's studies in the Ivy Kingdom, and the state of current affairs. Women hadn't necessarily been *unequally* subjugated before Queen Kaylah's rule, but their powers had been suppressed, ignored, or undiscovered compared to what they now were.

Having grown up in hiding in the human world, Leah hadn't learned much about who she was or what she was capable of until she met her boyfriend and other green folk like them. Part of why Leah hadn't learned more about herself had been her mother's fault, as the usurper's wife living in exile. Another part of it had been her mother's lack of knowledge and expertise about female Ivy powers.

Leah found this topic particularly empowering. Ivy girls were now taught much more thoroughly than they used to be about all their powers. Rifting, coagulation, fertilizing, numbing—to name a few. And of course vine maneuvering.

Women's education was a heated topic in some Ivy circles. As recently as two decades ago, the schoolboys had been required to take extra classes while the girls sat them out. Now it was the other way around. Since the Ivy Kingdom no longer trained young boys to be assassins in the human world, their course loads had been slimmed down. Respectively, the discovery of extra female Ivy powers by Queen Kaylah now meant the girls had more classes to take. Some saw it as a burden they shouldn't have to deal with. Others felt it was their right to be taught in every aspect of their powers.

Leah was nineteen now, trying to figure out what she was going to do with the rest of her life. Advocating for girls being taught the full extent of their powers was something she could get behind.

Sure, she'd floundered when trying to fit in in the human world, and her grand introduction to her home realm had been far from ideal, but she wasn't ungrateful for what she was now being offered.

Queen Catrina made sure Leah's every need was seen to. She allowed her a certain level of autonomy, though not as much as Leah would like. As the queen and king's ward, Leah was afforded the best education, the most elegant opportunities, and was reassured they would help her step out on her own someday.

Once class ended, Leah said her goodbyes to her instructor and her 'friends.' They had long since learned she wasn't a hugger.

Leah's personal escort—her security detail—stuck by her side once she exited the classroom. They walked silently down the second-floor hallways of the brick academy. Other students nodded at her and her escort as they passed, not all of them making eye contact.

She was mostly numb to that kind of thing now. She'd usually been the kind to pass under the radar in the human world, at least when she wasn't getting in trouble. Now, she couldn't hide, no matter how much she wanted to. The occasional scathing remark reached her ear, muttered purposefully loud enough to bother her. But the majority of criticism about Leah reached her by accident— the gossip of classmates from outside her toilet stall, or the comment of a dignitary around the corner in the palace.

Though, most signs of disapproval for Leah's very existence were much more subtle than words. It was in the averted gaze in the hallway, the pointing and cowering child in the marketplace, the strangers who would cross the lane when they saw her and her escort coming, the Seeders that would look her dead in the eye and flash green eyes at her, or the poorly attended Boman events she'd dared to make an appearance at.

Her boyfriend's mom, Rachel, had once called Leah's dad a monster. He had been. Not in the comical ghoulish way, but a genuine piece of living garbage. And Leah's mom, Beata, had turned a blind eye to the atrocities he'd committed, and had even helped him commit crimes. She was still in prison, serving her life sentence.

Sometimes Leah felt like she might as well wear a black sash, the words *Monsters' Daughter* embroidered with bright red thread.

But everyone already knew who she was.

Leah politely waved at a few classmates as she and her escort left the building. Guys were civil, but none of them even tried to talk to her. It was also public knowledge that she and Marcus had been back together for some time.

Just the thought of him made her smile. As did the thought of him visiting her at the palace for the weekend. And the thought of the plans they'd hatched.

"Are you needing anything from the market or elsewhere before returning home, miss?" her escort asked.

"Yes. I did want to swing by the market."

As they strolled down cobblestone streets, Leah ignored the people around her, the noise, the beautiful weather.

As much as she'd become a recluse and hated being around people because of the constant scrutiny, she enjoyed the freedom of being away from the palace. No officials or servants, or little princes or princesses underfoot. No one correcting her posture or language.

Once they arrived at the small nearby market, Leah quickly zeroed in on what she wanted. Marcus was in charge of bringing something for his visit that she couldn't get away with buying, not with her constant escort. She was only responsible for pampering herself this time.

Needing to not be too obvious about her desired purchases, she took some time browsing under the awnings of each vendor. She sniffed a few perfumes, wanting something new for the special weekend. Today was almost exactly two years since Marcus had taken her back after the whole assassination fiasco. They were celebrating their anniversary.

Another shopper stepped close to Leah, reaching for a bottle of perfume. Leah's escort cut her off.

"Please allow for some space, ma'am."

The woman looked at Leah, then rolled her eyes. "Last I checked, this is a free kingdom, and she *isn't* actually royalty." She stalked away.

"Sorry," Leah weakly called after her. She didn't bother with more than that, since the woman continued to walk away.

Leah couldn't win. There had never been a right answer for what should happen to her. She didn't like that she still had an escort every time she left the palace, especially since many people felt she didn't deserve the attention, or that the kingdom's resources shouldn't be used to pay for her security detail. But the fact of the matter was … some people still wanted her dead. She'd come a long way in the last two years, but the bullseye on her back may never go away.

It had been a gutting day when she'd had that conversation with the queen and king. She'd felt confident in her ability to protect herself against an attack, but they'd confessed they'd received multiple death threats against Leah. Some people thought she ought to have been executed as an example for trying to kill Kaylah. Many thought she embodied and embraced the twisted beliefs and prejudices of her parents. Given that fact, Leah didn't feel safe venturing out on her own.

She picked a rose-scented perfume and reached for the money in her silk satchel. After plucking out the coins needed, she hefted them in her hand, reluctant. None of this money was hers. She couldn't exactly get a job at a burger joint to earn her keep right now.

Servants, guards, food, clothes—all paid for by the Crown.

Leah glanced at her escort. Even though they were probably necessary, they drew so much attention to her. And perhaps it *was* over the top.

You should put the perfume back. You don't deserve it. You already have some at home.

And she really didn't need to buy anything at the market herself. She could have had a servant add it to their shopping list. To avoid a much longer trip back to the palace, she ought to only purchase the bare minimum, due to rifting limitations.

Moments away from putting the money back in her satchel and returning the bottle, Leah decided against it. This was a special celebration. She wanted to pick the perfume out herself, and it wasn't like it was that large.

She wouldn't steal it, either. She hadn't ever stolen anything in the Green Lands, not that the itch didn't come now and then. It took a massive amount of resolve in times like this to not scratch that itch, but she was determined to make a new life for herself, and to not undo all the hard work she'd put into her image.

Handing over the coins, she thanked the seller, then slipped the bottle into her satchel.

A few minutes later, Leah scoured the shelves at a clothing vendor's booth. Her escort gave her a little space as she surveyed the unmentionables. She quickly found something thin and cute, and paid for it, again tucking it into her satchel.

"Alright, I'm ready to go home."

***

Leah walked through the cave rift—the one closest to the palace, right on the edge of the Mother Vine protective border.

She hadn't returned to the human world in the last two years, though they now trusted she wouldn't run away, and Catrina and Stephan had issued her a passport and fake human ID in case she did want to go at some point. She was an adult now. But she didn't have anything to go back to in the human world.

Each footstep toward the palace was refreshing, exciting. She had a bounce in her step as she mused on the new purchases in her satchel, and her plans for that night.

As they neared the side entrance she usually used, a handsome figure leaned against the stone doorway. Brown curly locks framed a smiling face. His arms were crossed against his chest.

Leah ran to him, squealing.

"Hey, beautiful," Marcus said, opening his arms.

She squeezed him tight, breathing in his cologne. Marcus was her home, her person. The day to her night. She never smiled as widely or as genuinely as she did when she was with him. And she almost always had to wait until the weekends to see him.

He released her and kissed her on the cheek. "Let's head inside."

They didn't particularly care for the palace guards to watch their reunions, and her escort had already stepped inside. The moment Leah and Marcus entered the massive stone building and the door shut, he pulled her close, not allowing an inch between them, laying a kiss on her. She dug her hands into his hair, pressing against him.

Marcus was happiness. He was hope. He was everything to Leah.

He'd meant so much to her back in the human world, but he was so much more to her now. His kindness and forgiving nature were unparalleled.

After a minute, he leaned back, catching his breath and resting his hands on her hips. "That dress is stunning."

She grinned. She'd specifically chosen this one to see him in. It was light and flowy, with a soft pink floral print. "You say that about all my dresses."

He grinned in return. "Then it must be the girl in the dress who's stunning."

She gave him another smooch. "I love you."

"Love you too."

As much as she wanted to kiss his lips for days, and do a few other things, there was a guard or servant lurking around the corner. There always was, on Catrina's orders, to supervise the two of them.

Leah rolled her shoulder to keep her satchel's cord from slipping. "I picked up something special to celebrate our anniversary."

He arched an eyebrow. "Really? What is that?"

She leaned in, planting a kiss on his neck. "I guess you'll find out, if our timing is right."

He slid his hands onto her lower back. "I will be doing *everything* in my power to make sure that timing is right."

There had been plotting between the two. And if they'd worked it all out right, there would *finally* be passion.

Chapter 2

Two Weeks Later

LEAH SAT IN AN ARMCHAIR in her chambers, staring at the wall, more than a little sick to her stomach. Her heart raced. Marcus was coming for his weekly visit to the palace.

She was excited to see him, and dreading it at the same time. Things had been good between them. Great, in fact. Two years ago, they'd started off slow, taking almost three whole months to kiss after he forgave her for using him. Marcus still lived with his parents, and was studying under his father, Guillen, and other leaders, wanting to make his own way, working in law and public policy.

Leah had done a lot of pondering over the last little while. Sure, some people would never approve of her, but she wanted to make a name for herself, as Marcus had once challenged her to do. She wanted to be an expert with her powers, and teach other girls and women to do the same. At least she had *thought* that was what she wanted.

But things were about to change.

Leah was used to change. Not that she liked it, or was good at it, but that had been how she'd had to live her life on the run. The most difficult change she'd ever made was moving to the Green Lands after discovering her parents' true identities. She still visited her mom in prison once a month. She'd only visited her dad in the royal graveyard once—that had been all she'd ever wanted or needed after discovering the truth of the man.

This particular change might not be quite that big of a revelation and shift in her way of life, but it was right up there. Leah hadn't told anyone yet, but she was pregnant. Ivy women were able to tell very early, and Leah couldn't deny the signs.

A knock sounded on her door, and Leah forced herself to stand and open it.

"He's here, miss," Robyn, her favorite servant, announced.

Leah forced a smile. "Thank you." She followed Robyn out, calming her breathing. She had to tell Marcus tonight. He deserved to know. They needed to figure things out.

Robyn led her to the smaller sitting room, where Marcus waited with a giant smile. He jumped up and pulled Leah in close.

"I missed you!" he said.

"You too." She bit her lip.

He placed his hands on her hips and laid a reunion kiss on her like he always did. Dating in the Green Lands was hard if you didn't live close. You couldn't simply text or call; it was archaic.

"Sorry I'm late." He tucked a strand of hair behind her ear.

"You're fine. Just in time for dinner."

"Mmm. Anything good on the menu tonight?" He sat back down on the sofa and guided her onto his lap.

Leah straightened her dress. At first, she'd felt silly wearing dresses so much, just because people associated that with a 'proper' lady living at the palace, but she'd warmed up to them.

I'll have to sort my closet to wear bigger sizes. Ivy pregnancies only lasted eight months, and she was two weeks along.

She tried to focus on the moment at hand. "Um, the menu… Chef Kristoff's best stew, I believe."

"Delicious. Almost as delicious as you are." He grinned, then snuck another kiss.

Her heart couldn't handle his flirtations, and luckily, she didn't have to respond.

Another servant entered. "Dinner is served."

Leah and Marcus held hands as they strolled to the dining hall. Meals at the palace were always a mixed bag. The queen and king had three little kids, with a fourth on the way. You never knew when family members would swing by, or when they'd be hosting government officials or dignitaries. Luckily, tonight would be pretty quiet. Other than the northern Boman ambassador there for the night, it would only be the royal family, Leah, and Marcus.

She had remembered right that the stew was being served. Leah stirred it in her bowl, picking out the potatoes first. Conversation was lively amongst everyone but Leah, though she tried to contribute. She paid particular attention to the ambassador. He lived in one of the Boman colonies, by choice. A blond in his thirties, he wore a wedding ring. She perked up when he mentioned having kids. That was what this child would be—a Boman, born without powers. The gene that caused the condition popped up randomly and was rare in the general populace, but Bomanism was always passed down to the children of a Boman.

Leah glanced at Marcus; he conversed easily, talking about his recent studies. Her chest only hurt more at how excited he was about a new internship opportunity.

She had always been bad for him. Even though she'd spent the last two years trying to reinvent herself, and had finally seemed to find her way, she was going to hurt him. People who loved his family hated Leah. People who loved Leah's parents hated Marcus and his family. Not that it was anyone's freaking business what they did or who they loved, and not that they had social media or tabloids in the Green Lands, but green folk knew how to gossip.

The rumor mill was always pumping out something about Leah, and about their relationship. Sadly, most of the rumors about Leah were actually true. Even *she* sometimes followed the logic and questioned why Marcus was still with her.

Leah picked up her roll, nibbling tiny pieces as well as she could manage. There was a lull in conversation, so she spoke up. "Ambassador Grayas, what's it like raising Bomen in the colonies?"

The man addressed her with a smile. "I suppose it depends on who you ask. Some say we're doing an injustice by 'separating' them from their peers with powers. But you'd have to be blind to say everything is equal in the main territories, even after all this time." He turned to the queen and king, bowing his head. "No offense, Your Majesties."

Catrina and Stephan nodded. They may be a bit strict for Leah's liking, but they were always polite and proper.

Catrina dabbed her mouth with a napkin. "That's why we're always pleased to get feedback from you. It's easier to say than do, when it comes to laws and education for such a small minority."

Look at me—helping with the numbers game. Adding to the Boman population, and we're only nineteen. Leah swallowed another bite of roll before taking a swig of water.

"And how are things for non-Bomen living out there?" She'd considered a dozen options already for her unexpected new future, but life in Boman lands was sadly not something she could seriously entertain.

Ambassador Grayas smiled again. "It may be wishful thinking on my part, but I'd like to believe non-Bomen enjoy living there, too. Takes some getting used to, away from the kingdom, but we each have our reasons."

She appreciated his kindness and smiles. She didn't get those from many adult Bomen. Leah's grandparents on her mother's side had been in charge of the 'stunt' communities, the old quasi slave communities. One of the few blessings of having her mom lie to her her entire childhood, keeping her true identity as an Ivy from her, was that her mom's bigotry hadn't rubbed off on her. She hadn't developed an opinion on Bomen until she'd met Marcus and Jake.

But life in Boman lands? Another opportunity Marcus, and now their child, could never have—life with others of their kind—if they stayed with Leah. She would *never* be accepted by the general Boman populace, even if she loved one and gave birth to one.

Most of the rest of dinner, Leah pushed the stew around in her bowl. She couldn't live in Seeder lands, either. She'd enjoyed meeting Saff when Leah had visited the Seeder nation the prior summer, but other eyes hadn't been too friendly once they realized whose child Leah was.

Leah was seriously reconsidering life in the human world now. A fresh start sounded appealing, until she considered the logistics of leaving her new home. She had no money, no one to lean on.

"Are you alright, Leah?" Catrina asked across the dining table.

Leah looked up. "Yeah, of course."

"Not hungry?"

Leah set her spoon down and sat back in her seat. "Yeah, sorry. I might have snuck a late snack from the kitchen." That was a lie, but between nerves and maternal sickness, she could only stomach so much. *Seeders have it so easy.* They didn't have menstrual cycles, didn't get morning/maternal sickness. Granted, what they considered 'birth' wasn't exactly what she had grown up knowing that act to be.

"Aha. Kristoff will be disappointed." Catrina playfully wagged a finger at her.

"Sorry."

After the waitstaff cleared the dinner dishes, they served a raspberry mousse. Leah turned it down, instead sipping water.

Once dessert was cleared, Leah and Marcus were able to slip away and let the 'adults' talk more. They strolled onto the palace grounds to their favorite spot. Tall hedges surrounded a vibrant flower garden and a viewing bench.

The couple sat down, and Leah took a deep breath of the invigorating air. Marcus pulled her in close. She smiled at the warmth of his body, and at the purple and green lightning bugs dancing in a tall tree in the distance.

"You're quiet tonight," he said.

"Mmm. Guess so. Got lots on my mind."

"Like what?"

Leah swallowed hard. This wasn't the right moment. Not yet. "What else? Studies."

"Yeah? What's your focus this week?"

"Mostly coagulation." It was all bookwork and lectures.

"Cool. What about it?"

She shrugged. "Not my favorite, but I see its use. I preferred the discussions we had on the ethics and methods of teaching various powers at young ages." Truthfully, though, she didn't want to talk about her week anymore. How could she even entertain her dream of mastering her powers and teaching them, when her own child would be deprived of them? It didn't seem right anymore. "What about your week? Sounds much more exciting."

Marcus kissed her cheek. "I'm stoked to get this opportunity with Governor Scanlon!"

She wore a soft smile. "You've worked hard for it. I'm proud of you."

He held her tighter.

"That's pretty far north. For how long?"

"Still not sure yet. Two to four months minimum. And yeah, it's in the far north, but that doesn't mean I won't make my weekly visits." He nuzzled her neck. "I never want to miss my time with you."

She frowned even as he trailed kisses down her neck.

"Not in the mood?"

Leah laid her head on his chest. "Just tired. I like how peaceful it is right here, right now."

He gently rubbed her arm. "I can be okay with that."

After several minutes of cuddling, he spoke up again. "Whatcha thinkin' about?"

"Hmmm." She figured she'd answer truthfully. "The future. And my visit next week with my mom." She and her mom had come to an agreement—her mom would try to hide her disappointment that Leah loved a Boman, and Leah would try to look past the fact that her mom was a murderer and bigot. It felt like a bit of an uneven trade, but it somehow worked.

Leah *needed* her mom in her life. She already felt like an orphan with her dad gone, her mom in prison for life. But … eventually, her mom would find out that Marcus had knocked her up, and she'd be even more disappointed. There was no winning for Leah.

"I see. Those visits can be hard." After a minute he added, "Wanna know what I'm thinking?"

"What?"

"How happy I am to be here right now. And how much I love you."

Her lips twitched upwards.

He stroked her thigh. "And how amazing it was to sneak into your chambers a couple weeks ago."

She slid a hand to her belly, the weight of the decision ahead pressing on her. "Yeah. I think a lot about that night, too."

***

Leah couldn't get herself to tell Marcus the first night of his visit. Not when he'd been in such a great mood. But she wouldn't be able to keep it to herself for much longer.

Instead, she'd stayed up for hours in her chambers, examining her entire situation. She was pregnant; this she knew for certain. She'd been taught enough to read the signs, and Ivy women's bodies kinda yelled the fact at them. Since finding out a few days ago, Leah had carefully researched the birth control tonic Marcus had bought for her. It probably would have worked, had they been a little more careful about the instructions.

She couldn't blame Marcus—it had been his first time, and he'd been nervous about buying the right thing in the first place, and doing so while keeping it hidden, without drawing any attention to himself. She didn't blame herself all that much either, as this was her first time with someone who could actually get her pregnant. They were equally to blame for not being more careful or adding extra protection.

Eventually, she stressed herself out way too much, and finally passed out in bed well past midnight.

They met again for breakfast in the dining hall. Marcus excitedly chatted with the Boman ambassador. Leah dared to try to eat some breakfast. She spread some whipped coconut honey on her toast and savored the first bite. Subtle, sweet, and mellow—just right. After a few minutes of letting it settle in her stomach, she risked trying something else. She reached for a boiled quail egg—a rare delicacy in the Green Lands. She cracked and peeled it. After splitting the little thing in half, Leah reached for the salt. The smell of the yolk wafted to her nose, and her stomach lurched. Swallowing, she choked down the toast trying to make its way back up. When she realized it was futile, she dropped the egg on her plate.

"Excuse me," she squeaked out before holding her breath and standing. Trying to appear as calm and ladylike as possible, she clasped her hands before her and strode to the door. Fighting her nausea with everything she had, she made a mad dash down the hallway to the nearest lavatory, barely arriving at the toilet in time. She retched over and over again.

With the contents of her stomach expelled, she sat on the cool tile floor, leaning against the wall. She couldn't do this alone. She didn't even know if she could do this at all.

After ages on the floor, miserable but aware that her abrupt departure and prolonged absence would draw attention, she forced herself up, flushed the toilet, washed her hands, and splashed cool water on her face. She took a few slow, steady breaths and exited the lavatory.

"Hey."

She gasped, clutching her chest.

Marcus chuckled. "Sorry. Didn't mean to scare you."

She glanced to her left. "How long have you been there?" Had he heard too much?

He shrugged. "A couple minutes? Wanted to check on you after you went missing like that."

She calmed her nerves. "I'm fine. Just … a little under the weather."

"Anything I can do to help?" Frowning, he reached out and held her hand.

"No, but thanks. I think I'm going to lie down for a bit. Took forever to fall asleep last night." It was partially true. Her nausea was no doubt worse because she'd slept so little and so poorly.

"Okay. I'll, uh, be hanging out with the kids, then?" He was a great cousin to the little prince and princesses.

"Sounds good."

Chapter 3

LEAH RETURNED TO HER CHAMBERS and lay down. She found rest surprisingly quickly, and woke to a knock at her door.

"Yeah, um…" She brushed her hair out of her face, sitting up in bed, then raising her voice. "Yeah, you can come in."

The door creaked open, and Robyn peeked her head in, her long red curls dangling over her shoulder. "Marcus is inquiring about you."

Leah rubbed her face with her hands. "I'm fine." Her stomach ached a bit from throwing up earlier.

"Is it alright if he comes in?" Robyn asked.

"Sure." Leah pulled back the covers and stood while Robyn called to Marcus in the corridor.

Marcus entered and gave her a hug. He'd only ever been in here a handful of times before. They sat on a settee while Robyn busied herself with making the bed. It wasn't Robyn's job to do, and Leah was perfectly capable of making her own bed (though not nearly as neatly as the housekeeping staff did), but Robyn knew how to tactfully do her duty as a part-time chaperone.

Marcus wasn't allowed in Leah's chambers unchaperoned, and the reverse was true for Leah in Marcus's chambers when he came for visits. With Marcus in her chambers now, Robyn would be there to babysit the entire time.

"What's wrong?" Marcus asked.

Leah paused. 'My body is creating your child, and I'm in the middle of freaking out about it and the rest of my life' didn't sound like the right thing to say at the moment, especially with a servant nearby, even if it was Robyn.

"Like I said, just tired."

He eyed her. "When you didn't show up for lunch… Well, Aunt Catrina had a tray made up for you. Do you want to eat in here?"

It's past lunchtime already? "I'm fine, really. I'll grab something to eat later."

The words had no sooner rolled off her tongue than her stomach betrayed her with the loudest growl ever, and Marcus raised a skeptical eyebrow.

"Or maybe I'm more hungry than I thought." She glanced at Robyn, who was fluffing a pillow. "How about I get changed into something more comfortable and meet you in the small study?"

"Okay. I'll be waiting for you." He kissed her forehead and left.

Robyn exited the room after him, taking her usual place outside Leah's door while she changed.

Leah put on a pair of shorts and a comfy shirt, suitable attire for lounging around when it was just herself, Marcus, and the servants, with the possibility of running across the actual royal family. When she walked into the small study, Marcus sat at a table with her lunch tray. She crossed the room to join him, first sipping some water.

"Thanks for waking me. I love a good lunch date." She smiled.

"Of course." He pointed at the pastry on the tray. "That's really good."

She picked it up, tearing off a small chunk. "How was your time with the kids?"

He narrowed his eyes, bobbing his head. "I'd say pretty good. I became a duke today."

Leah grinned. "Really? And how did that happen? I know my nap was long, but an entire ceremony and everything to make it official?"

He leaned back in his chair, crossing his legs. "Oh yeah. You'll be sad you missed it. The whole kingdom showed up and everything."

She choked back a laugh. Dukes and duchesses were only given their titles directly from the queen, as a special status symbol for services to the kingdom. "And what did you do to earn it?"

"I'm the best in all the realm at building blanket forts. Prince Leon made it official."

Leah chortled. "Prince Leon? He has no right to issue that title, no matter how good you are at blanket forts."

Marcus looked downright indignant. "How dare you!" He put a hand to his chest. "I am *amazing* at it. And no, a four-year-old nonheir to the throne does not hold that authority, but I believe him when he says he'll convince Aunt Catrina to make it official."

She hummed. "But you said I missed the entire ceremony while I napped?"

He winked, then his gaze traveled to her hands. "You gonna eat?"

She hadn't yet taken a bite. After the quail egg that morning, she was nervous about eating anything at all, but starting with a pastry might be safe. She tried the portion she'd pulled off; it was slightly sweet with a hint of cinnamon. "You're right. That is good."

He smiled as she nibbled off another corner. "Are we still on for the boat ride tonight?"

With all her stressing, she'd almost forgotten about it. He'd arranged for them to have a special romantic boat ride on the palace lake. The thought of wobbling or rowing made her queasy all over again, but she tried to force a smile. "Yeah."

He looked like he didn't quite buy it. "Okay…"

She averted her gaze, taking another sip of her water. "The weather's nice today, though, right?" That was a pretty weak attempt at small talk. This was the Green Lands, a realm in perpetual spring. It was almost always a nice day.

"Yeah. It's beautiful. Like you." His voice was soft, almost distant or concerned, his smile only half there. "You do know that, right? That I think you're gorgeous? Inside and out. Clothed or … not clothed." He blushed a little. "And no matter what."

He'd never once made her feel less than gorgeous. Not once. And he'd definitely made his sentiments clear the night they'd finally shared a bed.

"I think you're rather handsome yourself."

This time he gave her a more confident smile. He shifted on his chair, sitting straighter. "And you—are you happy with the way you look?"

The question sounded much more baited this time. *That's … an odd thing to ask…* She'd always felt fairly comfortable in her own skin, even with weight fluctuations or most hairstyles. She still liked her green eyes and black hair, though not quite as much as she had before she'd found out who her parents were. "Yes…?"

He pursed his lips, not responding.

Now she *did* feel a little uncomfortable in her skin. Would he not see her the same way when she was big and pregnant? She furrowed her brow. "Why are you asking that?"

He bit his lip, then looked at her tray again. "You … didn't eat much last weekend when I came to visit. Or now…"

She breathed a sigh of relief. He thought she was on a diet? Why would she be? Because he'd seen her naked? "I'm not trying to lose weight. I don't have any … eating problems, either." Maybe she should tell him here and now, but again it didn't feel right.

"Just like my nap… I've been stressed, okay?"

He nodded. "Okay."

She made a concerted effort to polish off most of her tray. There were some lovely herb-roasted chickpeas, a baked apple, and a colorful salad with poppyseed dressing. She finished half of a tropical chia seed pudding before she had to stop.

More than once, a servant entered the room to check on them and her status. Leah drained her glass of water as another servant entered and whisked away her tray.

Leah and Marcus shifted to a settee in the study and cuddled, chatting about their weeks some more.

As she shared her opinion on a topic she'd covered in her studies, he just stared at her lovingly, tickling the palms of her hands. "I think that's great." He glanced at a pendulum clock in the corner of the room. "Oh, are we still on for the boat ride? I was thinking of making a last-minute change to the picnic menu, and I should let the kitchen know."

She tried to hide a frown. He was so excited to go out on the lake. But then again, he was excited for the rest of his life and career. All of a sudden, the richness of that chia seed pudding wasn't settling right in her stomach. All she could imagine was upchucking repeatedly over the edge of the boat and then standing, bowing, and announcing that she'd ruined their date night, his reputation, and his future. At least they wouldn't be teenage parents… They'd both be twenty by the time she delivered.

"I, uh… I'm still kinda wiped out. Could I take a rain check on that? And we could do something a little more low-key tonight?"

He smiled, though it didn't reach his eyes. "Sure."

***

Leah felt cruddy canceling their date plans, but she felt cruddy in every way possible already. Marcus was patient as always, and they chatted and cuddled, and even went for a short stroll on the grounds. She kept waiting for a 'right moment' to pop up, but it may never. He was visiting on a three-day weekend this time, but that didn't mean she could handle another entire day of anxiety.

And she couldn't keep the secret for long anyway. Green folk were blessed with great health. Something like a prolonged stomach bug was rare, and if Marcus had noticed she'd been acting off, it was only a matter of time before others would.

After dinner. No more putting it off.

Dinner was nice, and fairly quiet. One of the twins—the princesses—was fussy, but it was a casual evening anyway, with just the royal family and Leah and Marcus.

"I thought you two were going to the lake tonight," King Stephan commented.

Leah's stomach churned, this time with nerves.

"Um…" Marcus shrugged. "Leah's tired. Maybe we'll do it tomorrow."

Catrina frowned. "Sorry to hear that. Make sure to head to bed early so you're well rested."

With her mouth full of food, Leah gave her a polite smile and nodded. It was a bit of a trek to the lake, and she doubted Marcus would be up to it even after a good night's rest, what with the bombshell she'd be dropping on him that night.

"What time are you leaving for Capital City, darling?" Catrina asked Stephan.

He clicked his tongue. "Before daylight. There's a lot to cover at that assembly."

As dinner came to an end, Leah's gut twisted tighter and tighter. She had to turn down dessert. Marcus threw a quick glance her way. If he still took that as a sign she was on some kind of crazy diet, she'd soon be dispelling that notion completely.

"Do you want to play billiards, and go to bed early?" Marcus asked Leah as servants cleared the table.

"How about another walk in the gardens?"

He smiled. "I'm down."

***

They rarely stole kisses in the palace itself. Usually, they snuck out to the gardens for more alone time. Of course, a servant or guard was always nearby to act as chaperone, but being outdoors meant fewer eyes in general, and less chance of an accidental audience.

Leah's hands became clammy as the couple strolled to their favorite bench. They walked in silence, their fingers intertwined.

She loved him. Irrevocably. She prayed he'd feel the same way after she told him they were going to be parents so young.

Once they got to their bench, he pulled her onto his lap. She carefully unwrapped his arms from around her and moved to the side.

He gave her a questioning glance. "Are you really okay?"

Her throat bobbed, her heart thumping against her ribs. "Not really."

Frowning, he took her hands. "You can tell me anything."

"I, um…" She pursed her lips, gathering her courage. "I'm … pregnant."

His eyes widened, his face paled, and his grip on her hands loosened.

And he said nothing. Absolutely nothing.

It may have been only thirty seconds before he responded, but it certainly felt more like thirty minutes. She'd kinda hoped that initial look of shock would melt into an adoring smile. He was great with his young cousins, after all. But there was no smile. Only shock, possibly horror. And each second of his silence chipped at something in her heart, at her hope that things in her life could still work out.

Marcus's expression wasn't one of acceptance, or of satisfaction, as though he'd sabotaged his girlfriend's birth control tonic, or had understood she'd taken it wrong. It was the undeniable look of someone who was watching their reputation and dreams being ripped from them.

Marcus was the golden child of the realm. Leah was the black eye, the stain, Soren's heir.

"You're sure…" He gazed at her stomach. "I…"

Heat rose in her cheeks. "You better not finish that sentence the way I think you're going to." She'd slept with more than a couple of guys before him, but none since she'd met him, and she would *never* cheat on him.

Marcus furrowed his brow. "What are you talking about?"

She cocked her head, taking her hands back. "Am I sure you're the father?"

He scrunched his face. "I wasn't going to say that!"

"Then what were you going to say?"

"Just … asking that you're sure…"

She huffed. "Yes. I know. And before you ask how far along I am, I'm going to take a wild guess that it's about two weeks."

Shaking his head, he covered his mouth. "But it was only once. Well, you know… And we were careful."

She gritted her teeth, her frustration growing. "It only *takes* once, and obviously not careful enough."

He gestured at her, exasperated. "Why are you mad at *me*? I didn't do it on purpose."

The implication hurt more than he could ever realize. "Are you saying *I* did?"

He bolted upright, pacing. "I didn't say that. Why are you mad at me?"

Nothing about this exchange had gone well, and she didn't really have an answer for him. "I… I just… Sorry."

A whistle came from over the hedge, a thoughtful advance warning. Piot was often assigned as the evening chaperone to patrol the gardens when Marcus visited, and had the kindness to alert them before he'd appear from behind a hedge to catch them making out.

Both Leah and Marcus looked toward the opening of the hedge in anticipation. Piot rounded the corner, and gave them a smile and a polite nod. "Marcus. Leah."

They both politely nodded back.

"Hi," she said weakly.

After another nod, Piot left again.

Marcus sat back down next to Leah, his voice calmer and quieter. "So, what are you thinking?"

"I don't know." Her tone was nearly as panicked as she was.

His mouth hung open a moment, and his eyes once again drifted to her stomach. "Are you going to keep it?"

"I don't know," she repeated. Despite all the time she'd had to think about it, she didn't have a single answer for any other questions he might ask, either.

Silence filled the space between them. After a moment of contemplation, he spoke again. "Well, if you decide not to keep it… You know, Tobias and Cam have talked about adopting, and—"

"No!" She spat out the word before she'd even acknowledged to herself why. Marcus was suggesting she give their baby to his brother and sister-in-law?! "No. I'm not giving it up. I'm keeping it."

"Okay. Okay." His tone was soothing. The tiniest of smiles tugged at his lips. "We'll do the right thing."

Something in her knew what he'd meant by that, and it didn't sit well with her at all. What was the *right* thing? The *wrong* thing? Leah had … changed … since her arrival in the Green Lands. Her moral compass had adjusted a bit. Was her shoplifting habit in the human world bad? Yes. Had she always thought so? No. Was her habit of lying, sometimes just for fun, wrong? Yes. Had she always thought so? Not exactly.

But Marcus, he was a different breed. His moral compass had always pointed due north. And the 'right' thing here meant preserving the impeccable image of the royal family they were both tied to.

"And what is the 'right' thing to do, Marcus?"

His smile widened. "We'll get married."

"No."

He frowned. "Why not?"

"Really? You have no idea how flattering that is to hear, do you? Every girl *dreams* of the guy that knocked her up saying, 'Well, I guess we're just gonna have to do the right thing.'"

He was unamused. "So now I'm only the guy that got you pregnant? As if we haven't dated for over two years? As if we haven't talked plenty about marriage and having kids someday."

"Yeah, *someday*. Down the road. *Way* down the road. When you had your career sorted, and I'd figured out what the heck I was going to do."

"Well, those plans are out the window now, aren't they?"

"I'm not going to be some stupid hillbilly shotgun bride!"

His confusion was understandable, despite how thoroughly he'd been prepared for his foreign exchange year in the human world.

"I'm not being forced to marry just because I'm pregnant."

He studied her face. "You're not exactly flattered by my proposal. I'm sorry I didn't spout off the engagement ballad. But how do you think I feel when my girlfriend, who supposedly loves me, shoots me down without even a second of consideration?"

"Supposedly?" Her voice broke, and tears gathered in the corners of her eyes. "Yeah, because two weeks ago meant nothing to me, right? I'll be in the study if you decide you want to stop being a jackass." She stood and stalked off, wiping at her eyes.

Chapter 4

A HALF HOUR LATER, Leah still sat in the study, wiping away tears. A servant had been kind enough to fetch her a handkerchief when they'd spotted her crying.

Who knew if Marcus would even join her? He'd essentially broken up with her for an entire month when they were a new couple, when he'd found out about her shoplifting habit.

She stared out the window, aching inside, focused on the lingering punch of color on the horizon as the sun set.

"I love you," Marcus said softly from behind her.

She sniffled, continuing to stare out the window.

The door clicked. "You know that, right?"

"Yeah," she half whispered. "I know."

He joined her on the settee, leaning against the window. "I'm sorry I didn't handle that the best."

"Me too."

"That's why you haven't been eating much? You've been sick?"

She nodded.

"Can I help?"

Her heart melted, and she hugged him. "I love you."

He gave her his signature squeeze.

After a moment more in his embrace, she leaned back. "There's not really anything you can do right now."

"Let me know if that changes?"

"Will do."

He took her hands. "So… Keeping the baby?"

"Yes." She was as sure of her answer now as she'd been when she'd said it earlier. Her heart ached at the notion of someone else raising this child. Accident or not, it was hers. It was theirs.

"But…" He pursed his lips. "No marriage."

She looked down at their hands. "I'm not saying never. I just … don't want to be pressured into it."

"But do you want to do this together?"

She gazed into his warm brown eyes. "Yes." She couldn't fathom not having him by her side as she sorted through the mess of her life in this realm, as she carried and raised their child. She couldn't fathom not having her best friend there through it all.

"Then I'm yours."

She lunged forward, giving him a kiss. He held her by the nape of the neck, and she got lost there for just the briefest of moments.

Once their lips parted, she took a cleansing breath.

He rested a hand on her knee. "Not exactly the weekend we planned, huh?"

She frowned. "Sorry about the lake."

Giving her a half-smile, he rubbed her knee. "We've got plenty of other excitement instead, don't we?"

"That's one way of putting it." She mirrored his smile.

"Please … try to be patient with me. Kind of my first time with this sort of thing."

"Yeah. Same. Definitely my first rodeo." It didn't happen often, but she sometimes caught herself using a human idiom he wasn't familiar with. "A rodeo's—"

"I've heard my mom use that one before."

A servant knocked and entered, lighting sconces in the room and bidding them good night.

Leah and Marcus stayed up for hours discussing things. They didn't come to any solid answers on what they were going to do, but they discussed options. He'd continue with his internship, and she would continue with her education. And despite how much they both dreaded the prospect, they would have to inform Catrina and Stephan of their news and plans. The queen and king would *not* be happy.

As Leah and Marcus prepared to turn in for the night, they walked the candlelit corridors of the quiet palace, hand in hand. They reached the hallway where they had to part ways, and hugged once more.

Marcus caressed her cheek and kissed her on the forehead. "Love you."

She smiled. "You too."

***

Leah tossed and turned in bed, unable to calm her mind. Life would be so much easier if there were a manual, if there were signs posted telling her to 'go this way.'

She and Marcus had agreed to sleep on the discussion they'd had, and reconvene in the morning. They planned to tell Catrina and Stephan together once the king returned from an assembly late the next evening.

But Leah couldn't handle just lying there in bed again, stressing about things, and wondering if Marcus was in his chambers freaking out about the news.

Throwing on a robe, she set her mind to go see him. It would be a tricky feat, but she'd be doing essentially what Marcus had done to sneak into her chambers, getting them into this mess in the first place.

She cracked her door open and slipped into the hallway. Light on her feet, she made her move toward the storage closet. A mere two yards away, she halted when a door clicked behind her.

"Miss Elonto? What are you doing up? Did you need something?"

Leah's heart dropped. She turned. "Robyn? What are you doing here at this time of night?"

Robyn stepped into the candlelight. "Covering a shift for Lily. Did you need something?"

Leah paused. She could lie. She could say she'd been sleepwalking, or that she needed a new towel from the storage closet for some reason in the middle of the night. She *couldn't* pretend she was sneaking to the kitchen for a late snack, since she'd been walking in the wrong direction.

She liked Robyn, and felt she could be trusted. People would find out soon enough anyway. Though … she wasn't sure Robyn knew about the palace's hidden passageways, so she treaded lightly.

"I … need … to go take care of something in private," Leah said.

Robyn arched an eyebrow. "I might be able to help you if you'd like to elaborate."

Leah wrung her hands. "No, I… I kinda need you to … look the other way."

"Hmm… Looking the other way is not something I can do much of in my position."

"Please?" She was so desperate. "If you need to go take a quick bathroom break, and then … not check in my room…"

"Miss Elonto." Robyn's tone was more serious. "Please explain what you have in mind at this hour."

Hugging herself, Leah considered her options. She could let her plans go, but she couldn't stop that yearning, that nagging feeling telling her she had to be with Marcus right now. "I need to see Marcus."

"Absolutely not."

"I'm not asking you to lie. I just need you to not … proactively tattle on me."

"Leah," Robyn said softly, "I have to follow Her Majesty's orders when it comes to your curfew and visitations. You know that."

Leah was close to crying. Whether from hormones or desperation or exhaustion, she didn't know. "Please? I need to see him. I'll be back before your shift is over, long before they ring the breakfast bell."

Silently, Robyn shook her head.

"I need to be with him. I'm … pregnant."

Robyn's mouth hung open for a moment. "Does Her Majesty know?"

"Not yet. We're going to tell her tomorrow. But I need to see him." Leah wiped a tear from the corner of her eye. "Please just pretend you didn't see me leave, and I'll be back before anyone would know I'm missing."

Frowning, Robyn shifted from one foot to another. "Even if I did that, how would you get past all the other guards and servants on night patrols? They're not as likely to be sympathetic."

Leah hesitated. "I … know how to get there without getting caught."

Robyn's gaze drifted to the storage closet behind Leah.

She does know about the passageways. The palace was Leah's residence, but sometimes she still felt more like a guest than a resident herself. No one from inside the palace had ever told her about the passageways.

"You're asking for trouble, child," Robyn said, almost in a whisper.

"I'm already in trouble," Leah replied, her stomach in knots.

After a long pensive moment, Robyn finally replied. "You and I need to be perfectly clear with one another. We never had this conversation, and I never saw you sneaking out of your room. I will *never* lie to Her Majesty. For you or anyone else."

Leah's shoulders slumped.

"But I could stand to go use the toilet. I have no reason to check your room or to suspect you snuck out. I don't expect to see you until very early this morning. Much earlier than the change of shift or breakfast bells?"

Leah's tension eased, and she almost even hugged Robyn, not that hugging the staff was allowed. "Thank you!"

Robyn shook her head. "Don't thank me. But don't get me in trouble either."

"I won't!"

Robyn scanned her. "And if you ever need to talk about it, I'd be happy to answer any questions you have about pregnancy, at least based on my experiences with my two."

This time Leah did hug her. "Thank you!"

"Sure thing. Now, I'm heading down the hallway. And I'm assuming you'll be back in your bed where you belong." Robyn released her, and Leah stood in place until the hallway door clicked shut behind Robyn.

Leah quickly pulled open the supply closet door and shut herself inside. Her heart raced in the dark, but she persevered and carefully felt her way past the shelves to the back of the closet. She crouched, finding the little lever by the floorboard. When she pulled the lever, a barely perceptible *squeak* announced her success.

She'd snuck out and explored this route before, but had been much more careful to avoid detection.

Leah slid the panel to the side, slipping through the narrow entryway, then slid it back into place. She really should have brought a candle to see better, but she'd spaced it with the moonlight and candlelight in her chambers and the hallway. She'd do fine once her eyes adjusted, and with the few tiny windows along the corridors.

She knew her way around here anyway. She hadn't explored much of the maze of tunnels and offshoots, mostly just what was needed to find a path between her chambers and the ones Marcus was usually assigned when he came to visit.

After a while spent groping the cold stone walls and guiding herself at the right turns, she arrived at the door closest to Marcus's chambers. This door wasn't as close to his room as the first door was to hers, and it required a touch more precision with the timing.

Cupping her ear to the door, Leah listened for noise on the other side, though she hadn't expected any. This particular doorway was hidden behind the curtains of a small theater and concert hall. No one would be in there at this time of night. Even then, she was careful to keep noise to the minimum as she popped the door open and stepped into the room.

She was still two hallways away from Marcus's room.

They'd spent months planning their romantic rendezvous, and it had even become a game. Based on previous observations, there were usually more guards and servants patrolling the area around Leah's chambers.

Leah sighed, pausing with her hand on the doorknob. It definitely wasn't a game this time. She twisted the knob, listening intently as she opened the door just a hair. The night was still.

Shutting the door behind her, Leah hastened down the long hallway, with only the soft *pitter-patter* of her bare feet to give her away.

As she neared the corner, someone sneezed.

Shoot.

She stopped dead in her tracks, her gaze darting around the hallway. She chose the nearest door and pulled it open, ducking inside.

A bathroom… That could be good, since it could be locked, which she did immediately. Or it could be bad, if the sneezer needed to use it!

Calming her breathing, Leah waited. And waited. And panicked as footsteps thumped closer. She held her breath, her ear pressed to the door. She finally loosed that breath after the footsteps passed her.

She waited a few minutes, mentally mapping the routes she and Marcus had discussed. The timing had to be right. She had to wait long enough for that person to be out of earshot, but couldn't dawdle, because the next patrol might not be far behind.

Leah stepped back out into the hallway and turned the corner, running to the next doorway and taking less care to open it and step inside.

Luckily, no one was in this hallway either. She passed the first door and headed straight to Marcus's, trying the handle. Unluckily, it was locked. She knocked, hopefully loud enough that he would hear it, but others wouldn't.

She danced from foot to foot, wringing her hands, waiting for Marcus. She'd just done all that maneuvering to get to him, drawing Robyn into this mess, and she'd lose it if he didn't answer, if he was fast asleep, if she got caught.

The lock clicked from the other side, giving her reason to smile, and the door opened.

"Yeah?" Marcus asked.

Leah pushed her way in, closing and locking the door behind her.

"Leah," he breathed as she turned and fell into his arms.

"I needed to be with you," she said, her hands splayed across his bare back. The last time she'd snuck into his room, it had also been for comfort, though it had been at his parents' house. He'd also been wearing only boxers on that occasion.

Marcus nuzzled her neck, squeezing her tighter, not giving a verbal answer.

He was her home. He was happiness and hope. She'd reconsidered her crazy idea to sneak over to see him a handful of times as she'd navigated the palace, but the warmth of his perfect hug steadied her heart and confirmed she'd made the right choice.

Eventually, Marcus pulled back. "What's the matter?" His gaze flickered to her stomach, and his hands rested on her sides. "Is everything okay?"

She smiled, her heart melting. "I'm fine. *We're* fine. I just … needed to be with you."

He matched her smile. "I like the idea of that."

"Can we cuddle for a couple of hours? Then I can sneak back with plenty of time before the breakfast bell."

"Yeah." He led her by the hand to his bed. The moonlight through stained glass windows cast a beautiful pattern on the floor. She took off her robe to be more comfortable, and slid under the sheets with him.

They kissed a little, and talked a bit, but mostly just held each other. She was still lost and anxious, and could only imagine how he felt after finding out.

They checked his clock every once in a while. Every time she nodded off, she woke to a kiss on her cheek or forehead, and Marcus would ask if that was a sign she ought to head back to her chambers. She didn't want to. She didn't want to ever leave his side again.

Her arms and legs wrapped around him, she fixated on the windows. They truly were breathtaking—the stained glass in his room depicted a cherry tree in full bloom. A hint of daylight started to glow behind the windowpanes. She needed to head back soon, even though she didn't want to.

A loud knock on the door startled them. Leah's gaze shot to the clock. She still had plenty of time before she needed to be back in her own chambers.

Marcus gave her a panicked look as a second louder knock came at the door.

"Stay under the blanket," he said, covering her up.

Leah held her breath, listening. The door creaked open.

"Um… Hi…" His voice held no confidence. "Hi, Aunt Catrina."

Chapter 5

LEAH'S HEART FROZE AT MARCUS'S WORDS. She stayed under his comforter, completely still.

"*Get. Dressed,*" Catrina ordered, her voice low and harsh. "And have Leah get dressed. The three of us need to have a conversation *right now.*"

"Oh crap," Leah whispered.

"Yeah, um, I mean … she's…" Marcus grappled for a response. Leah hadn't gotten *undressed*, but Marcus was only in his boxers, and their level of clothedness probably didn't matter in the grand scheme of things when Leah ought not to be there in the first place…

"Now," Catrina repeated.

"Yes, ma'am."

The door clicked closed, and Leah pulled back the comforter. They exchanged a panicked glance as he reached for pants and a shirt.

"Why is she even visiting this early?" Leah asked, grabbing her robe.

Marcus frowned, shaking his head. "No idea."

"What are we going to say?" Leah's heart pumped faster than she could come up with answers.

"We're just going to have to tell her now…"

She hugged him, and a thousand scenarios raced through her mind. In five minutes' time, she might be kicked out, homeless. She might be forbidden from being with Marcus, forced to raise their child alone. Possibly exiled again to the human world, permanently.

He gave her a quick kiss. "It'll be fine. We were going to tell her today anyway, right?"

What world are you living in? Sitting down with Queen Catrina to break the news was a completely different thing than Leah being found in his bed, in direct defiance of the queen's orders.

Marcus took Leah's hand, and they stepped into the hallway together.

Queen Catrina was still in a silk nightgown, her long brown hair pinned up for curls. Her arms were crossed, and her expression was also cross. But instead of starting to lay into them, she remained silent, sizing them up.

"Well…" Marcus was the first to speak.

Catrina's gaze snapped to Leah. "I don't ask much of you. I have *always* given you choices. On your education, your therapy, what public appearances you make… And I've always tried to respect your choice to be together. I don't ask much. But the rules were crystal clear—the expectations have never been muddy for the two of you." She looked at Marcus. "Were the rules ever ambiguous?"

He swallowed. "No, ma'am."

Catrina focused on Leah, expectant.

Leah gritted her teeth. Yes, Catrina had allowed her a level of autonomy, but she had plenty of rules surrounding Leah and how she should act, dress, talk, *everything*.

Ivy society wasn't exceptionally prudish. Lots of people waited to have sex until they were married, but it didn't mean there wasn't also a decent chunk of the population that thought it was fine to live together unwed. Even Queen Kaylah had done that with her husband for two years before they'd wed, though their situation had been far from typical, and he hadn't been capable of accidentally getting her pregnant…

"No, Your Majesty," Leah answered, averting her gaze.

"That's right. Crystal clear." Pain and pleading were etched into her voice. "You have come *so far* with your public image. And now this." She shook her head. "Here I thought: 'Since I'm already awake, I'll go check on Leah, because she hasn't been feeling well.' And then I was rewarded with *this*."

Maybe she only knew that Leah had snuck into Marcus's room, and didn't know about the pregnancy part yet? Perhaps they should let this blow over before throwing that gem at her…

"We weren't … actually doing anything just now," Leah said. "We were only talking."

Catrina's eyes narrowed. "Frankly, I don't care to know what you were doing together last night. But I do know that 'only talking' doesn't end with you getting pregnant."

Yep. She knew. Marcus gripped Leah's hand tighter.

Robyn had to have told Catrina. While the betrayal hurt, Leah wasn't mad at her. She'd outright told Leah she wouldn't lie to the queen.

"Where did it happen?" Catrina asked, no doubt wanting to know *how many* rules had been broken.

Leah and Marcus remained silent.

"Where—"

"Here, in the palace," Marcus quietly answered.

Catrina pursed her lips. "I want names. Every servant or guard who knew you were sneaking around, disobeying orders."

"No one knew," Leah said.

Catrina cocked her head, clearly disbelieving. "Have you developed powers no one is familiar with? You can walk these halls without notice? When I've stationed chaperones? You've mastered invisibility now?"

"No," Leah said wryly.

"Then how, pray tell, did you sneak around the palace without a servant catching you?"

Leah's lips parted, but words failed to come for a moment. "I… We… The hidden passageways."

Rolling her shoulders, Catrina again shook her head. "And how do you even know about those?"

"I told her," Marcus lied.

"Really?" Catrina drawled. "As much as I love you, Marcus, I know you were never told about them. Only residents of the palace and those employed here are informed of their existence. They pose a security risk."

"I'm a resident," Leah countered. "Why wasn't I told? What if there was a fire, and I needed to escape?"

"Then a servant would have helped you out of one of the *many* other exits or, if needed, through the passageways. So, I'm going to ask you again. How did you even discover them?"

"Well, I…" Leah took her hand back from Marcus, hugging herself.

"Like I said, Aunt Catrina—"

"My mom told me about them," Leah confessed. "She told me my dad would sometimes sneak her into the palace before his parents warmed up to her."

Catrina's lip curled. "*Not* the best examples to be following. I shouldn't have to point that out."

Leah's stomach knotted. No, that hadn't been the wisest choice. Her mom had also escaped out those tunnels when the palace had been under attack the night her dad was captured.

"Did Robyn know you used the tunnels?" Catrina asked.

"It doesn't matter," Leah said.

"It does. I need to know who on my staff I'm able to rely on. You may not have grown up in this realm, but you've had more than enough lessons to understand what security at this palace means. Your parents might not have been able to murder your grandparents had the staff been more loyal.

"And when it comes to the security of the position I hold, and the safety of my family, my children, the people I love," Catrina's voice grew louder, "then I will *not* hesitate to dismiss anyone who would put them at risk!"

Leah recoiled a bit at that, her heart numb. Leah wasn't counted as a resident, or as a family member. Marcus was Catrina's nephew, but Leah? She was just Catrina's evil cousin's daughter, her ward, the object of Catrina's pity, her public relations project.

At this point, Leah knew in her heart she was homeless. But Robyn didn't deserve more trouble for knowing Leah had used the passageways. "Robyn didn't know. Don't fire her."

"And did *any* of the servants know you were using them? Robyn's already been dismissed for lying to me."

Leah's jaw dropped. "What?! That's not fair! She didn't lie to you. She told you where I was this morning, right?"

"Yes, but a lie of omission is still a lie, and she knew where you'd snuck off to without doing a thing about it, without proactively informing me."

"That's... No! You can't do that." Robyn was nice, and competent, and had just been showing Leah some compassion in a time when she was freaked out.

Catrina rested her hands on her hips. "I can't? I make the rules here."

Leah clenched her jaw. She was used to a sweet and caring Catrina, and a sometimes-exhausted version of her in private with the young kids and too little sleep. She'd also witnessed the more regal Catrina at formal events and with important guests. Leah hadn't yet seen this side—the *true* side of Catrina that had doubted Leah from the start, hidden under a mask of kindness.

"I will not ask again. Who else—" Catrina started.

"No one knew!" Leah shouted.

Catrina eyed her, then straightened. "I hope that's true. Back to the topic of your pregnancy. Are you keeping the child?"

Marcus slid a hand onto Leah's back. "Yes."

"Alright. Then we'll find time in my schedule today to discuss wedding details."

Marcus kept quiet.

"We're not planning a wedding right now," Leah said.

Looking mildly surprised, Catrina tilted her head. "And why not?"

Leah swallowed. "All you care about is public image, and that's already screwed now, isn't it? If you rush a wedding, people will suspect. If people with half a brain can do math, they'll know I'm already two weeks along. So why should I be forced into it before I'm ready?"

"Better to mitigate damage now than—"

A knock at the end of the corridor cut her off. The door popped open. "My apologies, Your Majesty."

"I asked for privacy, Tain," Catrina said.

"I know, my apologies. A high-priority memo arrived from that human ambassador."

Catrina blew out a puff of air. "Thank you. I'll be right out."

She faced the couple. "We'll continue this discussion later. Both of you properly dress, then see my aide to find out when we can schedule that."

"I'm not going to change my mind," Leah said.

Catrina only stared back at her.

"Give us some time to sort it all out, Aunt Catrina. We just found out."

"We don't always have the luxury of time when it comes to damage control, Marcus."

Leah needed to know where she stood in this mess, how far Catrina was willing to go if she'd fired her servant over such a small white lie. "Are you going to kick me out if I don't marry him?"

"Would that motivate you?"

"No." And it wouldn't. Leah was far too stubborn for that.

"We're going to take our time..." Marcus said. "But Leah and I are going to share a room from now on."

They'd discussed asking for that, but now was hardly the right time to assert that, and apparently Catrina and Leah were of the same mind.

Catrina wasn't accustomed to either of them breaking her rules, or standing up to her. Her exasperation wasn't veiled in the slightest. "You don't get to dictate what happens in my home, Marcus."

Leah was tired of cowering, of apologizing, of lying, of feeling this way—all of it. It had been a mistake. Her pregnancy wouldn't win her points in the public eye, but she still deserved a choice in the matter of her marital status. And Catrina ought not to be talking down to Marcus. Robyn shouldn't have lost her job.

Heat rose in Leah's cheeks and ears. "You don't have to be a bitch about it!"

A barely audible gasp came from Marcus. Leah flinched out of habit, but she hadn't needed to. Catrina could be strict, but she wasn't the type to smack someone she was angry with, the way Cheryl had with Leah when she was younger.

But if looks could kill, Leah would be in a body bag.

"Watch how you address your queen. Both of you, get properly dressed."

Leah choked down the lump in her throat. "Yes, Your Majesty."

"Yes, Your Majesty," Marcus echoed.

A hint of hurt flickered in Catrina's expression. Leah had never once heard him address his aunt so formally in private.

Without another word, Catrina turned and strode down the corridor, opening the door. "Please escort Miss Eleana to her chambers discreetly."

"Yes, Your Majesty."

As the guard headed toward the couple, Marcus pulled Leah into a hug. "We'll be okay," he whispered.

She wished she could believe that.

"Please come with me, miss."

Leah pressed her forehead to Marcus's. "I love you."

He cracked a tiny smile. "I love you too."

"Miss…"

She let Marcus go, and followed the guard down the hallway.

***

Leah perched on the edge of her bed, hands in her lap. The morning could be going better. Why did this have to be so messy?

She'd been sent back to her room like a little kid to get dressed. Then she was supposed to wait around all day until Catrina could squeeze her in for a meeting to demand again that she marry Marcus?

Sounds delightful… But how much choice did she really have in the matter?

Leah went to her walk-in closet, deciding what to wear.

"Where's my most revealing dress?" she asked herself. A 'proper' lady trying to improve her reputation should look sharp and not show too much skin. She'd disagreed with Catrina about her attire from day one.

As she surveyed the closet, an ache took hold of Leah's heart. Too many of these dresses were 'appropriate.' There was nothing wrong with them, per se, but they weren't Leah. When had she allowed herself to become that girl? Wearing what Catrina would like to the balls, just to avoid a disagreement. Simply going along with it to save time and energy.

Turning her back on the dresses, Leah returned to her bed. She tucked her knees up under her chin, and allowed herself to cry. Who even was she anymore?

Her past was a patchwork of mistakes and pain. Her new future—murky and uphill. Who she was in the present—a lie coated in manners and frills.

After wiping away her tears, she slowly approached the closet again, leaning in the doorway. She usually dressed based on the occasions of the day. Marcus's romantic boat ride was out of the question now. The only things on the agenda as of right now were waiting around and lectures.

Leah's wardrobe was stunning. She'd acquired so many pieces in her two years here. From the flowing cobalt blue ball gown, to the forest green drop-waist dress with intricate Ivy-style embroidery.

But none of it was truly hers.

Hadn't Leah told Marcus two years ago that she'd never be the girl they wanted her to be? That she'd advocate for herself about what she wanted to wear, wanted to do, wanted to become?

Becoming a teenage bride wasn't on her list. Being the palace puppet wasn't either.

Leah didn't want to wear any of these clothes; they'd been purchased and commissioned with Catrina's money, with the taxes of the kingdom. But Leah couldn't simply protest by staying in her pajamas against direct orders, or by streaking through the palace.

The smallest of smiles crossed her lips as she remembered her old friends. Crouching, Leah opened a drawer deep in the closet. Her old human-world clothes greeted her—the shirt and jeans she'd originally brought with her when she'd rifted into the Green Lands. She pulled them from the drawer, hugging them.

She hadn't worn these clothes in ages, and who knew how long they'd fit before she outgrew them with her pregnancy.

One leg at a time, Leah put her jeans on, then tugged her t-shirt over her head. Each inch of fabric against her skin was an old friend reminding her of a time in her life when she was free from so much obligation and care.

"Are you ready, miss?" a servant called through the door.

Leah loosed a breath. *No.* "Just a moment."

She stood in front of the gilded mirror, smoothing the creases in her shirt. Her hand glided to her stomach, and she almost cried again. She loved Marcus. An accidental pregnancy wouldn't change that, but she wasn't ready to just hop to the next step right now.

And something deep within her was wrong, something she couldn't explain, didn't understand, couldn't yet grasp.

A part of her faltered as her bright green eyes stared back at her. She'd run away from home before.

And she could do it again.

Leah glanced around her chambers. The room was beautiful, ornate, decorated with the few personalized touches she'd been allowed. How could something this bright be such a stifling prison?

Run. Run. Run, the voices in her head told her. *Get out.*

She was used to burning her bridges. She was used to having a reputation. She could weather those storms again.

How desperately she wanted to sneak into the passageways, to find her way out of the palace, to disappear forever. Just a girl. Just a girl with a child. Not Soren and Beata's daughter. Not Matron Kaylah's niece. Not Marcus's girlfriend.

Marcus. He was the only reason she paused. That, and the fact that she now would likely have someone keeping an eye on her every moment she wasn't in her chambers or the restroom.

But she needed to leave. Maybe for a week, as a palate cleanser, giving herself more time to process her situation.

Leah quickly set to work, scouring her drawers and shelves. What if she did leave? What if she *and* Marcus left? Just for a little while… Leah would only take her belongings. But what actually belonged to her? If Catrina had her searched, would a birthday gift from the queen and king somehow incriminate her as a thief? Because they'd decide it was theirs? She longed to pocket her throwing knives from Marcus, but marching angrily around the palace with them didn't seem like the wisest thing to do. Catrina would probably think she was taking after her parents and planning a coup. What about other gifts from Marcus?

Leah shook her head. She itched to get out of here, to keep things simple. She yearned for freedom.

She grabbed only one thing, tucking it into her sock and covering it with her jeans—her unused passport with a fake human-world ID tucked inside.

The servant knocked on her door.

"I'm coming," Leah replied. She took one last look at her room. At *the* room. It wasn't hers anymore.

It never really had been.

Chapter 6

AT THE CORNER WHERE THEIR corridors met, Marcus stood waiting for Leah. She forced a smile. His eyes studied her, her outfit included, and his confusion at her choice of apparel was apparent.

"Hi," he said, taking her hand. "You okay?"

She bit her lip, glancing at the servants around them. "Of course. We need to meet with Her Majesty's aide, right?"

"Yeah. Let's go."

A servant led them through the hallways. All was silent as they walked. It felt like a death march. Marcus tightly gripped her hand the entire way, once giving her a questioning glance. She only shook her head. They needed privacy for this conversation.

After being led to Catrina's outer office, the couple was met by her aide on duty. "Her Majesty's in meetings most of the day, as expected, but we've carved out some time to hold a private discussion between the three of you right before lunch."

Leah groaned. She didn't want to have this stupid discussion at all, but to have to wait around for hours?

"Okay," Marcus replied, always the more level-headed of the two. "Thanks."

As the couple left the office, they agreed to grab an early breakfast from the kitchen. With Stephan away and Catrina in meetings, there wouldn't be a proper meal in the dining hall anyway.

Leah and Marcus took their breakfast trays to the small study, always escorted, and ate their food in relative silence.

She didn't eat much, her stomach in knots, and a little queasy. After a servant cleared their trays, the couple went for a long and slow stroll in the gardens. Marcus was still uncharacteristically quiet, but so was Leah.

"Are you nervous?" she asked.

He waited a moment to respond. "I guess that depends on what you're asking about…"

"About your aunt…"

He shook his head. "Aunt Catrina only wants what's best for us."

She hid her frustration. So now them getting married wasn't just the 'right' thing to do, it was the 'best' thing to do. "She wants what's best for *you*, and what's best for the kingdom, but me? Not so much."

Marcus frowned. "Come on, don't be like that. We'll get it sorted."

Sorted? Like her life was a messy room that could be folded and stacked and organized and tidied up? She'd tried that! She *did* appreciate more stability in her life, and enjoyed many things about the Ivy Kingdom, but hated fitting into a mold forced on her by her notoriety and, frankly, by Marcus's family's notoriety.

Leah's life had become a scoreboard.

Say the wrong thing at a public gathering: negative one to five points, depending on how bad it was and how much the rumors spread.

Forget to curtsy to the queen and king at a ball: negative three points, because it probably meant she didn't respect them and was planning to assassinate them.

Be found in any sort of compromising situation with her long-term boyfriend: negative three points, since she shouldn't be tarnishing his impeccable reputation.

The 'scoreboard' wasn't really discussed, but rules had been set, expectations reiterated, and criticism occasionally given.

But Leah didn't say anything. She didn't want to argue with Marcus right now. She needed him.

He continued to be lost in thought, anyway.

Approaching a massive hedge at the edge of the garden, she yearned to keep walking, to find herself at the rifting cave at the edge of the palace grounds, to simply disappear.

Leah wrapped her arms around her midsection. "I want to go," she whispered.

"Where?" he asked.

"Away. I don't want to deal with this right now." Even as the words left her lips, she knew how childish that sounded. Actions had risks and consequences.

"She just wants to talk." Marcus rubbed her arm. "She wants to help."

It took everything Leah had to not roll her eyes. When things were calm, he was the realm's best boyfriend—attentive, sweet, passionate, funny, dorky. When it came to his family and their place in society, he sometimes wore rose-colored glasses, or failed to see exactly how hard it was for Leah.

"Sure," she muttered, turning back to the palace. Only when they were halfway back did he take her hand, and she softened a degree.

***

Catrina sat in her office, a kind but perhaps not fully genuine smile on her lips. "Hopefully you've both had some time to calm down and discuss things properly." Her gaze traveled over Leah in her human-world clothes.

Leah bit her tongue, the heat already rising in her cheeks.

Marcus said nothing.

"We're not going to make any huge decisions in one day," Leah answered.

"Surely you two have talked about marriage before…" Catrina arched a single eyebrow, a little more pointedly at Marcus.

"Please don't," he practically whispered, gently shaking his head.

Catrina sat back in her chair, blowing out a breath.

"We're not going to get married just to make you happy or to avoid a scandal," Leah said.

Catrina pursed her lips.

"We're nineteen. We're adults. We can do what we want."

Nodding, Catrina crossed her legs. "Then please act like one."

Watch your posture. Remember the governor's name. Don't forget to curtsy. Avoid looking like you're making frivolous purchases. Keep criticism to yourself.

Leah stood. "You have enough appointments today. We don't want to burden you."

"Sit down, Leah." Catrina pointed to the chair.

"No," Leah spat out with finality. Her passport was still tucked into her sock, and she was ready for its unused status to change. "I'm going." She threw a pleading look at Marcus to join her.

He frowned, only mouthing the word, "Please."

She wasn't going to fight him, too. Leah stormed across the room, pulling the door open.

"Eleana!" Catrina yelled, and the guards outside the room closed in on her.

Leah whipped around. "Let me go. You don't want me here, so I'm going."

Catrina pointed again to the chair. Marcus ran a hand through his hair, slumping in his own seat.

"One way or another, I am going," Leah said, her voice almost shaking. "I'm done with you, and I'm done with this place."

She glanced at the guards over her shoulder; they were poised with wrists at the ready to tie her up with vines if need be.

Catrina threw her hands in the air. "Fine. Go have another temper tantrum. Marcus and I could stand to have an adult conversation."

Marcus buried his face in his hands, but remained seated.

Leah's heart begged for Marcus to join her, to show a united front, but she needed to get out of here, and she wasn't going to wait for him. The moment the guards stepped aside, Leah made a beeline for the exit. After several hallways and a couple of sets of stairs, she slammed the door behind her and breathed in the fresh air. Only a little winded from the stairs, she marched forward.

"Temper tantrum," she muttered.

She got an odd glance from a servant or two tending the grounds as she kept mumbling to herself and striding through the gardens.

After several minutes, she was past the gardens and into the forest, ducking under tree branches.

"Leah!" Marcus's voice twisted her heart, but she only slowed a little.

"Leah! Wait up!"

She didn't, but he eventually caught up to her, winded, grabbing her hand.

"Hey, wait a second."

She took her hand back and continued walking. "Like I said, I'm going."

"And I'm going with you." He strode beside her, putting an arm around her. "Where are we going?"

She wanted to cry again. "Where do you think? The rifting cave."

"Okay."

They were still a couple dozen yards away when a horn rang through the air, and they both halted.

Fear raced through Leah. She'd only heard that horn once before, during a security drill. Surely no one was attacking the palace right now.

And then her knees got shaky. Catrina thought *she* was the threat? She was just scared and angry, and wanting to leave.

"What did she say after I left?" Leah asked.

He looked flustered. "It doesn't really matter. I … wanted to come after you and told her I was leaving, too."

In no time flat, soldiers ran through the woods, closing in on them. Even though electronics didn't work in the Green Lands, green folk had their ways of communicating. Guards in palace towers and lookouts high in the trees knew how to efficiently convey messages with codes and mirrors.

As the soldiers approached Leah and Marcus, the couple held up their hands, though Marcus didn't have his as high. Flashbacks tore through Leah's mind. Of gasps in a dining room. Of guards shoving her down a mansion hallway. Of being strapped to a chair for hours as she was bombarded with information about her parents. Of how much she'd thrown up when she'd come to accept the truth.

She didn't want to go back. If Marcus weren't next to her, if she weren't pregnant, if she didn't know better, she would have fought these soldiers. Tooth and nail. And she would have lost.

"Come with us please," one soldier said.

Leah gritted her teeth. Marcus took her hand, squeezing it. "It's really not that big of a deal to hear her out."

It wasn't to him. Neither of their aunts had ever discussed executing *him*.

"Fine." As they returned to the palace with several escorts, numbness overtook Leah. At least the archers positioned high above them didn't have their arrows aimed at her, so that was a good sign.

***

"I am trying to be patient," Catrina said, standing tall in her office again. "And I am not the enemy." Her soft blue eyes competed against her firm tone.

"Neither am I." Leah stood as well, refusing to take a seat. "But that didn't stop you from siccing your soldiers on me, did it?"

"Eleana!" Catrina scolded. "It doesn't have to be this way. We've treated you like family since the moment you moved in with us. Family dinners, outings, holidays…"

"But you're not my family. And I want to leave."

Catrina shook her head. "If you're going to leave this way, then—"

"Then what? You'll cut me off? I don't need your money." That was a lie. "I don't need your servants, or your palace." She shoved her hands into her pockets. "I don't need any of it."

Turning to Marcus, Catrina gestured at Leah. "Marcus?"

His expression was the epitome of discomfort. Only in that moment did it really dawn on Leah how hard this might be for him. He was being asked to choose between following his pregnant girlfriend and his own aunt, his queen.

"This doesn't have anything to do with him," Leah said, hoping to take some pressure off him. "Either throw me in the dungeon like a tyrant, or let me go. Last I checked, I'm a free citizen in this kingdom, and I haven't actually done anything wrong."

Catrina eyed her, considering. "If you want to go, then go. But you better understand the implications. You better remember the promises you've made about security measures at this palace."

Leah huffed. "Like I have anyone to tell them to."

"Passageways included."

"Done." She looked at Marcus. "I'm heading out. Again."

Marcus took her hand.

"You'll leave from the front gate," Catrina added. "You're no longer permitted to use the palace's cave."

An emotional door had officially been slammed in Leah's face. She and Marcus were to do the walk of shame, taking the much longer way out on foot.

Leah held back her tears, squared her shoulders, and choked down the lump in her throat. "Fine."

***

Their escort was mortifying. They hadn't stopped at their chambers for anything. And when the palace gates creaked closed behind them, Leah almost crumpled on the spot.

But she didn't. She gathered her thoughts and took a deep breath. She was *actually* homeless now.

It would be a long walk to reach a major highway.

Marcus had his hand on her back. "Do you want to take a rickshaw?"

There were always a few lining the central path between the palace and highway.

"No. I don't." She needed to work off some steam. And at least pretend to be as strong as she was stubborn.

"Alright," he said softly.

About a mile down the path, they neared the highway. Their walk had been done in silence, punctuated by the crunch of their footsteps on gravel and the occasional songbird flying above. Honey bees buzzed nearby.

Leah was thirsty, and *desperately* wanted a nap. And frankly, she didn't know where they were headed.

"Where … are we going?" She was the homeless one, not him. He still had a home with his parents, *and* a temporary home already lined up for him for his internship up north.

He kissed her temple. "I have an idea. But…" He hesitated. "We should stop by my parents' place first."

She cringed, wilting. "Do we have to?"

Marcus blew out a long breath, tucking her hair behind her ears. "The family talks. And I'd rather give them the news myself before Aunt Catrina sends word."

Frowning, Leah nodded. He deserved as much, no matter how little she wanted to see anyone in either of their families right now. Rachel and Guillen had forbidden them from sleeping together long before they'd even gotten back together as a couple. But unlike the motivations behind Catrina's orders to wait until marriage, Marcus's parents had set that expectation out of love and concern for him.

Leah had understood that. They genuinely had been astoundingly forgiving of her, accepting her into their home and family. That generosity, however, wasn't likely to extend to her anymore once they found out Leah was about to tarnish their perfect little boy's reputation.

Leah's thoughts turned to her own mother, and she couldn't hold back tears this time. She cried silently, allowing memories of a prison visit months prior to flood her mind. There was so much pain there. She still hadn't shared details of that visit with Marcus. Like a lot of her trauma, she'd buried it and tried to forget it.

She sniffled, and Marcus rubbed her back. "We'll be fine. I have a plan, I swear."

Sniffling again, she nodded. Glancing at him, she stopped thinking about herself. Why did she have to love him? If she were less selfish, she would have let him go long ago.

"I'm sorry," she whispered.

"For what?"

He was *so* close to his family. His parents, brother, aunt and uncle—the whole lot of them.

"For driving a wedge between you and your aunt."

He pressed his lips together, looking straight forward.

They neared another rickshaw, and he asked again if she was interested in taking it. It was several miles now to the nearest rifting cave, and she was crashing from her adrenaline high. She accepted, and he pulled coins from his wallet for the driver.

After they slid in and the driver began pedaling, Marcus squeezed her hand. "I will always choose you." He smiled softly, then kissed her cheek. Quiet enough for the driver not to overhear, Marcus added, "And I'll always choose our baby."

Chapter 7

AFTER THE RICKSHAW CAME TO a stop at the nearest rifting cave, Leah and Marcus stood in line to go through. The cave was somewhat busy, and gazes caught on the couple now and then. That was expected, completely normal. Perhaps not at that particular cave, though, since they'd never been forbidden from using the palace's private cave. What onlookers saw—his arm supportively around her, faint smiles—was far from properly representing the chaos of the day. Eventually, their turn came, and Leah rifted first. With the help of a Seeder employee, Marcus rifted next.

Leah was tired. It would be another half-hour walk from the cave to Marcus's parents' house, and they could have rented bikes, or paid for a rickshaw to get them there faster, but she didn't want to get there faster.

She didn't want to disappoint more people today. Didn't want to see the looks on his parents' faces.

So, they plodded on. Marcus kept his arm around her, but there wasn't much conversation to be had.

"What are your plans?" she finally asked. "Where are we going to stay? What are we going to do?" She wasn't fond of the idea of him wasting his money on an inn for her, and while she was always welcome to stay in the family guest house on Rachel and Guillen's property, she imagined that open invitation was about to come to an abrupt close.

Marcus smiled. "For starters, we can stay at Tobias and Cam's cottage."

Leah arched an eyebrow. "Really?" They lived in the human world, but visited on a somewhat regular basis, and always stayed in their Ivy Kingdom cottage on visits.

"Yep. They told me I could crash over there if I ever needed some space from Mom and Dad."

"I just … don't want to impose."

He rubbed her arm. "They're not expected to come visit for several weeks. We'll be fine."

Drawing a deep breath, she relaxed a little. She was a cloud in the wind right now—floating, directionless, not tethered or grounded. They at least had a starting point.

But they had to talk to his parents first.

***

Leah's legs filled with lead as they stepped onto the grounds. Marcus's hand on her back wasn't exactly *shoving* her forward … but it was definitely doing its part to keep her upright and on her current trajectory up the lane.

"It'll be fine," Marcus whispered into her ear. "Try to be calm about it."

The lack of perfect calmness in his voice did his statement no favors. Telling his aunt he'd gotten Leah pregnant was one thing, even if his aunt was the queen. But breaking the news to his parents…

Rachel greeted them with a smile and a hug. "I love surprise visits!"

"It's good to see you too." Leah wore the best smile she could muster.

They sat in the living room, and Marcus grabbed some crackers from the kitchen to snack on, giving Leah some. He also brought her a glass of water, which she was immensely grateful for.

"So… Just dropping by because…?" Rachel asked.

Marcus cleared his throat. "Well, we, uh… When will Dad be home?"

Rachel glanced at a clock on the wall, crossing her legs. "Shouldn't be long."

"Cool…" Marcus sat back on the sofa. "I had a nice visit with Ambassador Grayas at the palace."

Leah snuggled up to him, taking sips of water. Marcus's small talk—as if life were normal—was difficult for Leah to hear, but it did the job of filling the time before Guillen would get home.

Rachel looked so young. And she *was* young. She was going to become a grandma before her fortieth birthday.

Leah's stomach churned. Maybe she should have just listened to Catrina. Should have given in. Maybe they should have eloped and lied about the date, and then everyone would be more forgiving?

People looked to the royal family expecting perfection. Wise decisions, ideal families, no missteps. Marcus and Tobias had gotten tons of attention during Kaylah's rule, as the nephews to the queen who had no children of her own. They had less focus on them now with Catrina in control, and with her bearing children, but Rachel and Guillen were still war heroes, and Leah was still a black mark.

There would *always* be high expectations.

"Anything exciting with you, Leah?" Rachel asked.

"Oh, well…" She let out a nervous chuckle. "You know, the usual…"

The front door squeaked, and Leah didn't know whether to be relieved the small talk would be over, or more nervous since they now had to fess up.

"Hey, honey," Guillen called from the foyer. Entering the room, he wore a bright smile. "Hi, you two. I expected you'd be staying the bulk of your weekend at the palace."

"Yeah, well ... plans changed," Marcus replied with a hint of unease in his voice.

Guillen sat opposite them, next to Rachel. "Well, I certainly wasn't complaining. Any fun plans?"

Leah placed a hand on Marcus's knee, squeezing it. He rested his hand on hers. "We kinda need to talk."

Rachel surveyed them, her eyes narrowing slightly. "Okay…"

"Um…" His voice was higher, all confidence stripped from it. "Well, we… Things, um, aren't going as planned, exactly…"

Guillen's eyes flickered to Leah's hand on Marcus's knee. "Go on."

"We're, uh… Well, Leah's … um… She's…." Marcus swallowed. "Pregnant," he whispered.

Rachel's eyes grew wide, immediately looking at Leah.

"That is *not* what we were expecting to hear," Guillen said calmly.

Rachel pinched the bridge of her nose. "Where, when, how, why?"

Marcus glanced at Leah. "At the palace."

Honestly, if they were going to sneak around, they should have done it on one of Leah's visits here, because it would have made things ten times easier, and likely wouldn't have ticked Catrina off so much. But Leah couldn't have imagined doing so. She'd betrayed their family once, when they'd first welcomed her into this home. Sneaking around Rachel and Guillen's house would have felt like much more of a betrayal.

"And she's a little over two weeks along."

While Guillen did a better job of veiling his reaction, Rachel was pretty obvious in her disapproval. "How and why did this happen?"

"How?" Marcus asked in a higher octave, squirming in his seat.

"I know how babies are made, Marcus." Rachel crossed her arms. "But this is unbelievable."

The rest of the conversation went much more calmly than it had at the palace. Rachel and Guillen shared their disappointment, and reiterated the rules, and expectations the family had had for the couple. Marcus and Leah explained that it was an accident, that they were adults, and that they were keeping the baby.

Rachel focused on Leah's hand. "You're not engaged?"

"No." Marcus's response was swift, with perhaps a hint of … disappointment?

Of course he was disappointed. He was doing a decent job of supporting Leah, but he was just trying not to get crushed between a rock and a hard place with his family's reputation and Leah's proposal denial.

Rachel's brow furrowed. "Why not?" The question had been aimed at Leah.

Leah looked away. "Because we're not."

"Why?" There was something in Rachel's tone this time that Leah couldn't fully discern. Her expression was a bit confusing as well. Why didn't Leah love Marcus enough to accept his proposal right away? Why wasn't Leah immediately falling into line and marching to the beat of the royal family's drum?

They eyed each other for a minute. "Because I'm not ready," Leah finally answered with as much conviction as she could, without sounding confrontational.

Guillen sighed, rubbing his face. "Then what's the plan?"

Leah stood, unable to bear more discussion about plans they didn't have. Marcus followed suit.

"We wanted to be the ones to tell you before Her Majesty did," Leah said. She started to walk out of the room.

"We'll keep you updated," Marcus said, trailing after her.

His parents didn't come after them, didn't demand more answers.

The moment the young couple stepped out the front door, Leah fell into Marcus's arms, crying. Every moment of her life was a disappointment to others. Every ounce of her existence unwanted. The entire realm would have been happier if she would have never been born.

Marcus held her tight, rubbing her back. "Come on. Let's go to the cottage and rest for a bit."

***

The cottage was a tiny one-bedroom setup, and they'd been there to visit before, but it felt intrusive to sort through Tobias and Camry's things while they were away.

Leah sat on the sofa in the main room while Marcus surveyed the pantry and checked out the cellar. Worn out, practically in a trance, Leah stared at a bookshelf.

After a little while, Marcus joined her, kissing her cheek. "There's enough to piece together a few meals with whatever is growing wild in the garden, but I'll want to swing by the market."

She numbly nodded.

He pulled her into an embrace, wrapping his arms around her from behind. "Look at that pretty painting. I wonder what amazing couple gifted that to Tobias and Cam…"

Leah scoffed. "You picked it out with your dad."

"But it was intended as a gift from you and me."

She frowned. "You mean the day before I ruined their wedding by trying to kill Kaylah?"

Marcus remained silent for a moment. "We've all moved on from that. You should too."

Something deep in her soul ached. But had they? Who was 'we all'? Not the entire realm. Not Queen Catrina, since she hadn't even trusted Leah with knowledge of the palace's hidden passageways. Not even Tobias. He'd never actually said the words 'I forgive you.' At family gatherings he was polite, albeit a smidge cold, but nowhere near as friendly as he'd been when they'd first met. Marcus had been right when he'd told Leah that Tobias knew how to hold grudges. Camry, his wife, was much more generous. Granted, she was human, and hadn't grown up with the royal family dynamic and expectations the brothers had.

"Are you sure they'll be okay with us staying here?" Leah asked.

63

"Yeah. Of course."

Leah had nowhere else to go. She hadn't grabbed any money, any extra clothes, any ... anything, other than the passport still tucked away in her sock.

"Alright," she said, resigned to the idea, given her lack of options at the moment.

"I love you," Marcus whispered into her ear.

"I know."

"I looove you," he said in a singsong voice.

"I looove you too."

He nuzzled her neck. "I love you." His voice was comically deep this time, and she finally smiled.

"Mhmm?"

His arms tightened around her waist. "I love you both."

She melted right there on the spot, snuggling with more ease into his arms. "Thank you."

He kissed her neck.

Lying in his arms, she half expected a servant or soldier to come crashing into the cottage as a chaperone. Or to drag them back to the palace to pick out wedding linens. But they didn't. No footsteps clicked in stone hallways. No dignitaries visited who Leah needed to remember the names of.

Just silence. Just being held by her best friend. Before she knew it, she'd nodded off.

***

Leah woke disoriented, taking a minute to find her bearings. She'd never slept in the cottage, so she panicked a bit, but then the warmth of Marcus's body behind her brought a smile to her face. He was her home. Anywhere with Marcus could be home.

"Are you awake?" she whispered. No response, only soft breaths.

She carefully pulled his arms away from her so she could slip off the sofa. Marcus's hands suddenly pulled her back down. "Mmm, but you're warm."

She chuckled. "Yes, but I'm also hungry."

He trailed more kisses down her neck. "Fine. Be that way."

She stood, taking a moment to play with a couple of his curly locks before walking to the kitchen.

After returning with more water and a bowl of dried apricots to share, she faced Marcus, sitting cross-legged. "Where do we go from here?"

With a contemplative look, Marcus focused on the apricot he squished between his fingers. "I don't know. You tell me."

Leah swallowed hard. Just because they were pregnant and cut off from the palace didn't mean their lives had come to a screeching halt, did it? They could still keep moving forward… Minus the fact that Leah seriously doubted Catrina would have her tutors come to the little cottage, she also didn't have money for further tuition at the academy. She didn't even know how much it was or what the payment schedule was. It was more affordable and flexible than colleges in the United States back in the human world, but students still paid something to attend classes…

But Marcus had options. He had a stipend—an allowance from his family's investments. He still had his internship, which started the following week, and presumably work with his dad until then.

"You should keep working," she said. He deserved to pursue his passions and career goals. No one really knew about the pregnancy yet, and it wasn't like anyone in their families would leak that information to make things worse for Marcus.

Marcus nodded. "And you?"

"I'll…" She wasn't up to the scrutiny of the public right now.

He gave her an understanding look.

"I'm going to take some time to rest until the maternal sickness passes, and…" She glanced out the window toward the small backyard. "I'll work in the garden to help save on groceries."

He gave her a weak smile. "Sure."

After a little more snacking, they decided they needed some real food. Leah was anxious about leaving the house. The idea of being out in public without an escort, or being around people at all, was too much to stomach. Marcus volunteered to go alone.

In the hour or so that passed during his absence, Leah more fully explored the cottage. She ought to have asked him to buy more clothes for her, but she didn't know how much money he had on hand, or if he'd know how to buy her size without her trying the clothes on. Handcrafted clothing here varied a lot more than mass-produced goods back in the human world.

Leah shrugged it off, running her fingers over the embroidered waistline of a cute shirt she remembered Camry wearing ages ago. Camry had once offered to let Leah borrow her clothes, so that would have to do for now. While she was in the closet, she finally took her passport out and tucked it away for safekeeping.

The bookshelf in the main room was fairly full, which was a normal sight in the place of a wealthy family like Marcus's, but apparently not all that common in regular green-folk homes. Printing and binding were still old-school without electricity, and the paper degraded far less quickly in this realm than the human world. That meant the library systems here were generous and extensive. So Leah had been told, at least; she hadn't had much opportunity to see or learn all of that for herself.

She dared to step into the backyard and stroll around a bit. The garden was unkempt, which wasn't surprising since Tobias and Camry weren't there often. Rachel and Guillen usually had a gardener come well in advance to tidy things up if the couple was planning an extended visit.

Taking off her shoes, Leah roamed through the cool grassy yard. Despite being in a wealthy part of town, it was low-key on this property, a refreshing change of pace.

Now if only time could freeze, and this cottage was a few miles away from civilization…

Standing under a healthy chestnut tree, she got an idea. Holding her hands up, she shot vines out of her wrists, wrapping them around a sturdy branch. Disconnecting the vines at her wrists, she then extended more and quickly wove it together, making a less-than-ideal but better-than-nothing swing. She tested its hold, then carefully sat, smiling.

She softly swung, staring at the Outer Rim mountains in the far distance and the setting sun. Streaks of violet and fuchsia painted the sky, and she thought of the palace. What had they eaten for dinner? What had King Stephan thought of this whole debacle?

As it grew later, Leah started to worry. Marcus should've been back already. She considered slipping her shoes back on and trekking to the market alone, but a pair of hands suddenly gripping her sides stopped her from getting off the swing.

She startled and looked over her shoulder. Marcus laid a kiss on her.

"I was getting worried. What took you so long?"

He smiled. "Just putting up the food and preparing us something fresh."

She frowned. "You should have gotten me. I'm more than willing to help." She'd never cooked in the palace, understandably, but she often joined Rachel in the kitchen when visiting their place, and she'd helped her mom cook all the time in the human world.

"That's okay. I figured you could use a breather after today." He nodded at the cottage. "Want to see what I made?"

"Yeah." She got up, and they walked inside. He'd lit candles already, and the two of them ate the salads he'd prepared while discussing the market and the next day. He still had his third day off work, so they had nothing on the agenda.

As the dark of night enveloped the evening, Leah drank a mint tea, which helped with her nausea. She was still beat, though, mostly from the emotional roller coaster.

After the stress of the day, it was a bit awkward climbing into bed together this time, but they easily found their place, snuggling up and quickly dozing off.

Chapter 8

LEAH WOKE EARLY, THOUGH NOT as early as she normally would.

No servants knocked on her door. No breakfast bell rang through the halls. As much as a pampered life was superior in some ways, it couldn't hold a candle to waking up next to Marcus.

She watched his chest rise and fall. This wasn't their first time sharing a bed, but it was the first time they'd actually spent the whole night together.

Her happiness wavered. Had she placed all her happiness on him? Did she lean on him too much? His reputation, now his money? His kindness? Was she just using him again?

What had he told her two years ago when they'd broken up? 'I'm not your crutch.'

Closing her eyes, she pushed out those memories. She'd deserved his anger. And she'd done her best to make her own way, right? She'd become studious, without needing him to keep her on track like he had in high school.

Though ... now she might become the equivalent of a college dropout.

She breathed deeply, restoring her smile and focusing on his face. Leaning over, she gently pressed her lips against his. It took him a moment, but he soon kissed back, sliding his hands along her back to pull her in. He moaned, deepening the kiss.

After a minute or two of kissing, he gazed into her eyes, smiling wide. "First time being kissed awake… That's something I could get used to."

She agreed.

His hand trailed to her hip. "There's something else we haven't had a chance to do in the morning."

It wasn't like she needed to worry about birth control tonic anymore. "I vote we give it a try."

*****

They lay under the covers, sharing a smile. "I love you," he said.

"I love you too." They were good at this. She'd slept with enough guys in high school to know the difference, and what Marcus lacked in experience, he made up for with passion and sweetness.

He tickled her exposed shoulder, his mouth agape for a moment. "Please marry me."

Something in her tightened, and she looked away. Each time someone brought up marriage now, it was like a vise in her chest gripped a smidge tighter. And with each addition of pressure, an anger rose in her, a part of her that fought harder to push back.

Maybe she was emotionally claustrophobic. Was that a thing?

It was probably just the stress of trying to prove herself in the Green Lands, and attempting to follow all the rules laid out for her. If people would stop bringing it up, she wouldn't push back. Right?

Part of her feared that wasn't the case. Perhaps she'd met her limit long ago. After an entire childhood of being lied to, of having zero say in where they would live, or when they would move. Of living moving box to moving box, town to town. Of not being allowed to have social media accounts like every single kid her age did. Of losing her friends and being forced to cut ties every time they relocated.

"No," she said softly, getting out of bed and grabbing a towel. He should understand that he needed to be patient with her. He should understand *her* by now.

Hadn't she been clear—crystal clear—years ago when they'd danced together for the first time at a ball, that she would never be the girl Ivy royal society wanted? She'd be herself. She'd dress the way she wanted, and act the way she wanted.

But she'd given in on so many things. And maybe he'd come to love *that* Leah too much.

She made a beeline for the solar-heated shower.

He got out of bed, following her to the bathroom, stopping her from shutting the door. "Come on." He frowned. "You act like we've never talked about this."

Sighing, she leaned in the doorway. Was this what he wanted? To get married so they could have sex all the time? To get married to appease the kingdom and his family? To keep his name less tarnished?

Or was he just that nice of a guy? The stay-with-the-girl-you-knocked-up-no-matter-what kind of guy? All obligation?

"We never did talk about *this*, Marcus. This version of things. Of me getting pregnant years before I was planning to start a family, and then having everyone in the realm pressure me into getting married."

"I'm not asking because you're pregnant. I'm asking because I love you."

In the back of her mind, a voice rose from her childhood, that of a woman in prison. *You did this on purpose. You were afraid he would leave. You just don't want to admit it to yourself.*

She swallowed as another voice took its turn. *You were always a slut. This was bound to happen. You only exist to burden others.*

"Maybe I'll consider it when people stop pressuring me into it." She forced the door closed before she began to cry. She spent half her shower doing exactly that—quietly sobbing into her knees.

***

Leah stepped out with a towel around her. Marcus still waited in the hallway, his head on his knees in a similar fashion to how she'd sat in the shower.

He looked up with a cautious expression. "I'm sorry … if you feel pressured, okay?"

She averted her gaze. "Thank you."

Standing, he gave her a kiss on the cheek and took a turn in the shower while she dressed.

They made breakfast together—an apple salad similar to a Waldorf salad, but with a different dressing. They juiced some kittlefruit and oranges to accompany it. Only the repeated *thud* of the knife on a wooden cutting board really sliced through the thick silence between them.

"I don't want to fight," he whispered.

"Me either."

She took the bowl from his hands, setting it down, and pulled him into a long hug.

It was much needed, as was their refreshing meal. Afterward, they enjoyed some downtime playing a card game.

Leah laid down a card. "Would you mind going back to the market today? At the very least, I do need some new underwear of my own."

He lifted an eyebrow. "Yeah, guess you're not wearing Cam's, huh?"

She grimaced. "No. I'll wash the pair I wore yesterday, but," she shifted in her seat, "jeans and commando—not so fun."

Marcus's grin was mischievous. "If we're going to share a place, and you're going to go without wearing those, then I don't see why you need to wear anything at all."

He was getting way too comfortable with this lifestyle already. He rarely made her blush, but he'd succeeded. "Stop it." She pursed her lips. "Does that mean you're not wearing anything under those pants, either?"

He squinted playfully. "Wanna find out?"

She giggled, throwing a card at him.

Placing her card on the correct pile, he cleared his throat. "No, I had a couple pairs of spare clothes over here already, in case I ever wanted to crash here when we had guests over."

Lucky for him. He had a stash of clothes at the palace for his visits too.

"I don't mind going to the market. Though it might be as odd picking you up underwear as it was the…"

The birth control tonic.

"Well, anyway…" He looked at his hand, rearranging his cards. "I'll pick you up some. Since I only have a couple of pairs here, I'll swing by my place to get some of my own clothes."

She internally groaned. Couldn't they just avoid family? Boycott the rest of the world and live in a reality where it was only the two of them and no pressure? No conflict?

But it *would* be a waste of money for him to buy new clothes when his parents' place was only a mile away.

"I'll try to just slip in and out if I can, okay?"

She nodded.

***

Marcus returned a few hours later, hands full of tote bags holding clothes. Luckily, neither of his parents had been home, so he'd been able to grab some of his own things without any conflict.

Leah rifled through the things he'd gotten her. She couldn't help but smirk. He was like a kid in a candy store, having bought her a wide array of colors. "Interesting choices," she commented. "Was there a discount for less fabric?"

He busted out laughing. "That's what you get for letting me pick."

She kept smiling, putting them away in a drawer. They honestly weren't all that different from what she'd often worn in the human world, and she'd felt too awkward to buy that style as the ward of the queen and king. "I'll let it slide this once." She winked.

Marcus continued hanging up his clothes, putting a few pieces up on the shelf of the closet. "And if you want more clothes of your own instead of borrowing Cam's, let me know."

She perched on the edge of the bed. "I'm fine." She'd never liked taking charity. Granted, borrowing Camry's clothes was *also* accepting charity, but it wasn't wasteful…

"You *are* fine," he said playfully.

It was moments like these that gave her a glimpse of who they used to be amidst the chaos of the last couple of days and weeks. It was almost even better in a way, because they were legitimately sharing a room, and so far, she didn't hate it in the slightest. As an only child, she'd been worried about having to share.

"What in the?" Marcus reached above his head in the closet, pulling out Leah's passport. "How did Tobias and Cam get back to the human world if they forgot—"

Leah swallowed, frozen as he flipped it open to read *her* name.

He looked at her, confused and obviously hurt. "When you were heading to the cave by the palace, you were going to the human world? I thought you were just going to rift to… Well, I guess I didn't know where…"

She gingerly took the book from his hands, frowning. "I wasn't going to… Not necessarily… Honestly, I wasn't thinking straight. I didn't know where I was going, either."

He weakly nodded, but it was clear he didn't believe her.

"I swear. I wasn't going to leave you." She wasn't going to. Except she kind of had… But it wasn't like she'd planned on *actually* leaving him, on breaking things off.

But maybe he thought she was lying again. Because that certainly had never happened in their relationship before…

She set the passport on the bed and stood, taking his face in her hands. "I wasn't going to leave you."

He searched her eyes. "Okay." His voice didn't hold much more conviction than it had before.

She stole a peck on the lips, and he gave her a half-smile. So she kissed him again and again, hoping to lighten the mood.

"Alright. I get it." He wore a more convincing smile this time. "Do you want me to put that back up there?"

"Um, don't worry about it. I'm kinda starving already." She held him by the waist. "Would you mind fixing a snack for us?"

He stole one more glance at the passport. "Sure."

Once he left the room, Leah stared at the passport, her heart pounding. The way he'd looked at it made her worried he'd take it so she *couldn't* leave.

Picking it up, she ran her thumb over the gold embossing—a blossom surrounded by an ivy leaf resting on a handprint. An old impulse came to visit—one she'd long since tackled and overcome. Stealing, and then hiding the plunder in her bedroom.

It was ridiculous, really. It wasn't stealing. This passport was *hers*. But the need for secrecy, for hiding, for keeping herself safe, for relying on herself, came so naturally in the moment.

As more chopping and stirring echoed from the kitchen, Leah scoured the room for a good hiding spot. She ended up tucking it away in Camry's underwear drawer, assuming Marcus wouldn't have the guts to search through his sister-in-law's private things.

She then closed the closet door, and since it had taken her a while to decide on a hiding spot, she busied herself with making the bed.

No sooner had she replaced the pillows than Marcus came back into the room, stirring a large bowl. He glanced at the closed closet, no doubt wondering why it had taken her so long to join him.

She smiled. "I guess I've gotten too used to a tidy bed at the palace."

"Yeah." He nodded for her to join him. "Come with."

The rest of the day was spent peacefully. There was a slight bit of anxiety and tension between them, but they were just settling into new circumstances. It was reasonable to assume it would take some adjusting.

She was surprised when they headed to bed that he didn't want to do more than cuddle, but she wasn't terribly in the mood, either. It had been a weird day, to say the least.

She didn't sleep the best, her mind running through all the problems with no solutions in sight. But she did eventually nod off.

Only to be awoken bright and early by a knock on the front door. She stilled, making sure it was actually a knock and not something from her dreams.

Another knock.

"Marcus." She shook him awake. "Someone's at the door."

He blinked. "What?"

"Someone's at the door."

Rubbing his face, he groaned. "Yeah. Let me get dressed. I'm not opening doors in boxers anymore."

He stood, grabbing a pair of pants.

"Marcus?" a male voice called from a distance.

Leah froze. "Is that your dad?"

Chapter 9

MARCUS'S FACE WENT PALE AS he tugged on his pants. "Yeah, sounds like him."

Why couldn't his family leave them alone to sort things out? Give them a little privacy?

"How did he even know to find us here?"

It was probably pretty obvious. If they weren't staying at the palace or his family's estate, then the cottage would be the most likely answer.

Marcus pulled out a shirt, an apologetic look on his face. "I … left my parents a note when I went to grab my clothes. Just in case they were worried…"

She let out a frustrated sigh, and he frowned.

"Marcus?" Guillen called again.

Marcus ran from the bedroom, and the front door squeaked open. "Dad… Hey…"

"Are you still coming to work with me?"

Leah glanced at the clock in the corner of the bedroom, blowing out a breath. They'd agreed he would go back to work as usual, and his three-day weekend was up, so they shouldn't have been surprised.

"Yeah, of course. Let me brush my teeth," Marcus said.

After a few footsteps padded down the hallway, water splashed from the direction of the bathroom, and Leah worried he might not even say goodbye. But he reappeared in the bedroom for a moment, giving her a kiss. "I'll be back right after work, alright?"

She sat up in bed. "Yeah. Have a good day."

Half expecting Guillen to mention that he knew Leah was hiding away in the bedroom, Leah was surprised when the front door clicked closed without a single mention of her. Though … just because they hadn't talked about her while they were within hearing range didn't mean they wouldn't be discussing Leah on their trip to and from work.

She groaned, sliding down in bed, throwing the covers over her head, and falling back asleep.

***

It was quiet when she woke, but that extra sleep was exceptionally refreshing. Leah threw on some of Camry's pajamas. After a trip to the bathroom, she settled on cooking a decent breakfast. The pancakes she made on the griddle were fine, but her mouth watered at the thought of bacon. Oh, how she missed bacon after more than two years without it!

She blankly stabbed at the last pancake on her plate, dragging it through the dregs of crushed raspberries. Bacon—she and her mom had cooked up bacon for a nice last meal together before she'd betrayed her mom, before she'd run away with Marcus.

Before she'd tried to kill Kaylah, and had gotten her mom caught after nearly two decades in hiding.

Leah couldn't hold back tears. It was probably just hormones. Ivy pregnancies and births were very similar to that of humans. Never had Leah been more jealous of Seeders than when she found out Seeder girls didn't even have to endure periods. And here she was—knocked up, nauseous, and moody.

But it wasn't really fair to blame it all on hormones. One of Leah's 'talents' was shoving down her trauma, just to let it build and bubble over. But that wouldn't happen this time.

Leah was fine. She'd come to terms with the truth about her parents and the atrocities they'd taken part in during the old war. She'd … ignored the truth bomb her mom had dropped on her a few months ago about Leah's conception.

A hollowness threatened to take hold, but Leah wouldn't allow that.

Standing from the little breakfast nook, she refilled her water glass. She'd said she would tend to the garden, but didn't have it in her right now. Instead, she turned to the main room and perused the books on the shelf. They ought to keep her mind off everything.

The books were about seventy/thirty fiction to nonfiction. Tobias didn't seem so stuffy that he'd enjoy reading nonfiction on his visits to his home realm, so these had probably been collected by or gifted to Camry—informational tidbits to help the human fit in.

Leah related to Camry so much on that, having grown up *thinking* she was human. Then again, Leah had spent the last two years with the highest caliber of tutors and educators.

Nonfiction sounded boring, not the escape she wanted. But, she reasoned, if she took some time to read it, that would supplement her current education. She wasn't dropping out. She was … doing independent study.

Leah pulled a book off the shelf; the spine was dandelion yellow. *Seeders: Past, Present, & Future.* It had likely been gifted by someone from Rachel's side of the family.

She cozied up on the sofa, pulling a light afghan over her lap. Then she got lost in words and pictures for hours. She took a few bathroom breaks, and a late lunch, but for the most part simply soaked up all the culture and history there.

A knock from behind startled her as she turned a page. She was of half a mind to ignore it and pretend she wasn't home, but if someone was dropping by a rarely used cottage, they probably already knew Leah was there.

Setting her book and blanket down, Leah approached the door. She regretted going to answer it once the face of her visitor came into view. Leah wilted. Guillen coming to collect Marcus for work was one thing, but why would Rachel drop by?

It was too late to duck and hide away, as Rachel had seen her too. Leah put on a pleasant smile and opened the door. "Hi."

Rachel donned a bright smile of her own, holding a huge basket of produce. "Hi, Leah." Her gaze rested on the clothes Leah wore.

Great. Not only was she sinking Marcus's reputation and future, and had become a school dropout, but Leah was braless, wearing someone else's pajamas in someone else's home. She was a leech. Rachel had to be imagining she'd spent half the day kicking her feet up and eating bonbons.

"I was studying… About Seeders, actually." Leah jabbed a thumb over her shoulder. "And Camry said I could borrow her clothes before, and Tobias offered to let us stay here." *Not really* us, *per se, but Marcus…*

"Looks comfy, and I'm sure she wouldn't mind," Rachel said. "Mind if I come in and help you put away the food? It's from our garden. We really should do a better job of tending to the one here for surprise visits."

Yes, I mind. Leah wished for peace and quiet, and a judgment-free sanctuary. But Rachel was the last person she could ever say no to. "Sure, be my guest."

Rachel came inside, basket in hand, and headed straight for the kitchen. She started unloading fruits and vegetables, a pair of mangos here, a bunch of carrots there.

Leah stood and watched. "I can do that. Marcus can bring the basket back later tonight…"

Waving a dismissive hand, Rachel kept unpacking. "Nonsense. I don't mind."

Maybe Rachel was bored. She didn't work full-time anymore, and hadn't for a while. Most of her work was charity work, and her schedule was sporadic. Though, perhaps this was an olive branch? Or it was a way of being nosy and making Leah feel guilty.

Once the basket was emptied, Rachel picked up Leah's dirty breakfast and lunch plates, putting them in the sink, and then proceeded to mortify Leah by lifting her hand to the water pump.

"Please don't," Leah practically begged. "I know how to do my own dishes. I'd rather you not."

"I don't mind. I just want to help."

"Please. I'm not a spoiled palace brat."

Rachel chuckled. "I'm guessing the only dishes you've helped with in this realm were at our place, because the palace staff would be utterly insulted if you tried to do your own dishes."

Leah frowned, and Rachel matched with a frown of her own. "I didn't mean it as an insult. I've spent a good amount of time in that palace. I'm just saying I know how it works there."

She left the dishes alone, facing Leah. "Can we sit and chat for a little while?"

That certainly didn't bode well for the 'get her out so I can enjoy peace and quiet' strategy, but Leah again couldn't say no. "Sure."

They moved to the sofa, and Rachel smiled when she spotted the book Leah had been reading. Leah tucked her knees up under her chin, holding her legs.

Rachel loosed a breath. "How are you doing?"

"I'm fine. Maternal sickness, but it could be worse."

Rachel nodded. "Is that what's keeping you from your studies today?"

Leah averted her gaze. "I needed to take a day off."

"Understandable." Rachel plucked a speck of lint from her shirt. "Catrina's worried about you."

Leah met her gaze, her hairs standing on end. "You guys have … talked to her?"

"She sent a note to make sure you were okay."

That had to be a fat lie. Catrina had sent a note to ensure Leah wasn't out there giving away palace secrets, or instigating a rebellion of discontented citizens, pitchforks in hand and headed straight for the secret passageways.

"Do you love my son?" Rachel asked softly.

That was unfair, and a low blow. Now Leah suddenly didn't love Marcus, just because she wasn't ready to marry him? Every relationship Leah had been in before him was short and shallow, and mostly physical. Marcus was everything to her. He was the day to her night. "Of course I do."

Rachel chewed on her lip. "Then why don't you want to marry him?"

The vise tightened, and Leah clenched her jaw. She tried to speak calmly. "Because I'm not ready right now."

Looking into her lap, fidgeting with her hands, Rachel remained silent for a little while. "I know better than anyone how complicated it can be to date and marry into the Ivy royal family. It's very stressful. And … you knew what was expected of you when the two of you started dating again."

Leah's stomach knotted. Maybe she should have waited to tell everyone she was pregnant until she started to show—then she would have a forty-three-step plan sorted out about how she could smooth everything over without inconveniencing everyone.

"I'm sorry I'm not what you want for your son," Leah said. Flashbacks from years ago came to her. *I'm sorry I'll never be who you want me to be.* Her mom had then reassured her that she'd always love Leah, no matter what. Why was it easier for a convicted murderer to love Leah than all these upright citizens and war heroes? And then another voice reminded her of one of her darkest days. *You came into my home. You broke my son's heart. You jeopardized my husband's respectability.*

"Don't say that," Rachel insisted. "I love you like a daughter. I wish you were ready to be one."

Sometimes it was hard to know which voices to listen to. The scathing ones always felt more genuine, because the kind ones were more likely to make her look like a fool. It was particularly hard to know which to believe when the voices originated from the same source.

"And I just want my grandchild to be welcomed into this world with a supportive family," Rachel added.

"So, what does that mean for them if we don't push this under the rug and have a shotgun wedding?"

Rachel shrugged. "We'll still love them, and you. It would just be less complicated if you and Marcus took the next step sooner than later."

If this was Rachel's sole intention for her visit—to wear Leah down—then this conversation was over. "I understood the expectations when Marcus and I got back together. But he understood that I came with complications. We're adults now. Let us be."

Rachel's expression conveyed that she'd gotten the message. "I only wanted to help." She stood. "You know where to find us if you need anything."

She grabbed the empty basket from the kitchen and headed for the door. "Have a good rest of your day." Her voice was still kind, but the tension was thick.

Leah remained seated. "You too."

The door closed behind Rachel, and Leah rested her forehead on her knees. "I hate this," she muttered.

After a few minutes of gathering her thoughts, Leah got up and dressed, then set to work tidying and dusting every inch of the cottage. If they were going to get surprise visitors multiple times a day, she might as well make it look like she wasn't a useless blob and complete disappointment.

Luckily, no other visitors dropped by. Leah was just getting dinner started when Marcus returned. She gave him a genuine smile, wrapping her arms around his neck and weaving her fingers through his hair.

"Mmm." His smile was bright as he leaned in, kissing her. "I love this." He slid his arms around her waist. "Sharing our mornings and nights together. Not having to wait until the weekends." He snuck another kiss. "If I'd known how good this would feel, I'd have suggested we move in together at least a year ago."

She rolled her eyes, despite agreeing with him. "Yeah, because that would have been allowed by the committee of public scrutiny and familial obligations."

He wrinkled his nose.

"Help me with dinner?" she asked.

"Sure." He washed his hands, and they worked side by side.

"So… How was work?" she cautiously asked.

He trimmed a floret of broccoli from the stem. "Good. The usual."

"And conversation with your dad?"

He hesitated, trimming off another floret. "Good. The usual."

She passed him a skeptical glance out of the corner of her eye.

Marcus shrugged. "It was fine. I told him we were going to stay here a while and figure things out."

Leah continued plucking grapes from the stems. "How long is 'a while'? We have less than a week until you go off to start your internship up north…" There wasn't a rifting cave all that close to where he would be working, and his employer would be paying room and board. They'd planned for him to continue visiting her on the weekends when she was still living at the palace.

"We'll see. A day at a time, right?"

She nodded. "Your mom dropped by today."

"That tracks. I was curious why we have so much more fresh food. How did that go?"

"Oh, ya know. About as expected."

"What's that supposed to mean?"

She stepped behind him, using the water pump to rinse the grapes. "Trying to help. And trying to guilt us into rushing things."

"I'm sure she wasn't trying to guilt you into anything."

Why? Why did this have to happen? His family had been so supportive before she'd gotten pregnant. And now, she just wanted him to pick *her*. Not mediate. Not justify their actions.

Leah remained silent, not wanting a fight or to sour the mood.

"Have you thought more about what you're going to do with your time?" he asked. "About your studies?"

"Yep. Independent studies. I spent a good portion of today reading."

"I mean real studies."

She cocked her head, defensive. "You can be well educated without a degree or formal education, without some stupid stamp of approval." She tried to keep her tone even. "What's so special about a teacher lecturing as opposed to reading what one wrote in a book?"

He held up his hands. "Okay. So you're not keen to go back to tutors and the academy."

She frowned. It wasn't like she'd hated them.

Marcus turned, checking the heat of the coal stove. "I'm just saying, if you wanted to continue what you were doing before, I'm sure Aunt Catrina would be reasonable."

"No." If Leah never saw Catrina again, it would be too soon.

"You wouldn't even have to talk to her. You could write a letter."

"No."

He sighed, putting a pan on the stove and drizzling some olive oil into it. "Fine."

Another moment of silence passed, and she set to peeling an orange for their fruit salad.

"Do you want an escort here at the cottage?" he asked.

"What? You want to pay for a security detail? No one but the family knows I'm here so far, right?"

"Yes. Well, no. My dad asked me to ask you. The palace would still help keep you covered."

Queen Catrina's brother, Sir Guillen. Rachel had already mentioned a note. It was *so* nice to be the topic of everyone's conversations…

"I don't need an escort."

"So, you're not going back to the academy, and if I'm heading up north, you'll stay here?"

It hurt that he didn't even entertain the option of taking her with him. But he still wanted to get married; was still on his family's side of the argument about 'mitigating the damage' and 'preventing the fallout.' If there was one thing she downright *loathed* about dating Marcus, it was that the royal family was held to such a high standard compared to any other group of people.

But she considered his question. She didn't have anywhere else to go, anything else she was comfortable doing right now. "That's the plan for now. I'll get the garden going so I don't have to go to the market, and I'll study from here."

He dropped the broccoli into the sizzling pan. "Alright."

Chapter 10

THE REST OF THE WEEK was nice. Better than nice. Leah kept herself busy during the days, mostly with reading. No matter how boring the book was, she made herself finish it. Textbooks and history books were unsurprisingly dry. But finishing them, marking them off, gave her a purpose. No one could say she was being lazy.

And the mornings and nights were stellar. They may not be on a honeymoon, but she and Marcus sure acted like it. When they shared those quiet moments of pillow talk each night, and the smile-filled mornings alone, not a single part of Leah doubted if she loved Marcus, or if he loved her.

As they neared the weekend, however, she was a bundle of nerves. They ate breakfast at the table one morning. "You, uh, haven't started packing…" she said, spearing a piece of asparagus in her hash.

"I can't carry much through a rift…" He raised an eyebrow, taking a sip of orange juice.

"I thought you were catching a train."

He grinned. "I figured I'd spend an extra day with you, and I'll just buy new stuff up there."

She frowned. Sure, he had money, but she didn't like being a financial burden.

"Ouch," he said playfully. "I thought you'd enjoy spending more time with me, but here you are trying to get rid of me."

She rolled her eyes. "I'll tie you up, and not let you go at all."

He chuckled. "You can tie me up with your vines any day."

Her cheeks warmed. "I'm happy to have you here, but I feel bad that you're going to have to make unnecessary purchases."

"Don't worry about it. I'll have my stipend *and* a steady paycheck."

Nodding, she tried to allow herself to not take on that guilt.

"I'm going to swing by my parents' place tonight after work, though, so you can have more money here for anything you need during the week."

You're using him. He's just a tool. This baby is only a tool.

Leah closed her eyes, forcing the lies out of her head. "I don't need your money."

Marcus's mouth hung open for a moment, and she imagined his protest. She'd told him that back in high school, that she didn't want him to pay for dates when she and her mom had run into hard times financially. Or maybe he was thinking that if she'd finally agree to marry him, it would be *their* money, and not *his*.

"I just," she shrugged, "don't have any need for money if I'm not going to the market, right? No escort. I'll be fine."

He pushed around the food on his plate. "You're going to tend to the garden, then?"

Yeah, she'd said she was going to. When he was home, she spent all of her time with him. During daylight, she'd been spending it napping away her maternal sickness or reading. "Yes. I'm going to clean up the garden."

"Then I'll make sure the pantry's well-stocked before I go." He rocked his head back and forth. "But I'm still going to leave you with money, for emergencies."

She grudgingly accepted.

***

The day before Marcus started his internship, he was pure nervous energy. He kept checking that Leah had everything she needed, and tidied up his things, helping her fold up the freshly line-dried laundry. While he saved a lot of time by not taking the train, he'd still have to walk or ride to the local rifting cave, and then once he got to the other side, he'd need to buy new things, and make his way to the rural town he'd be living in.

The time was passing too quickly, and he was stressed. Her heart was going away for the week, and she wanted to leave them both with a reminder of how much they'd enjoyed their time together, and what they had to look forward to the next weekend.

She pulled him into the bedroom, kissing him hard. Backing herself onto the bed, she tangled her fingers in his hair, and extended vines to tug his shirt up.

He pulled away. "You're killing me. I don't have time."

She frowned. "Yes you do. It's not like there's a train schedule you need to abide by."

He raised an eyebrow. "My parents."

She internally groaned. His parents were *not* what she wanted to hear about while in bed and trying to get hot and bothered. "What about them?"

"They're seeing me off at the cave. I don't want to be late."

She leaned back on the bed, propping herself up on her elbows and retracting her vines. "When did you plan that?"

"I told you." He furrowed his brow.

"No. You didn't."

"I'm sure I did."

She huffed. No, he hadn't. "They'll survive if you're late."

He straightened his shirt. "And they'll probably guess what we were doing to make me late."

Leah pointed to her stomach. "Your child in there. They know. We've been staying here together. I think they know."

Tucking his hands into his pockets, he frowned. "C'mon. This internship is a big deal for me. My parents were already planning to see me off at the train station before I changed my plans to stay longer with you."

Why did she have to compete for his attention? Why couldn't he be an orphan like her, with no family to come between them?

"Fine," she said weakly.

He rubbed her knees. "I want you to be proud of me, happy for me."

"I am. You love what you do. You're a hard worker. You'll do great things."

"You can come to the cave to see me off, too…"

And leave with his parents after he walked through? *No thank you.* "That's okay. I'll stay here."

He pursed his lips. "If that's what you want."

She simply smiled. Marcus held out his hands, and she accepted. He pulled her to standing again, hugging her tight.

Then he gave her a solid kiss. Once their lips parted, he crouched down, lifting her shirt. He pressed his lips to her stomach. "You be nice to her," he lectured Leah's stomach.

Tears instantly pooled in her eyes, her heart melting.

When he stood tall again, his smile was warm and bright. "What?"

"I don't want you to go," she whispered. *Ever.*

He tucked her hair behind her ears. "It's only a week. We've been apart way more than we've been together." He stole another kiss. "And I will make it up to you, spending *every* free second together next weekend." He leaned forward, nibbling her ear. "Maybe I'll even bring back new half-priced clothing for you."

Okay, *that* brought a genuine smile to her face. "Go on. Don't be late."

He winked, and she walked him to the door. They exchanged 'I love yous,' and then he walked away.

He was her home, happiness, and hope. It was hard to see all of that walk away. He looked back once and waved before turning the corner. She forced a smile and waved back. And then he was gone.

And she was alone. Utterly alone.

***

Other than crickets singing in the early evening, it was quiet. To distract herself, Leah picked up another book, this time from the fiction options. *Valeska and the Wandering Soldier.* It was a bit of a slow-paced read, but she started to get into it. After she'd devoured a dozen chapters, her candle was burning low. It was time to call it a night. What she wouldn't do to get a text from him like when they'd dated in high school. 'Got here safe. Sweet dreams.'

She lay awake in bed half the night. After she finally fell asleep, a loud *thump* woke her. Her heart racing, Leah stayed in bed, silent and still. Another *thump*, and a slow *screech*.

Was someone trying to break in? Scare her? Now she kind of wished she'd taken Marcus up on the offer to have an escort. Sneaking out of bed with vines at the ready, Leah tiptoed to the front door and peeked out the window. Then rolled her eyes.

A storm, knocking a tree branch against the window.

She ruffled her hair, yawned, and went back to bed.

Owing to her rough night, Leah slept in much later than usual. It was closer to lunchtime when she dragged herself out of bed, but it wasn't like she had a set schedule anymore. She tried not to frown at that.

She was fine. How many people dreamed of this kind of life? No responsibilities.

As her stomach protested the lack of food, she slid a hand to it. No responsibilities *yet*.

Leah peeled a banana, deciding what else to eat, and was halfway through it when she glanced into the backyard.

Most of the garden resided in planter boxes. Rachel leaned over one, a pile of weeds beside her.

Rachel dug into the soil with a trowel, dropped a seed in, and covered it up. With a watering can, she moistened the soil, then she placed her hands over the seed. Her hands glowed with Seeder energy, and soon enough, a sprout emerged. Seeder powers were pretty amazing. The first time Leah had seen Marcus's mom actually *fly*, she was floored.

Rachel repeated the process with another seed. While it was nice to get help in sorting out the garden, it also rubbed Leah the wrong way. It was like the dirty dishes the other day. She could do it herself, and she didn't need Rachel stepping in to take care of it. It just made her feel guilty and inadequate. Had Marcus asked his mom to come over because he'd resented that Leah hadn't been working on the garden?

Leah huffed, taking another bite of her banana and setting it down. She got dressed for the day, refusing to let Rachel see her in 'lounging clothes,' and joined her in the backyard.

"Hey, there," she said on her approach.

Rachel looked up with a bright smile. "Hi, stranger. Didn't want to disturb you."

"Thanks." Leah fidgeted with her hands. "I appreciate the help, but I really can take care of this myself. It was at the top of my to-do list today."

"I don't mind. I don't have any plans until this evening." She continued working.

Leah flexed her hands. *Fine. We'll do it your way.* She bent and picked up the pile of weeds, taking them to the composting area. Then she set to work on weeding the box next to Rachel.

"Did you want to fertilize these so they'll grow faster?" Rachel asked.

Looking up, Leah hesitated. "Well, I… I could try, but I can't guarantee I wouldn't kill them."

Rachel chuckled. "You won't kill them. That's a basic Ivy power. You mastered that forever ago."

That was true. But Ivy women's powers were mostly chemical, and so were Leah's hormones. She'd learned after coming to the Green Lands that Ivy women's powers could be a bit unpredictable when they were pregnant. "Yes, but I haven't tried it on a plant since I got pregnant."

"Right…" Rachel replied in an awkward tone, as though she should have thought of that herself. "But we can test it. If it dies, it dies, and then we replant."

Yeah, that was *exactly* what Leah needed—for Rachel to nurture life, and Leah to destroy it in front of her. For Leah to cause these new sprouts to wilt and wither. For her to poison instead of fertilize, and taint the soil. "I'd rather read up on how to do it first, thanks."

There were books out there on how to master your chemical arts during pregnancy. Queen Catrina no doubt had one on her nightstand right now. Then again, Mrs. Perfect probably had that mastered with her first pregnancy, and wouldn't need tips for her third.

"Okay." Rachel covered another seed with soil.

Leah shook her head, yanking on a stubborn invasive vine. Rachel had to be imagining Leah a coward for not being willing to try, to not perform in front of her. And Leah almost gave in, but her pride kept her back, and she envisioned Rachel taking Leah's destruction of new life as evidence of what a horrible girlfriend she was, what a horrible wife and mother she would be. She was already destroying the life of Rachel's baby boy.

Leah's side of the family only knew how to destroy. Marcus's knew how to build.

But Leah kept pulling up weeds in silence. Why was Rachel doing this? She'd always been kind and welcoming and forgiving, not overbearing.

"Do you want me to pick up a book on Ivy powers during pregnancy?" Rachel offered.

No. You're already doing too much. "I'm fine. I planned to stop by the library to get one."

"I'd love to accompany you, especially since you don't have your escort. You know—girl time."

Leah steadied her breathing, plunging a trowel into the soil to dig up a deep root. "I'll let you know."

More silence passed, and Leah eventually took her weeds to the compost pile. Rachel had moved over and started working in the newly cleared bed.

"What are you planting?" Leah asked. She'd be the one eating most of the produce while Marcus was away during the weeks, becoming a big shot. It was a little presumptuous that Rachel hadn't even asked Leah what she wanted planted.

"A little of this and that. The first box has a couple types of squashes. I'm planning for tomatoes in this box." She smiled. "And some moon melons, because I know how much you and Marcus like them."

Okay, fine. So you remember what foods I like.

"And lots of radishes if we have enough space, since Tobias and Camry love them."

Right. This is their house, not mine. Why was every action, every word, like a Seeder dart to Leah's heart? Why did the simple fact she'd gotten pregnant now make her emotions paper-thin?

People loved Marcus. They tolerated Leah.

With her mind turning to her mom, Leah sniffled. Even the few who truly loved her didn't always want her, weren't really proud of her.

"You alright?" Rachel asked.

"Yeah. Just hungry, should have had more to eat."

"Go grab something. I can handle this myself."

Leah accepted. She did need to eat and pee, but she was mostly ready to be alone again.

After fixing a lettuce wrap, Leah watched Rachel from the window. Rachel was laser-focused on the work at hand. Leah was lost in thought in her own world as well.

Why was no one trying to convince Leah to give up the baby? Rachel surely hadn't wanted to become a grandmother so young. And she wanted her son to become an important person like her husband. It had to be incredibly painful for Rachel to even be around Leah after the torture Leah's dad had inflicted on her.

But Marcus had forgiven Leah, and cared for her. And that was it, right? Marcus was simply respecting Leah's wishes to keep the baby, and everyone was respecting Marcus's choice. It wasn't about liking Leah or caring about her opinions. It was about Marcus.

After polishing off her last bite, Leah decided she was done with gardening for the day, and with having uninvited company. She walked outside, tucking her hands into her pockets. Rachel gave her yet another smile. "Just about finished with this section."

"I, uh, I'm pretty tired, actually." Leah rocked on the balls of her feet. "I was going to take a nap. You know, tired from the baby and all that."

Rachel set down the watering can. "Right. Don't worry about it." She grinned. "I've got my Seeder energy fueling me. I can take care of this."

Leah pursed her lips. "I'd feel guilty if I wasn't helping."

Only then did it seem to click with Rachel. She gave an understanding nod. "It wouldn't hurt to give myself a little extra time to get cleaned up and ready for my function tonight."

Swinging her arms with nervous energy, Leah nodded in return. "Thanks for coming over, though. I've got lots of food in the house to last me a while."

"Sounds good." Rachel gathered the gardening tools. "You know where to find me or Guillen if you need anything. Healing … someone to shop with … or to pick up books for you … or anything, alright?"

I'm an adult. I can take care of myself. "Thanks. I'll let you know."

After heading inside, Leah read instead of napping. It was nice to get lost in a fictional world where no one knew her name. Where she didn't exist. Where *other people* were the main characters, and it was *their* problems that had to be overcome.

***

As Leah crawled into bed, she tried to shut off her brain. She hadn't been very 'gracious' with Rachel, or so Catrina would have said.

Leah was ungrateful. But was she? She acknowledged how lucky she was to have been taken in at the palace. How fortunate she was to be alive in the first place.

She rolled over in bed. How many people could relate to that? How many knew what it felt like to have your right to live deliberated over by dignitaries, by your own family members? Knew what it meant to betray those you loved, and be betrayed by them?

Leah was a tool. No, her mom hadn't trained her to be an assassin, to attack Kaylah as Kaylah had originally thought, but Leah was still a tool. She created chaos in peace. And had once created peace in chaos, but no one knew about that truth, not even Marcus, because that triumph was drowned in pain. In pain and a promise.

She was lucky to be allowed to live. Honestly, she'd be lucky to be allowed to keep her own child. Soren's heir, Soren's legacy.

Scoffing, Leah pondered that one. Maybe she should consent to marrying Marcus. At this point, it would be easier to make everyone else happier. And that was probably what they were waiting on… If Leah and Marcus didn't work out, who would everyone side with? Would Leah even get to keep the baby?

But if I marry him now, isn't that just proving the point that I'm using him, manipulating him? That—like her dad, like her parents—she treated people like tools?

Even after she finally fell asleep, Leah's nightmare of a life haunted her. Her mind gave her a front-row seat to the day she'd learned the truth about her parents. The day she'd lost her mind and almost become a murderer.

*

Leah, Queen Kaylah, and Leah's mom, Beata, sat together in the manor after the botched wedding luncheon. Leah's eyes were puffy from crying, her throat sore from screaming. The truth was sinking in. And she was sinking too.

Despite everything she'd learned about her mom, Leah couldn't turn her back on her. "I love you too," she said, then faced Kaylah. "What's going to happen to us?"

Kaylah glanced between the two. "It hasn't been decided yet."

Leah had nothing left. No parents. No family. No friends. No Marcus. No trust. No self. Her heart and hope were gone. "If you kill her, you should kill me too."

"No!" Beata screamed.

Kaylah furrowed her brow. "Why would you say that?"

Leah exhaled. "Because I never would have been born if you'd caught my mom when you did my dad. Why should it be any different now?"

Kaylah spun. "Is that what you told her?! No wonder she tried to kill me!"

Beata returned her anger. "You would have put me right next to Soren. Don't deny it!"

Kaylah balled her fists. "I would like to think I'd have given you the benefit of the doubt, to confirm whether you were pregnant first!"

"So, what? I'd give birth. You'd take her straight away and make her an orphan then? That's better, right?"

Kaylah narrowed her eyes. "Did you get knocked up hoping for a pardon?"

"No!"

Leah trembled, the last ounce of her identity crumbling before her. "Can I please go?" she begged.

*

Over two years later, that scene still tore through her mind, awake or sleeping. But now, Leah had more information. Her mom *hadn't* gotten pregnant hoping for a pardon. Her parents hadn't planned to get pregnant either. Nor was Leah an accident.

The truth of Leah's conception, if the realm knew it, would bring thunderous applause. And in so doing, would shatter her more than she already was.

Somewhere between rest and restlessness, her mom's words whispered to her: *You and me, we're the same.*

Chapter 11

THE REST OF THE WEEK was fine. Leah read nonfiction books during the mornings, and fiction during the evenings. For an hour or two around lunch each day, she did more work in the garden. She was surprised Rachel didn't stop by to help more since she'd seemed so insistent, but then she dared to poke her head out the front door, and found a letter Rachel had left her at some point.

Let us know if you need anything. Love, Rachel & Guillen

Leah didn't need anything. Sure, the fresh food was dwindling, and the garden was growing slowly because she hadn't dared to try fertilizing it with her vines, and she still hadn't picked up the book from the library about Ivy powers during pregnancy. But she was fine. She didn't need anything from anyone.

As the weekend approached, Leah's smile came back. She looked forward to spending every available moment with Marcus.

It was already dark by the time he returned to the cottage, but his face was heavenly and happy. They took a few minutes to talk about their weeks, mostly about his adventure with his internship, and then made their way to the bedroom. She fell asleep wearing only the new bracelet he'd brought her back, and she'd be okay if that was all she wore for the entire weekend.

The next morning, she mentioned how scruffy his face was, so he took time to shave. He was finishing up while she brushed her teeth in the bathroom.

"You know…" he said playfully. "I figured out why you don't want to marry me."

The vise tightened.

He wiggled his razor. "No *marry* me because you're not used to waking up next to the *hairy* me."

She looked away. Bad puns and rhymes were kinda their thing, but it was insensitive to keep bringing marriage up.

"Hey." His voice was soft. "It's just a joke."

"I don't like that kind of joke."

He took her hand, rubbing it with his thumb. "Sorry."

"Yeah. I'm gonna get dressed and check on the garden."

"I'll meet you out there."

Leah doubted anything in the garden actually needed attention; she'd mostly wanted to take a moment to enjoy her makeshift swing. She walked herself forward and backward, seated on the swing, her feet never leaving the ground.

Marcus joined her, holding her from behind and kissing her neck. "Mmm. Do you need any luck today?" He grazed her neck with his lips again.

"Don't you dare give me a raspberry."

"Ouch! Here I am, trying to help…"

She rolled her eyes and smirked at the same time. "Always trying to help."

"I could give you a good-luck raspberry on your belly."

That made her wrinkle her nose.

"For the baby." He stuck out his tongue.

She chuckled softly. "He or she can wait to enjoy that once they properly meet you."

He beamed. He was going to be a good dad. She hated fighting with him, and luckily, their fights were usually short.

Usually.

Marcus gently pulled her back on the swing. "So, what are our plans this weekend?"

"Plans?"

"Yeah. I've got to go to the market for a few things, right?"

"Well, yeah."

"Do you want to get out of the house and come with?"

She winced. "Would you hate it if I didn't?"

"That's fine. You grow a mini-us, and I can easily drop by the market solo."

She'd venture out there again. She would. Just … not right now.

"Any other plans?" he asked.

"No…"

He stopped swinging her, and stood in front of her. "How do you feel about dropping by my parents' place? Maybe for dinner?"

She frowned, her hands dropping from the swing's vines into her lap. "You said it would just be you and me this weekend. You promised."

"I… Well, you know… It's only a couple of hours. C'mon."

"You *promised*," she said, deflated.

"I know." He rubbed the bracelet on her wrist. "But they're excited to hear all about my internship, too."

Trying to keep calm, she took a breath. "Did you already tell them we'd come by?"

"No. But I told them I'd ask you."

She huffed, stood, and stomped back inside the cottage. *Men are stupid.*

"What was that about?" he asked, entering behind her.

"You told them you'd ask me?"

"Yeah. I didn't want to make the decision without you." He was clueless.

"And if we don't go, then they'll know it's all my fault."

He pressed his lips together.

"Yeah," she said.

"Sorry."

She rubbed her face, then tugged on her hair. "I've had enough time with your mom this week."

Don't you love my son? Why won't you marry him? I know better than you. Let me do the chores you're too lazy to do.

Marcus narrowed his eyes. "What's that supposed to mean?"

"She's dropped by twice, uninvited."

"She was only trying to help, and support us."

"Support you, Marcus. You."

He folded his arms. "My mom *loves* you. She's trying to make the best of this, okay? It would be good for you to spend more time together."

"Why? She and I were fine before we moved into this place."

"Because she knows what it's like to marry into the royal family. She understands what the pressure is like. She understands a lot of what you're going through and just wants to help."

Leah clenched her fists. Marriage, again. Pressure? Rachel was a saint who didn't tarnish the royal line. Understood Leah? Guillen couldn't even get Rachel pregnant. She had no idea what this felt like!

Someone with a perfect little tight-knit happy family like Marcus would never understand what it was like to be an orphan, to come from such a broken family.

He'd wanted the thrill of dating Leah. Of sneaking around at the palace. He liked the bad girl in the bedroom. But he didn't really want Leah for a wife, not the way she was. He wanted a girl like his mom.

"I am *not* your mother," she snapped.

His tone matched hers. "I didn't say you were. Why do you have to get so worked up about this? You know, this is your fault."

Heat rose in her cheeks.

He continued. "You didn't like Aunt Catrina's rules. Fine. But you didn't have to be so … *crazy*. You didn't have to call her a bitch."

"*My* fault?" Her voice shook. "*You* got the wrong birth control tonic for me. You were supposed to buy the clove one, *not* the tea tree one."

His eyes grew wide as he realized his mistake. The clove was effective for short-term. The tea tree was for long-term and should have been taken regularly for a while to work. "Then why didn't you tell me before we did anything?"

"Because I didn't look up the difference until I recognized my symptoms days later!"

His face was apologetic, but then he dredged deeper. "It was a mistake. But that doesn't mean you can walk all over people trying to help you."

She rolled her eyes.

"You don't like being compared to my mom?" he said. "Would you rather I compare you to *yours?*"

That was dangerous ground.

"What's that supposed to mean?"

"Just … never mind." He swiped a hand through the air, heading to the bedroom.

No. Never mind? You didn't get to insult someone, comparing them to a somewhat neglectful, somewhat homicidal person, and then simply say 'never mind.'

She followed him. "What about my mom? Where does she even play into this?"

"I don't want to argue."

"Too late."

He eyed her for far too long. "Fine. Let's get it out. Let's say what needs to be said."

She planted her hands on her hips. "Go for it. I'm dying to know."

"I don't say anything about your visits to your mother, but I hope you understand that she will *never* get to meet our child."

Leah hadn't considered it all that much. And while she agreed in concept, she didn't like being told what she could or could not do.

So instead of doing the wise thing, she doubled down, she dug her heels in.

"You don't get to tell me what I can or can't do, Marcus."

He was just as upset as she was. "I do on this."

"Yeah?" Maybe she really did need a palate cleanser, and not just from his family, but from him, too. "If you say so. I'll stay away from my mom. Far away. I'm glad I thought to bring my passport."

Shock flooded his features. "The human world? No!"

"I could go. I could disappear. You wouldn't have to worry about me ruining your reputation or career, or getting between you and your mom. My mom and I survived just fine over there for years without anyone finding us."

"Yeah, that worked out great, didn't it?!"

She clenched her fists. "No one's stopping me." Catrina hadn't stopped her from leaving the palace, and she probably would be content with Leah disappearing altogether.

He looked her dead in the eyes, his voice calm but firm. "I could stop you. And you know it."

A lead weight slammed down in her gut. That was the exact kind of threat she'd heard him utter once before. Only once. *I think we both know this could get* much *worse for you.* She hadn't understood Marcus's threat to Tanner back in high school, but she did now.

That was the kind of flex the nephew to the queen could make. *He* wouldn't stop Leah from leaving. She was stronger than him with her powers. He could *have* her stopped.

And he was right. Not a single part of her doubted in that moment that Catrina would choose him, that everyone would.

Leah grasped at straws. "You don't even have proof the baby's yours. Maybe it's not. Maybe you don't deserve to have a say in anything I or my baby do."

He reached for ammunition, and found it. "Wouldn't surprise me. You did sleep around before me, right?"

Exactly one person knew how much that insult would hurt. She'd only confided in *one* person the details of her sex life. And that one person also knew that not all of her sexual encounters had been fully consensual.

She choked on her words, unable to reply. He was that one person.

"But I think we both know that's mine." He glanced at her stomach. "We both know it will come out a Boman like its father. And that there's not a *single* Boman in the entire realm, on the entire planet, other than me, that would ever screw you."

And that was it. With white-hot rage, her hand flew through the air, her palm connecting with his face with the loudest *slap* she'd ever heard.

Marcus stumbled back onto the bed, clutching his cheek, his mouth agape.

She held back a whimper, realizing what she'd just done. "Get out."

His nostrils flared as he stared at her. "Done." He got up, and she sidestepped out of the way. Grabbing his wallet from a basket near the door, he turned to her. "I'll be up north if you come to your senses."

As her heart broke completely, she gritted out her goodbye. "Don't hold your breath."

He slammed the door behind him as he exited. She watched out the window, hugging herself, her heart racing, her breathing rapid.

Only when he was far down the lane did she allow herself to fall apart.

She crumpled to the floor, sobbing and hyperventilating.

Her hand stung.

He shouldn't have said half of the things he'd said. But she'd just made things immeasurably worse for herself. His aunt was the queen. Slap a commoner—that's assault. Slap a member of the royal family?

And even if Catrina let Leah off the hook, the court of public opinion never would. She'd hit a Boman. After trying for two years to prove she wasn't an unstable bigoted assassin like her parents, she'd smacked her boyfriend.

And it hadn't been a regular slap. Her Ivy energy had boosted that. She'd used her powers against him. She'd used powers against someone born without them.

Leah would never recover from this.

Breathing and crying too hard, she threw up on the wood floor.

***

Much later, Leah had cleaned up her mess. She was too jittery to do anything other than go into the backyard and power-weed, yanking out everything in sight from the garden beds still needing to be overhauled. As she took the last of the weeds to the compost pile, her eyes fixed on the bracelet she wore, the one Marcus had just brought her.

She'd done the wrong thing. But so had he. He had no right to use her past mistakes against her. With tears in her eyes, she undid the clasp and let it fall into the compost heap.

After returning to the cottage, she made peppermint tea to soothe her stomach, and a light meal. And then she stared at the wall, replaying their entire day together. How had they made love that morning, and by noon, thrown away everything?

Leah flexed and unflexed her hand time and time again. She'd hit him. She'd *hit* him. After growing up with an abusive 'aunt,' Leah had promised herself she would *never* be that person. Anger didn't justify physical violence. But she didn't cry again. She was too hollow and hopeless to find tears. She just stared at her hands as the sun set.

Darkness fell. Marcus didn't return, and no one came for Leah. She needed to sleep this all off like the nightmare it was. Using a striker, she lit a beeswax candle, then took it to the bedroom.

It was comfy, and she desperately needed that rest, but the magnet had been flipped, and her safe haven now pushed her away instead of drawing her in. The thought of lying alone in the bed they'd shared was too much. She grabbed a pillow and quilt, tucking them under her arm, and picked up the candle, returning to the living room and crashing on the sofa.

Chapter 12

LEAH WOKE LATE AGAIN. What was there to do or look forward to? Absolutely nothing. She stared at the bookshelf and couldn't imagine picking up a single one of those books.

Eventually, after multiple loud protests from her stomach, she found the will to roll off the sofa and get food.

As she surveyed the mostly empty counter, something through the window caught her eye—movement from the backyard.

And then her jaw dropped. Rachel was back, finishing up more seeds in the freshly cleared area of the garden. Leah's breathing became shallow. There was exactly a zero percent chance she was going to join her out there. Not after her fight with Marcus yesterday. She took a step back, hoping to slip past the windows and hide. And then Rachel glanced in her direction.

Crap. Leah swallowed and continued her retreat.

Marcus wasn't due back north yet. He might have been mad enough to storm off to the closest rifting cave and spend the rest of his free weekend there, but he might just as easily be staying at his parents' place.

Leah sat cross-legged on the bedroom floor, resting her face in her palms, waiting for Rachel to go away. How much time passed, Leah was unsure, but longer than a few minutes later, and sooner than she'd imagined (approximately when hell would freeze over), a knock sounded on the back door. Rachel's audacity…

What was Leah going to do? Huddle on the bedroom floor forever? Rachel and Guillen had bought this cottage for Tobias and Camry; they had a spare key. She and Leah had made eye contact— she knew Leah was inside.

Praying to whatever deities may exist out there, Leah hoisted herself up and approached the back door.

She shyly opened it. "Hi."

Rachel was all business, no smiles. "Everything's planted." She reached down, lifting a giant basket of fruits and vegetables far too easily. Leah's Ivy energy made her perhaps twice as strong as Marcus if she focused, but Rachel's Seeder energy was easily double that of Leah's.

"Here," Rachel said. "This should last you a while."

"Thanks…" A little perplexed, Leah accepted it.

But Rachel didn't keep her waiting. "I don't know why you getting pregnant makes me the bad guy here, Leah. I don't."

Leah set the basket behind her. *Okay, so maybe she just thinks I'm frustrated because I didn't go to dinner or the cave? Or she picked up on it when she helped in the garden last?*

Leah sighed. "I don't expect you to understand. It's complicated. You can't … get pregnant." How could Rachel understand? Seeders didn't go through that whole thing like Ivies or humans did. And Ivies—even Ivy Bomen—couldn't reproduce with Seeders, so she and Guillen could fool around together every day of their lives without any sort of birth control or protection, without the fear of an accidental pregnancy. Leah *had* hoped Catrina would be more understanding, given she herself was pregnant right now, but she'd been born an heir to the throne, and hadn't married or started popping out kids until she was in her thirties.

Rachel nodded. "You know, Leah…" She pursed her lips, considering. "You're not the only one that's gone through hard things, or has had tough decisions to make. It's bold of you to assume I can't relate to you in any way. Or that I've never wished to experience the miracle of life in that way." There was a hint of sadness in her voice that Leah hadn't heard before.

Humbled, Leah softly apologized.

Tucking her hands in her pockets, Rachel opened her mouth again. "Has my son ever hurt you?"

Leah's heart skipped a beat. "No… Not physically."

Visibly agitated, Rachel eyed her. "So, when you hurt my son, it wasn't in self-defense?"

Leah froze, absolutely paralyzed. He had told his mom. Fear raced through Leah as she recalled with perfect clarity the most terrifying part of the day when she'd tried to assassinate Kaylah. It hadn't been Kaylah who had really frightened Leah, or even the guards who had yanked Leah away. It had been Marcus's mom.

Rachel's eyes had glowed an unnatural Seeder-green that day. *I liked you, Leah. And so did Marcus. But I've had to kill for my family. I won't let anyone hurt them.*

Her would-be future mother-in-law had essentially threatened Leah's life that day. And Leah had earned it. Had she again?

"I didn't mean to," Leah breathed.

Rachel was a war hero, as was Guillen. Leah felt two inches tall right now, easily squished under an angry boot—no Seeder blades or throwing knives necessary.

Rachel's expression was tense, but all she did was shake her head and walk away toward the side gate, which led to the front yard.

Only then did Leah let out a shaky breath, shutting and locking the door. She hefted the huge basket of produce and lugged it to the kitchen.

Still calming down, she braced herself against the counter. *Why did he have to do that?* How immature was Marcus to run to his parents and tattle on Leah? Their whole argument had started because he'd made her the bad guy with his parents over a stupid dinner visit. But now? Now he'd dragged them *fully* into their relationship.

Unable to force herself to unpack the groceries yet, she turned to the living room, ready to flop back on the sofa.

And then something caught her eye from the front door window.

"Seriously?!" It wasn't Rachel. Rachel had worn a lavender shirt; this figure wore a dark green shirt, simply standing there, not knocking.

Leah stalked to the front door, pulling it open. "Excuse me, can I help—"

The figure turned, a familiar middle-aged blond smiling back at Leah.

She didn't return the smile. "Wren? What are you doing here?" He'd been one of her regularly assigned escorts. She was nervous to hear the answer.

He nodded. "Miss Eleana. Just doing my job." He pulled an envelope from his jacket pocket, handing it to her.

She anxiously eyed the wax seal on it—Queen Catrina's.

Carefully pulling the seal off, Leah unfolded it and read the letter. It was short. She was unimpressed. "Do you know what this says?"

Wren gave a shy look indicating he did, which made sense.

"Tell her my answer is no."

"Miss Eleana…"

"No. And my name is Leah. We're not at the palace. You can call me Leah."

"Leah," he replied softly. "It would be in your best interest—"

"Her letter said it was a *request* to come to the palace to speak with her. A request can be denied. It's not a command, demand, order, or edict. I can say no, and I do." She handed him back the letter. "I have nothing to say to her. You're lucky you still have a job after working with me. Other servants aren't so lucky. That's your queen for you."

All duty, Wren nodded, tucking the letter back into his pocket. "Then I'll continue my appointment here."

"This is only a one-bedroom cottage. I don't have anywhere for you to sleep…"

"Your escorts are being put up at the nearest inn."

Great. More expense on my behalf that people can balk at.

"I'm not inviting you in, and I intend to go nowhere, so I hope you enjoy standing outside, rain or shine."

He gave her a patient smile. Or maybe it was condescending? "I do my duty as needed, miss."

Duty. Always about duty. "It's Leah. Have a good day."

She closed the door and dove back under the quilt on the sofa. And there she planned to stay the rest of the day. Maybe the rest of her life. Under guard, a pariah, she'd remain there until she and her unborn child died of old age and sheer spite.

***

The next few days were quiet. Leah *wanted* peace and quiet. Though perhaps not *quite* so much… Especially when it left her to her guilt and anger and thoughts.

So, she threw herself back into the books. She binged most of the fiction books first, throwing in the occasional nonfiction book, skimming over the parts that mentioned her parents. She was tired of hearing about them.

Her entire week consisted of reading, snacking, gardening, and trying to forget how much she missed Marcus. And hated him. And hated herself.

It gutted her each time she walked by the empty bedroom. Her heart ached each time she found herself with her hand on her stomach, or wanted to talk about something happening in a book she was reading, just to realize she had no one to talk to.

Her escorts were positioned at the front door around the clock. She gave them a chair to at least be able to relax. It wasn't their fault Catrina had ordered them to keep her locked up.

As the weekend approached, Leah decided to take care of something she'd been neglecting—writing a letter. She visited her mom in prison monthly, and her visit was already past due. Her mom understood Leah's life was busy, or at least that it had been, so it wasn't like they met on the same day every month, but still. Leah didn't want to worry her.

Sitting at the breakfast nook, Leah hovered a pen over paper. She needed to explain why she wasn't coming to visit. She really did need to just leave the cottage, but some overly cautious part of her feared that if she left, she might never come back. She was a squatter right now, and maybe the escorts were the family's way of drawing her out so they could evict her.

And she didn't have it in her to break the pregnancy news to her mom yet, especially not in a letter. Her mom had stressed that she would always love Leah. Would she now? As Leah rested a hand on her slowly growing stomach, her lips formed a faint smile. It was an odd connection she couldn't explain. Then her smile faded. Could her mom ever love a Boman grandchild, given Beata and her family's part in history as oppressors of Bomen?

This was definitely a conversation to have in private and in person. With the way things were going, how long would it be until Leah was comfortable going out to visit her mom again?

Hey Mom,

Sorry I haven't been able to visit. Things are going great at the academy and with studies.

She scratched out each word, recalling the runaway note she'd once left for her mom in the human world.

My schedule's been so crazy. I'll be touring a bit, and Marcus's family surprised me with some fun getaway plans, and I'll probably spend some time visiting him on his internship, so I just wanted you to know what I was up to if I'm not able to visit you for a little while. If I can't come by, I'll definitely drop you a letter. I hope you're doing alright.

Love you,

Eleana

It was bad to lie. While Leah had always technically known that, she hadn't always strictly followed the rule to not lie. Was it wrong to lie now?

She folded the letter, addressed it, and opened the front door.

"Miss." Wren nodded in greeting.

"Wren." She held the letter tight in her hand. It now dawned on her that she hadn't even taken five steps out the front door since arriving at the cottage. Sure, she'd explored the entirety of the large backyard, but she'd been holed up pretty tight here.

"Going somewhere?" he asked.

As she was still in pajamas, surely he knew the answer to that. But her legs didn't move. The backyard was mostly private, with brick walls and bushes. The front yard was so exposed.

"Would you like me to take that to the postbox?" he asked.

She gave him an appreciative frown. "Thanks."

The postbox was only a few yards down the walk, but she was grateful for the gesture.

"I needed to stretch my legs anyway." He strolled to the edge of the property, deposited the letter, and turned back with a smile. "You're making my job too hard."

She returned the smile. "You like to read, right, Wren?" He'd snuck a book out of his pocket now and then while standing guard.

"That I do."

"Have you ever read *Valeska and the Wandering Soldier*?"

"Of course."

"Is it part of a series?" she asked. "That was kind of an abrupt ending."

His eyes widened. "There are nine books in that series. You've only read the first?"

She'd read several novels from the collection at the cottage by now, but there hadn't been a sequel to this book, and the ending had stuck with her. "Yeah. We only have the one here."

"Well, you definitely ought to check out the others." He paused, surveying her. "If you'd like to dress, I'd happily escort you to the library."

She frowned again. "That's … okay. Thanks for the offer." Resting her hand on the door handle, she prepared to go back inside.

"It's a pity." His voice was playful as he sat on the chair. "If I were you, I'd *die* to know what happens to the mutant Seeder troop we never hear from again in book one."

"Right?! Like, what even was the—" She stopped as a smirk slid onto his face. She cocked her head. "What happens to them?"

Wren shook his head, pulling his current read out of a pocket. "I don't give spoilers, Miss Eleana. I'm strictly against them."

They both knew what he was doing. It had usually been all business with her escorts during her time at the palace, but if she had to pick favorites, he'd be in her top two.

Still, she was nowhere courageous enough to venture from the cottage yet. "Maybe down the road. Thanks, though."

"Let me know when you're ready."

She wished him a good day and headed inside. It was only a silly book. She didn't *need* to know more. And she hadn't finished all the other books in the cottage yet anyway.

Settling on the sofa, Leah picked up her current read. She struggled to get back into it, her mind on the cliffhanger of *Valeska and the Wandering Soldier*, and on her letter to her mom, and the fact that she hadn't heard from Marcus all week.

Maybe… Maybe he'd realize how hurtful he'd been, how much of an idiot he'd been. Maybe he'd just needed the week to cool off, and he'd come back and apologize.

She flexed the hand she'd used to slap him, tears forming in her eyes. And then she'd apologize too, once he came back.

If he came back.

They'd 'taken a break' in the human world for an entire month when he'd found out she had a shoplifting habit. By the time he would come around after she hit him, she would probably be celebrating their child's fifth birthday.

Leah sniffled, took a sip of water, and forced herself to reread the last page she'd read without taking anything in.

***

Marcus didn't visit that first weekend. Leah cried herself to sleep each night.

She didn't need him. She didn't need anyone. Her life had been a revolving door of boyfriends, family, and acquaintances. Marcus was no exception. He'd stayed longer than most people in her life, but that simply meant it would take longer to get over him.

Leah didn't need Marcus. She could be a single mom like hers had been, and a better one. At least that was what she told herself every time she was on the brink of tears again.

Naps, garden, books—they became her daily life. She was fine. Just fine. Her maternal sickness was even finally easing up.

A few days down the road, a knock at the door startled her as she prepared a snack. She peeked around the corner, spotting none other than Wren at the front door, waving an envelope.

Leah wiped her hands on her jeans and ran to the front door. She took the envelope from him and immediately recognized the prison's stationery. She smiled, happy to get a quick response from her mom. "Thanks."

"You're welcome."

She paused, suddenly self-conscious. *What kind of person smiles about getting a letter from a war criminal?* She folded it and tucked it into her pocket. "So, what book are you reading today?"

Wren perched on his chair. "*Saltzer's Triangle.*"

"Never heard of it." She had admittedly not been a bookworm before this fiasco, with human literature or green-folk.

"If you liked *Valeska and the Wandering Soldier*, you might enjoy it."

She shrugged. "Cool. I just finished *The Hippo Ride.*"

Wren arched an eyebrow, clearly intrigued. All animal life in the Green Lands was small. Nothing that large and beastly resided here, but most green folk had a fascination for, or at least curiosity about, the human world.

"You know what a hippo is, right?" she asked.

"I do."

Leah sat on the step near him. "So, it's…" She almost called it urban fantasy, but that was her human-world childhood kicking in. Wren was born and raised Ivy. Since the book was written by an Ivy author, but the setting was the human world, she guessed it would be considered high fantasy for them? "Well, it's all in the human world."

"Did you like it?"

Leah briefly described the plot, which she'd rather enjoyed, but struggled to get past some of the glaring worldbuilding errors. It was obvious the author hadn't done any research. Hippos weren't bright purple, nor could they fly, though since it was fantasy, she could forgive those. But the descriptions of the setting—New York City—were horrendous. The characters walked through cornfields, and sharks swam in rivers that snaked through the metropolis.

She and Wren chatted for some time about whether the author had intended it to be read comedically or if those were in fact errors. She genuinely didn't think they were intentional.

"Well…" Wren pursed his lips. "I'll have to check it out and see if I agree with you on that."

Leah pointed to the door behind her. "Do you want to borrow this copy?"

He was hesitant.

She was sure Tobias and Camry would understand, as long as he didn't take it off their property. It wasn't like they were around often enough to enjoy it, as this was their second home and they were usually over at Rachel and Guillen's place when visiting the realm anyway.

But she understood his reluctance. He was already being paid by the queen to sit around and read fiction right now instead of using his extensive training to ensure Leah wasn't being murdered. Accepting a book was probably pushing things a bit too far.

In that moment, though, she realized how at ease she'd been, just sitting down to talk books with someone. She realized how lonely she truly was, how much she missed interactions after being surrounded by servants at the palace.

"Well, if you do decide to find a copy at the library, let me know, and we could … talk … about what you think… If you want."

His expression was kind and thoughtful. He had to know, right? Even if he was in the dark about what Leah was going through, he'd been there for eight hours a day, and she'd yet to leave the property, hadn't had a single visitor. The escorts always exchanged information at the change of shift, so the others would know she hadn't left, either.

Leah stood, ready to go inside.

"You know, Miss Eleana, I think I'll take you up on it."

She instantly smiled.

"I'll probably finish my current book midshift today, and I didn't bring a new one. I'd love to borrow that book. Unless…" He cleared his throat. "Unless you'd prefer to go to the library. Then we could both get a new book to read."

She gave him a look to say she knew exactly what he was trying to do, and he chuckled. Hopping inside, she grabbed the book and handed it to him. "But if I catch you dog-earing that, Tobias and Camry might kill me."

"Dog-ear?"

Then *she* chuckled. "Dogs—human pets… Sometimes their ears flop over like that." She demonstrated with her hands on her head. "Don't bend the pages."

He gasped. "I would never!" He gave her a bright, toothy smile. "I'll take good care of this."

"I hope you like it."

"Do most dogs do that? With the ears? I haven't spent much time over there on vacations."

"Um… A decent number, I guess? I'm not really a dog expert."

"Did you ever have a dog companion when you lived in the human world?"

She tried not to frown. "No. We moved around too much, and it would have been too much to keep track of." Not only had she wished for a dog as a kid, but questions like that reminded her too well that everyone in the realm knew her past. She and Wren hadn't ever conversed so casually before, but whether he thought it a sob story to pity or a sensational story to savor, he was far more aware of her story than she was of his.

"That's a shame," he said politely.

"Yeah." She rubbed the pocket she'd forgotten her mom's letter was tucked in. "I guess I'll get back to what I was doing. Thanks for my letter and for the chat. Enjoy the book."

Closing the front door behind her, Leah drew a deep breath. She quickly finished making the snack she'd been preparing before the letter came, then sat down to eat and read.

Her mom's letter was nice and long, which was unsurprising, as she had all the time in the world serving her life sentence. She expressed how much she missed Leah, the good things she'd been doing for community service from the confines of the prison, how she hoped Leah could visit soon despite her busy schedule. She seemed to have bought Leah's lies about what she was up to.

At the bottom of the letter, Leah kept reading the same words over and over.

Love always.

But did her mom really? Always? And would she really? Always?

Chapter 13

MARCUS DIDN'T VISIT THE NEXT weekend either. Leah was fine. Just fine.

She was fine because she *didn't* struggle to sleep. At least … not *that much*. And she was fine as she devoured more books, and found herself discussing them on a regular basis with Wren.

And she was absolutely, most definitely fine when she took down the large painting that had been a wedding gift from her and Marcus, relocating it to the bedroom closet so she wouldn't have to look at it every day.

She was a little less fine when she spent a good two hours straight staring at a photo of Tobias and Camry's human-world wedding. She'd been absent, having ruined their first wedding attempt. She analyzed Marcus's smile in the photo. She'd used him. She'd manipulated him.

And … then she bawled and turned the framed picture facedown on the bedroom dresser.

She was ashamed the first time she realized she'd lost track of the days, of what day of the week it even was. They all blended together.

The garden grew slowly. Painfully slowly. But she wasn't starving yet.

One day, Leah knelt at the garden box of tomato plants, using her own vines to wrap around stakes in the corners. She contained the growing plants, leaning them against her vines for support. She and her mom had never planted anything in all their years in the human world. They'd moved too often to be able to harvest anything they would have sown, and neither of them had really been the green-thumb type anyway. Luckily, there was a booklet in the nonfiction part of the bookshelf that addressed gardening basics.

She hadn't been inside more than five minutes before a knock at the front door surprised her. It wasn't one of Wren's special knocks, either.

When she reached the door, her stomach knotted. Guillen. Why not? One by one, every member of Marcus's family and the royal family would inevitably try to convince Leah to do the 'proper' thing and marry Marcus, to put aside her own reservations. Or … he could be there as a government official about her battering a Boman…

Nervous, she opened the door. "Hi, Guill— Um … Sir Guillen."

Guillen pressed his lips into a thin line. "Huh… We've never been that formal before, you and I…" His voice held its usual calm, but his eyes searched her.

"Well, I…" She just stood there. He had to know about her slapping his son. He had to have been fed up that she was squatting at his other son's property, her life and career prospects wasting away one day at a time.

"I'm not usually one to invite myself in, but could we talk?" he asked.

She gulped. "Sure, come in." As she perched on the edge of the sofa, he eased down on a chair opposite her. His gaze took in her bedding—still a mess on the sofa—and her shame was complete.

"Is, uh…" he started.

"It's more comfortable than the bed, that's all." That was a blatant lie. Night after night on the sofa was taking a toll on her back, but she still couldn't fathom spending another night in that bedroom without Marcus.

Guillen rubbed his knee, his expression somewhat skeptical. "We'll have to see about replacing that mattress, if it's not comfortable."

"No, it's… I rotate between them."

He silently nodded. "How are you doing, Leah?"

"I'm fine."

"Is that an American human fine? Or a real fine?"

She furrowed her brow.

"A polite lie? Or a genuine answer?"

She averted her gaze, fidgeting with her hands. "How can I help you?"

Guillen's voice was ever so soft. "You're his world. You know that, right?"

That wasn't fair. And that wasn't true. Marcus would be here with her if that were true.

"You've seen him?" she asked, still not looking Guillen in the eye.

"Yes."

She couldn't bring herself to ask how Marcus was doing. If he was fine, she'd die on the spot. If he was miserable, she'd feel he deserved it, but somehow also feel more miserable herself.

Guillen blew out a long breath. "My sister wants what's best for you."

Leah's jaw tightened. *Right. Defending his little sister, the queen.*

"*And* she wants what's best for the kingdom…"

Crossing her arms, Leah remained silent.

"She's not perfect," he said. "She… Well, she was more sheltered than I was about some things growing up. And she's trying her best. I wish you'd go speak with her."

Over my dead body.

"Right… I'm not her messenger. That isn't why I came today."

Leah finally met his gaze, curious, worried.

Guillen ruffled his hair. "Here's the thing, Leah. I might be the only person in the family who will say this, but I feel it's important."

She hated when people talked that way—'the family,' as opposed to 'Marcus's family' and 'Leah's family.' It reminded her that, no matter how distant it was, they were already related. Marcus was her second cousin through adoption. Guillen was her first cousin once removed. Had she understood what any of that meant when she'd moved to the Green Lands? Heck no. Had she researched it thoroughly and made sure marrying second cousins through adoption was legal and not completely freaky after they'd discovered they were? Absolutely.

Guillen continued. "If you don't love my son, I don't want you to marry him."

She didn't know whether to be relieved or insulted. It hadn't been a matter of not loving Marcus, right? This whole disaster had come about because…

"I know what it's like to be raised in a home where…" Guillen spoke slowly, deliberately. "Where my parents were not equals."

A knife to the chest. No, Leah was not Marcus's equal. Not in breeding or education. Not in action or reputation. She never had been, and she never would be. *You're only using him*, a voice not completely her own whispered.

"My parents didn't share mutual respect," Guillen said. "There was an imbalance of power, and just…" He pursed his lips, taking a long while to speak again. "I may be partial here, but I don't want my son in an unhappy marriage."

She willed herself not to cry.

"And frankly, if the two of you aren't meant to be together, then you and that child deserve better, too."

His soft blue eyes were piercing, thoughtful. It took everything she had to breathe normally, to not fall apart on the spot.

Interlacing his fingers, Guillen asked, "Do you want that baby?"

"Yes," she croaked.

This whole exchange was painful. His kind tone, his gentle mannerisms. "Then … congratulations."

He hadn't said it with an ounce of sarcasm or malice, but it sent her into full-on tears. No one had congratulated her yet. She hadn't even thought of it that way for herself.

Scooting to the edge of his seat, Guillen wore an expression of concern and compassion. "Do you want a hug?"

Even as tears cascaded down her cheeks, she shook her head.

"Can I help?"

She didn't like people to see her cry. "No."

"Okay…"

After a minute of her trying to regain her composure, he stood and strode to the bathroom, returning with a handkerchief.

Leah calmed herself. "Thanks."

"Of course." He stayed standing. "You know where he's staying up north, right? I could get you the address…"

She sniffled. "He knows where I'm staying too."

Guillen's smile was an ironic one. "Perhaps you two are matched. You certainly both know how to be … a fair bit stubborn."

She blew her nose.

"Anyway," he said, resting his hand on the door handle, "it's a common trait with us Elontas, Elannas, and Elontos… I'll get out of your hair. Please let Rachel and me know if you need anything."

She nodded to be polite.

"We love you, Leah."

She choked back more tears, unable to reciprocate. Desperately wanting a hug, but far too proud to ask.

"Have a good rest of your day." He opened the door, uttered a goodbye to Wren, and closed the door behind him.

Leah stood and peeked out the door's window as Guillen strolled down the lane. She unintentionally caught Wren's gaze for the briefest moment. He examined her, a pitying frown on his lips. Ashamed, she ignored him and returned to the sofa.

She had permission to not marry Marcus if she didn't want to. Why hadn't the weight lifted?

It doesn't matter, a brutal, icy voice whispered in her mind. *You will never deserve Marcus, and you don't deserve his child. You should have never even been born.*

***

The next morning, Wren's signature knock roused Leah from the sofa. She greeted him, still ashamed he'd seen her on the verge of losing it the day before.

"Miss Eleana." He gave her a single polite nod, as always. And then he handed her a book.

Holding it in both hands, she read the title. "*Valeska and the Lost Troop?*" She met his gaze. "Is this…?"

He gave her an encouraging smile. "The second book in the series?"

She could have hugged him, not that she would. Before Catrina had fully realized Leah was not a hugger (at least not with anyone other than Marcus and her mom), she'd established the rule that Leah should not hug any of the servants or staff. It wasn't proper. And when she had—that night when she'd been relieved to have Robyn's help—she'd cost Robyn her job. Maybe her poison wasn't limited to her vines; maybe her hugs and very essence were poison to people, imparting misfortune.

"Thank you," she breathed, clutching the book to her chest.

"It's from the library, though, so no dog … earing it." He winked.

"You went to the library for me?"

He swatted a dismissive hand through the air. "Of course not. I was already going there to pick up a new read."

She glanced sideways at a book right inside the cottage, resting on the entryway table. "Did you decide not to finish this one?" He'd bookmarked it halfway through, returning it to her at the end of his shift the day before. It was another book she'd loaned him from Tobias and Camry's collection.

"Well…" Wren cleared his throat. "I sometimes read more than one at a time…"

She handed him the book, and as she met his kind hazel eyes, nothing more needed to be said, other than "Thank you."

"Happy to, miss." He gave her another polite nod, and she stepped inside, ready to finally devour the next book in this intriguing series.

The beginning was a tad slow, and her mind wandered. Was it sad that she had almost even come to consider Wren a friend? Thinking on it, she hadn't really made friends with any of her peers in the Green Lands, not in all this time.

Sure, she'd learned to socialize at balls, and she had her 'friends' at the academy. And Marcus's friends had tolerated her. But she'd become so much closer to the palace staff, honestly. Most of them were older than her, but she could relate to them in a different way. They weren't royalty; they were normal citizens. And that was how she'd always been raised—by a single mom and a hateful 'aunt,' the three of them scraping by.

Leah drew a deep breath, setting the book down after reading the same paragraph a dozen times.

Where were those 'friends' from the academy now? Did any of them even care that she'd stopped attending classes? Probably not. If they did, and they'd inquired as to Leah's location, was Catrina intentionally keeping that information private? Withholding outside contact from Leah until she capitulated to Catrina's demands? Or hiding the truth about Leah's pregnancy because she was so ashamed of it?

Lifting her shirt to expose her belly, Leah stared at it, gently caressing it. She could feel the life within her, even if she wasn't really showing yet. There was perhaps a *little* pooch there.

Just like with Leah's own birth, no one would want this baby to be born. Why did she? Why did she want to inflict herself and her reputation upon this child, just like Leah had always suffered because of her parents' choices?

Life was beautiful. Having already envisioned what the baby would look like, Leah knew this little girl or boy couldn't be anything but adorable. Maybe, in some way, she wanted to keep the baby because she was lonely.

That's not a good reason to have a child.

She swallowed. Perhaps she wanted it because she did still love Marcus, despite everything that had happened, and it was a piece of him.

You sound like your mother.

She bit the insides of her cheeks, still gently massaging her stomach.

He's already left you. You burn bridges. You push people away.

Her throat tightened.

You're selfish. That baby would be better off without you. Everyone would be.

She sniffled, wiping away a tear and promptly pulling her shirt back down.

"Shut up," she whispered, picking up the book again and finding her page. Pushing away the world and the worries, she dug back into *Valeska and the Lost Troop*, promising herself today would be a good day.

***

Despite Leah rationing it out, her food supply was getting dangerously low. The garden was taking ages to mature. She ought to suck it up and go to the market. Wren was more than willing to escort her.

Yet, the thought of being around so many people was crippling.

Maybe Wren would go to the market for her, like he had the library?

I can't ask him to do that. That wasn't his job. He wasn't a shopping servant; he was an escort, a guard, a protector.

But … he *had* gone to the library for her…

Leah finished book two by the next day, and thoroughly enjoyed it. She returned the book to Wren, and they chatted a bit about the writing and plot.

"Would you like the next one?" he asked.

"Yes!"

"Would you like me to take you to pick it up?" he asked cautiously.

She bit her lip. She was an adult, and she should act like one. But…

Ending her long hesitant pause, he said, "If not, that's alright. I was already planning to go to the library after my shift."

She gave him a sad, thankful smile. Then it shrank, her nerves taking hold. "If … if you're willing to exchange this book for me, would you be willing to pick me up another one?"

"I can do that. You want books three and four at the same time?"

Her heart racing, she picked at her nails. "Well, um, no. Actually, yes, that would be nice. But … something else, too. A nonfiction book."

"I don't see why not."

She studied his face. He already had a faint five-o'clock shadow. His crisp uniform reminded her exactly how much of their 'friendship' was a job for him.

"Do you know … why I'm here?" she asked. It still hadn't really been discussed between the two.

He squared his shoulders. "It's not really my place, miss."

He had to know something, though, right? "What were you told when she sent you to this cottage? About why I'm not living at the palace anymore?"

Wren's mouth opened slightly, and stayed open for a bit. "I don't know much, Miss Eleana. Obviously, Her Majesty and you are not seeing eye to eye…"

Obviously. Once a week, Catrina sent the same 'request' to come visit with her at the palace. And each time, Leah had declined.

Leah bolstered her courage. The garden *would* grow faster if she knew how to manage her powers during pregnancy, if she could safely and efficiently fertilize it. "I need a book … about …" She wrapped her arms around herself. "About Ivy powers during pregnancy."

Wren's eyes flickered to her arms covering her stomach, just for a moment. "Oh." His tone conveyed genuine surprise. "Well, I'm sure I could find something… And be discreet about it."

She took a full breath, relief washing over her. "Thank you."

He narrowed his eyes slightly. "I'm trusting Her Majesty knows this?"

Leah nodded.

He looked at her, his mind obviously working. Would he ask if Marcus was the father? If Marcus knew? If it had anything to do with why Marcus had abandoned her? "I'll see what I can find, then," was all he said.

"Thanks again."

Chapter 14

WREN BROUGHT LEAH FOUR BOOKS from the library—two more of *Valeska's Adventures*, and two about Ivy powers during pregnancy.

She set to work in the garden after skimming the sections on fertilizing abilities.

She ought not to have skimmed. The first plant grew limp and yellow. So, she returned to the cottage and thoroughly studied the texts.

Ivy powers were primarily chemical, mostly having to do with one's train of thought. There was a good deal of meditation required to manage female Ivy powers well during pregnancy.

Between devouring more of *Valeska's Adventures* over the next few days, and practicing meditation exercises, Leah was doing alright.

She finally gave it another go in the garden, extending vine tendrils from her wrists into the soil. She closed her eyes, breathing deeply, envisioning Ivy energy mingling with her Ivy chemicals. She channeled them down from her mind, to her arm, to her vines. Slowly, making sure she wasn't giving too much, she released the mixture into the soil through the small leaves lining her vines.

The change wasn't immediate, but she sat back on the grass to watch. It wasn't a grass yard, really, not in the way she was used to in the human world, in the US. It was a blend of grasses, clovers, and tiny wildflowers. It was cool to the touch, soft under her weight.

The excitement of watching a garden grow was akin to that of watching paint dry. But the sun was bright, the breeze light, the wild buzzing bees happy.

In the end, after a half hour, perhaps a full hour, she could've sworn the fertilizer was working, that the tomato plant she'd tried with looked greener, the vine slightly thicker.

She smiled, content. By the time dusk had come, she'd fertilized the whole garden. She couldn't stay here forever, but the garden would be left after she figured out her life, as a thank you to Tobias and Camry.

***

After exchanging more books with Wren the next morning, Leah strolled into the garden, her stomach growling, her mouth watering at the prospect of a faster growing garden.

It wasn't an exact science, and there wouldn't be a massive change in the plant growth overnight, especially not with Leah's limited experience.

But she smiled at the bright green garden that greeted her. Plucking a low-hanging plum from a tree, she admired her work. The spinach was broad and leafy, ready to harvest. All the other plants were looking healthy as well, though she'd hoped for more blossoms to peek out.

Reminding herself to be patient, she finished her plum. Raising her hands above her head, Leah shot out vines from her wrists, wrapping them around a sturdy branch. Flooding her arms, shoulders, and back with energy, she pulled herself up and perched on the branch, cautiously balancing herself against the trunk. With hands and vines, she harvested several plums, filling her pockets and easing some down to the ground. After getting back down, she harvested some spinach as well, and returned inside. Plums and spinach weren't exactly a delectable breakfast, but they would do until the other produce came in.

***

Books and watching the garden consumed more of her days. The garden had transformed into a veritable forest of lush leaves and thick stems and vines.

But … Leah grew worried. Healthy leaves were great for spinach and lettuce, not as good for squash and tomatoes. There were no buds.

Her heart sank as she recalled more from her studies about fertilizing. This was her fault. She'd thought initially that she had mastered this power, and maybe she had, and it was just the pregnancy causing the problem. But she'd forgotten to consider the differences between the various plants' needs. Too much nitrogen in the mix, and you got all leaves, no fruit.

"Seriously?" she uttered, frowning. She tightened her ponytail, considering her options.

Leah hadn't become a master gardener overnight, and hadn't even used those skills a single time at the palace. She hadn't needed to. Now, she could refertilize, adding more chemicals to try to balance it out, but she might screw up again and make things worse.

Her mouth watered at the fruits and vegetables she could start eating again if she could just get it right. And if she didn't… Stepping forward, she rubbed a leaf of a tomato plant. There was nothing quite like the herbaceous aroma of tomato leaf. Ivies weren't susceptible to many poisons. Eating leaves from the nightshade family wouldn't harm Leah… She tore off a small leaf and tasted it.

Chewing it around in her mouth, she grimaced. It didn't taste nearly as pleasant as it smelled, and the texture was less than appealing. Still, she forced herself to swallow it.

Sighing, Leah resolved to try to fix the chemicals. She only experimented on a fourth of the garden this time, aiming to not make the same mistake of ruining all the crops.

Shaking her head, she harvested more plums and spinach. At least she hadn't tried fertilizing the trees or bushes.

Energy drained from the exertion of fertilizing, she went inside to eat and nap.

***

The garden was … depressing. The correction Leah had given some of the crops seemed to be helping—they were now budding. So, she carefully applied her fertilizer to the rest of them, ensuring her concoction of Ivy energy and chemicals was well-balanced. But how long would it take for these to produce something she could actually eat?

The spinach had all been plucked, but she planted more. For now, she was scrounging what little fruit was still on the trees, and pimple berries from a bush, and picking through the limited dry storage left in the cottage.

She wasn't consuming nearly enough calories, especially not for someone with child. But she'd be okay. She'd be fine. Leah was always fine.

***

Leah's stomach complained early one morning. Low on energy, she rolled out of her little blanket on the sofa and ambled to the tiny kitchen.

Visions of rich banquets at the palace danced in her memories. She could almost even smell some of the exquisite food she'd become accustomed to.

Pulling herself back to her sad reality, Leah surveyed her meager spread. A healthy handful of buckwheat groats, a small container of coarse cornmeal, half a bottle of oil, seasonings, a precious bag of dried fruit.

She glanced through the kitchen window to the backyard. She'd be fine. This was the Green Lands. This realm was like a paradise. New berries matured each day, fresh sprouts emerged regularly, and things would work out.

Envisioning the worst, she pictured herself kneeling on the grass, harvesting clover—it was technically edible. That much she remembered from her courses.

Leah fought the truth tugging at her. She was doing this to herself. She was imprisoning and debasing and starving herself. No one was doing this to her.

She could trudge the mile to Rachel and Guillen's home to grovel for their forgiveness, to ask for food, to ask Rachel to come back and use her powers to boost the plants' growth.

She could take Wren up on his constant offer to leave the cottage and go to the market. Marcus had stormed out without taking the extra coins he'd brought.

She wouldn't be doing any of those things. Leah was done asking for help. Done taking people's charity and money and simply accepting that she had no other choice.

Everyone was probably aware of her status right now anyway. Perhaps that was part of the 'family plan,' to starve Leah out until she gave in to Catrina's demands.

Leah guzzled extra water and counted out a scant handful of the dried fruit. She sat at the table, nibbling and sipping. Water was good for her anyway, especially since she was pregnant.

Soon enough, Wren's signature knock sounded on the front door.

When she opened it, he gave her a half-smile, as well as the next Valeska book, and a letter from her mom.

"Thanks," she said.

He wasn't his usual self. Not bright or cheerful. He looked like he was prepared to deliver bad news.

"Is anything wrong?" she asked.

Wren bunched his eyebrows. "What do you say to us finally venturing away from here today? Checking out the library and market?"

She flipped the pages of the book in her hands. His trips to the library weren't part of his job, but had been out of the kindness of his heart. The reminder made her feel more guilty.

"I … can just reread the books I have here," she said.

"And the market?"

That water wouldn't keep her full for long. Somehow, kneeling on all fours and eating clover from the dirt like a cow seemed less intimidating than being in public right now.

"I'm fine."

Standing tall, Wren crossed his arms. "The cold storage in a place like this can't be all that large. I'd imagine the pantry's not all that expansive, either."

She swallowed. "They're surprisingly large for a cottage this size." That was a complete lie.

He nodded, eyeing her. "And you know we patrol the entire property regularly, right? That includes the backyard?"

Her anxiety doubled. *Please don't. Just let it go.* "I know."

"I couldn't help but notice the garden's perhaps not meeting demand," he said.

"It's doing better, thanks to the books you borrowed for me." She turned to head inside.

Resting a hand on the doorframe, Wren stopped her. "We should get you food until the garden produces more."

"No." She stood there, unwilling to budge on the topic. *You've always been a burden, a mistake.*

"If you don't have proper food, I will have to inform Her Majesty." His tone was matter-of-fact.

She spun on him, her heart aching at the betrayal. "Don't you dare. I don't want help. I don't need help. I'll be fine."

"My assignment is to keep you safe," he said, sparing a quick glance at her stomach. "To keep you both safe. And if you're not getting enough to—"

"I'm fine!" she snapped, her eyes burning. "I can take care of myself. I can take care of myself and my child, and it's none of your concern. And Catrina can keep her nose out of my business."

He loosed a soft sigh. "She cares about you."

"No. She doesn't. She cares about appearances. I'm sure she's happy to be rid of me. Everyone is." Marcus, his parents, her 'friends' at the academy. "Queen Catrina doesn't care about me." Her voice shook as tears pricked at her eyes. "Nobody does."

"Miss Eleana—" he started with gentle chastisement.

Leah shoved the book he'd just given her back into his hand, pushing past him, and slammed the door closed, locking it tight.

She lay back down on the sofa, trying to find a comfortable position, slowly breaking into a fit of tears. And her mind fixated on that hidden passport.

What game was she playing? Marcus hadn't so much as sent a single letter after leaving.

She yearned to give that passport a maiden voyage to the human world. To escape this all. Marcus may never come back to her.

But a sinking anxiety stopped her from considering it too seriously. Catrina had probably reinstated the order that Leah was prohibited from leaving the realm, like she'd been for ages after her attempt on Kaylah's life.

Plus, going to the human world likely meant permanently cutting ties with this realm. Right now, she didn't have a lot to lose in that move. Except for contact with her mom as she rotted away in prison all alone.

Leah unfolded the new letter from her mom, soaking it up, cherishing each word. There wasn't anything particularly exciting about it.

As with the last letter, Leah kept reading those two words at the end. *Love always.*

Always? Really? Some things in life worked that way. Gravity *always* worked. The sun *always* rose in the morning. And Leah *always* … found a way to screw things up.

But love and relationships? There was no always with them. People left—by choice, consequence, or death. People lied. Her mother certainly had.

About so many things. More than anyone else in the realm even knew. But Leah now knew.

The next morning, Leah stepped out the back door, praying every branch, stem, and vine in the garden had miraculously become laden with fruit overnight.

She didn't make it far. Right outside the door sat a giant basket brimming with fresh produce and dried grains. Resting on the top, dead center, was the book Leah had shoved into Wren's hands the day before.

Frowning, she picked it up. A small letter stuck out the top. She unfolded it, her hurt forming a puddle in her chest as she read it. Two words: *I care.*

Numb, trying to sort through her emotions, she summoned Ivy energy to give her enough strength to pick up the giant basket and bring it inside.

After taking her time to munch on some strawberries and mull things over, she gathered her courage and opened the front door.

Wren didn't react, sitting and reading a book.

"Thank you," she said.

"You're welcome." He didn't look up.

It was uncomfortable. He had to think she was throwing a tantrum like a child, that she was unstable like her father had been.

"And I'm sorry," she added.

He looked at her, closing the book in his lap. "No apologies necessary."

"How much did it cost?" She could pay with the money Marcus had left behind.

"It was a gift. Consider it a present for you and your little one."

"Yeah. Thanks." She fidgeted with her hands. It was time to swallow her pride. Or at least a small portion of it. Time to force herself out of her cocoon of safety. "How about we…" It pained her to utter the promise. "We can go to the market on Sunday, if the garden isn't producing enough by then." It wouldn't, not that quickly. But his gift was more than enough to last until then.

He smiled. "I'll be ready."

"And thanks again for the book." It was number eight of nine in the series.

"Of course," he said. "I'll warn you that it's a slower pace than some of the others, but vital. Stick with it, and it'll make sense."

She returned his smile, more at ease over book talk. "Sounds good."

Chapter 15

A SOFT KNOCK STARTLED LEAH AWAKE. Squinting in the daylight, she searched for the clock on the wall. It was already almost noon.

Yawning and stretching, she forced herself to fully wake. She'd gotten so caught up in book eight of *Valeska's Adventures* the night before that she'd burned through one of the precious few candles still left in the cottage. She had no idea how late it had been when she'd finally finished the book, eventually shut off her mind, and nodded off.

Rubbing her face, she approached the front door. Another soft knock disturbed the silence. It was Wren's day off, and the other escorts didn't use playful special knocks like he did, but they weren't usually this quiet.

Pulling the curtain to the side, she peered through the window in the door. Panic flooded Leah as she stared straight at Camry, who gave her a smile. Leah's heart and lungs forgot their jobs.

Her jaw dropped as she sucked in a breath. Within the span of about three seconds, a mile-long list of horrors raced through her mind. She was wearing Camry's pajamas. She hadn't showered in a couple of days, and the bedding sprawled out on the sofa definitely needed a wash, too.

The painting in the bedroom closet. The empty wall now gaped in the absence of the wedding gift she'd taken down. Their wedding photo lay facedown in the bedroom. Leah's underwear was in one of their drawers, and… *Kill me now.* Her passport was still tucked away in Camry's underwear drawer.

That didn't even touch on the messy bathroom and the unfortunate garden experiment.

Mankind truly did not understand the full meaning of the word *mortified.*

And what was Leah to do? This was Camry's home! Leah couldn't simply pretend they weren't staring at each other right now. Couldn't ask her to wait while she scrubbed down the cottage and ran away with her tail tucked between her legs.

She forced herself to open the door. "Camry," she breathed.

Camry lunged for her, sweeping her up in a hug. "Hey, Leah."

Leah wilted. "Hey." She quickly pulled away, backing toward the sofa. "I'm so, so, so sorry. I didn't even realize what day it was, and…" She tugged the blanket from between the sofa cushion and back, folding it. "I should have… I'm just going to straighten up, and I'll get out of here."

"You don't need to leave," Camry said softly, tucking her chestnut hair behind her ear.

"No. I do," Leah insisted. Granted, she needed at least half a day to properly wash herself, the laundry, *and* the house. "I'll hurry." She glanced at the door. "Where's Tobias?"

"He's at Rachel and Guillen's."

Which probably meant they'd heard it all. That she was pregnant. That she'd smacked Marcus.

"Oh," Leah replied. "Well, I'll straighten up, and then you guys can have your place back."

"Leah," Camry said a little forcefully. "We're not kicking you out."

"No, I..." Her breathing was rapid as she shook her head, stacking the blanket on her pillow. How could she have lost track of time so badly that she'd completely forgotten they were coming to visit? And not only for a weekend? It was November, and they were gathering to celebrate Thanksgiving. "This is your home. I'm sorry."

Camry cocked her head. "Are you going back to the palace?"

Even if Leah groveled, begging to return after storming out the way she had, there wasn't a chance Catrina would allow her to move back after Leah hurt Marcus.

"No."

"Then, where will you go?" Camry asked cautiously.

Leah turned to her, quieting. She had *nowhere* to go. She should have been sorting that out while here, not just hoping that Marcus would come back to fix things for her, not spending all her time lost in books to escape. "I'll figure it out."

Camry took a seat in the armchair. "We already settled in at Rachel and Guillen's guesthouse. We knew you were staying here. And that's fine."

Biting the insides of her cheeks, Leah sat on the sofa. "You know?"

"That you're pregnant?"

As she met Camry's eyes and nodded, she recalled with perfect clarity the conversation she'd had with Marcus when she'd told him she was pregnant. He had wanted to give up their baby.

Well, if you decide not to keep it... You know, Tobias and Cam have talked about adopting...

He'd jumped right to offering up their child to his brother and sister-in-law. Was Camry there to accept his offer? Had he made a unilateral decision that Catrina would surely uphold, since Leah had proven herself an abusive, unsuitable mother?

"I, uh, yeah," Leah said. "Pregnant. I'm keeping it."

Camry nodded, unfazed. "That's what I heard. How are you feeling?"

Okay, so maybe I jumped to conclusions about Marcus just turning over our baby without proper warning or a discussion…

"Better. My maternal, er, morning sickness is all gone." She did the math. She was nine weeks along. Nine! She'd spent nearly seven weeks holed up in this cottage.

"I'm glad you're feeling better."

She was still beyond embarrassed to be disheveled and squatting in their cottage, even if it was her only option at this point. "I really am sorry."

"Don't be. I brought you a gift from back home, by the way." Camry smiled brightly, pulling a tube of lipstick from her jeans pocket.

Leah couldn't hold back a small smile herself as she accepted it. They'd originally shared a bonding moment over lipstick. "The human bringing the good stuff. Thank you."

Camry shrugged. "Not exactly a baby shower gift, but we've got time for that."

Turning it in her hand, Leah studied the sleek tube, admiring the shade Camry had picked out. It was a pretty pink with a slight brown undertone. "Thank you."

"We're having a big family get-together at Rachel and Guillen's place. Do you want to join us? No rush if you want to get dressed."

Camry and Eric—Kaylah's husband—were American humans. Rachel had been raised by a human mother as well. Most Ivies didn't celebrate human holidays, but this group did, and Leah had enjoyed that part of her old home. It was still too early to gather for Thanksgiving, so this was probably just to celebrate Tobias and Camry's arrival, but Leah couldn't face either of Marcus's parents right now. And things would only be going downhill with Tobias at this point. Leah wouldn't be attending, but that didn't stop her from asking what she needed to know. "Is Marcus over there?"

Camry pursed her lips. "Not yet, but I think he's planning to come."

"No, I…" She couldn't come up with an excuse. She what? Had plans? Needed to wash her hair? At least that one was true. "I'd rather not. But thank you."

Drawing a deep breath, Camry scooted to the edge of her chair. "Do you want to hang out, just you and me?"

"Maybe another time."

"Alright. No pressure. If you change your mind, you're welcome to come over. And we'll be here for the better part of a month, so there's plenty of time. You're obviously still invited for Thanksgiving."

Leah nodded. "Yeah. Thanks."

"Well, I'll," Camry gestured over her shoulder toward the door, "head out. I just wanted to see you and say hi, and invite you over."

"Thanks again."

Camry stood, seeing herself out.

Leah sat there, numb. She stared at the tube of lipstick, musing on its familiarity. It wasn't like natural Green Lands makeup. 'A gift from back home,' Camry had said. From Camry's home, the human world. Not Leah's home. It *had* been her childhood home, but she'd been unable to call it that after she tried to kill Kaylah. She'd forfeited her right to choose which realm, which world she would live in.

Leah had nothing waiting there for her anymore. Nothing and no one.

But she didn't here either. And over there, she could at least start a new life where she wasn't the daughter of Soren and Beata, wasn't tainted by their legacy.

A familiar eerie cold settled into Leah's chest as she started to cry. She was ready to leave. She was ready to run. If Marcus had wanted to fix things between them, he could have by now.

She yearned to disappear. But how? She had an escort posted at the door around the clock. It wouldn't be that hard to sneak over one of the brick walls in the backyard and drop into a neighbor's yard to get away. She'd snuck out of her own house more than once growing up, and she'd snuck a guy into her bedroom with her mom in the other room.

But then … what about the rifting?

She wasn't nervous about whether she could rift safely. Unlike Ivy poison and chemical arts, rifting only required Ivy energy, and that she had in spades, unhampered by her pregnancy.

Sniffling, Leah pondered her options. Sneak out and trek a few miles to the nearest rifting cave? And then what? Hand her passport to the cave employees and waltz through? Every living, breathing creature in the realm knew who Leah was, and Catrina had to have already made her passport null and void.

Most people were fight or flight. Leah was both.

She had only one option. It was illegal. She'd done illegal before, and she could do it again.

Leah set to work tidying up the cottage. She wouldn't take time to shower or wash things, but she could make it a little more presentable.

The bathroom wasn't *that* bad, all things considered. She placed her folded bedding on the end of the bed, sparing a momentary gut-wrenching frown, imagining him lying there beside her, holding her.

She retrieved the painting from the closet and hung it on the living room wall, hoping Camry hadn't noticed. She flipped their wedding picture upright, grabbed her passport from Camry's underwear drawer, and even tucked her own clean underwear in her jeans pockets after she dressed in her own clothes. The underwear was skimpy enough to all fit, and it wasn't like she could buy more anytime soon—Leah didn't have a single human penny to her name.

Last time, when she'd run away *to* the Green Lands, she'd crafted an elaborate plan. One that had imprisoned her and her mom.

Mom. Leah released a shaky breath. Maybe it was better this way. Yes, her mom was lonely in prison, but her mom's sisters and nieces and nephews sometimes visited…

Leah was leaving. This time, as she ran away *from* the Green Lands, she had no plan, but she at least knew how to get around, and could find a women's shelter…

After chucking her bamboo toothbrush, Leah peeked out the front- and back-door windows. Her escort stood guard, ever watchful, at the front door. Leah sketched out an apology on a piece of paper—a simple *I'm sorry for everything*—and left it next to her most recent read from the library.

She paused, her hand glued to the library book. She spared another glance at the front door. Her gut twisted as she considered Lycha, her current escort. Leah hadn't gotten to know her nearly as well as Wren, and she was glad Wren wasn't there right now, but it wasn't right for Lycha, either. She'd probably be canned like Robyn had been for helping Leah at the palace. No matter what, Leah was always sowing destruction, burning people in her wake.

And in that moment, she thought of her dad, Soren, of all people. Even *he* had been destroyed by Leah's existence, though he'd died never understanding that.

Slipping into the backyard, Leah picked a ripe pimple berry—white, mild, and creamy. She'd miss the unique plant life of the realm.

Her heart thumping wildly, she glanced between the handful of trees. She'd never actually rifted through a tree. It was illegal from the human world, as it required the sacrifice of the tree. Other than in the case of emergency, it wasn't even allowed in the Green Lands unless it was on your own property.

They could add this to the list of her offenses. She could handle knowing she'd be penned into the history books as a disappointment like her parents. That was the legacy she'd inherited.

Ivies, at least in the old days before rifting caves had become commonplace, generally preferred to rift through pine trees. Apparently, the energy worked differently depending on the tree, and the process imparted a flavor to the rifter. Pine trees allowed rifting with more ease, and tasted faintly of vanilla.

Tobias and Camry had no pines on their property. Leah didn't care how much energy it required or how nasty a rift might taste, as long as she could get away.

Leah stepped up to the plum tree, drawing a breath. She was really going to do this. She was making a true fugitive of herself. She was breaking the tree-rifting ban and taking her child without Marcus's permission.

Crying a little harder, she glided her hand across the rough bark of the tree. If she actually went through with this, it was a one-way ticket, unless she wanted to join her mom in prison and have her child taken from her.

Even if she wanted to tree rift home in the future, she'd be unable to return with her child after they were born. They'd require a Seeder employee at a cave to open a rift for them, and a specialty Boman jade for her child.

She wasn't giving up this child, nor was she going to come back in shackles.

"You can do this," she whispered.

As she extended her vine, touching it to the trunk, memories tugged at her. Kara, the Ivy girl who had taught her to rift in high school—they'd never talked again after Leah left the human world. Marcus—how calming it had been when he'd wrapped his arms around her when she'd been frustrated when practicing.

A muffled squeak escaped Leah's lips, and she forced down the lump in her throat.

Do it. Leave. Be a coward.

Leah pressed her vine harder against the bark, summoning her energy, focusing on the lower central channel for her energy as she'd been taught.

They don't need you here anymore. They don't want you. For good or bad, your part in this realm is done.

Tears cascaded down her cheeks as she directed her Ivy energy to her extended vine. It pulsated, lingering at the tip of her vine, waiting for her to make the final choice, to commit.

I'm not giving up. I'm giving up Soren's legacy, Beata's legacy. And this child will get the fresh start I never did.

And then she did it. Leah pushed her Ivy energy past her vine and into the tree. It instantly connected, and a coppery tang filled her mouth. Her energy mingled with that of the tree, and she slowly dragged her vine down, opening a rift, a seam between the realms.

Only a few inches into forming the rift, Leah struggled. Not physically.

The bark already hinted at peeling back, at being singed. She was stealing the life of this tree, the same one that had sustained her during her time here.

As she paused, all the self-doubt, the self-hatred, the secrets and lies and torment bombarded her. It was hell in her mind.

The same kind of hell she'd faced, the darkened haze she'd gone through, when she'd made the immeasurably rash decision to try to take her own aunt's life.

Leah reeled her vine back in, panting. And then she sank onto her knees, rested her forehead against the tree trunk, and sobbed.

And sobbed.

Why was she so broken, so wrong, so destructive?

She knew the answer to that. She'd been made that way from the beginning. It was in her very nature.

Wrapping her arms around her stomach, she stayed there. Her tears watering the ground wouldn't undo the damage she'd done to the tree, but it was the only penance she could offer. And she had nowhere to go, nothing to do, other than to let it all out.

It could have been minutes, but it felt more like hours that she knelt there, until she was interrupted.

Chapter 16

SHE RECOGNIZED THE VOICE. "Leah?"

Leah quieted and stilled, praying Kaylah would go away, that like a child closing their eyes and thinking they're invisible, Leah could be ignored.

"Leah?" This time Kaylah's voice was filled with urgent concern, not searching curiosity. "Are you okay?"

"Leave me alone," Leah pleaded.

"That's the last thing I'm going to do." She rested a warm hand on Leah's back. "Are you hurt?"

"Leave me alone," Leah repeated weakly.

"It looks like I've already done that for too long," Kaylah said. "Come on." A second hand grasped Leah's arm. "Let's go inside."

There was no point in fighting it. Matron Kaylah would have an escort as well who could back her up.

It took extra energy for Leah to force herself up, but Kaylah's hands were strong and supportive.

A strange man, probably Kaylah's escort, her personal bodyguard, watched on as they entered the house. Kaylah sat her down on the sofa, and eased herself onto the armchair. "Are you hurt?" Kaylah asked, her face painted with concern.

Leah averted her gaze, staring at her hands. "I'm fine."

"That's … not exactly true, is it?"

Picking at her nails, Leah shrugged. "I'll be fine."

Warmth and caring infusing her words, Kaylah said, "Let me take you home."

All of Leah's tears had been cried. She looked up, puffy-eyed, and stated the simple but devastating truth. "I don't have a home. I never have." She couldn't recall a single postal code from her years in the human world. Not a single address where she'd lived. She and her mom and abusive 'aunt' Cheryl had moved too often, and changed phone numbers too often, to keep any of that straight.

"You're coming home with me," Kaylah said, exuding compassion. "You'll *always* have a home with me and Eric."

Leah sat there, half considering, half wishing she was in a void somewhere, not having to exist or think or feel at the moment.

"Come on." Kaylah stood, surveying the small living room. "What do we need to pack?"

"Nothing here is mine."

"That makes things easier." She stepped toward the kitchen. "Have you eaten?"

Leah's humiliation from Camry's visit had been so complete that she hadn't even thought of grabbing a bite before taking off. "No."

"Well, now, that won't do. I'm a bit peckish, too, so let me pick out a little something for the both of us." Kaylah's tone had become more cheerful. A false kind of cheerful, but she wore the mask well. Leah didn't protest.

Carrying a bagful of food from the kitchen, Kaylah rejoined Leah, her eyes resting on the folded letter Leah had scribbled out.

Leah didn't even have it in her to protest as Kaylah unfolded it and read it. She didn't say anything, but instead folded it back up and tucked it in a pocket of her dress.

"Great. We've got snacks. Anything else?"

Leah pointed to the book. "That's the library's."

"We'll see that it's returned."

Frowning, Leah added, "Please don't fire my escort."

Kaylah raised her eyebrows. "No one gets fired today unless you say so."

A measure of relief lightened Leah's load.

Squaring her shoulders, Kaylah stretched out a hand. "Let's go."

***

The escort on duty seemed a bit confused as they left, as Leah asked her to tell Wren thank you. Kaylah told one of her two bodyguards to inform Eric that she was taking Leah home.

She and Leah slid into the rickshaw together. "We'll be traveling to my estate, the less public roads, please," Kaylah instructed.

The driver began pedaling, and they were on their way.

"We're not going to the local cave to rift?" Leah asked. Kaylah lived far into the country. It might take days, between rickshaw driver breaks and transfers.

Kaylah hung the bag of food on a hook in front of them. After a moment of silence, she angled her body to face Leah. "Here's the thing, kiddo: most green folk your age only know what an Ivy tree rift looks like from stories and textbook diagrams, but when I was your age, I was making them every other day."

She'd noticed the damage Leah had done to the tree. They were taking hours and days to return to Kaylah's place because she didn't trust Leah to take a cave rift, nor should she. She was still a flight risk.

"Will I be in trouble for … the damage?" She'd understood the repercussions of opening an illegal tree rift, but wasn't sure if there was some sort of lesser punishment for having only formed a partial rift.

Scooching closer to Leah, Kaylah faced forward, sliding an arm around her shoulders. "I saw nothing."

"But the damage… Will it … die?"

"It'll be fine. It'll scar, but it'll bounce back." She squeezed Leah. "It will bounce back, and so will you."

"I hate my life," Leah confessed.

The rickshaw jostled as they hit a bump, and the driver apologized.

"Sometimes we all do," Kaylah said, giving Leah another light reassuring squeeze.

Worn out and grateful, Leah rested her head on Kaylah's shoulder and closed her eyes.

***

A half hour later, Leah woke to another bump in the road. She straightened and listened as Kaylah discussed travel plans with one of her bodyguards. The rickshaw was flanked on either side with a bodyguard on a bike, which had to look absolutely ridiculous for most humans to behold, but that was the life of the Green Lands, where electricity didn't properly work, even after years of joint Ivy/Seeder/human experimentation. Matron Kaylah, a retired queen, still had bodyguards with her nearly everywhere she went.

Done talking with her guard, Kaylah gave her attention to Leah. "You should eat something."

Leah pulled an apple from the bag and took a bite.

"Did the nap help?"

"A little."

Kaylah took an apple out for herself. "Good."

"Why were you even there?"

Holding out a finger, Kaylah finished her bite. "I happened to be in the area."

"In the area for a family gathering while Tobias and Camry are in-realm?"

"Hmm… As the rather barbaric human saying goes: two birds, one stone." Kaylah held her apple in her lap. "I wanted to come see you when Catrina sent word about your pregnancy, but it also sounded like you wanted everyone to get out of your hair while you sorted things…”

Leah nodded, chewing in silence. Kaylah wasn't much of a retired queen by the way she packed her schedule with causes and events. She'd probably just arrived at Rachel and Guillen's place using a cave, and was missing a weekend with her favorite people, her husband included.

“If I promise to take a rift to the cave closest to your estate, you could return and still enjoy time with the family,” Leah said.

“Hmm… One step at a time. I'm okay with what we've got planned right now. Girl time—just you and me.”

Right… “You don't have to lie to me, and I don't have to ruin your weekend.”

“You couldn't if you tried.” Kaylah crunched down into her apple once more. “Plus, road trips are good for the soul.”

The rest of the day, they traveled in relative silence. Leah was grateful to not have Kaylah pry or prod. At each major city, or sooner as needed, the rickshaw driver took a break, and the women would stretch their legs. Leah's bladder was happy for the breaks as well.

They sat down for a warm meal at dinnertime on the outskirts of a town along the way. Despite it being a simple meal, it was divine after what she'd been scraping by on at the cottage. They chatted, though it was all fairly surface level—about the food, the scenery.

As the sun began to set, they pulled into another town and drove straight to an inn. The innkeeper had already been alerted to Kaylah's stay, and fawned over her on their arrival.

Kaylah requested they fetch some nightclothes and a fresh change for the next day for both herself and Leah.

The room was a two-bed suite, likely as nice as they got at inns along the path out in the middle of nowhere.

An employee of the inn rushed to light the lamps of the room, offering to draw a warm bath. Kaylah accepted.

Leah eased herself onto one of the beds and ate another light snack from the bag Kaylah had packed.

After fresh clothes had been secured from a local shop, Kaylah recommended Leah bathe, and she'd take a turn in the morning.

Whether the offer came from Kaylah having had to endure hours next to Leah's unshowered self, or to allow Leah to soak away the stress of a day as the hot mess du jour, Leah didn't want to know.

"You'll be okay in there?" Kaylah shyly asked before Leah closed the bathroom door.

Leah's heart hurt. She'd like to think Kaylah was concerned she'd slip on the wet floor, but it was probably more about Leah being reckless, and Kaylah being concerned all over again that Leah had been suicidal. They'd visited that particular concern enough shortly after Leah had tried to murder her.

"I'll be fine," Leah reassured her. "I'll leave it unlocked in case I slip."

Kaylah gave her a smile. "Thank you."

By the time Leah emerged, Kaylah had dressed in nightclothes, braiding her hair to the side. Her long hair was as black as Leah's or Beata's.

Leah combed out her wet hair. "It feels good to be clean."

Smiling again, Kaylah finished her braid. She pointed to a pitcher of water. "Stay hydrated."

After pouring herself a glass, Leah sat cross-legged on her bed, facing Kaylah.

"How's the baby?" Kaylah asked.

"She's good." The thought of the child growing within her tugged her lips upwards.

Kaylah arched an eyebrow. "She? A little predictive mother's intuition?"

Leah shrugged. "I guess I've just started to imagine it's a 'she' instead of an 'it' or 'they.' I'd be happy either way, though."

"You know…" Kaylah took a sip of her own water. "As you recall, I was super excited to find out I was an aunt…"

Nodding, Leah pursed her lips. "As *I* recall, it took a little bit. Or did you secretly like me trying to murder you?"

Kaylah donned a feisty grin. "Tosh! What aunt doesn't have a niece trying to snuff her out?"

Leah chuckled, and Kaylah winked. Dark humor had been their path to stop walking on eggshells around each other, though they never talked like this with anyone else in the room unless it was Eric. People would be too appalled at how unapologetic Leah sounded after trying to assassinate everyone's favorite queen.

"Go on, tell me how much you loved finding out about me," Leah prompted.

"As I was saying…" Kaylah flourished a hand in the air. "I thought it was fantastic to be an aunt. But I hope you don't get offended that I'm a smidge more excited about that little gremlin." She pointed at Leah's stomach.

"Really?" It sounded like there was a catch.

"Really. I mean, I'm arguably a great aunt, but now, I'll be a *great* great-aunt." She paused. "Not like a great-great-aunt, like super old, but you know what I mean. I'm great, and I'll be a great-aunt."

"Very humble, too."

Kaylah beamed.

"But please tell me you are not going to refer to my child as a gremlin."

"All children are gremlins," Kaylah stated matter-of-factly. And the funny thing was, Leah had heard Kaylah use those terms interchangeably just like that, ever since she'd met her. In private only, of course.

Kaylah continued, "I mean, diapers and screaming?" She shuddered. "I changed Marcus's once after he was adopted. Uh-uh. *Never* again."

It hurt to hear his name. Leah set her water glass down. "Are you telling me a retired queen won't deign to change her great-niece or nephew's diaper now and then?"

Wrinkling her nose, Kaylah didn't respond. Leah chuckled again.

"Fine. But if you're going to be a *great* great-aunt, then you probably shouldn't call her a gremlin like all the other kids out there. She's special."

Kaylah held a hand to her heart, playful. "I don't make the rules. No exceptions. No matter how much I will love it, that thing is a stink bomb in the making."

Leah sighed dramatically. "Then it's not my fault if I accidentally let it slip that the kingdom's hero refers to her subjects' little ones as gremlins."

"You wouldn't dare! Plus, which of us would they believe?"

Unable to mask it this time, Leah frowned. That remark hit too close to home after Marcus's threat to pull rank on her about leaving for the human world.

Kaylah's demeanor instantly changed, but she didn't ask.

"I'm pretty tired." Leah pulled back her covers.

"Yeah, same." Kaylah didn't budge from her spot. "What did you mean by your note at the cottage? That you were sorry for everything?"

Fighting fresh tears, Leah only shook her head.

Kaylah didn't press the matter. "This is a fun girl's trip, not an inquisition."

After Leah crawled into bed, Kaylah snuffed the lamps.

"Good night, Leah."

"Good night."

"Love you, kiddo."

Leah still hesitated with that one. "Thanks."

Chapter 17

LEAH'S EYELIDS FLUTTERED OPEN. She was exhausted and sore. It took her a moment to remember where she was. Kaylah was already up, sitting against the headboard of her bed, staring across the room, studying the wall.

Shifting to sit up, Leah caught Kaylah's attention.

Kaylah smiled warmly. "Good morning, sunshine."

Popping her neck, Leah returned the greeting. This bed was so soft and comfortable compared to the cottage sofa; the bare walls and new layout a refreshing change.

"I ordered us breakfast in the room," Kaylah said.

"Thanks."

Kaylah turned on the bed, facing Leah. "We should talk about a few things before we head out today, while we have some privacy away from the guards and driver."

Leah tensed. "Yeah?"

Searching her eyes, Kaylah cocked her head. "Nothing bad."

Swallowing, Leah nodded.

"I think we should have a little more direction about what we're doing here. Did you, or … do you have any plans? For the future right now?"

Did she have plans and goals and aspirations? Or had she thrown her life away and given up?

"I'll figure it out," Leah said.

"I'm not trying to rush you. I just want to make sure we're on the same page. I want to make sure you have everything you need, and that I'm not cramping your style."

Something akin to a half-hearted bitter laugh made its way up Leah's throat. "I have no style to cramp." A little more humbly, remorsefully, she added, "I don't exactly have plans right now." She stared down at her hands, pushing back her cuticles with her fingernails.

"That's fine," Kaylah replied, all kindness and reassurance. "I do want to set some rules about living on the estate."

A weight pressed into Leah's chest. Was this going to be like living at the palace all over again? Being told how to talk, sit, stand, and breathe? Who she could hug, or share any affection with?

"Nothing big," Kaylah continued. "You'll be staying in the house proper."

"I really don't mind staying in the guest cabin." Out of the way, away from people.

"No. In the house proper."

They met eyes, Leah gnawing on her lower lip. She wasn't being forced out into public, but Kaylah wasn't about to let her remain a hermit.

"You can have the entire second floor of the east wing if you'd like."

"Sure."

Kaylah gave her a single nod. "When Eric and I are home, I'd like you to eat at least one meal with us a day. You're welcome to join us for all of them if you'd like, but I'd like at least one."

Not in any position to protest or bargain, Leah only nodded her agreement.

"And you and I will enjoy a weekly picnic together, just the two of us."

Leah arched an eyebrow at this one.

Smoothing the bedding around her, Kaylah said, "We've got a lot of missed bonding opportunities to make up for."

Yeah, Leah's entire childhood. And they'd spent plenty of time in each other's company over the last two-plus years, but most of that had been at official, public, or family gatherings. Not all that much one-on-one time.

"Okay."

Kaylah squinted at her. "I'm going to try to not be offended that your agreement to my terms sounds like you'd rather have all your teeth pulled."

Leah gave her a cheesy smile.

A knock at the door announced their breakfast had arrived. The inn's staff carried in a mouthwatering buffet of hot porridge and hash, fresh berries and cut melons, and a bright medley of sauteed vegetables. It was much more food than the two of them needed, and no doubt a more generous and refined spread than any of the other customers were being offered. But that was the perk of traveling with royalty, of being around Matron Kaylah.

None of the staff even passed Leah any contemptuous glances, though a couple of their gazes caught on her a little longer than she would have liked.

After they had done all of their bowing and curtsying, had deposited the dishes on a long table in the corner of the room and poured glasses of juice for the two women, they left them to scoop up.

Sitting at a small table by a large window, Leah and Kaylah dug in.

"So, anyway…" Kaylah said, spearing a chunk of honeydew with her fork. "Let me know what you need, and we'll make sure it's taken care of."

"I'll need some clothes."

"Of course, we'll take care of clothes and toiletries and all that."

Leah ate a spoonful of porridge. "I can do some extra chores to pay for them."

Kaylah looked no less than offended. "I'm bringing you home to live with me, not hiring you as a servant."

Leah didn't have it in her to ask if the funds she'd received as Catrina's ward were still assigned to her, or if Kaylah was taking on her expenses from her own pocket. And she was too weak to object, to let her pride be upset for leeching off Kaylah and Eric.

So, Leah just ate another spoonful of porridge. As she did so, she pondered her current situation further. How long she'd be at Kaylah's place, she didn't know. But something in her was more at ease at the idea of staying there a while, compared to any of the alternatives. Just until she could sort things out and make her own way.

Leah took a swig of white grape juice. "Will Catrina know I'm staying at your place?" She might already.

"Yes." Kaylah met Leah's look of frustration with a calm reply. "We only keep tabs on you for your safety. She'll know you're with family and won't have to worry about you."

Leah choked down a scoff. Catrina wasn't so much concerned about Leah as she was concerned about what Leah might do. That was a moot point right now, but Leah wanted to make sure Catrina knew they were completely done. "Could… Would you ask for my things to be delivered to your place?" She didn't have much of her own, but at minimum, her knife-throwing set was completely hers.

Kaylah finished chewing her bite. "Yes, I'll send for all that."

"Thanks."

They kept eating. Leah asked what would become of her escorts, wanting to make sure no one lost their job because she'd left the care of the palace. Kaylah assured her they'd be kept on as staff at the palace, that Catrina always had extra people staffed. Leah hoped that was true, still regretting costing Robyn her job.

After they'd both had their fill, they set out for another long day on the road. The scenery was tranquil, soothing. Leah had been at Kaylah and Eric's estate a handful of times over the last two-plus years, but never by rickshaw. It wasn't far from the end of a train line or a rifting cave, and she'd always taken either of them before.

Her view was full of pastel pink flowers on rolling hills, pineapple trees near ponds, and chatterbirds swooping in the sky. She allowed herself to admire the Green Lands, the Ivy Kingdom and its beauty. She was usually so busy with tutors and the academy, official functions, time with Marcus and his family, that she forgot what it could feel like to simply *be*.

The break from chaos wasn't healing, exactly, but it was quiet. The kind of quiet where she found herself almost even smiling as she imagined her child in her arms someday. The kind of quiet where she found her thoughts drifting to the child's father, and everything else that sucked. It was usually around those times—when her heart sank, her mind stuttered under the stress—that Kaylah conveniently wanted to muse about something from her childhood, or take a break to stretch their legs and let the rickshaw driver rest.

Leah knew what Kaylah was doing. And she let her.

They traveled all day, staying at another inn they reached at dusk.

The next day, they rode past dusk, lanterns on the rickshaw lighting their way. There was no need for an inn when they were so close to Kaylah's estate.

Dim candlelight danced in a few windows as they approached, lit by servants waiting for their arrival. Kaylah had sent word to them and Eric, who she'd left at Rachel and Guillen's house.

Shortly after the pair stepped into the main entryway, Eric rounded the corner, squeezing Kaylah tight, then turned to Leah with a soft smile.

He tucked his hands in his pockets, his arms straight and rigid. "I know you're not much of a hugger, but would you like one?"

She wrung her hands. "No thank you."

"That's perfectly fine. I'm glad you ladies made such good time, and got here in one piece."

Kaylah's escorts entered behind them, handing the few items Leah and Kaylah had collected along the way to her staff, and wishing everyone a good night.

One servant lingered at the door to the hallway.

"Acacia will take you to your room and help you get settled," Eric said.

"Thanks."

Kaylah had made it clear this was no imposition, but having Eric waiting up for them reminded Leah how much of an interruption her breakdown was causing. They were both giving up time with family—their closest friends—to coddle Leah. "I don't mind if you two go back to Rachel and Guillen's to visit while Tobias and Camry are in-realm."

The couple traded a glance. "They'll be around for a while. We'll see. We're excited to spend time with *you*," Kaylah insisted.

Eric slid an arm around Kaylah's waist. "We didn't move out to the middle of nowhere to be around large groups of people all the time. We really don't mind."

"Okay. Thanks again, for everything." She swallowed. "Have a good night." She followed Acacia down the hallway and up a flight of stairs.

Leah had only stayed the night at the estate once, and it had been in a smaller guest room on the opposite end of the house from where Marcus had slept that night. Acacia guided her to a much larger room this time, with an en suite bathroom and a door to an adjoining room. Leah explained she didn't need a huge room, but Acacia stated she was giving her the one she'd been instructed to. You couldn't really argue much with staff just doing their job.

The woman bid her good night as well, and Leah sat on the large soft bed, taking in the room in the light of a lamp. The room was smaller than what she'd been given in the palace, but still three times the size of any of the bedrooms she'd had in the human world.

Sore and tired from hours and days in a rickshaw, she barely scraped up her energy to use the bathroom and brush her teeth before she passed out on the bed.

***

Leah woke to a knock on the door. Daylight peeked past the edge of curtains covering the windows. Groggy, Leah rubbed her eyes and cleared her throat. "Yeah, just a second."

After rolling out of bed, she was greeted by another servant. "Sorry to wake you, miss. Matron Kaylah asked me to see that you're well, and to set your things up in your room, if that's alright?"

"Of course. And I'm fine." Her things? New things Kaylah had bought for her, or stuff from the palace?

The servant gave her a bright smile. "Lovely. Breakfast can be made for you down in the breakfast room whenever you're ready." She reached down for a large bag. "And I'm sure I'll have this all unpacked for you by the time you've eaten."

Leah considered telling her she could unpack her own things, but she'd learned at the palace to allow the servants to do their jobs. Plus, she was starving. "Sounds good."

Entering the room, the servant added, "Since the closet here is smaller than what you're used to at the palace, we already placed your finer things in the attached room next door."

That threw Leah off. "Wait, what?"

The servant gestured to the door connecting this room to the next. "Over there. The ball gowns and whatnot."

Leah furrowed her brow, heading next door. She was utterly shocked to find an armoire plumb full of her fancier dresses, as well as a couple of loaded-down makeshift racks set up alongside the wall.

Some items had been placed on a shelf, perfumes and her throwing knives included.

Perching on the edge of the bed in there, Leah shook her head. *I can't believe it.*

She'd expected Queen Catrina to send her things at Kaylah's request, but not *everything* that had been in her chambers. Leah took a few moments to size it up before the servant appeared at the door. "We can rearrange it if you'd like. We'll be moving another armoire in here, but Her Highness didn't want the noise of it banging around down the hallway waking you."

Leah numbly nodded, looking at the dresses on the rack. The organization of the items didn't matter all that much to her; it was the fact Catrina had sent *all* of them that still had her uneasy.

Memories flooded Leah with each dress she studied. Embroidered, beaded, and lacy—they were all beautiful, all likely one of a kind. She'd worn them to balls and official functions where she'd needed to make a good impression. There were plenty of everyday dresses as well.

Some of the dresses held better memories than others. She just sat there and stared. Why had Catrina sent them? Leah hadn't paid for them, and in a lot of ways, they weren't even a wardrobe—they were a uniform.

Was Catrina being kind by sending them? Perhaps. Or was she sending a message to Leah? That she was done with Leah. Done with trying to help her. Done with trying to reach out to her. Done with Leah's ungrateful, selfish, stupid self. Done with the girl who was going to sink her nephew's reputation because she couldn't keep her legs closed as ordered.

Leah's gaze fixed on a deep plum dress with a sweetheart neckline. She ached. She'd worn that one to her first ball. Marcus had saved her from her misery that night.

"Leah?" Kaylah's voice was soft from the doorway, and Leah's attention snapped to her.

"Hey."

"Everything okay?" Kaylah asked cautiously.

"Of course." Leah sniffled, wiping away a tear. "I was just…" She drew a deep breath. "Why did she send all of these? It's not like I'm planning to go to any big events right now, and I won't fit into them soon, anyway." She was forming a baby bump, and it was likely already too tight of a squeeze into some of the more formfitting ones.

"I'm sure she expected you'd want them all in one place. And you may fit into them again someday."

Leah huffed. "They're not even mine. It's not like I paid for them."

Kaylah inclined her head. "They were bought for you, tailored for you. They're yours." She paused. "But if you'd rather, I could have them stored elsewhere for now."

Leah didn't want to cause the servants any extra trouble. "It's fine."

"How about we grab something to eat?"

Standing, Leah followed her downstairs to the breakfast room. Eric was off elsewhere, but Kaylah sat to eat with her.

The multigrain toast and melon-pomegranate smoothie bowl were delightful.

"Did you sleep well?" Kaylah asked, sipping water.

"Yeah. Like a rock."

She smiled wide. "Good."

Leah took another bite of her toast. "Is this our one mandatory meal of the day?"

Kaylah pursed her lips, scooping a spoonful of her smoothie. "How about we spend two together on your first day?"

It wasn't like Leah had plans, or grounds to deny her request. "That works."

Other than shared meals, what was Leah going to do with her time? She should be sorting out her life, but just the thought of that was beyond daunting. "Do you mind if I look around in your library?" There was an entire room dedicated to books—every inch of the walls lined with full shelves, comfy armchairs and sofas taking up the center of the room.

"Be my guest." Kaylah ate another spoonful. "Looking for anything in particular? Or just perusing?"

Leah shrugged. "I guess perusing." Though ... she hadn't gotten the chance to check out the last book in the *Valeska's Adventures* series... "Are you familiar with *Valeska's Adventures*?"

Kaylah softly scraped the bottom of her bowl. "I sure am. I doubt there's an Ivy who isn't."

"Do you have it?"

Twisting her lips, Kaylah searched her mind. "I don't think so."

Leah frowned, and Kaylah raised her eyebrows in question.

"Well, I just finished book eight, and it's a nine-book series."

"Aha. I'll see what I can do about that."

Smiling, Leah reached for her glass of water. "Thank you."

"Anytime."

Chapter 18

THE NEXT FEW DAYS WERE spent in the library, on solo strolls around the expansive grounds, and with a healthy amount of napping when Leah felt like it.

Leah reconsidered the options for her future. They all relied so heavily on one person—Marcus. Her gut twisted, and her anger grew every time she recalled the things he'd said and done. Her heart hurt at the broken promise he'd given her the day she'd permanently left the palace. *I'll always choose you. And I'll always choose our baby.*

She almost wrote him a letter, on more than one occasion. But *he* hadn't bothered to, and he was perfectly capable of doing so.

At the end of the week, Leah and Kaylah set out on the first of their agreed-upon picnics. They settled down on a large blanket near a swimming pond.

"Thanks for joining me." Kaylah smiled.

Leah hadn't had much choice in the matter, but she wasn't about to insult her hostess. "Yeah, this pond is so pretty."

"First, I have a gift for you." Kaylah pulled a linen-wrapped package from the picnic basket.

"For what?"

"Because. And I promised…"

Leah unwrapped the gift, surprised to find the final book in the *Valeska's Adventures* series in pristine condition. Leah studied it. It looked brand new, not like a public library copy. Then she opened the front cover. Clear as day, an inscription had been penned on the title page. *To Leah—Enjoy the adventure.* And it was signed by the author.

Her jaw dropped as she ran her fingers over the writing. "This is for me?"

"I didn't realize you were such a bookworm."

"I'm not. Well, I wasn't…" Not until she'd walled herself off in that cottage. "Thank you." She'd never had something special like this.

"The author doesn't usually do signed books, but being me has some perks."

Leah shook her head, fixated on the book. "Thank you."

After a minute, Leah set the book down, helping Kaylah unpack their lunch. "I really like it here," Leah confessed. "More than at the palace."

Kaylah blew out a puff of air. "You didn't grow up with that lifestyle. I'm sure it was a hard transition. I wish…" She hesitated. "Do you think you would have preferred to move in with me and Eric if you'd been given the choice when you first moved over here?"

"I … think that would have been hard at the time."

Silence hung thick in the air. She'd hated Kaylah, and she'd hated herself for what she'd tried to do.

"You know," Kaylah continued, "when we discussed what would be best for you, Catrina and Stephan were quick to offer their home."

Leah bit the insides of her cheeks. The day they'd sat in a room and discussed whether Leah and her mom would live or die for their crimes…

Kaylah gingerly opened a glass jar of peaches. She explained how Catrina truly did want the best for Leah, and how she still wished Leah would go speak with her at the palace. Leah tried not to be annoyed. "You have to make a lot of tough calls as a queen," Kaylah said.

Leah shook her head, staring at the spoon in her hand.

"Leah, I understand you're frustrated with her, with the rules." Kaylah's voice was kind but not hesitant. "But you've learned about our history. Every day of my reign, and Catrina's, we've had to be mindful about dotting our *I's*, and crossing our *T's*. It's one thing to rule a kingdom and keep up an air of professionalism. It's a whole nother issue to recover from decades, even centuries of brutality."

If Leah were more levelheaded, she would acknowledge the truth of that statement. She would also admit that even a queen was allowed a bad day. Catrina hadn't been herself that morning, just like Leah hadn't been herself when she'd slapped Marcus. Maybe the kids had kept Catrina up half the night, or her own maternal sickness had. Maybe she'd been stressed to her limits by her unending daily obligations. Maybe she had been shocked at Leah's defiance because she'd never fully understood how messy Leah's life had been before coming to the Green Lands—she'd hidden that part of herself well before that morning.

But Leah had never been all that levelheaded, and it wouldn't destroy the kingdom for someone to back her up when she desperately needed it.

Pursing her lips, Leah met Kaylah's gaze. "Is this what our picnics are going to be? Telling me why I'm wrong about everything?"

Kaylah sighed. "No. That's all I'll say about things with Catrina."

"Good. And you know, people hate me for what my parents did, but that's not my fault. I mean, obviously … the whole attempted murder thing was kinda my fault." Her cheeks warmed, but she was still stuck on the way Catrina had handled the palace's secret passageways. "Catrina even treated me different. I wasn't planning a coup. I was just trying to… It's not fair."

Kaylah frowned. "It's not. And honestly, I don't even consider your parents the worst Ivy rulers."

Leah cocked her head in disbelief. Her own dad had tortured Kaylah for days.

"I'm serious. Yes, they did horrible things, but most of what people detest were their *plans* to do things. What they *hoped* to do with Bomen, Seeders, and Ivy society as a whole. But if you ask me, I'd say Queen Lavinia was the worst we've had."

The name was familiar, one Leah had read since coming to the realm.

Kaylah spelled out her meaning. "A huge manipulation of her people, and a legitimate attempt at genocide against the Seeders."

Leah couldn't help but think of Rachel at the mention of her people. Seeder lands had been poisoned, and that poison had been lethal to every single unbloomed Seeder girl—vulnerable as teenagers or younger without their powers yet.

"Yeah, that really is worse than what my parents did."

"Plus, I look at it this way: your mother and father tried to steal my throne, but that's not any worse than your father's and my great-grandmother killing an entire downline of heirs to switch the Mother Vines' allegiance for her takeover."

"True." Leah turned the spoon in her hand. "We should bring those up more in public education, then people will hate me less."

Kaylah frowned again. "People mostly focus on your parents and what they did because it's such recent history."

Leah shifted on the blanket, crossing her legs. "So, in a hundred years' time, people will be more forgiving and might even like me?" That did a whole lot of good for Leah right now...

"Mmm." Kaylah skirted answering that one with a single understanding look. "Things will get better." She glanced at the food. "But this won't if it warms up, so let's dig in."

They sat in silence for a few minutes, munching on pastries, peaches, and broccoli slaw.

"Do you want me to arrange a counselor for you to see?" Kaylah offered.

Leah shook her head. She'd seen one for a while after the whole botched assassination debacle, but Leah had eventually come to dislike the sessions. Perhaps she'd adopted her mom's distrust of therapists, but Leah had started to fear her information hadn't been completely private with the counselor, that some of it might be given to the queen to ensure Leah was safe and proper.

She'd completely stopped counseling after a particularly painful visit with her mom at the prison. Leah had needed to bury that memory, the feelings that had torn her in half that day.

"Should I keep this baby?" Leah asked. "Or should I…"

Kaylah surveyed her, finishing a bite. "I thought you wanted to."

Leah swallowed a lump in her throat. "I do." But as much as she'd grown attached to the baby, and as much as she loved her mom, she couldn't lie to herself. More than once, *especially* in the last few months, Leah had wished her mom had never conceived her. Had found it in her to drop Leah off somewhere to be adopted as a baby.

"If you want to keep it, then you should."

"I might be a horrible mom," Leah confessed, heartbroken. "And she wouldn't have to live a crazy life like me if I gave her away, and she never knew she was my child."

"It's hard having notoriety. Marcus and Tobias know what that's like, growing up, and they're happy."

That comparison was nowhere near fitting. Their parents had been a controversial pair at the end of the war, and to some extent still were, but they were hailed as heroes. Even those who still clung to outdated beliefs were generally happy the war had ended, because it meant not sending their sons and fathers, husbands and brothers off to die in war.

"And I don't see why you'd be a horrible mother," Kaylah added.

The royal family was talking about Leah, this much she knew. But she wasn't sure to what extent. "How much do you know about why Marcus left me at the cottage?"

Kaylah cleared her throat. "I just know … that you're pregnant, and had a falling out with Catrina, and then Marcus … and his family. And that you haven't seen him in a couple of months?"

Tears pricked at the corners of Leah's eyes. "He… He said … some awful things. And I… I hit him."

"Oh." Kaylah didn't show judgment or shock.

"I hit him *hard*." Leah wiped away a tear. That single action had taught her that she was capable of becoming something she'd sworn to never become—an abuser, like Cheryl. It had taught Leah that her simmering anger could go too far. What if she got frustrated some day and took it out on her own child? It was a terrifying thought.

"I didn't really mean to, but I'm pretty sure I used my Ivy energy when I hit him, when I slapped him."

"I see…" Crimes committed against Bomen carried heavier sentences, and regular green folk with powers had to be considerate of those born without them. "Have you two ever fought like that before?"

"No."

"Then … if you're basing how good of a mother you'll be off of *one* incident…"

Leah twisted her lips, unwilling to accept the leniency.

Kaylah wouldn't have it. "Every single parent out there, no matter how kind and competent, has done something wrong. They've screamed at their crying child after they both got a sleepless night, or they've forgotten something important, left something hot or sharp within reach. No one's perfect. And whether as a parent or as someone in a serious relationship, it's their responsibility to ensure it never happens again."

"It won't."

Kaylah nodded, not responding for a while. "I'm sorry he said … whatever he said, if it was bad enough for that to happen."

Surprised with herself, Leah felt immense relief at that. It bugged her sometimes when Marcus called Kaylah 'Aunt Kaylah.' Because she was actually *Leah's* aunt, not his. Kaylah was only his honorary aunt. But blood wasn't always thicker, and Marcus had grown up around Kaylah as the golden child, and Leah had only been in her life a couple of years, after trying to kill her.

But she felt safe in Kaylah's presence right now, as though she might be the only person who wouldn't pick sides.

"You know, he's … immature," Leah vented, setting down her plate and spoon. "He doesn't always get how hard this is for me. And the way he… He wants me to marry him, but he won't even put me before his mom. Isn't that what adults are supposed to do? I'm carrying his child, but he cares more about what his parents think, or what Catrina thinks." She huffed, then added a couple more examples of instances that frustrated her.

Kaylah heard her out, not interrupting. She set down her plate and spoon as well. "You *are* both still young. But … you're right. Some of that was pretty crappy." She drew a deep breath. "One thing you have to remember is that he grew up in a healthy, happy home. He's gone through some unique and hard experiences, but not nearly the way you have. And…" She shrugged slightly. "When children go through a lot at a young age like you did, they're forced to grow up faster."

Leah had told Kaylah about Cheryl's abuse, and Kaylah was well aware of the fact that Leah and her mom had moved a ton in the human world, but Leah hadn't told her even half of everything, hadn't told her anything about the sexual assaults she'd endured.

"I'm not excusing him," Kaylah said. "I'm only saying … we all mature at different rates, and he can catch up."

Leah hoped that was true. In her heart of hearts, she still yearned for him to be next to her in that huge bed, to share meals and smiles with her, to share dreams and a future with her.

"Have you written him?" Kaylah asked softly.

Shaking her head, Leah frowned. "He hasn't written me either."

"Well, when you're ready, we could spare the paper." Kaylah smiled. "Because you two are one of my favorite couples." It was public knowledge Kaylah was a bit of a romantic, a bit of a matchmaker.

"I'll try to remember that."

"I also have some spare notebooks if you're interested. I know Rachel has found journaling helpful … if you don't want to do counseling again."

Leah fought to not roll her eyes at yet another comparison to Rachel.

"I know… Not your favorite person right now, but I figured I'd throw it out there. You've both been through a lot. And I really do think she'll be a great support for you two and the baby. It sounds like you just need to set some boundaries."

"Yeah, we'll see."

Soon enough, a breeze blew in, the sky threatening to mist, so they packed up and returned to the house.

Leah ended up making her way to the sitting room and grabbing some stationery. After returning to her room, she penned two letters. One to her mom, to let her know she was safe and doing well, still unable to visit her. The other to Marcus, apologizing for hitting him, asking him to visit her at Kaylah's.

Only one of those letters made it to servants' hands to send in the post. The other was deposited in Leah's bedside drawer while she mulled over the matter.

Chapter 19

IF HER PRIDE WASN'T DEAD SET against it, Leah might be able to entertain the idea of staying at Kaylah and Eric's estate forever. Kaylah continued to insist that Leah had the invitation to do so, and that everyone needed to accept help at times in their lives. Humble pie was a tough meal to swallow, and Leah wasn't sure she'd ever fully accept help without guilt or grudge.

But she did take her time in the library. She finished the *Valeska's Adventures* series, and reread them all again.

Kaylah and Eric stayed with Leah at their manor for Thanksgiving, a few of the staff members and their families joining them. The pumpkin pie was divine, even the crust.

On Leah's daily stroll about the grounds, she always carried a book with her; many from Kaylah's private library hadn't even been read by their owners. Granted, Kaylah and Eric were politicians, retired rulers, so a lot of their collection was dry reading, so Leah steered clear of those. Marcus might have enjoyed them, though, given his political aspirations and current internship.

Leah hiked the little hill in the back woods, made a vine hammock for herself in said woods, and soaked often in the swimming pond.

She stood a dead log up against a pair of healthy trees to use as a target. When her anger or frustration festered too much, her throwing knives got good use. She pelted them into the log time and time again. When feeling a little less violent, Leah practiced extending her vines around her palms, and squeezing them—Kaylah's tip of something she'd done many a time under the table during frustrating negotiations.

Three weeks after arriving, Kaylah and Leah held their weekly picnic, this time in the pavilion near the pond. Kaylah and Eric were having an old friend visit them, another mutual friend of Rachel's.

"And I mean it when I say you don't have to stay holed up in your room," Kaylah said. "It won't be awkward."

"Okay." Even as the word left her lips, Leah fully intended to do just that—hide away in her room.

***

Kaylah's Seeder friend was expected to arrive the next day for a few-day visit. Leah had met her only once before.

As soon as Leah woke, she dressed and searched the manor for Kaylah, having forgotten to ask her an important question about their agenda while the guest would be there. Eventually, Leah poked her head into the sitting room, where Kaylah already conversed with the woman—a strawberry blonde.

"Oh, sorry," Leah said. She hadn't meant to intrude, and she hadn't expected the visitor to arrive so early in the morning.

"Come on in!" Kaylah said, gesturing for her to enter.

"Well, I… I didn't mean to barge in."

"Come on. I insist."

Leah nervously entered, sucking in her gut. At three months pregnant, she was definitely starting to show. She sat down on a settee opposite the two, putting on a smile. "Good morning. And good to see you, Mrs. Murialsdotter."

"You can call me Saff." She smiled. "I didn't think you'd remember me."

In truth, Leah hadn't remembered her last name, but Kaylah had reminded her of it the day before. "I still don't know a ton of Seeders by name, but I remember you."

"I hope that's not a bad thing." Saff and Kaylah shared a playful glance.

"It's not." Leah straightened her shirt, afraid to expose her bump.

"You know, the two of you should have a chat while you're here, Saff," Kaylah said.

"Honestly, I'm going to be pretty busy," Leah lied. "I didn't mean to get in the way."

"I don't mind." Saff crossed her legs.

"Saff doesn't bite," Kaylah added. "Though…" She narrowed her eyes at Saff. "The first time we met, she *did* want to kill me."

Before she realized what she was saying, Leah grinned. "So, we *do* have something in common."

Saff's eyes grew wide, and her jaw slacked. Leah was about to explain how she and Kaylah joked about the assassination attempt that way, but she halted once Kaylah started to cackle, full-on cackle.

Leah's cheeks were warm, but Saff's face relaxed.

And Kaylah kept howling with laughter.

Leah shrugged at Saff. "That's just kinda how we roll."

Saff gave her a gentle smile as Kaylah finally took a breath.

"Gosh, I love you, kiddo," Kaylah said.

And in that moment, Leah was safe. How many people could forgive someone who had tried to take their life? And then rescue them and take them in?

"Love you too," Leah shyly confessed.

Kaylah's smile faded, replaced by a look of deep appreciation, as though she'd just been gifted the Christmas present she'd always wanted. As though she'd craved to hear that from her only niece for quite some time.

Leah still wasn't used to throwing the L-word around, and now Kaylah was the third person she'd ever used it on. And perhaps this wasn't the best time to get mushy, with a guest in the room. "Anyway, I really was going to get back to my book." She'd already forgotten her question. "But, uh, Saff, I'd be happy to chat if you'd like later."

"Sounds good."

***

Seeders were an odd bunch. If they chose to have children, they had twenty-four. No more, no less, and all at once. Was that why Kaylah had wanted them to chat? Because Saff had so many kids, and Leah was about to become a mom? That would require Leah to divulge that secret, assuming Saff didn't already know.

After lunch, Saff suggested they walk the grounds. Leah was always happy to do that.

"I love visiting Kaylah's estate." Saff walked with her hands behind her back. "Seeder lands are beautiful, but it just hits differently over here."

"Yeah, it's nice here."

After a moment of silence, Saff spoke again. "Was there something in particular you wanted to talk about?"

"I kinda thought you knew why Kaylah suggested we talk…"

"Nope." Saff chuckled. "I'm sure there's some puzzle to put together between you and me. Kaylah always has her reasons."

It was probably about the pregnancy thing. But really, Saff couldn't relate that much. Seeders carried their seedlings—their children—in their bodies for a week max. Not the eight months Ivies did. And the numbers game was definitely off-kilter.

But Saff had more value than just as a mother. Leah leaned into that. "Maybe it's that I spend so much time in the kingdom, and could stand to learn more about Seeders."

Saff flourished her hands. "At your service."

Leah gave her a half-smile. "Well, maybe this is selfish, because I'm a little curious about … what Seeders currently think of me."

For good or bad, most of that feedback had always been either blatantly shoved in Leah's face (through obscene gestures, scowls and flashes of glowing eyes, or otherwise), or fed to her by the palace.

"Well…" Saff bobbed her head. "Like Ivies or humans, Seeders don't all agree on everything."

That was a politician's answer if Leah had ever heard one. "So, they still hate me for my parents, and trying to take out Kaylah."

"Well, I…" Saff paused. "It's not like you're the topic of discussion every day. Most of the time, we all just go about our business. I'm sure things appear worse than they are to you because, well, it's your everyday reality."

Yeah, one I can't escape. "But when I *am* the topic of discussion?"

Saff breathed deeply. "Some say you're brave. Others…"

That sentence needed no conclusion, and it wasn't like Leah and Saff were close enough to be so frank.

"Are you thinking about doing some more travel in Seeder lands? Or doing some studies over there? I could help set you up."

Leah scoffed. "No one wants me over there. I wouldn't want to push my luck."

"Well, *I* like you."

That kind of validation from someone even older than her mom was like nails on a chalkboard. "Thanks. Now you just need to get the memo to the rest of your nation, and people can chill out."

Saff chuckled softly again. "Honestly, I can understand how some people struggle to accept you. They either have rumors to go on, or official royal tours with carefully crafted speeches. Maybe you *should* spend some time over there, and let people see the real you." She smirked. "Anyone that can joke about murdering Kaylah and get her to howl like that is redeemable in my eyes, and approachable. And Rachel likes you…"

Until her son knocked me up and I slapped him.

Leah folded her arms across her stomach. "Yeah. Get people to see the real me."

They walked for a while longer, and Leah couldn't help herself. "Is it… What's it like having twenty-four kids? Not the physical act, but raising them. Keeping them straight and caring for them all. Do you ever go crazy?" Her kids were about to all become teenagers.

With a sideways glance and the hint of another smirk on her lips, Saff said, "One kid or twenty-four, you go crazy. But I get why Ivies and humans find that kind of life so outlandish. What you have to remember is our lifestyle, our culture. Everything for Seeders is about family and community. Aunts, uncles, and grandparents are constantly around to help. It's a team effort."

Leah nodded.

"Are you and Marcus considering having kids down the road? Assuming things keep going the direction they've been going?"

Leah's heart dropped into her stomach. The direction they'd been going? "We've talked about it."

"I'd say you two have a nice support group, then, don't you?"

Did they? Marcus did. "Yeah."

Children and family support… Leah's mom still didn't know she was pregnant with Marcus's child, with a Boman. Just the night before, Leah had received another letter from her mom. That last line still haunted her. It was the one thing Leah had always needed to hear from her mom, and now always struggled to believe. *Love always.*

Leah was far too polite to ask Saff, but how many times in her stress or frustration had she ever wished she hadn't had a clutch of kids? How many times, if any, had she regretted that decision?

As much as Leah wanted to ask more about kids, she wasn't ready to divulge her little secret to a woman she barely knew. Overall, it was a pleasant walk, and gave her a couple of things to think over.

***

Saff's visit was only for a few days. By the time she left to return home, Leah had been at Kaylah's for a month.

Leah and Kaylah held their weekly picnic. It was nice chatting over meals with Eric, too, but Leah was growing fond of this special time with just her and her aunt. Though, she'd had some rough nightmares the night before, and was a bit on edge emotionally for this one.

"You really didn't have to hide away in your room so much." Kaylah gave her a playful look of scolding before taking a bite of strawberry.

"I know."

"You okay?"

Leah stirred her chia seed pudding. "I'm fine."

Kaylah leaned on an elbow. "Did you ever … send a letter to Marcus?"

Frowning, Leah shook her head. "He hasn't sent one to me either." Not that she hadn't thought about her letter to him, or reread it a dozen times. She was thirteen weeks along. In three weeks, she'd hit her halfway point in this pregnancy. She'd decided that if he hadn't sent her a letter by the halfway mark, she would have to be the one to suck it up, to swallow her pride, and reach out. She couldn't keep going on like this, not knowing what her future held, not knowing how to move forward. Not knowing if moving forward meant doing so without him.

"He loves you," Kaylah reassured her.

Leah choked down the pain in that statement, battling the demons from her dreams. "No he doesn't. People tolerate or pity me; they don't love me."

"Not true," Kaylah said adamantly. "Eric and I love you, and the family loves you…" She sat up. "And I've known Marcus long enough to know that he loves you, and that you two are just … stubborn, and this will blow over."

That deep anguish of defeat whispered to Leah that it was all a lie.

"Your mother loves you," Kaylah added.

Leah sniffled, shaking her head. "Not really."

Kaylah seemed confused, rightfully. "I knew the moment I saw her at the wedding venue that she *loved* you. She was ready to die for you, Leah."

And even as she *knew* that was true, Leah shook her head. Because it hadn't *always* been the truth.

With the haunt of a whisper, her mom's words had tortured her in her sleep last night. *You and me, we're the same.*

"What's wrong?" Kaylah asked.

Leah's throat bobbed. "Did my mom ever tell you about my conception?"

Kaylah looked surprised at the turn of conversation. "We never really discussed it much."

Leah had her confirmation. No one knew her mom's secret, other than Leah.

"She did ... *imply* ... that perhaps her pregnancy was an accident," Kaylah said.

Leah nodded. She'd kinda guessed that too.

"That doesn't mean she doesn't love you, Leah. Your pregnancy wasn't planned either, but that doesn't mean you don't love your child, or that you won't be a great mother."

The comparison was gutting, visceral, and in no time flat, Leah's eyes blurred with tears. "That's not how it happened."

Kaylah searched her face. "That's not how what happened?"

Leah swallowed hard. "My parents didn't plan me. But I wasn't an accident. *My mom* planned me." She looked down, picking at her nails. "He made it clear when they were dating that he wouldn't be faithful, and she agreed to that. She told herself she could be okay with it, as long as he made her number one. But after a while, she got jealous. She grew tired of him taking lovers." Leah dug a finger into her knee. "And she did what no woman should ever do. She stopped taking her birth control tonic, and lied. She made him get her pregnant, and lied about it being an accident to try to keep him closer."

When Leah looked up, Kaylah grimaced.

Soren had been a monster, a piece of trash that had only ever used people as tools. Perhaps he and Beata had truly been meant for each other, because Leah had been Beata's tool.

"And you know, it worked. Too well. My dad did *one* decent thing in his life; he got protective of his wife and unborn child. But then it backfired. My mom wasn't a strategist. He took care of that part of the war. But he started to act more … erratic, less predictable. He stretched the army and assassin networks too thin. He put his focus in the wrong places." Her heart ached at the confession. "They lost the war because of me. He died giving her more time to get away because of *me*."

Kaylah wore a deep frown. "I know it's hard, and I… I know it's a barely there silver lining, but that saved my life. I have no doubt he would have killed me eventually. And it saved *a lot* of other lives."

"I know," Leah croaked. If the realm knew that Leah had helped cause Soren and Beata's downfall, they'd sing a different tune. She had no doubt they'd suddenly be a lot more forgiving to her, and even to her mom. But sharing that truth with the realm would mean accepting the piercing duality of it. Accepting the other half, or trying not to, had been destroying Leah since the day her mom had let this fact slip.

"Don't get me wrong," Leah continued. "I know they were wrong and horrible and misguided, and it's good they lost the war. But my mom is the only person that *ever* loved me growing up. She was the *only* person even remotely there for me."

Sharply engraved in the back of her mind, Leah still recalled her conversation the night she'd found her mom's journal in the human world, had discovered her parents had been rulers of some mysterious realm.

Leah had asked: "If you knew then, what you know now, that this would happen, would you have done things differently?"

Her mom had replied wistfully: "Absolutely."

"Worse than being an accident, is being a regret," Leah told Kaylah.

Kaylah looked instantly perturbed. "Your mother said that?! That she regrets having you?"

"No, she didn't." And she hadn't. She'd only spilled her secret by accident on a random prison visit, and still professed on every visit and in every letter since, that she still loved Leah, and *always* would. "But you didn't see the way she was when I was a kid. Emotionally checking out, writing in a journal, mourning my dad day and night. She wouldn't even tell me his name!" It hadn't only been sorrow that had stunted her mom all those years; it had also been guilt. "Wouldn't you, at least a little bit, regret or resent your own child if they were the reason Eric died?"

"I'm not a mother, so I can't say for sure, but I certainly hope not."

But Leah had already answered that for herself months ago. As much as part of her was getting excited for the new life growing inside her, she had regrets. No resentment, but there *were* regrets. "You know, my mom used to say we were so much alike. We look a lot alike, we like the same movies, we both … started having sex around the same age. And I know it's not the same as what happened with my dad, but this baby, associated with me, and not conceived according to the high royal expectations, is going to take Marcus down a notch."

Kaylah looked her dead in the eyes. "You both made a choice to have sex. It's just as much his responsibility as yours, no matter who has the better or worse reputation."

"Yeah?" Leah wiped away her tears with the back of her hands. "You can't imagine what people are going to say? That Soren's daughter got knocked up on purpose because Marcus got tired of her? Realized he could do better? That I did this to trap him?"

"You're not like your mother. If you say it was an honest mistake, I believe you."

"And everyone else?" Leah challenged. "When they all know I manipulated him before? Lied to him to get close to you? When I proved I was crazy?"

"Leah." Kaylah's voice was soft, pleading, understanding. "It'll be okay."

"Right. Because a formal notice from the palace soothes all unease, rights all wrongs." She shook her head. Kaylah had commented about the strict palace rules and it being harder for Leah because she hadn't been raised royal. It was true. Kaylah was made of tougher stuff. She could handle the constant scrutiny. Leah had thought she could, had thought she was strong, but that had always been a facade, a lie.

"I'm here for you, okay?" Kaylah reassured her.

The floodgates of guilt and pain and grief had already opened for Leah, and she was far from done. She hadn't expected her pregnancy to trigger so much in her, but it had. It had shaken her to her core.

As those gates remained open, her heart raw, Leah struggled to breathe, tears continuing to cascade. "Everything is my fault. I have no one to blame but me. I built my own prison. And *every* time I think back to my life in the human world—the life I left behind—I realize I'm the one to blame.

"Because when my mom was too depressed, sad about losing my dad and not being able to see her family, not able to enjoy the ambient energy of the realm—it was my fault. And every time Cheryl hit me, grabbed me, pulled my hair, made me feel worthless—it was because my mom was too wrapped up in being sad because my very existence got my dad killed, so she didn't want to see it, didn't want to believe it."

"That's on her," Kaylah retorted.

"Every time we had to move because I acted out or because my mom was afraid of us getting discovered, every time I had to leave friends behind, every time I *hated* it—my fault.

"Every time I made stupid decisions—shoplifting, lying, sneaking out to parties—my fault."

"She was a neglectful parent," Kaylah replied.

Leah sniffled, catching a breath. "Every time I was an idiot with a guy, letting things go too far, getting hurt, earning a reputation as a slut, just because I wanted friendship and love and attention… That was my fault too. If I had never been conceived, my dad wouldn't have acted rash in the war, my mom wouldn't have lost him, wouldn't have grieved, and my life wouldn't be a living hell."

Now even Kaylah was crying. "He might have lost the war anyway. Don't internalize all that blame."

Despite her need to shove it all down, to pretend she'd never learned the truth of what her mom had done to deceive her dad, Leah had analyzed it. Knowing and feeling were two different things. Her heart and mind were oil and water.

Leah pointed to her head. "I know that here." She pointed to her heart. "But this tells me I'm lying to myself."

An unborn child held no fault because of their parents' decisions. A little girl was blameless for the neglect of her mom.

But Leah couldn't win. Couldn't accept that she had any role in ending the war, in one of the best things to happen for peace in the realm in *centuries*, without also accepting that she was scum.

Kaylah scooped Leah into a tight hug. "I'll never be anything but grateful for you."

Leah sobbed. Even as tears spilled down her cheeks onto Kaylah's back, as snot fell ungraciously onto the retired queen's shirt, as huffs and whimpers escaped Leah's lips, she sobbed.

Chapter 20

AFTER A MORTIFYINGLY LONG AMOUNT of time, Leah's crying had quieted. She leaned back, and Kaylah released her. Leah tried not to be embarrassed. "Sorry."

"Don't be. How can I help you?"

Leah loosed a breath. "I have no idea."

"Does ... Marcus know?"

"No. I haven't told anyone about that. And I'm not ready for anyone to know." Her mom had pleaded with her not to share the truth of her conception with anyone.

Despite Kaylah's nod, she looked as though she didn't fully agree with that call.

"And please don't do anything with my mom, or say anything to her either." As far as Leah knew, Kaylah never visited her mom in prison, but Kaylah *did* still have some sway politically.

Kaylah didn't respond, but her expression hinted she wanted to tear Beata a new one.

"I know I should hate her, but she's the only person that's always been there for me. Even if it was ... not always what I needed." Leah sniffled once more. "She didn't tell me that to be mean. She let it slip on accident. She doesn't even realize I feel this way."

"She should, Leah. *She* deserves to feel the weight of her decisions, not you. She should be protecting you, not the other way around."

Leah frowned, glancing down at the picnic blanket. Her mom was so lonely in prison. And no one knew her mom the way Leah did. Her mom could do better, could become a better person. "Please."

Kaylah sighed. "Fine."

They continued to eat their picnic in relative silence. Leah reached for a cloth napkin at one point to wipe her hands on, but she'd used them all for tissues.

"You know, kiddo..." Kaylah scooped a spoonful of pudding. "Going back to the whole you-becoming-a-mother thing? I think you'll be a great one. You're more mature than your mother was, and you know what mistakes to avoid."

"Thanks." It hurt to be both compared *and* contrasted to her mom.

"I kinda thought you and Marcus were..." Kaylah rocked her head back and forth. "You know, talking about tying the knot."

Leah picked at a pastry. "Well, yeah, we've talked about it. But I was in school, and he was going off on his internship and focusing on his career, and..." She shrugged. "I guess it's a good thing I was never really a princess, because I suck at dating or even being remotely related to royalty."

Kaylah gave her a small grin. "I *was* a real princess, and I *still* sucked at it."

Leah chuckled.

***

When she retired to her room that night, Leah lay there, her arms spread wide across the massive bed. What did she want? To be in

Marcus's arms. To have him warming her, kissing her, telling her it would all be okay.

But he wasn't there. She considered her letter in the bedside drawer. Perhaps she ought to not wait until this arbitrary four-month mark in her pregnancy to send it to him.

Though … she did want to hold off a bit. She needed to process everything she'd just thrown at Kaylah, process what she wanted, and if the contents of the letter would change.

As much as she hated the idea of journaling like her mom and Rachel had, it made sense to write out her thoughts.

The next morning, Leah took Kaylah's suggestion to start one. She didn't even know how to journal.

Do people just write 'Dear Diary' and treat the book like it's a person they're telling their story to? Or maybe that's only diaries… What's the difference between a diary and a journal?

Had she been in the human world, she'd have whipped out her phone and looked up all those questions on the internet. As she was in a realm without electricity, she had to do what came to her. It made sense to start from square one.

So … before I was born…

The weather was tepid, the breeze light, as she sat under the pavilion and wrote. She had to admit it was cathartic. And she also had to admit that she needed a handkerchief, or two, or a dozen, if she was going to take this up.

But she spent hours pouring her soul into that thing. It was her witness. It was her warden. It was her shame and hope and sorrow.

Only when she shivered did she realize she was squinting, the light of the day fading. And she was famished.

Tucking the notebook under her arm, she headed inside. Having eaten breakfast on her own, as well as a meager snack she'd taken out with her, she made a beeline for the dining room. She halted at Eric's voice. "You're sure she'll be okay?"

"Yeah," Kaylah replied. "Sometimes we just need time and space to heal."

Leah clutched her journal, rounding the corner. "Sorry I'm late." She was *abominably* late. Kaylah and Eric's plates had been cleared, and they had dessert sitting untouched in front of them.

"I didn't mean to break my promise." She'd missed a full day of meals, not spending any with them.

Kaylah smiled, gesturing at the food dishes still on the table, and at Leah's empty dinner plate. "A little birdie told us you were busy jotting in that notebook of yours. We figured you'd join us when the light was all gone, or that pregnant body of yours forced you to seek nourishment."

Leah matched her smile, sitting down and setting the journal on the chair beside her. "Thanks."

As Leah scooped mashed potatoes onto her plate, Kaylah leaned her head on Eric's shoulder. They sat extra close during private meals, a far cry from the formal affairs they often attended. "In case you heard us on your way in, I was telling Eric why you were out there. Not any specifics, just that we had a good chat yesterday."

Eric raised his hands in a gesture of 'it's not my business if you don't want it to be my business.'

Leah liked Eric, and he'd never acted as though he judged Leah, but she was grateful Kaylah hadn't shared anything. Leah was still ashamed to be a mess. "Thanks." Though she *was* surprised. They didn't seem like the kind of couple that kept secrets from one another, or perhaps Leah didn't know them as well as she thought. They were diplomats, after all. Eric had technically been Kaylah's consort, and Kaylah had probably kept plenty of information from him during their reign. But as Leah started eating those perfectly creamy mashed potatoes, she doubted that.

She did love Kaylah. That she had saved her that day in the backyard of the cottage, that she was being impartial and helpful, and kind. That she was willing to keep Leah's secrets. And in that moment, Leah realized...

"Have you ever had servants follow me into the woods?"

"You're sturdy," Kaylah said. "We figured you'd make it back in one piece. They've only ever checked on you by tracking you down to make sure you were okay if you were gone for too long and missed a meal."

Leah nodded, scooping another spoonful, her mind in those woods. Kaylah had let her wander those woods to her heart's content, full-well knowing Leah had made an attempt at tree rifting to the human world to escape. Any number of those trees could have been Leah's ticket out of here, but she hadn't thought to do it.

She felt safe at Kaylah's. She felt free without the cage.

Just earlier that day, she could've sworn she'd felt the baby move for the first time. It had been heartwarming, and painful. Her journal entry echoed that of her own mother's, one penned long ago.

I felt the baby for the first time today. How is it the best things can bring the most pain? I'll do anything to keep it safe. But it reminds me so much of him.

Leah knew what she needed. And she needed to change that letter to Marcus.

***

Leah kept reading and writing. Kaylah and Eric ordered maternity clothes for her. Leah had rewritten her letter to Marcus, but hadn't worked up the guts yet to send it, or to discuss her plans with Kaylah.

She could take a little more time, no rash decisions like her dad. Instead of rushing into things, she added another project to her to-do list. One that brought a smile to her face. With more movement in her growing belly, she was sure she could feel the baby now, and she wanted to do something special for her.

She started to write her stories. Stories about a brave little Ivy girl taking on a variety of adventures and challenges. She wrote little boy stories, too, in case she was wrong about the gender. She couldn't draw worth beans, though, so hopefully her future child could appreciate stick figures that looked like someone drew them with their eyes closed.

***

The pavilion had become one of her favorite spots to journal. The midday sun was warm on her back as she scratched out her feelings about having to move cross-country during Christmas one year. In the present, Christmas was just a few days away.

A male voice cleared his throat from just outside the pavilion.

"I packed a lunch," Leah said. "I'm fine, thanks."

"I'm glad to hear that," a hesitant and familiar voice replied.

Leah's heart ceased to beat as she looked up, taking in those warm brown eyes, that curly brown hair. "Marcus," she breathed.

Chapter 21

FROZEN IN PLACE, LEAH GAPED. "Marcus?" she repeated.

His hands were in his pockets, his arms rigid. "In the flesh."

"What are you doing here?"

"We should … talk."

And like that, her heart dropped to her gut. Any conversation that started like that between a couple didn't bode well. "Then say what you need to say." *Just rip off the bandage.*

He furrowed his brow. "Well, I figured *we* would talk. Not just me. Mind if I sit?"

Leah rubbed her face. "Go ahead." She closed her journal, setting it beside her as Marcus took the bench opposite her under the pavilion.

"You look great," he said, all hesitance. His eyes flashed to her stomach, and he frowned. Was that regret for getting her pregnant? Fear of her reaction about whatever he'd concluded alone? Or guilt for leaving her alone without a shred of news for eleven of the fifteen weeks she'd been pregnant?

"I think we should lay it all out there," he said. "And be honest."

"Sounds like a good start."

"And if I'm honest…" He bobbed his head. "I'm only here because Kaylah sent me a letter."

So, maybe Kaylah wasn't so great at secrets and not meddling. "What did she say?"

Marcus twisted his lips. "It was pretty succinct. That I should stop being a jackass and come visit my pregnant girlfriend."

Okay, fine. She liked Kaylah again. "About time."

"You could have visited me too." He tilted his head. "Or written a letter."

This was going to be a long chat, and a difficult one. "A lot could have been done differently. Like not dragging your parents into this mess."

He narrowed his eyes. "What do you mean?"

"You and me, we can work through problems, but once you drag family members into it, they pick sides, and they won't be on my side. You didn't need to tell them that I…" She paused, feeling every bit wrong. People who were hurt had a right to speak up, and denying him that would have been wrong, but it still wasn't right that he'd turned his parents even more on Leah. "I am *so* sorry I hurt you, and I will *never* do that again. To you, or anyone else." She rested a hand on her stomach. "I swear." She wouldn't be like the fake aunt she'd suffered under growing up.

Marcus acknowledged her words with hurt in his eyes. "I didn't tell them about that. I haven't told anyone."

"I thought we agreed to be honest. Your mom knew I hurt you. No one else was in the room to know that."

He drew a deep breath. "I told her to not say anything. I asked her to leave it alone, and give you some space."

"So, you did tell them."

"Leah, you slapped me *hard*."

Her soul shrank to the size of a mushroom. "I know. And I'm sorry."

"I didn't have to walk far down the lane before I realized I was bruising. And the last thing I needed was for everyone to notice a famous Boman with a formerly homicidal girlfriend developing a giant bruise on his face. There aren't exactly Seeder healers around every corner, so I walked to my parents' place."

Leah frowned.

"I wouldn't tell her how I got it. But she put it together when I asked her to make sure you had more food because I wouldn't be back for a while. I told her not to say anything."

Leah was at a loss for words.

"I didn't drag them into this, not intentionally."

"You shouldn't have said what you did before it happened, before you left." It didn't excuse her actions, but he had been beyond cruel.

This time he frowned, his throat bobbing. "I know. I'm sorry. I... I was trying so hard, but you were making me choose, and then you were going to leave me."

"I wasn't. And I told you that."

"Then why did you have your passport with you? Why did you hide it again after I found it?"

He *had* searched. "I wasn't going to leave you. It was just an option, one I prepared for when I was panicking."

Looking her dead in the eye, he kept a measured but unhappy tone. "You threatened to take our child and disappear in the human world like your mom did."

So many objections assaulted her. What about the fact that he'd threatened to cage her? Or literally any topic that touched on her painful feelings with her mom at the moment...

She chose the moment where this had all really started to go downhill. "Just admit you don't want this baby, Marcus."

His expression was incredulous. "Why would you think that?"

"You clearly didn't have a mirror when you had pure terror on your face as I told you I was pregnant. And you didn't want it."

"I never said I didn't want it."

"Maybe you didn't say it that way, but you made it abundantly clear."

He spoke through clenched teeth, his nostrils flaring. "I never said it, because I never *once* thought it."

She threw her hands up. "The first chance you got, you suggested we give her to your brother and sister-in-law to adopt."

"Really?!" Marcus's jaw dropped. "I'm sorry I didn't say the right words, or give you the right facial expression. You had time to process before telling me you were pregnant. You got my raw reaction. And you weren't sure you wanted to keep the baby." He gestured at her. "And if you didn't plan to keep it, you'd what? Put it up for adoption? Why the hell would that bother an adopted Boman to imagine their Boman child put up for adoption? Wondering if their birth parents hated them for the sheer fact they were born without powers?"

She should have thought of that. He didn't speak often or resentfully about his being adopted, but he'd shared how it had hurt finding out the way he'd been dropped off at an orphanage as an infant, in the way unwanted Bomen used to be.

"And honestly," he continued, "I panicked. I didn't think I could be a single dad, but I grasped on to the best option I could think of at the moment. Tobias and Cam have talked about adoption. And if they adopted it…" He paused, looking down at his hands. "Then maybe I could still be in its life."

Tears coated her eyes. "You should have said that."

He shrugged. "With your next breath, you decided you wanted to keep it, so I didn't think it mattered."

Leah scooped herself another helping of humble pie. "I should have been more understanding about all the Boman stuff."

Her mom's words replayed in her mind. *You and me, we're the same.* And that hurt—another comparison. While Soren had been the war strategist, Beata had played her role as his queen. They hadn't ruled long at all, but after their downfall, plans had been found for what they'd wanted to do with Bomen after they'd eradicated the Seeder threat. It was disgusting, and it had been planned and penned by

Leah's mom, Beata—the daughter of the leaders of the former quasi slave communities.

Leah loved Marcus. She'd grown up around humans, who didn't have powers. It had never meant anything to her that he didn't have them. But she'd been culturally deaf, utterly insensitive. She needed to do better about considering his needs, too, and that of their future child. And not just because the realm would skewer her if she made a misstep as the parent of a Boman.

"I'm really sorry."

He looked at his hands again. "Thanks."

What more was there to say? "I know you don't like choosing between me and your family, but you broke promises."

"I know. I'm sorry. I thought my mom could help."

Leah fidgeted with her hands. "Did you … have your aunt send the escorts? To make sure I couldn't leave?" They'd appeared the day after he'd left, after he'd threatened to make sure she didn't leave the realm.

He hesitated. "Not exactly. When you stormed away from the palace and I hung back, I asked Aunt Catrina to give you some space. You were acting kinda crazy, and nervous. I told her we'd be fine without your escorts while we stayed at the cottage. And then when I left the cottage, my mom wanted to make sure you were safe, so she asked Catrina to station them there for you. They were already assigned to protect you."

"They were only there on regular duty? I could have rifted to the human world with my passport?"

"I don't know," he admitted. "I haven't talked to Aunt Catrina since we left together."

She took a cleansing breath, the nightmare of misunderstanding between them laid bare. "It's already terrifying to know what kind of repercussions having your child will bring down on me, and I should have considered that more seriously before we got back together, but I'd like to think we can still sort this out."

"Leah…" He ruffled his hair. "No offense, but people bring up our relationship to me, too. It's not like I've never had someone express what a bad idea dating you is. After all we've been through. After our family's history. But I have *always* looked past that."

That stung. And he had no right to dismiss her so casually. "There's a *big* difference in our situations, though. Because *you* have always retained the ability to walk away from me and my reputation. I've never had that option in this realm, and I never will. If you broke up with me and left me for good, people would pat you on the back. I would continue to be Soren and Beata's murderous child. Any semblance of a decent reputation comes from dating you, and from 'official memos' from the palace PR team. Or from pretending to be something I'm not. I stay with you because I love you, but I'm not ignorant of the fact that I rely so heavily on you. And I hate relying on anyone." For money, for reputation, for anything. In a cage.

He sighed. "You're right. It would suck having your parents."

It did, but it was time she came clean about her parents too. "It bugs me when you talk about my mom. Especially when you compare us."

And then she let it out. Having had some time to process, and already having confessed it all to Kaylah, she explained her heartache, fears, and hurt about how her mom had betrayed her dad, and how Leah had shouldered that blame.

He mostly sat through it with head shakes and a sympathetic frown.

"I know your mom is better than mine, but I'd rather not be compared to either." She sniffled.

"I get it." He fidgeted with his hands. "Can I hug you?"

"Yes." She choked down fresh tears as they stood, meeting in the middle.

Kaylah's hugs were healing. Marcus's hugs were something otherworldly.

"I am *so* sorry," he whispered into her ear. "I'm never leaving you again. *Never.* I'll do better."

Marcus was home. He was happiness. He was the day to her night.

"I'm sorry too." She savored the warmth of his arms around her.

"This kinda feels weird," he said after a while, a smile in his voice. "Hugging you with a bump between us."

She wore a smile that she imagined matched his. "It's only going to get weirder."

"I love you," he said.

"I love you too." She leaned back, and they locked eyes. His lips begged to be kissed, so she did just that. He didn't hesitate in returning the kiss, a hand holding her hips, the other weaving into her black hair.

For that moment, it was only the two of them in that realm. The two of them, the scent of daffodils in the distance, and their hearts beating wildly in unison.

And even as they pulled apart, she wanted more. She *needed* more. "What do you say to us…"

You're nothing but a slut, Cheryl's voice taunted, a memory from her past.

There were worse things Leah could be. She could be like Cheryl. Leah promptly told the bitter old hag in her head—the one who was actually rotting away in a prison cell—where she could go, and what she could do with herself.

"What do you say to us finishing this conversation in my bedroom?" She'd wilt on the spot if he refused her. She *needed* that kind of connection with him, that happiness and hope she'd had when they'd first arrived at the cottage.

He gave her a shy smile. "Really?"

"Really."

Blinking, he looked down. "That won't hurt you or the baby?"

She rolled her eyes. "I'm pregnant. Not dying."

"Then let's see how it goes."

Chapter 22

THINGS WENT WELL BACK IN Leah's room. *Very* well. That side of things had never been a problem in their relationship—the passion, the physical side. But this time was different. There was more sweetness, gentleness, intention. She loved Marcus with everything she had.

They lay cuddling under the sheets, staring into each other's eyes. "We're not half bad at this, are we?" he said.

She bit her lip. "No, we're not." She ran a caressing hand across his shoulder. "But sex doesn't fix everything… If anything, for the two of us, it kinda makes things…" She didn't want to say worse, not about their child. "More complicated."

Marcus pursed his lips. "Yeah."

"So… Assuming we both do better at being considerate, and communicating, and controlling our tempers… Where do we go from here?"

"I took the week off, told them I needed to take care of some family business." He stroked her hip with his thumb, a pensive look on his face. "I know the family wouldn't like it, but would you want to join me up north? Move in with me? See how things go?"

Her heart was full of gratitude at the invitation, but it wasn't enough. "There will be rumors."

"I know."

It felt like they'd be digging a bigger hole, digging deeper at making their families unhappy, at causing more drama. "Is it going to be that much different than hiding away here or at the cottage? I guess with the exception of spending our nights together…"

He drew a deep breath. "Option B: we go to the human world, assuming you still want to."

"Really?" Her stomach flipped. "For how long? Just this week?"

His gaze was soft, his expression sincere. "For as long as you want. As long as it takes."

"But what about your internship?"

Something flashed across his face. Guilt? Frustration? "Like you said—I've always been able to walk away unscathed. And I think I get it now. With hardly any advance notice, I told them I was taking a week off for personal reasons. And you know what they said? 'Take all the time you need. We'll hold your position for you.'"

"That's really nice of them."

He wrinkled his nose. "Too nice. Do you know how many people applied for that position? *A lot.* And I doubt they would have extended that offer to anyone who wasn't Guillen's son, and Catrina's nephew."

He'd talked about that with Leah before—wanting to stand on his own two feet. But he hadn't seemed to fully understand his privilege until now.

"That's kind of how politics go, right? It's about who you know?" she said.

Letting out a soft sigh, he shook his head. "I guess I still need to figure out how I want to fit into the politics game, because it's not just about wanting to do good, as much as I want it to be. Neither of us can escape our parents' legacies. The difference is … mine will always give me a leg up, and yours will always be ready to tear you down."

She gave him a tender kiss on the lips. "You'd really be okay with spending time in the human world? How much time does 'as long as you want' entail?"

"I told you before Tobias's wedding that I'd be willing to live in the human world, for the right person. And if that's what it takes to make you happy, then we can stay there. Because *you're* the right person."

That gesture meant more to her than the world, especially considering what he was willing to give up.

He continued. "And even if this is a trial run, to see if you and I can really make this work…" He slid a hand to her belly. "Even if you and I don't get…"

Married?

"Well, if we can't sort out our problems, and we have to … go our separate ways…" His voice was strained, pained. "Then we'll know we gave it a fair shot. And we'll figure out how to still get along, right?"

"Yeah." Her heart was heavy at discussing the fact they may not be able to resolve their differences in the long run. They *were* both stubborn, and so different.

"No matter what, we're always going to be family," he said.

That little part of her that got the ick at technicalities squirmed. Their relationship was legal in all fifty US states, and no one in the Green Lands thought much of them being second cousins, through adoption or not, but still… "Please don't bring up the shared family members thing when we're in bed like this."

He furrowed his brow. "I wasn't. I meant that no matter what, even if we go our separate ways, I will *always* be this child's father, and you'll always be its mother. We'll always be a family in that way, always there for him. Or her."

And in that moment, something clicked for Leah. Something deep, visceral, primal. She couldn't change the facts of her parentage, of her past. Wishing things had been different wouldn't do any good. Fearing the unknown future hadn't benefited her either. But she craved family, one of her own. One she could create and mold and nurture to be what she wished she'd grown up with. It was already staring her in the face, and growing within her.

"I'll marry you."

Marcus's eyes grew wide. "Really?" His stare was cautious. "You mean it?"

"Yes. I… I still don't want to be pressured to do it *tomorrow*, or in front of thousands or anything, but … yes."

"Whatever you want!" And then he laid a kiss on her that would make anyone blush.

Eventually, he released her and untangled himself. "I have something for you." Sliding out of bed, he grabbed something from his clothes on the dresser. "Close your eyes."

She did as directed. A heartbeat later, the bed dipped again beside her, and his warm hands took hers. He parted her fingers, and slipped a ring on. "You can open them."

In shock, she stared at the ring. It was an Ivy design—white gold with thin details, one of a kind. "You came prepared with a ring?" With how many times she'd turned him down, and with how badly they'd become separated, that had been a lucky shot in the dark.

"Not exactly," he said softly. He hesitated, hurt or embarrassed. "I've had that with me for at least four months."

She did the math. Her pregnancy was a week shy of four months along. "You bought this before we got pregnant?"

He averted his gaze. "Yeah. I, uh, well, I was going to ask on the special boat ride."

Boat ride? "Oh," she said in a barely audible whisper. He'd planned a special boat ride and dinner, one they'd had to cancel because of her maternal sickness. The one they'd canceled on the same day she broke the news to him.

"Actually, um…" He swallowed. "I first was going to ask you the night I snuck into your chambers, but then it didn't feel right. Like it was a reward or something. 'Congratulations… We finally slept together… Enjoy this new ring!' And then there's the whole what-story-do-we-tell-our-future-kids thing. I didn't want it to be weird that we were *naked* when I proposed."

She smirked. "You mean like right now, when we're naked again, and you just slipped a ring on my finger?"

"Riiiight… I vote we omit the bedroom facts from this proposal and reunion story. This all happened at the pavilion."

She admired her ring once more. "I agree." It wasn't a harmful lie.

His voice softened again. "And about what we tell him, the baby, someday… About how this all went down? I don't want him to ever feel unwanted."

She gazed into his warm brown eyes. No, as an adopted child, Marcus would naturally *not* want his child to experience that same pain of rejection. As a deceptively conceived child, she *wished* she'd only been an accident. "I agree. People will do the math, and stories will come out—they always do. But as far as this child will ever know, it was unplanned, but *not* unwanted. Never unwanted."

He kissed her on the head, and they slipped more deeply under the covers, cuddling. She stared at her ring. It felt weird, but right.

And then something nagged at her. There was *something* about the looks Catrina and his parents had given them when they'd announced the pregnancy. A sharpness to the looks and questions they'd aimed at Leah about the young couple *not* being engaged. "Did anyone know you were planning to propose?"

"Yeah," he confessed. "My parents, and Aunt Catrina and Uncle Stephan. Uncle Stephan helped me coordinate the staff for the boat."

She let out a frustrated sigh. "Is that why they looked at me confused, even *offended* when they asked why we weren't engaged? Because they knew it was already going to happen?"

"Um… Maybe?"

She covered her face with her hands. "And you don't see why that made me the bad guy? Why everyone questioned if I really loved you?"

"Um…"

Turning to face him, she couldn't hide her frustration. "Why didn't you say something? Why didn't you pull out the ring and show me that you weren't proposing just because I was pregnant?!"

He frowned, wearing a look of devastation. "I screwed up. But I… The way you shot me down? That *destroyed* me. You were *adamant* about the fact that you didn't want to marry me. And with each mention of marriage, the thought disgusted you more and more. So, I stopped bringing it up. I asked family to stop asking, to stop bugging you."

That vise that had twisted tighter with each mention, each hint…

She hadn't appreciated the pressure. "Don't most couples *talk* about engagement before it happens? How often is it actually a surprise?"

"We talked about it. I missed you like crazy, Leah. I wanted to see you more often than on the weekends. And I figured when we started to talk about 'when' we got married instead of 'if' we got married, that you might be okay with pushing up our timeline." He quickly added, "On marriage. Not … kids… So that sorta happened in the wrong order."

To that, she couldn't help but chuckle.

But she did have to sigh again. "I need you to man up, Marcus. This baby is yours, and we both need you. You can't make me out to be the bad guy here. I'm already the bad guy in everyone's eyes. And you can't just disappear for weeks or months at a time because you got your feelings hurt." She tried to be calm, remembering what Kaylah had said about Marcus's easier childhood meaning he hadn't been forced to grow up as fast as Leah had. Yes, she'd been as stubborn as he had been, but she'd tortured herself over it. He hadn't seemed to realize the consequences of his mistakes.

"I'll do better," he promised.

After a little more time in bed, they decided to get up. It wasn't even dinnertime, and the staff had to have informed Kaylah and Eric that Marcus was on the property…

As Leah slipped into pants, Marcus commented on her new wardrobe.

"Yeah, Kaylah helped me get some stuff that's bigger." Leah liked this deep purple shirt and the way it flared out a bit. "Sad to say, but the dress I wore to our first ball is *definitely* not going to fit me right now."

He grinned, buttoning his pants. "No offense, but I'd rather see you wearing *nothing* over any of those dresses."

"You don't blush as much as you used to."

His grin only widened.

"But you're still a nerd."

"You love it."

She eased herself down on a chair to put her sandals on. "I do." Admiring him as he combed his hair with his hands at the mirror, she couldn't resist a smirk at the irony—he hadn't been her type until she'd had no other choice than to date him. She'd never been attracted to guys like him before.

All sorted, he approached her, then knelt in front of her. "Can I see the belly?"

She lifted her shirt a bit. He gently slid his hands onto her bump, and beamed. He leaned in and kissed it ever so softly; it sent shivers up her spine, set the butterflies in her stomach loose again.

"Hey, little guy," he said. "Sorry I was gone." He lifted his gaze to Leah. "That won't happen again."

She rested her hands on his. "You think it's a boy?"

Marcus shrugged. "Maybe because I'm used to having a brother."

"I told Kaylah I thought it was a girl."

"Hmm… I guess we'll see. How does it feel? Everything's okay?"

"Yeah." She squeezed his hands. "I felt her move recently."

A subtle frown played on his lips as he nodded. "I'm sorry I missed it. I'll be around for all the other firsts."

***

They discussed a couple more things about their future, but some of it needed to be done with Kaylah.

Emerging from Leah's bedroom, they made their way to the dining room. A couple of servants busied themselves already with arranging the place settings for dinner. But … there were only two settings.

"Is Kaylah or Eric gone for the night?" It wasn't like they'd babysat Leah the entire time she'd been there; they still came and went on occasion…

"No," one of the men answered. "They're taking dinner on their balcony tonight."

Kaylah. She'd sent for Marcus, and now they were leaving them to eat alone. She really was a matchmaker.

Leah didn't hate the idea of time alone with Marcus, but she was also excited for the next steps. "Do you mind if they join us?" she whispered.

"That's fine," Marcus replied.

"Could you let them know we'd like them to join us? Assuming they want to?"

"Yes, ma'am. We'll pass that along. Dinner will be served in about an hour."

While there was definitely temptation to spend that next hour back in Leah's room, Leah and Marcus decided they'd worked up enough of an appetite for now, in case Kaylah and Eric came looking for them before dinner.

Instead, they snuggled in the library, with her sitting on his lap, him nuzzling her neck.

"I want to hear all about your internship."

Marcus explained how he'd spent the better part of the last three months—learning public policies, formal manners, how laws were handled between the elected officials and the queen and king. Politics weren't really Leah's cup of tea, but she listened intently.

"And … you?" he asked, drawing a spiral on her thigh.

"Oh, ya know… The equivalent of a college dropout still… I don't know." Her shoulders slumped. "It feels wrong to focus so much on powers when our baby won't have any."

"Hmm…"

She smiled. "But I've been reading a lot. And I've even written a few books."

He raised his eyebrows high. "What?"

"Well, it's not like they're novels, but more like little stories for us to read to her." She rested a hand on her bump.

Marcus trailed kisses down her neck. "That's brilliant. Can I see them?"

Leah cringed at the thought of anyone reading or seeing them in their current state. "Uh… Maybe down the road. They could be better. And the drawings are, well, *interesting.*"

After a while, they were summoned for dinner by one of the servants. The servant informed them that Kaylah and Eric would be taking dinner with them.

And now, Leah and Marcus were about to discover if they could actually make their plans work.

Chapter 23

KAYLAH AND ERIC STOOD FROM the table and exchanged hugs with Marcus after he and Leah entered the dining room. "Thanks for inviting us to dinner," Kaylah said.

Leah squinted as they all took their seats. "Mmhmm… We had an agreement. I can't believe you were going to back out of a shared meal together."

Kaylah grinned wickedly as she unfolded her napkin, placing it on her lap. She was the master orchestrator, and Leah could never be mad at her again.

"Congratulations, you two," Eric said, taking a sip of his wine. "On…?"

"Your engagement. That's what your ring means, right?"

Leah blushed. She hadn't realized they would have noticed so quickly. But then again, they were diplomats. They knew how to read people and pick up on small details. "Thanks."

Marcus sent a smile her way. "Thanks."

They began serving themselves from the generous spread on the table—rice pilaf, roasted yams, a black bean spread with flatbread, and more.

"Bacon," Leah whispered. *Bacon. Ham. Steak. Chicken. Meat!* The human world had more meat, and that reminder made Leah's mouth water.

"Busy mentally planning the wedding?" Kaylah kidded. "Or are we needing to change Christmas plans?"

Leah had zoned out. "I was just thinking about, well, yeah, some of our plans for the future." She treaded lightly, nervously. "Marcus and I are hoping to leave and spend some time in the human world."

In unison, Kaylah and Eric's gazes dropped to their plates, Kaylah's lips pressed into a thin line. And Leah's heart stuttered. "Am I not allowed to leave?"

Kaylah drew a deep breath, her silverware clinking as she set it down. "Catrina … put orders in place when you left the palace, when the two of you left and refused to go talk to her."

"I can't leave either?" Marcus asked.

"The orders only pertain to Leah," Eric said, giving her an apologetic glance.

"It was just a security measure," Kaylah said. "And I'm sure if you two want to pay her a visit, she'd lift it."

Leah groaned internally. This wasn't the start they wanted, not if their reunion and future plans involved sitting down with the queen to be lectured, scolded, and possibly punished or forced into something they weren't ready for yet.

"Can't you do anything about it?" Leah asked. "You know, as Matron?"

Kaylah sat up straighter. "I'm not the queen anymore. My authority doesn't override her orders."

"But you still have pull," Marcus countered. "Diplomatic visas and whatnot?"

It might not be fair to drag Kaylah into their mess, but Leah still held out hope. "We figured you two would understand, with how you kept your relationship a secret when Eric first moved to the Green Lands. You two didn't want people to have their noses in your business."

Eric winced. "Those were different times and circumstances."

Kaylah studied the couple. "We can try."

"Thank you!" Leah said, all smiles.

"When are we planning on this?" Kaylah asked.

"Maybe a couple of days?" Leah said. That way Kaylah and Eric could enjoy time with family during Christmas. They'd allow Kaylah to tell the family a partial truth—that the young couple had made up and were choosing to spend their time alone getting reacquainted. They'd just omit the human-world part of the equation. "As much under the radar as possible, but we have some things to take care of."

Then Kaylah asked which property the couple would be staying at in the human world, as the royal family had a handful they kept up. Leah and Marcus wanted freedom, a clean break from their families. They weren't planning on staying at any of them. And they weren't planning on using either of their allowances, their stipend money.

Kaylah swirled her wineglass. "But neither of you have ever paid bills."

"I'm getting a job first thing," Marcus said.

"As am I. Until the baby comes, at least," Leah added. Her mom hadn't allowed her to help when they were in a pinch back in the human world.

"It's … pricey to step out on your own. Especially in the human world. They have nasty inflation, and neither of you have marketable skills or job experience you can lean on, not to put too fine a point on it."

Kaylah's skepticism was logical, but Leah and Marcus were determined. "We'll make it work," Leah said.

"Until we leave, I was planning on staying here," Marcus said.

"We assumed as much," Eric replied. "You both always have an open invitation in our home."

"And we were planning on having me stay in Leah's room," Marcus added, his tone landing between the fear he'd exuded about breaking the pregnancy news to his parents, and the boldness with which he'd outright told Catrina they'd planned to room together at the palace.

"Obviously," Kaylah said.

"And if my parents or Aunt Catrina ask?" Marcus asked. Technically, Leah and Marcus were still breaking their rules.

Kaylah gave him a smirk. "If there's one thing I've learned while wearing a tiara and a crown, it's how to lie without lying."

"Okay…" Marcus still had a nervous edge to his voice, and Leah tried not to be annoyed by it.

Kaylah, however, *didn't* try to mask her feelings. "You are adults. You're going to have a child together. You are engaged. It's not my place to babysit you and make sure you look just right for the PR portraits." She pointed her dinner knife at Marcus from across the table. "And I care more about what my niece wants right now than what your aunt wants. And so should you."

Well, this is awkward. The room went silent. That was a little harsh on Marcus, but it meant the world to Leah to have someone in her corner, to have someone sticking up for her.

"I want Leah happy," Marcus muttered.

Kaylah looked between them and added, perhaps to keep things in perspective, to keep things fair, "And you better not hurt my nephew."

Leah ached inside. Was that about her slapping Marcus? Whether or not it was, she wouldn't hurt him again, and intended to not hurt his heart again either. "Yes, ma'am."

With a single nod, Kaylah continued her meal, as did the others. Leah and Marcus only exchanged a small glance about the awkwardness of being put in their places.

The rest of the meal was much less tense. Dessert was served— a selection of pastries and fruit puddings.

"Did anyone ever tell you the story about ornery little Marcus and that tree house in his parents' backyard?" Kaylah asked Leah, selecting a pastry.

The tree house they'd made out in? "Um… No."

"You see, Marcus can be stubborn, as we all know." Kaylah tore off a piece of her pastry. "So, the tree house…"

"She doesn't need to know about that," Marcus said, squirming in his seat.

"No, I think I do."

Kaylah grinned. "Oh, she does."

Marcus groaned, and Eric snickered knowingly.

"When he was little, whenever he'd get in a fight with Tobias or his parents, whenever he'd get in trouble, he'd climb that tree and refuse to come down."

Leah smiled, picturing him as a little boy defiantly climbing up and sticking it out.

"All there is to the story," Marcus declared.

"Not even close." Kaylah's tone was honey-thick. "One day, Little Marcus was particularly angry about something, climbed up to that tree house, and hunkered down. For hours. But he'd enjoyed plenty of juice and water earlier that day."

Marcus was most definitely blushing. "The end."

"But he wasn't coming down from that tree. He pronounced he never would. And when he couldn't hold his little bladder any longer…"

He covered his face, slumping into his chair. "Kill me now."

Kaylah flourished a hand in the air. "He watered the lawn from up in the tree house. As any dignified member of the royal family would be expected to."

Leah choked on a laugh.

"And he still refused to come down, even after skipping dinner. After multiple attempts to talk him down, Guillen went to the shed and brought out an axe."

Leah's eyes grew wide.

"He wouldn't have hurt Marcus, but a single solid blow to that tree trunk had Marcus surrendering in no time flat."

"I was *little*," Marcus defended.

"And I thought he'd learned his lesson about running away from problems."

"I did. I have," he said humbly at the subtle reproach.

Returning to her jovial tone, Kaylah smiled at Leah again. "The best part? The new gardener was out touring the grounds that day as Marcus performed his 'waterfall.' Saw the whole thing."

"I didn't know!" Marcus laughed.

Leah joined in with a laugh. "I hear plenty of stories about Marcus as a kid, but you and I need to talk more. I have a feeling everyone's gatekeeping all the juicy stuff."

"That's it," Marcus said. "Change of plans. We're headed to the human world first thing in the morning." He and Leah shared a grin.

The rest of the evening was filled with easy conversation as they enjoyed their small family reunion. Once the two couples said good night, Marcus and Leah continued to discuss their plans and rekindle their flame in the privacy of her room. *Their* room.

Chapter 24

LEAH WOKE THE NEXT MORNING to a soft kiss on her bare shoulder.

"Good morning, gorgeous," Marcus whispered, his voice groggy.

She moaned. This wasn't a dream, but it sure felt like it. "Good morning."

He kissed her shoulder again. "Are we still on for our plans today?"

Drawing a deep breath and stretching, she finally opened her eyes. A soft glow from behind the curtains lit the room. She turned to face Marcus. "Yes. We have to hope Kaylah can get an exception for us. I don't want to derail everything." Leah didn't want to talk contingency plans.

He slid a hand to her hip. "Okay. And you're sure you don't want to just write your mom a letter?"

Leah's heart was heavy. She wasn't really ready to see her mom, and didn't want to lie to her. But Beata had to be lonely and worried that Leah hadn't come to visit in months. And the couple didn't know how long they were going to stay in the human world.

"I need to see her. I just have to."

"Okay."

"And I promise, no funny business with rifting," Leah added. The prison was quite a ways away, but Kaylah and Eric trusted that Leah wasn't a flight risk at the moment, and a cave rift would be the quickest way to get there. Eric and a couple of their bodyguards would be escorting her.

Marcus gazed into her eyes. "I trust you. I look forward to seeing you again tonight."

***

Dressed in a shirt that did a decent job of concealing her growing belly, Leah set out on the daunting trip to visit her mom. The shirt hid her stomach well enough, and didn't scream 'I'm a maternity shirt hiding something.'

Preparing to walk into the public gaze, Leah had slipped her engagement ring into her pocket, and was ready to exhaust every ounce of her Ivy energy, if needed, to engage her core, to suck in her gut as far as possible, to appear completely normal.

Eric did a good job soothing her nerves on the ride to the cave, shooting the breeze about the weather, about recent scientific discussions the United Green Folk Alliance had been working through with some humans.

Leah tried not to be insulted when the employees didn't let her create her own rift at the cave. Since the destination a person rifted to was determined by what the rifter envisioned, what they mentally dialed in when rifting, the cave employees had no way of ensuring Leah wasn't leaving the realm, wasn't disobeying Catrina's ban on her going to the human world.

So, Leah and Eric went through the same Seeder-created rift, exiting at a familiar cave nearest the prison her mom was being held in. Luckily, Cheryl was locked up to rot elsewhere.

Leah's heart beating wildly, her hands clammy, she straightened her shirt, made sure she was still standing tall and sucking in her gut, and strode alongside Eric to the prison. He gave her frequent calm, reassuring smiles.

More there for support and security than anything, Eric stayed in the waiting area. Leah always visited her mom alone. The guards guided her into the visiting room, with one stationed in the corner. They didn't usually require that, but perhaps that had been another of Catrina's requirements. It *was* Beata who had told Leah about the palace's secret passageways, after all.

Leah paced the small room—like most buildings in the Ivy Kingdom, it was built of stone. The walls, floor, and ceiling were all grey, depressing. A water spigot and glasses were situated on a ledge in the corner. Sweating, nervous, Leah filled a glass for herself and sipped.

"Sweetheart!" Beata said from behind, all excitement and warmth.

Setting her glass down, Leah turned and gave her mom a hug. *Suck it in. She can't notice.*

It didn't exactly feel *good* to hug her mom, but bittersweet. "Hey, Mom. Sorry I was away for so long."

Her mom squeezed tighter. "You have a life to live. That's okay. I'm just glad you're alright."

After a minute, they finally broke apart and sat at a small wooden table. Leah wasn't too fond of having the guard still in the room, having eyes on her, but she didn't have much choice in the matter.

Beata took Leah's hands in her own, a mirror image of Leah, only older and with dark brown eyes. And she did look older, like she'd aged more than she ought to have since Leah's last visit, but that might have just been Leah's guilt tricking her senses.

"You *are* okay, right?" Beata asked.

"Of course. I'd tell you."

Beata's hesitant expression implied she knew Leah better than that, that they were both inept at baring their souls.

"I'm good," Leah calmly stressed. "How are you?"

She always tried to listen to her mom, tried to show interest. The modern Ivy prison system was strict on making sure prisoners were treated fairly, that fights didn't break out, that there wasn't abuse. Leah didn't worry about that so much anymore. Her mom was allowed to work on projects within the prison for community service during her life sentence, as a small way she could make amends for her crimes, as a way to keep busy and have meaning in her life. But it was dull, day after day, life on repeat.

Her mom summed up the past few months, and Leah did her best to listen, despite her nerves, despite the strain on her energy to keep her facade and keep her stomach tight.

"I want to hear more about your adventures, though!" Beata said.

Leah slowly exhaled. "I'll have to tell you more next time. I hate to say it, but I have somewhere I have to be later today."

Beata frowned.

It killed Leah to do this, to lie straight to her mom's face. It was just like she'd done when running away to this realm, and now she was doing it to run back to the human world. Running away with Marcus.

"Either way, I'm always glad to see you." Beata gave her a smile.

"Me too." Leah gathered her courage, and leaned in a bit. Hopefully not so much that the guard caught on that it was a conspiratorial stance. "I know I haven't been able to visit for a while, and I'm … going to be gone for a while again…" She cringed.

Beata looked confused. "More traveling? You'll send word?"

Leah swallowed the lump in her throat. "Well, um… I changed my plans, and I got accepted into a university in the human world." She quickly whispered, "Please don't say anything." She indicated with her eyes that she meant the guard, that she didn't want anyone to know.

"Oh." Beata searched her expression. "I know you've had it rough because of your father and me, and the 'incident,' but you… Why over there?"

"I miss it. You know… Electricity, meat, cars, human holidays. I thought I'd give it a try."

Beata nodded. "It's what you grew up with. But you'll still write? Come back when you can on school breaks?"

Leah's stomach knotted. She and Marcus were separating from the family for now—a full cutoff. "I … might not."

Profound sorrow filled Beata's eyes, torturing Leah. Leah pitied her *so* much. "I'm sorry. I don't know. I'm not sure when I'll be back or send word. It may be sooner than not. I just wanted to give you a heads-up."

Beata rallied a weak smile. "Okay."

Taking a shallow breath, desperately fighting to both breathe and relax while simultaneously clenching her muscles, Leah prepared for the second part of what she needed to say. "I've told you Marcus and I have talked about marriage, right?"

They didn't discuss Marcus much on their visits, mostly to avoid contention.

Looking down at her hands, Beata cleared her throat. "Yes, you've mentioned it."

"I don't have any official announcements, but I need you to … get on board. Because I love him, and he's going to continue to be in my life." Leah *knew* her mom could do better, could become a better person, could grow and overcome her prejudices. And Beata hating Marcus for being a Boman was one thing, but the thought of her hating their child? Leah couldn't handle that. It almost destroyed her knowing her own mom might have regretted or resented *her* growing up.

Beata didn't reply.

"You say you want me to be happy," Leah said.

"I do. But can he protect you? Are you equals? Does someone without powers even understand you?"

Leah's jaw tensed. "He makes me happy. He understands me and is equal to me in different ways. Were you and Dad equals?"

"That was different." And it had been. While many still didn't believe it, didn't *want* to believe it, Leah was convinced Soren had been a rare form of Ivy, born with extra powers like King Stephan was.

"Not really," Leah replied. She sighed, unhappy with the way the conversation was going. She wasn't there to convince her mom, just to hopefully point her in the right direction, giving her a nudge to reconsider her prejudices, so she'd be prepared for the big news down the road. Because the road was short, and permanent decisions hung in the balance. "I'm asking you to try to see things from a different perspective, okay? That's all I'm asking. Because someday when I come to visit, I'm going to have a ring on my finger, and when that day happens, I don't want to have to choose between you and Marcus." *And it's going to be a heck of a lot sooner than you think.*

"And I might have his kids someday. We know they'll look like me." Leah looked so much like her mother because of the family genes in their line, because of the ancient clan they'd descended from. "But they would be like Marcus." She searched her mom's dark brown eyes. "Will you hate my children? Will I have to tell my children their grandmother hates them?"

Beata averted her gaze, her mouth open for a moment. "I couldn't hate any part of you, Eleana. I will *always* love you."

"That's not true if you hate Marcus."

"Then maybe you should reconsider your choice. I'm sure there are tons of nice Ivy guys out there who aren't *stunts*."

Leah bristled. Stunt was an old term—stunted—and not a kind one. "Bomen, Mom. They're called Bomen."

Her mother looked her dead in the eyes. "Why are you so determined to make your life harder? Loving one of them, with our family history? You will *never* be accepted into their little circle."

It hurt that it was true. Bomen were a tight-knit group. And Leah wouldn't just be another standard Ivy with powers going to playgroups with other moms who had Boman children. They wouldn't be soccer moms hanging out. Not with Leah's family history. But she'd loved Marcus too much to consider the easy path. Nothing in her life had been easy.

Sitting taller, Leah gathered herself. "I came here to let you know that I'm okay. That I'll be gone for a while. And to give you the courtesy of knowing that I would still like you in my life down the road. But if you ask me to choose…" Tears threatened to emerge. "If you ask me to choose, you may not like my choice. Please don't make me choose."

Beata studied her, not responding. She had to know that something was in the works, that a proposal was imminent if Leah was broaching the topic. She even glanced at Leah's hands, checking for a ring.

Leah guzzled the rest of her glass of water. "Like I said, I've got somewhere to be." She stood, and her mom followed suit.

"I love you," her mom said softly, awkwardly opening her arms.

Leah gave her another hug. "I love you too."

She couldn't stay long, couldn't handle the stress, and she refused to cry, refused to turn into a ball of mush in that visitors' room. She released her mom. "Sorry I couldn't stay longer, but I really have to go." She added a little more uncomfortably, "Happy holidays."

"You too, sweetheart."

As Leah reached for the door, Beata spoke again. "Your last letters came from Kaylah's estate…"

That was a can of worms Leah wasn't about to open. "Long story. I'll tell you all about it when I come next time. Love you."

And then she left, clicking the door closed behind her. As a guard guided her back to the waiting room, Leah fought tears with every step. That hadn't gone well, and would probably make her mom worry even more. She hadn't even told her what she'd planned to study at this fictitious university. Hadn't explained herself. The brevity of the conversation hadn't been reassuring to her mom at all. But at least there was something, and hopefully some kind of a seed planted about changing her thoughts on Bomen?

When Leah entered the waiting room, Eric stood to greet her. His two bodyguards and a prison attendant were in the room as well, on the other side.

Leah faced the wall, releasing her tense muscles for a minute, angled away from the others who might notice too much. She tried to catch her breath, tried to not hyperventilate. Eric slid an arm around her shoulders. "Are you okay?"

"Yeah." She gulped for air. "I'm fine. I'll be fine."

"Do you need anything, Your Highness?" one of the others asked.

"No thank you," Eric answered.

Grateful for his support, Leah took another minute to gather herself before setting out again, heading straight back to his and Kaylah's estate.

***

Leah ambled along that last stretch of the path to Kaylah and Eric's home. Once they were within the gates at the end of a long dirt drive, she assured Eric she'd prefer to walk by herself, taking her time, that she was grateful for his support but no longer needed the escort.

Rubbing her belly, glad to not have to be sucking it in unnaturally anymore, she pondered on the last thing Eric had said to her at the prison before they'd left:

"Ready to go home?"

"Yeah, let's go home," she'd said. "Well, to your home."

"Your home too."

She wore a thoughtful smile. It was a transient home like any of the others she'd lived in her entire life. But she *did* like the way it felt there. It *felt* like a home. Yes, there were servants and visitors, but not the way there had been at the palace. And even with Marcus, they had enough privacy in the eastern wing to enjoy each other, but were close enough to be near family to chat or spend dinner together.

It wouldn't last forever, but it was nice.

Once she arrived at the house, a servant told her Marcus could be found out back at the pavilion. His primary task of the day had been to rift to the apartment he'd been staying in during his internship, pack up his things, and have them shipped here for safekeeping. He'd also collected his remaining pay, telling them he wasn't sure how long he'd be gone.

Strolling to the backyard, she found him at the pavilion, where he worked away at the other task of the day: writing letters.

"Stealing my favorite writing spot?" she asked on her approach.

He smiled wide, his gaze still fixed on his paper. "Great minds…"

She stepped up, slinging an arm around a pillar. "Do you want privacy?"

"You're fine." He glanced up. "Do you want to talk about your visit?"

She twisted her lips. "Hmm…"

He set the paper and pen on the bench next to him, holding out his arms. She smiled and accepted the offer, sitting on his lap.

"You okay?" he asked.

"I will be." *I hope.* "How was it, settling things up north?"

He shrugged. "It was fine. It was a little weird when they tried to pry, asking if there was anything wrong. It just felt like they wanted dirt on the family, you know?"

Leah wrinkled her nose.

"And…" He rubbed her thigh. "They reassured me they'll keep the position open for me, because I'm *such* a valuable asset." He rolled his eyes.

"You are."

He raised his eyebrows. "I'm a beginner intern."

"And you'll be brilliant in what you do someday. Even if your career has a … gap in it." She frowned, intertwining their fingers.

"Worth it."

Giving him a hesitant smile, she studied his warm brown eyes. "Are you sure you'll be okay with working construction in the human world? That's hard work."

"It pays well, doesn't require as many fancy fake IDs, and it's pretty much the only skill I can think of that can get me a job right away when we go over there."

His father had worked in construction before the war ended, and built the house he and Rachel now lived in. Marcus had been too young to help with that, but he had enjoyed spending time with his dad learning some of the basics with renovations over the years and improvements to the tree house.

"If you say so," she replied, kissing the palms of his hands.

"Is *that* it? You're afraid I'll get callouses? You don't want rough hands on your body?" He grinned mischievously.

She leaned in, brushing her lips against his ear with a sensual whisper that would have made the songbirds in the distance blush. "I've never complained about you being rough with me, have I?"

He groaned. "We have a lot to do today, and you are not going to make it easy on me."

"I bet there's a nice cozy spot out in these woods. I've never made love out in the open." As she whispered, his breathing became labored, and she poked out a vine, slithering it up his shoulder, to his neck, and then tickled his ear.

"Ack!" He wrenched his head away, and she giggled.

He threw her a dirty look, and she got off his lap, settling on the bench beside him. "There *is* a lot to do." It was already nearing dinnertime, and she had letters of her own to see to. They were both taking the day to write to Catrina and his parents—apologies, explanations.

After fetching paper and a pen for herself, Leah rejoined him, and they worked in silence, side by side.

Kaylah was gone all day, running errands, personal and official, with her charity work.

The next morning, Marcus and Leah ate with Eric. He said Kaylah had been delayed, but would be there by lunchtime.

Leah was a bundle of nerves, pacing around. She offered to pack up her things so Kaylah and Eric could have their guestrooms back, but Eric insisted it wasn't a bother, and it was something that could be dealt with when she and Marcus returned and had decided what they were going to do.

Kaylah returned right in time for lunch, and they all sat down together. "Some of your favorites." She smiled, gesturing to the dishes One was loaded with mashed potatoes, another with sliced moon melon.

As they ate, they discussed their plans for the evening. Leah was ready to get it over with. When the time came, they handed their letters to Kaylah, who promised she'd deliver them once the couple was out of the realm. Leah dressed in clothes that would help conceal her stomach, though she still planned to suck it in while in public. She and Marcus tucked away his internship earnings and anything else they could use that would fit in their pockets.

And they were set to go. Eric and Kaylah stood ready in the entryway; Eric planned to stay at the estate to help the group keep a lower profile.

"Before we go, Eric and I have something for the two of you," Kaylah said. She held out an envelope sealed with her official insignia.

Chapter 25

LEAH EYED THE ENVELOPE Kaylah offered. "What's that?"

"Open it, and you'll find out."

Leah took it from her, popping the green wax seal and opening the envelope. Out slid a single item: a shiny brand-new human-world debit card. The sticker was still on it. "No. We told you. No family money. We're doing this on our own." She held it out to Kaylah.

Kaylah did not take it back. Eric only shook his head, wrapping an arm around Kaylah's waist. Kaylah turned to Marcus. "How much do you have from your internship?"

"Three hundred bronze marks."

"The conversion rate is lousy, and that won't get you far."

"That's why I'm applying for jobs first thing tomorrow morning," Marcus replied.

"It takes time to find jobs, to find apartments, to get *approved* for an apartment. Especially around those human holidays."

Leah sighed. "And I'm going to—"

This time Kaylah turned on her. "It's your inheritance."

Leah scoffed. "I don't have an inheritance."

"Well, that's what I'm calling it. When you first came here, when we brought your mother and that other horrible woman in, they had cars; they had possessions. When we packed up their things, we sold a lot of it. It had no use over there. You deserve every penny of that."

Leah furrowed her brow. She hadn't thought of those logistics. "But that money would have gone to the queen's coffers to take care of me, right? That money has to be long gone for my upkeep."

Kaylah shrugged. "Your mother's car was a really nice model."

Hmm… Leah held up the card. "How much?"

"Enough to get you by for a while."

"*How much?*"

"I have pretty lucrative investments in the human world. Great interest rates. So, there's a … small bonus."

Leah held it out to her. "No. We don't want your charity."

"It's not charity. Christmas is in two days. It's part of your gifts."

Leah continued to hold it out to her.

Her expression firm, Kaylah remained still. "We *all* need a hand sometimes. Financial stress doesn't help in relationships." She gently cocked her head to the side. "You don't have to spend it. Keep it for emergencies."

Leah's pride fought tooth and nail, despite the perfect logic. "Fine," she grumbled, sliding it into her pocket. "But don't be offended when we return it someday completely full."

Kaylah only gave her a soft smile. "We won't be."

"I don't like you right now." Leah pouted. "But I still love you."

"Come here, kiddo." Kaylah reached for her, and the group exchanged hugs.

"All set, then," Marcus said, squaring his shoulders.

"One last thing." Kaylah pulled a ring off her finger. "I want you to take this with you. *Do not lose it.*"

"Are you serious?" Marcus asked in full disbelief.

Leah took a step back, nearly terrified of the offer. "That's *definitely* too far. Your royal ring?!" Only official Elontas—those in the proper Ivy royal family line of heirs—were assigned insignias, and they each had *one* ring. One official ring they wouldn't let someone pry from them.

"I can do with this as I please. You may need it."

Staring at it, Leah stood frozen. "We don't know how long we're going away for. *You* might need that. And people would think I stole it from you!" Even if this realm didn't know about her previous shoplifting habits, they'd think it.

Kaylah let out a composed breath. "Eric still has his. I trust you. And while this may not do you any good in the human world other than earn you a few bucks at a pawnshop, this will do nearly anything for you in a pinch in this realm. If you two have an emergency, all you need to do is rift over, or show the ring at a cave. It will stop a train. It will send people to track me down from anywhere. They will take care of you and do as you say, *then* verify that it wasn't stolen later." Her expression and tone were stone-cold sober. "Take it."

"Aunt Kaylah," Marcus interjected. "It's not like I'm banned from leaving the realm. If something happens, I can ask for help."

She was losing her patience. "I love you, but it is not the same. And you're about to defy your queen's explicit orders, nephew or not, by taking your fiancée out of the realm. And if you break your neck working construction, I have a feeling Leah would appreciate having a safe way to approach a rifting cave to call for a Seeder healer to make a special visit for you."

With that devastating vision dancing in her mind, Leah palmed the ring, sliding it into her pocket. "Okay. I'll make sure not to lose it."

***

The walk and ride to the rifting cave were beyond tense. Leah focused on sucking in her gut, breathing calmly, putting one foot in front of the other, and not crushing Marcus's hand.

Not wanting to involve more people than necessary, they lied to the customs official, stating Marcus and Leah were traveling domestically.

When they got to the rift coordinator, the panic fully set in. With Catrina's ban, Leah still wasn't allowed to create her own rift. And since Marcus was a Boman, he wasn't capable of making his own, either. They needed a Seeder to open a rift for them.

"We will be going to Selen, these two first," Kaylah calmly instructed the Seeder employee.

The employee gaped. "Um, Your Highness, we're not allowed to… What I mean is, the girl's not allowed to … leave the realm. Domestic only."

A bitterness lingered on Leah's tongue. The unused passport felt like a useless brick in her pocket right now.

"I understand the current orders," Kaylah said. "This is an exception."

The employee cringed. "Matron, all due respect, but the orders come from Her Majesty, and I can't lose my job."

"I'll make sure you won't."

When the employee wouldn't budge, Kaylah took them to the side to chat in private.

Marcus kissed Leah's shoulder, holding her arm tight. "It'll be fine. Everyone in this realm owes her."

"Yeah," Leah whispered. "Kinda wish she hadn't handed the crown over to your aunt already."

A couple of minutes later, Kaylah and the tense cave employee returned. "I appreciate your cooperation," Kaylah said.

Pursing their lips, the employee nodded curtly. "Selen?"

"Yes please."

The Seeder stepped into the center of the cave space and swiped a hand through the air. A shimmering rift opened, and Leah approached.

"What's holding up the line?" a voice called from behind.

Crap.

Kaylah looked Leah dead in the eyes. "Love you, kiddo. We'll be right behind you. *Go.*"

Leah panicked. Kaylah helped her with a gentle shove.

"Who is that? Hold up now, I need to see—"

The voice cut off the moment Leah entered the rift. Her field of vision swiftly transitioned from the back of a cave to a yellow glow, then into an inner cave. The lack of ambient Green Lands energy was an instant and staggering contrast.

Before Leah could process everything, the arrivals coordinator beckoned her to move forward. "Wait… What are *you* doing here?"

Correction. Leah hadn't been panicking before. *Now* she was panicking. "I, uh…" They'd hoped the human-world employees wouldn't care, or hadn't been informed of the ban. And if she had been any Regular Joe, she'd have waltzed right by with the employee assuming she'd shown her passport and it wasn't a big deal that she was there right now.

But Leah wasn't a Regular Joe. She was notorious.

Leah threw her thumb over her shoulder. "Kaylah's right behind me."

The employee looked insulted. "*Matron* Kaylah?"

Ugh. Why hadn't Leah at least used Kaylah's title? She sounded ungrateful. People didn't understand how close she'd grown to Kaylah, and that she was grateful she'd spared her life after the botched assassination attempt.

"Yes, Matron Kaylah."

The employee stared at the rift, disbelief plastered on their face.

Come on, guys. Marcus should have already come through, and then Kaylah through her own rift. *Come on.*

The rift closed.

"Right," the employee drawled.

"I swear. She's right behind me."

"How about you follow me, and we'll find out?"

Leah planted her feet. She wasn't going to be separated from Marcus. She wasn't going anywhere. "She'll be right through."

"Security!" the employee called out.

"Security? There's no need for security!"

"Please calmly follow them."

Leah clenched her fists, her mind racing. They didn't need a scene. They were trying to avoid a scene! Why weren't Marcus and Kaylah coming through?

"Send someone over to confirm. Kayl— Matron Kaylah will confirm it's okay for me to be here, that the order was … rescinded…" She used to be a much better liar.

The employee gave her an incredulous expression. Inter-realm rifts weren't something you sauntered back and forth through willy-nilly. Seeder or Ivy, you could only physically make a round trip between the realms once a day. Most of the cave employees probably lived in the Green Lands, and would be cutting their shift short by going back. Shift coordination was fine-tuned, and Leah was the wrench in the works they weren't willing to deal with.

A uniformed security officer approached. "Please come with me, Miss Elonto."

Leah shook her head. *Kaylah will be through in two seconds.* How many dozens of rifting caves were there in the entire Green Lands realm and human world combined? And *all* the employees knew Leah was banned? She didn't need the rumor mill churning about the ban, and then that she'd been taken into custody for directly disobeying her queen's orders.

The officer—a male Ivy—extended vines, wrapping them around her upper arm. "You can follow me, or we can do this the hard way."

Gutting memories flashed through her mind. Being shoved down a hallway at the wedding venue by Kaylah's bodyguards. Being strapped to a chair for hours.

Sweating, Leah could sense the Ivy energy burning and surging in her, her own vines prodding at her wrists. "*Get your vines off me,*" she muttered through clenched teeth, her voice low and threatening.

"I explained your options, Miss Elonto."

Should she pull out Kaylah's ring? *It will stop a train.* It would *force* them to rift over to check her story.

It didn't feel like the right moment to play that trump card. That ring was supposed to be for an emergency. This wasn't an emergency. She didn't need that ring right now, because Kaylah was just on the other side of a rift, arriving any moment. Right? "I'll come with you if you take your vines off me."

The officer considered. "Do you have any weapons on you?"

Leah's lip curled. *Seriously? Who did I come to assassinate? A no-name employee? Some random human?* "No."

Cautiously, the officer released her. "Hands where I can see them, and keep your vines to yourself."

"Done."

She followed the officer. He kept a close eye on her as he guided her to a small room and closed the door behind them.

"Matron Kaylah will be over to vouch for me."

"The orders come from the queen."

"Then there's a delay in the update on those orders. I was granted an exception."

He scoffed. "That's likely." He eyed her, pointing to a large wooden table in the room. "Empty your pockets."

Her passport? The debit card? Kaylah's ring that they'd assume she'd stolen? Her extra pair of *underwear* she'd tucked in there? "No."

"We're well within our rights, especially given your history."

"I was acquitted of all charges. I've been living in the palace. Official notices went around the *entire* realm explaining my innocence! Don't give me this 'given my history' shit! I don't have any weapons on me. I have no reason to."

He stared right at her, and with that scathing look, it was clear she really didn't have a place back there. People tolerated her because the government said to, but they didn't understand her, didn't respect her. "I can have a female come in and do a strip search."

Her face heated with rage. "Over my *dead body*. My *aunt* is just on the other side of a rift. And if anyone touches me... I'd hate to find out what she'd be willing to do for her only niece."

"The one who tried to murder her?" he said flatly.

Kaylah's forgiveness had never been anyone else's to give but hers. Nor had Marcus's or anyone else's. Green folk worshipped Kaylah, and loved Marcus. But they were so blind at times, even when Kaylah and Catrina had tried to clean up Leah's mess with their PR teams.

Luckily, the security officer did seem to weigh the relationship, and the faint possibility that Leah might not be making this all up. He didn't pull out the restraining straps normally used for Ivy vines.

Instead, he jutted his chin to the end of the table. "Over there. Sit down. Hands on the table. No sudden moves. We'll see how this pans out."

For the next several minutes, he interviewed Leah. He asked about her purpose there, and details about this 'change in orders' that didn't actually exist. After a few lies, she stopped answering his questions. She finally released her death grip on her Ivy energy clutching in her gut once she realized the table covered her stomach, and settled in, drawing patterns on the table. "Matron Kaylah will explain," she said over and over and over.

He eventually got tired of that phrase and left, locking her in the room.

A breath whooshed out of Leah, and she laid her forehead on the table. No one had luck like she did. What kind of cruel irony was it that she'd plotted and snuck into the Green Lands in the first place, and now she'd plotted and snuck out of that realm? Neither time had gone off without a hitch.

Leah was thirsty and ready for a good night's rest. There was a time difference when rifting, so it was still earlier in the day here, but she was beyond ready to call it a day and be done with this.

Eventually, her lungs didn't appreciate her bending so far forward, so she sat back in her chair, watching as time ticked by on an electric clock. She mused on that, on her old friend—electricity. How much had changed since she'd left the human world? Was there a new president in the United States? Had any major hurricanes or earthquakes happened? What was the weather like outside this cave?

One minute crawled by after another on that clock. More than a half hour later, the door *finally* opened again.

Chapter 26

MORE CALM THAN LEAH HAD expected him to be, Marcus stood at the door. "Are you okay?"

"Yeah." She stood and rushed into his arms. "What took so long?"

He sighed, threading his hand into her hair. "I'll tell you all about it later. Let's head out of here. Do you still have everything you came with?"

"Yes."

"Good. Let's go. Our ride is on its way."

"So, we can stay? Is Kaylah not going to say goodbye?"

He pursed his lips, shaking his head. "She's… Yeah, we can stay, but we should get going."

Leah wasn't about to argue with that. She took his hand and followed his lead. The cave was near silent; all employees they passed had their eyes on the couple.

They wove the reverse route Leah had taken two-plus years ago to get there, eventually ending up in the fake nature preserve's display room. They had a little while to look it over this time since they were waiting on a rideshare to take them away instead of going to a car in the parking garage. A giant tan moth with a broken wing hung lopsided off a single pin in the other wing. A coyote looked like it had been taxidermied by someone while blindfolded. They really did go to great lengths to deter humans by making this place dumpy.

A single cashier stood in the gift shop.

"What happened?" Leah whispered to Marcus.

He rolled his eyes. "A cave supervisor with balls the size of the Grand Sea? He came to see what was causing the holdup, and once he saw me, and you… He tried to uphold Aunt Catrina's orders, and wouldn't budge."

Could Leah have found a way to be content as a shotgun bride? Maybe she should have just sucked it up months ago… But that wouldn't have resolved everything. Not even close.

"That is *seriously* ballsy, with Kaylah there and everything."

"Right?"

"But where is she now? What happened? What took so long?"

Marcus ruffled his hair. "We were trying to minimize the damage, to keep it under wraps. In the end, she pretty much put both caves under lockdown, staff sworn to secrecy until she could bring proof from Aunt Catrina that her orders regarding you were rescinded."

Leah angled her head. "But they're allowing us to leave."

He rubbed the back of his neck, pulling a cell phone from his pocket. "Under the condition we carry this with us. For 'emergencies and updates.'"

She wilted. Her mom had tracked her via cell all her life. "You mean so they can track wherever we go?"

Huffing, he tucked it back into his pocket. "I swore I'd take it. It was either that or they'd send you back home until it was all sorted out."

Yuck. "I guess I'll take the phone."

He nodded. "So right now, I'm pretty sure *your* aunt is on her way to storm the palace to have a few choice words with *my* aunt.

And I'm putting my money on *yours* winning this one, or at least hoping… She was *scorched.*"

Catrina hadn't even fought in the old war. Kaylah had taken multiple lives. "I'm putting my money on Kaylah, too. Plus, Catrina wouldn't even be the queen yet if Kaylah hadn't given the position to her."

"Shh," he whispered.

"Right, sorry." The employee was still in the room, and that kind of talk wasn't ideal from the usurpers' daughter.

Marcus kissed Leah's forehead, and soon after, his phone dinged, notifying them that their ride was there.

They slipped into the back seat of a pristine blue car and headed out. They'd decided ahead of time to go to a somewhat familiar area, but not too close to where Tobias lived, or Marcus's grandparents. They'd be about an hour away.

Marcus rested a hand on her leg, and she leaned her head on his shoulder, dazed.

"Is that place any good?" the driver asked as he pulled away. "Such a weird out-of-the-way place for people to come and go without their own cars. And at the weirdest times of day. And around the holidays…" Caves were open around the clock.

"No. It sucks," Marcus said.

"Dang. Then they must pay for some good advertising, huh? To con people into checking it out?"

"Guess so."

After a couple more questions from the driver and disinterested answers from Marcus, the driver got the hint.

Leah closed her eyes and let herself simply be. Her life was a disaster. From conception to the foreseeable future. Part of her said the only way out of that would be to take that phone in Marcus's pocket and chuck it out the window, and tell the driver to drive any which way until sunset.

But that would be too rash. Rash decisions rarely paid off for Leah.

After a while in silence, the driver turned some music on.

"Are you okay?" Marcus whispered into her ear.

She swallowed. Being grabbed like that by the security officer…
And threatened to be strip-searched? *Not really.* "I will be." She rested
a hand on her relaxed baby bump. "I will be."

An hour later, they rolled up to a hotel in the city they'd chosen,
thanking their driver.

"You have that debit card Kaylah gave you?" Marcus asked as
they stood outside the hotel.

"Yeah… But didn't you exchange your Ivy money at the cave?"

He frowned. "I wanted to get you out of there."

And with that, she pulled it out, and peeled off the sticker. "Our
independence lasted long, didn't it?" She gave him an ironic smile,
and he chuckled.

They paid with the card, presenting fake IDs, and headed to
their room. Starving by now, Leah gulped down water while Marcus
ordered room service. If they were having to utilize Kaylah's
generosity already, they were going to enjoy a good meal. It kinda felt
like a last meal, given that the phone dangled over their heads like an
axe, so they ordered extra dessert.

Leah turned the debit card in her hand. "I swear Kaylah can see
the future."

Marcus plopped on the bed next to her. "I think if she could,
she'd have split us up and had a whisper rifter sworn to secrecy help
you get out."

She cringed. "If we'd decided to go that way, I could have just
tree rifted myself."

No, they'd wanted to do this smoothly, and as legally as possible.
Kaylah could smooth-talk, though apparently not everyone once
she'd passed on the crown and entered retirement. Bomen could
only rift through caves anyway, and Leah hadn't wanted to be
separated.

"How do you feel energy-wise?" Marcus asked.

Leah rubbed her face. "It's weird. I'm sure I'll get used to it." She hadn't known the Green Lands energy growing up. But the difference between realms was palpable. It had been invigorating as it flooded her upon her arrival when she originally went over there. Now, as she stepped back into the human world, she already understood why most green folk only came to *visit* over here. She'd wondered if that difference, that lack, had contributed to her mom's depression over the years, to Cheryl's bitterness toward Leah. Leah feared that for herself now. If her biology, her cravings to return to the realm and that unique energy, would trump her craving to be free.

Then again, if Catrina dispatched guards to drag the couple back, Leah wouldn't have to find out for herself.

"On a scale of one to ten, how much would you hate me if that phone smashed itself during the night?"

Marcus lifted an eyebrow.

"Fine. I'm just throwing it out there. If they're going to keep thinking I'm a villain, might as well see how badly we can blow things up."

He placed a soft kiss on her lips. "Kaylah will come through for us."

She snuggled up to him as they waited for their food. All she could think about was how she never wanted to go back, would *never* forgive Catrina, and how excited she was to eat meat-lover's pizza after two and a half years without it.

***

In the middle of the night, Leah's bladder happily reminded her she was pregnant. She reached for the striker on the nightstand to light a candle, only to remember she was in the human world. With a smile on her face, she clicked the button on the lamp next to her, then tiptoed to the restroom.

When she finished up in there, she decided to sneak one of the leftover breadsticks. As she was midchew, something caught her attention from across the hotel room. A tiny blinking red light—the cell phone.

Her gut twisted with dread. Was it a message from Catrina to make sure they were dressed because a dozen guards were on their way to drag them back?

Please leave us alone.

Leah sat on a chair next to the small table where they'd emptied their pockets into a pile. Drawing a deep breath, she grabbed the phone and turned the screen on. Two texts from an unknown number.

<Free as a kite, kiddos! Keep this phone and number for emergencies. Merry Christmas. Love you!>

<P.S. I'm not saying you have to, but if you wanted to name your gremlin after me, I wouldn't be mad. ;) >

Leah's heart swelled. They were free. Kaylah had come through for them. She hadn't signed her name, but it had to have been Kaylah. No one else would have called their unborn child a gremlin, and she wouldn't have sent a servant through a rift to type that. That was a private joke.

The timestamp showed it had been sent a couple of hours ago. Kaylah wasn't likely lingering in the human world for a response, but she might rift over now and then to get in cell phone range. Leah typed up her own message.

<And Happy New Year. Love you too!>

After sending it, Leah gingerly set the phone on the table. The room was silent other than Marcus's soft breathing behind her, the occasional hum of a car on the street, and the clunk from the ice machine down the hallway.

Leah sat there a moment, surveying their tiny cache of belongings, and considering the many tasks ahead of them in the next few days. She plucked out two of the things that made all the difference in the world right now: a debit card and a gold ring.

In that moment, Leah came to a realization that was both heartwarming and heart wrenching. Kaylah had done more for Leah in the two and a half years she'd known her than her mom had her entire life.

Even as she thought it, guilt rose within her. Her mom wasn't *all* bad. She *was* bad. She had let her husband do unspeakable things in war and in his personal life. And she'd manipulated him by getting pregnant with Leah. And she still clung to old prejudices.

But Beata had also kept Leah safe… *Somewhat* safe. Clothed and fed. And she'd done her best to keep Leah out of trouble with regards to shoplifting and school and boys. Yet, she had been grossly neglectful. She was horrible at communicating, at keeping harmful secrets. She had refused to see the things her aide was doing to Leah, refused to listen to Leah, calling her a drama queen about Cheryl's insults and abuse over the years. She'd taught Leah to run away from problems instead of trying to calmly face them.

Kaylah always gave Leah the benefit of the doubt. Space and freedom and a listening ear. Encouragement and even calling her out when needed, in a way that helped Leah.

Leah wiped away a tear, hugging herself. "Thank you," she whispered.

After another minute, she turned off the lamp and crawled into bed with Marcus, laying her head on his bare chest.

He stirred a little, and she adjusted her engagement ring, happy to wear it now that they were away from green folk. She kissed his chest. "We're free."

***

Marcus was over the moon the next day after he read the texts. After ordering more room service for breakfast, they had to prioritize their to-do list.

The Ivy money Marcus had brought would do no good in the human world. Green folk had allies amongst the humans—some minor politicians and scientists, some family members and friends—but for the most part, they were still very disconnected worlds. The only place to exchange that money was at rifting caves, and they didn't want to step foot in one until they were sure they were ready to return, just in case. They'd stop by an ATM to check how much Kaylah had loaded into that account.

They needed to look into apartments, apply for jobs, get new toiletries and clothes and personal phones, and figure out transportation. They took time to enjoy each other, but this wasn't a vacation. This was a trial run to ensure they could make things work between them.

They spent the next few days getting things lined up, taking a little extra time to celebrate Christmas. They didn't exchange gifts, but they took a stroll in the snow. It rarely snowed in these parts, and it was exciting to witness it after its absence in the Green Lands.

The ATM revealed that Kaylah had indeed been absurdly generous, and while they still intended to try to do as much of this as they could on their own, it was comforting to have a safety net. They purchased the necessities, and started applying for jobs and apartments. It was tricky, having no references, no listable work experience.

Ivy royalty had connections in the human world, and they could get you any sort of fake background you wanted. The old assassin networks had been dissolved long ago, but their connections were still helpful for green folk who wanted to explore the human world.

Marcus still had his fake persona intact from when he'd come over as a foreign exchange student. For Leah, they'd taken one of her most recent photos and made her a fake driver's license that they'd presented to her with her passport. Her mom had never let her get a license when she was a high schooler here.

But if a company did a background check, the couple didn't have much set up to help out. Marcus's job would be the easier one to come by. Hard labor paid well, trained on the job, and sometimes hired undocumented workers.

Soon enough, Marcus snagged a job, and they found an apartment. Without work or rental history, they paid a huge sum for a deposit on a dumpy third-story apartment in a busy neighborhood near a bus line. They quickly realized how naïve they'd been about finances.

Before moving into their apartment, they figured out how to disable the tracker on the phone they'd been given. Not wanting to worry Kaylah, they sent a text to her, letting her know they'd done that and were fine. A week later a text came in with a single heart emoji.

The couple didn't waste money on decorations, so the apartment walls remained bare, dozens of poorly plugged nail holes dotting them.

Furnishing their new place was an adventure. Most of the stuff was secondhand. Leah's Ivy energy, even when dimmed in the human world, became immensely helpful when they carried it all up the stairs to their place. She had to be extra careful to not use her vines in public—it had become second nature in the Green Lands, and they were useful for gripping things. Leah almost had a heart attack when she nearly dropped a couch they were carrying up the stairs. A pair of neighbors came running up to help, shocked a young pregnant girl was hefting a couch up to the third floor with her fiancé. She wasn't wearing shirts designed to hide her fast-growing belly anymore, and wasn't sucking in her gut. She chose to believe she was only getting bigger so fast because of the baby, and not because of the bacon and other things she'd missed and was now consuming on a regular basis…

Finding Leah a job was a harder task. She was trying for entry-level positions, but wasn't getting many callbacks or return emails. They considered breaking their no-contact rule with family to ask his brother or grandparents to be references, but they chose not to, at least not yet.

So as Marcus worked full-time, Leah spent her days applying for jobs, reading books she got from the local library, and journaling. In the evenings, they enjoyed cooking together, relaxing, and chatting.

Marcus came home from work, day after day, exhausted but happy. He admitted it was awkward to learn to use power tools, but he never complained about having to work a hard job, not once. Not when he'd fall asleep while sitting on the couch. Not when he came home with a gash on his arm that Leah could only help bandage and kiss better, when his Seeder mom could have instantly healed it with a mere touch of a finger.

Separated from the stress and scrutiny of their home realm, they were doing well.

Chapter 27

EVENTUALLY, LEAH LANDED a part-time job, working at a dollar store as a cashier. It didn't help all that much with the finances, but she at least had some satisfaction that she was contributing.

With her spare time, she gave something else a try. She'd enjoyed *Valeska's Adventures* so much, and found herself reading more often than not, so she decided to give writing a go. Not just the kids' stories back in the Green Lands that she hoped to finish for their child someday, but stories for an older audience. Maybe if she'd gotten into books in middle and high school, she'd have avoided a lot of the drama and trauma. Plus, *Valeska's Adventures* was pretty light on the romance, and Leah had a feeling she could do better.

With a notebook and pen, she started to write.

Things were genuinely going smoothly between Leah and Marcus. They were best friends. They took time on the weekends to go for walks. He endured her talking about books, and she always listened to his stories about what happened to coworkers she hadn't met on his worksite.

Were things perfect? No. They were still very different people from shockingly different backgrounds. They were young, and trying to figure out how to make things work. They both forgot to pay a utility bill, and had to pay an extra charge. The minutiae of sorting out things like who was going to pay the bills and how to remember to do it on time were daunting.

And they both still had their tempers. Leah remembered the tips Kaylah had given her about dealing with frustrations.

One evening after Marcus came home and showered, he sat on the floor while Leah massaged his shoulders. She used her Ivy energy to put some extra pressure into his knots. He squirmed a little as she did so, but was grateful.

"You're sure you don't want to go alone?" he asked.

Leah sighed. To try to make things work, to find a better way to meet in the middle and deal with stress, they'd looked into counseling. There was a local program available that helped with low-income sessions. A limited number of sessions were covered, so they'd agreed to take them as a couple.

She leaned forward on the couch, wrapping her arms around his neck, and rested her chin on his head. "Yeah, I'd rather go with you."

It was tempting to see a counselor for herself, because no one here would have preconceptions about who Leah was. They would have no background on her, would have no need to report to the queen or anyone else. But … Leah's heartache was deep and complex, and she'd have to walk on eggshells to discuss it with a human. 'So, when my dad was king… Oh, um, I mean… a CEO of a company you've never heard of…' 'After I tried to assassinate my aunt, the queen… No, I mean… Um…'

She'd either slip on that kind of information and earn a grippy-socks vacation because they thought she'd lost it, or she'd have to lie so much that she doubted any sort of soul-baring would be effective.

No, she'd sort through her stuff—someday, somehow. And in a way, she already was. Just voicing it with Kaylah and Marcus had been immensely helpful. Just jotting it in a journal helped her release her anger and think things through.

Marcus kissed her hand. "Okay. I'll make it work with my schedule."

The first session was mostly a meet and greet to discuss what they wanted out of counseling. The second session was surprisingly productive. Though, Leah was mortified to find herself crying in front of a stranger about how she felt regarding always losing people. She was honest about her mom being sent to prison for life, about her dad dying before she was born, about having to move all the time growing up. She was perhaps a *little* hazy on the details.

She and Marcus had agreed ahead of time to go out for ice cream after sessions to decompress, and it was a fun reminder of their original dates as high schoolers.

"I'm really sorry," Marcus said quietly, pushing his ice cream toppings around as they sat in the shop.

"It's okay. It was my fault, too," she reassured him. It was true. When they'd 'taken a break' in high school for an entire month, during Christmas Break, it had been because Marcus had wanted it. It had been torture for Leah, but she'd earned it by shoplifting. And him being gone for nearly half of her pregnancy? She could have reached out to him as easily as he could have to her.

"Still." He frowned. "I think her advice will help."

Leah nodded. They'd talked about how to pick their battles in their session that night, and also different fighting styles. It was weird to be told it was okay to fight, but that they needed to set boundaries. They needed to agree together on what was too far in an argument. Bringing up past mistakes and hurtful trauma was a no-go.

And Marcus was an avoider in arguments. In his heart, he was still that little boy who didn't want to deal with contention, and ran off to a tree house. But if he needed space and time to work through a problem, to properly handle it, then Leah agreed to give it to him, but there had to be rules. He could halt an argument and go for a walk, but he'd have to promise to not be gone for more than a couple of hours. They both needed boundaries.

Not once was a rationale given that they needed to handle things a certain way because of how it would affect Leah's public image, or Marcus's reputation, or the royal family's.

It was impartial. It was helpful. It was encouraging.

***

They didn't check the 'official' cell phone often, but they kept it plugged in on a side table.

Around Leah's five-month mark in her pregnancy, Marcus started to act antsy, staring at the phone.

What was going through his mind? Did she even want to know? Could she handle the truth?

At some point, she couldn't ignore it. One Sunday afternoon, Leah lay with her feet propped up on the armrest of the couch, her hands resting on her rapidly growing bump, her head in Marcus's lap as he gave her a relaxing scalp massage.

"Why do you keep looking at the phone?" she asked.

He pressed his lips together, hesitant. "I've been thinking a lot about Aunt Catrina, is all."

Leah's stomach tightened. "What about her?"

"That she's due any day. I've just been thinking it would be cool to know what she ends up having."

The vast majority of green folk still didn't come to the human world for health care, for obvious reasons. They didn't know the gender of Queen Catrina's baby, or if there would be multiples. Twins and triplets weren't uncommon for standard Ivies.

Leah closed her eyes, processing. She wanted nothing to do with Catrina, with official palace news, with any of it. They'd agreed upon a full cutoff. But … Catrina was his aunt, and they had always been close. And it would be a major cause for celebration in the Ivy Kingdom, so perhaps they should be aware of that sort of thing?

Drawing a cleansing breath, Leah opened her eyes. "I'd be okay with us texting Kaylah for an update once she's given birth…"

He instantly beamed. "Thanks!"

They texted the number they had for Kaylah, and a few days later got a reply. Catrina had given birth to another set of twin girls.

"Poor Leon," Marcus said. "Outnumbered four-to-one."

"Right? And *four* daughters, *four* downline heirs of her own. One more, and she's single-handedly taken care of the Elonta line!"

Ivy royalty had complex rules about names and titles, mostly based on the way the Mother Vines assigned their allegiance. The first five female Ivies after the queen in the Elonta bloodline held the power.

Leah's mom had never truly held the power of the Mother Vines, had never *truly* been a queen. She wasn't an Elonta. Leah was grateful to not be an Elonta or Elanna either. While these births were celebrated, it would no doubt stir up unwanted feelings and resentment in some of those further down the bloodline who were now taken a notch down because new heirs above them had not only claimed an exclusive title, but access to a power that only six people at a time could hold to any discernable degree.

Leah was fine being an entire realm away from those considerations. The enormous celebrations welcoming the new little princesses, and the subtle passive-aggressive greetings from Elontas or Elannas down the bloodline. But it brought her peace to see how much joy a little news from family back home brought Marcus.

***

Not much later, Leah's peace turned to guilt. How could she not feel guilty? Marcus's family was so close. He would never be living over here if it weren't to be with Leah. He'd said he would be willing to move to the human world permanently if that was what it took to make Leah happy, to make things work between them.

But part of her knew, no matter how much she wanted to deny it, that this was a *temporary* situation. Even if they did set up a permanent home here, would they never visit the Green Lands again? She couldn't do that to Marcus. Rachel wasn't capable—as a fully-rooted Seeder matriarch—of entering the human world anymore. They couldn't expect family to come to them. Marcus could go there. And what? Take the baby with him? Leave Leah behind because she couldn't stomach facing the public again? She'd always be the bad guy.

But every single time she imagined going anywhere near a rifting cave, she panicked.

Marcus had picked up some extra hours one Sunday, and Leah hadn't been put on the schedule that day at the dollar store. She lounged at home, cross-legged on their bed, writing in her journal.

If people only knew her—the real her. If they understood what she'd been through, how she'd misunderstood everything when she'd tried to kill Kaylah…

Leah had gone on tours with Catrina, had been formally presented and acquitted of any crimes. But people still judged.

Tapping her pen on the notebook, Leah recalled something that Saff of all people had said. Leah had asked Kaylah and Rachel's Seeder friend about current Seeder feelings regarding Leah.

As she'd suspected, Seeders had never grown that fond of her.

I can understand how some people struggle to accept you, Saff had said. *They either have rumors to go off of, or official royal tours with carefully crafted speeches.*

Yeah… Those 'carefully crafted' speeches had been dry and official and everything Leah wasn't. No matter how the palace's PR team packaged Leah, it had never felt authentic, and people probably saw that. Catrina had asked her more than once if she'd wanted to say anything for herself, but public speaking was *not* her thing. Even if she'd worked up the guts to try, she'd be a sweaty mess, likely stumbling over another preapproved message.

Leah lamented her position, until something clicked.

***

Marcus returned home a few hours later, coated in sawdust. Leah didn't wait for him to shower. She grabbed him and pulled him in for a kiss. He didn't hesitate to reciprocate. Holding her waist, he eventually pulled back. "If you want a little something more, I can take a quick shower…"

"No. Well, maybe a little later, but I couldn't wait. I think I know what I want to do…"

"Okay…"

"I want to write another book."

He set down his lunch bag and took a spot on the floor. "Another one for the baby, or like that older one you won't let me see?"

She wrinkled her nose. "You'll think it's crap."

Marcus rolled his eyes. "I'm sure it's not half as bad as you think."

"And if my writing *is* crap, you're going to lie and tell me it's good so I don't feel bad."

He clasped his hands, resting them in his lap. "I can be impartial. And my grammar is better than yours. I can proofread…"

It was true. He'd had a better education and had been a better student. "Maybe… But I'm not talking about fiction. I want to write a nonfiction book. An…" She cringed. "Autobiography of sorts? Or memoir? Something that tells my story. Something that gives me the opportunity to change the narrative. More personal?"

He furrowed his brow; she might die on the spot if he thought it was a stupid idea. 'Autobiography' sounded so dry. She wasn't even twenty yet. Presidents and other famous people had books like that published about them, not the villain's daughter, right?

"If you want to, you could give it a go?" Marcus said.

Not exactly a pat on the back.

"But how much are you willing to include?" he asked.

She sat on the couch, blowing out a puff of air. "I don't know yet. I'm still figuring that out." How much of her life did she want to share? How much did she *need to* for people to give her a chance? Would she divulge that she'd shoplifted? That she'd suffered sexual assault? And if she did, to what end? To what extent?

Leah picked at her nails. "I think the only way people will really give me a chance is if they learn more about me, directly from me. Not rumors. Not dry, carefully crafted speeches, you know?"

He nodded, still pensive. "But if you did that, you know it would have to be approved by Aunt Catrina. Royal family involvement and all…"

She frowned. "I know. But I'm willing to try."

Folding his arms, he shrugged. "It's your story. I support you however you want to go about it."

"And the fact that you're part of my story?" She glanced at her round protruding stomach. "A pretty big part of it?"

"I don't expect you to lie," he said softly. "But I *would* like to be able to read it. Have some say, perhaps?"

"Of course!"

"Then it's settled. If it makes you happy, and you think it can make things better for you and that little guy." He pointed at Leah's stomach. "Then I'm on board."

She smiled. "Good. How about you clean up, and I'll see about dinner." She stood, pulling down her shirt. "And then we'll decide what kind of *dessert* we want."

***

A few days later, Leah allowed Marcus to read her progress on the romantic adventure story she'd been working on. It made her cringe to share her work, so she sat on the bed outlining her life story while Marcus read her other book in the living room.

Leah had a lot of work to do. Her journal was helpful, but it wasn't perfectly organized chronologically or by topic, so she still needed to decide how she wanted to approach this.

The blinds were drawn closed, and the overhead light illuminated the room. She dug around the comforter with her bare toes.

"Are you kidding me?" Marcus said from the living room.

"What?"

"No." His voice was firm as he appeared at the bedroom doorway, holding her notebook. "No. Absolutely not."

She hid a grin. "What? You told me you liked my writing."

His eyes were wide. "Yeah. I do. You're actually really good. But this? *No.*"

She feigned innocence. "It's a rough draft. It'll get better."

"A sex scene?"

Releasing that grin, she kept a tone of confusion. "I thought that was some of my best writing yet."

Marcus glanced at the page. "I'll give you that. It's … not bad… But not exactly appropriate for the age range your books are supposed to be written for!"

Leah shrugged.

As he cocked his head to the side, it was more than evident he was willing to die on this hill. "People will assume you wrote this about *us.*"

She waved a dismissive hand. "Psh. That's the fiction one."

"If you ever publish this, *in either world,* green folk will find it and still make assumptions."

Drawing a deep breath, Leah stretched out her legs. Her tone was sweet and seductive. "Marcus… I didn't write that scene for any of these books. I wrote that for *you.*"

He slowly straightened, considering. "You promise? It's not for the books?"

"Yes."

"Okay…" He relaxed, holding the notebook in front of him again. "It is actually really…" He swallowed. "I don't think we've tried a couple of the things in here…"

With an absolute smirk, she replied, "No. We haven't."

He cleared his throat. "You know, I was thinking of going to the store. We're kinda low on bread. And I could … pick up some extra things…"

He understood the assignment.

"Only if you want to." She winked.

He looked like he could pounce right then and there. "I'll order a rideshare. Way faster than taking the bus at this time of night."

She acted casually disinterested. "Up to you. We *are* low on bread."

They shared a grin, and he left the doorway.

"Marcus?"

"What?"

"Can you pick me up some pickles, too?"

"Sure."

His keys clinked from the other room, and he reappeared in the bedroom doorway, a finger extended. "When you say pickles… Is that a … euphemism?"

She laughed. "Dill. The kind I've been eating a lot of."

He chuckled. "Okay. Pickles."

An hour later, he brought back two full grocery bags. Amongst the collection, he had remembered the pickles, but not the bread. That was fine. They had not, in fact, been low on bread.

Chapter 28

AS LEAH NEARED THE SEVEN-MONTH mark of her pregnancy, she and Marcus decided they could make do with her quitting her part-time job. It would be tight on finances, but he was bringing in a steady paycheck, and they still had Kaylah's money for emergencies.

Since Ivy pregnancies only lasted eight months, Leah was large. *Really* large. And tired of the comments and questions of strangers.

And she loved working on her books.

And … she was getting more nervous about the next steps.

From what she'd gathered, Ivy births were similar to human births, with some essential differences. Her mom had escaped the palace with aides who had helped her deliver Leah. Leah had Marcus, but the thought of delivering a child in secret like that was terrifying.

She was about to acknowledge they'd have to go back to the Green Lands for the birth. She was nowhere ready emotionally to go back there, but she didn't have much choice in the matter, not when it came to her safety and that of their child.

"How do you want to go about this?" Marcus asked, massaging her feet as they sat on the couch.

She frowned and groaned. Sneak back and see if they could retain some semblance of privacy somehow?

One of the phones dinged, and they both perked up. It wasn't one of their personal phones. They'd turned the sound up on the one they'd been given at the cave, so they wouldn't miss any pertinent updates.

Marcus grabbed it from its spot on the side table, clicking the screen on as he sat back down. He silently read, surprise on his face. "Well, that's an option." He handed the phone to Leah.

<Hope you kiddos are doing well. Would you like an Ivy nurse to come check you out and prepare for that gremlin?>

Leah smiled. "What do you think?"

Marcus held his hands up. "It's up to you."

Even if they'd still go back, advanced preparations would put Leah much more at ease. She still didn't trust her chemical powers, not after she'd botched the garden at the cottage. She'd felt bad when she couldn't even inject Marcus with numbing when he'd gotten an injury at work, because they weren't willing to experiment on him, not on a Boman.

She wished she'd have studied more from the library book Wren had checked out for her, other than just reading about fertilizing powers during pregnancy.

And in regard to her delivery, Leah didn't want pain. Ivies with powers metabolized things like alcohol and human painkillers a lot faster. Minimal pain during birth was natural for Ivy women, assuming they knew how to balance their energy and their chemical arts. But Leah was in the dark.

"Definitely." She typed out a response and sent it off.

A few minutes later, the phone dinged again with an address, date, and time for an appointment.

<Renting out a private exam room. You'll be in good hands. Love you two!>

Leah's heart warmed. Kaylah was in-realm, though likely more than an hour away at the cave. The address for the nurse's appointment was in the city nearest the cave.

She would've hugged Kaylah if they'd been closer.

***

Less than a week later, Leah and Marcus arrived at the clinic Kaylah had specified. Marcus's boss wasn't all that fond of him taking the afternoon off, but they hadn't been given options, and he wasn't about to miss this.

Leah was sweaty and nervous as they entered and checked in. The receptionist swiftly led them to a private room where a brunette stood and surveyed the equipment, looking sharp in a white button-up shirt and dark grey pencil skirt.

"Hi," Leah said as they popped into the room.

The woman turned.

"Olivia!" Marcus practically lunged for the woman, hugging her.

Olivia smiled. "Hey, Marcus. It's been too long."

Leah closed the door behind them, a little awkward about not knowing the woman.

"Leah, this is Olivia. The best nurse in the kingdom."

Leah shook her hand. "Nice to meet you. How do you guys know each other?" Olivia had to be about Guillen's age.

Olivia kept smiling. "I was the palace head nurse for a time, under Queen, well, Matron Kaylah."

"Oh."

"Take a seat." Olivia gestured to an exam table, and Leah settled onto the edge.

"Aunt Kaylah didn't say it would be you!" Marcus said, standing next to Leah.

Olivia busied herself again with the equipment in the room, inspecting. "Her Majesty and Her Highness were probably working out details, and we had to see if I could clear my schedule."

Leah was a bit iffy on the details of this woman. Never once had Leah been to a doctor, at least according to her recollection, in the human world. Her mom had been too paranoid about them doing an exam that would reveal her green-folk nature. Green folk with powers were also blessed with quick healing and good health.

So the idea of a stranger fiddling around with her body was … new, and uncomfortable.

It was also weird that this nurse and Marcus were close enough to hug.

"Did you leave the palace because the throne changed to Queen Catrina? Or to pursue pediatrics?"

"Neither," Olivia said, clicking on a machine. "But you don't have to worry. I've assisted with several births."

That wasn't reassuring. It wasn't even her specialty…

"She's the best there is," Marcus whispered, and Olivia blushed.

"Do you have kids of your own?" Leah asked.

Olivia faced her, an air of professionalism about her. "I never found the time to start a family of my own. But I assure you, I'll take good care of you." She paused, leaning back against the counter. "I head the Sanath Institute."

Leah's eyes grew wide. "Oh!" That was huge. "Oh." The Sanath Institute had the most progressive and prestigious nursing program in the entire Green Lands. She'd studied it when trying to peg down a career path. "That's amazing. I considered seeing if I could study there, but I realized how far behind everyone else I'd be since I didn't grow up knowing how to use my powers."

"I'm sure we could still get you an interview with the entrance board for consideration."

Leah rested her hands on her huge stomach, trying not to frown. It still didn't feel right to focus her career on powers when her child would be born without them. And she wasn't fond of the idea that she'd only be extended that special exception because of her connections to the royal family.

And, even though it wasn't doing anything for her financially at the moment, Leah was growing more attached to the idea of becoming a writer, a real author with books published.

"Thanks, I'll think about it." She gave Olivia a half-smile.

"Right." Olivia stood tall, gesturing to the machine she'd turned on. "I've trained on human equipment, and this is top of the line. Want an ultrasound? Just to take a peek?"

Leah instantly beamed. "Yes!" The human world had its perks.

As instructed, Leah lay back, and Marcus held her hand.

Olivia prepped a wand with gel, explaining a little about the equipment. The image might be a bit fuzzy due to Leah's Ivy energy, so it would help if Leah could force it away from her stomach where it naturally pooled to support and protect the baby. She channeled it to her extremities. It felt weird, as did the cool gel on the wand. But soon enough, little whooshes filtered through a speaker, and Leah had to fight not to cry. That was her baby. Her and Marcus's actual baby. A little heartbeat.

Marcus kissed her hand and squeezed it tighter.

"Mhmm," Olivia said, facing the screen. "Good job parting your energy. I've got a pretty clear view. And look at that Boman energy." Her voice was sweet, her bedside manner friendly.

"You can tell?" Leah asked. "The difference between an Ivy baby with powers and without?"

Olivia nodded, moving the wand. "Fainter glow. And if you're *really* looking for it, you *might* be able to check for vine nodules, but that's harder."

Leah was over the moon. It made it all so real.

"Did you two want to know their genders today?"

"We were talking about that, and—" *Wait, what?* 'Their' could have been interpreted as gender-neutral, but... "Did you just say genders, with an *S* at the end?"

Olivia smiled brightly. "Yes. Twins."

Leah's jaw dropped.

"Really?" Marcus asked, his voice as confused as Leah's.

"I thought all Bomen are single births…"

"Me too," Marcus echoed.

The *last* thing Leah needed was for more attention because she was having some sort of freaky pregnancy no one had ever heard of. Strike that—the *actual* last thing she needed was for people to assume she'd cheated on Marcus and these children were standard Ivies with powers…

"Can you count again?" Leah asked, a hint of panic in her voice.

Olivia hummed confidently, swiveling the screen. Clear as day—two babies. "See that fuzziness on the screen? That glow?" She pointed to their tiny heads and necks. "Boman glow. This is the third set of Bomen twins I've heard of, actually."

Leah breathed a smidge easier. At least she wasn't going in the history books as a first on this one. But then the reality of having twins smacked her. One was going to be enough to manage, an arm and a vine full. "Two?"

"Isn't that exciting?!" Marcus's tone echoed his sentiments.

Leah, however, was still stunned. She turned her head, enunciating clearly. "You don't get to be excited about that. You don't have to push them out of your body!"

His unadulterated joy was unwavering. "Twice the cute!"

"When you think about it, it's not that much extra work, because—" Olivia stopped and cleared her throat at Leah's reproachful glare, returning her attention to the screen.

"Come on. We've got this," Marcus added a little more calmly.

Leah looked at him. And then it hit her… She allowed his glee to rub off on her, to calm and reassure her. What she would've done to have him be this excited when she'd first broken the pregnancy news to him… She returned his smile.

"They're going to look just like you," he said. "Perfect." He kissed her forehead.

"I'm fairly confident in the genders, if you did want to know them," Olivia said.

They'd agreed to be surprised, but Leah was already surprised by the twins detail, and now she wanted as much information as possible for preparations. *No wonder I'm so huge. At least it's not all the bacon and tacos…*

She looked at Marcus. "I kinda want to know now."

"Sure, why not?"

Olivia pointed out the anatomy. "This one's a girl."

Leah threw Marcus a subtle 'I was right' look.

"And a boy."

Marcus snickered, nudging Leah. So, they both had guessed right.

After another minute of pointing out anatomy and answering questions about what the equipment showed, Olivia turned it off and sat on a stool in the corner of the room. "Do you know what your plans are? Have you been preparing with energy and chemical arts exercises?"

Leah bit her lip. "I didn't study… And I don't have a book about all of that… And Kaylah didn't exactly say what our options are…"

"Well… It's up to you." Olivia folded her arms. "I highly recommend starting the exercises right away, because that makes an Ivy birth massively easier. And *you're* going to be the only one who can regulate your pain. Another Ivy's numbing won't work on you when you're pregnant. It's tricky, but you have to self-regulate."

That sounded both oddly empowering, and frustratingly daunting. "Are you going to be able to teach me?"

"That's part of why I'm here. Were you planning to give birth over here?"

Leah blinked. "If it's an option, then absolutely."

"It is. If you've got the time, let's discuss it."

They spent the next hour forming a plan. Olivia would be rifting over to the human world on the weekends, and stationing another nurse she trusted over here during weekdays. The other nurse would meet with Leah to coach her on exercises in preparation.

The scanning equipment was ideal here, but the couple confessed they didn't live all that close. With Olivia sworn to secrecy, they told her what city they'd settled in, and she said she'd scout out another birthing location. Given Leah was a mother with powers, her pregnancy was very low risk, even with twins.

"And then the last week, both of us will plan to be here full time until these little ones arrive."

Leah was *so* relieved and much more confident in the path ahead of her. Marcus was excited and supportive.

But they also had to decide who would be clued in on their news, assuming they even had a choice in the matter. Catrina and Stephan would be notified, as well as Kaylah and Eric, and Rachel and Guillen. It didn't feel right to keep them all in the dark, and they'd keep the secret.

Leah and Marcus left the appointment after exchanging contact details with Olivia. She'd have the other nurse reach out soon about helping Leah prepare.

Needing groceries anyway, Leah and Marcus swung by the store on the way back to their apartment. Once home, they sat on the couch, enjoying a quart of rocky road ice cream straight from the carton.

"Here's to *two* of them." Leah held up her spoon, wide-eyed. Marcus grinned and clinked his spoon against hers.

This was perfect, absolutely perfect. They hadn't been ready to return to the Green Lands, and they'd be able to have the kids here. But a nagging feeling slowly brought Leah's spirits down.

Rachel. Leah remembered Rachel's reproach, how she'd shared that she had once yearned to experience the gift of life. Now she was becoming a first-time grandmother, and her future daughter-in-law was at fault for cutting her out of the equation.

Rachel wasn't the entitled type. With extra time and perspective, Leah now genuinely regretted how things had gone down between them at the cottage. Had Rachel been a bit overbearing? Yeah. And she'd reacted to the news in a way that had ruffled Leah's feathers.

But she'd been trying to help, and some of those problems were of Marcus's causing. Rachel was sweet and kind and forgiving. And unable to come to the human world. Even if Leah chose to make an exception to their no-contact rule with their families, Rachel couldn't be there for the birth.

Leah stared at her spoon, frowning. "Do you think your mom will ever forgive me for doing this over here?"

He matched her frown, his eyes conveying he understood. "She'll be sad. But she wants you to be happy, too."

And then Leah remembered everything her parents had put Rachel's family through, and how extraordinary it was that she had forgiven Leah, that she even tolerated Leah.

Neither a human-world birth laden with guilt nor a Green Lands birth filled with anxiety was ideal.

Marcus reached over, taking Leah's hand, and kissed her engagement ring. "This is about *our* family. You and me and our *mini-me*s."

She nodded, forcing a smile. She'd be able to come to terms with it. And then she gazed down at her ring. They hadn't held any real conversations about marriage since Marcus's proposal months ago. He was probably too scared of her running away again or thinking twice about it. But this had also been a bit of a trial run to see if they could make things work. She was confident now that they could.

"What do you want to do about the wedding?" she asked.

Chapter 29

MARCUS EYED LEAH, FINISHING ANOTHER spoonful of ice cream. "What about the wedding?"

"What do you want it to look like? Venue? Timeframe? People?"

He scrunched his eyebrows in thought. "I dunno. What do you want?"

"Nope. I asked you."

Sighing, he set down his spoon. "I always imagined, you know, the whole big wedding thing. My aunt *is* the queen, after all. But I know that's not what you want."

She mulled it over. It wasn't what she wanted at all. She'd faintly learned to *imagine* getting to a place where she was capable of enduring a giant ceremony with all eyes on her, back before she'd gotten pregnant, but now…

That didn't mean this was going to be one-sided. He deserved to get something he wanted, and maybe that was a sacrifice Leah could make. Or maybe even if it was something small in the Green Lands, his mom could be there, to make up for missing the birth?

"You know me: crowds and I don't get along. And I would have *literally* no one on my side of the wedding that wasn't already on your side, because I'm *absolutely* not inviting anyone from my mom's side of the family. But I can … do what you want…"

"That doesn't exactly sound like an ideal bridal situation."

Her heart was heavy. Couldn't she just have this special day without guilt? A bride getting what she wanted? "I know, but we agreed to compromise, to meet in the middle."

His eyes were warm, his voice soft. "All I've ever wanted was *you*."

She had to blush at that. Since they weren't eating the ice cream anymore, she put the lid back on and took it to the freezer. "You know, that's not completely true. You haven't *always* wanted me."

"Lies."

"Hmm." She nestled into his arms on the couch. "Exhibit A: dating that human girl after I asked you out."

"What? Exhibit A: I thought a super pretty and bold girl asked me to shoot archery, and I made an idiot of myself by calling it a date and finding out she did *not* consider it a date."

Leah let out a breathy chuckle. "But after I asked you on a real date, you went on *two* dates with some human girl! I was throwing myself at you!"

"Hey, now. I'd already asked her on the first, and I didn't want to be rude."

"And the second? That was *torture* waiting for you to decide."

"She asked, and I felt bad saying no."

"You admit you were spineless?"

His lips brushed against her ear as he whispered playfully. "You don't get to be mad, because you didn't even like me yet."

She pouted. "I liked you as a friend. And I *definitely* liked the way your butt looked in jeans…"

He nibbled her ear, exploring her body ever so gently with his hands. She was putty in his arms.

"So, what do *you* want?" he asked.

"Right now?"

He knew exactly what he was making her want.

Kissing the back of her head, he slid his hands to her giant stomach. "How about we figure that out in a few minutes? For now, what do you want with the wedding?"

Right. Yes. That…

"Honestly, I'm willing to compromise, but my ideal right now is just … us. Make it official. I kind of even would like to do it before the babies come. Is that weird? Would you hate having me this big for our wedding?"

"I'd be okay with all of that. I was the one who wanted to move up our timeline, remember?"

She narrowed her eyes, resting her head on his chest. "You'd really be okay with an elopement?"

"We're already halfway there."

***

There were two bridal shops in the area, and Leah went to them both. It was depressing. Unsurprisingly, they didn't have entire sections dedicated to dresses designed for superpregnant mothers. And the plus-size options were abysmal.

And she was shopping alone. Marcus offered to join her, but she wanted to keep *something* a surprise for the wedding. If she hadn't nearly died of mortification from her visit at the cottage, Leah might have considered breaking the no-family ban to shop with Camry.

This was one of those events she imagined she would have loved to do with her mom… At least … the mom she'd known before coming to the Green Lands.

At the first shop, a spiteful voice told her it was a joke for a slut like Leah to even consider a white dress. She almost listened to it. But she wanted white, so she reminded that voice to take a hike. She prayed that someday down the road, it would be faint enough for her to not keep hearing those kinds of comments.

At the second shop, her own guilt told her she didn't *need* a special dress to elope, and it wasn't her money to spend. This was going to go on Kaylah's card.

She tried to push past that one, because Kaylah would want her to be happy. But … it was a hefty fee they were quoting to take a frumpy plus-size option and rush fit it to her.

Leah stared at herself in a mirror, adorned in a ghastly lace-covered dress that was tight on her stomach and baggy everywhere else. She did *not* feel like a bride.

They still wanted to make a sale. "I think it's great you're doing it now; that way you and your babies can share their dad's last name, right?"

Leah laughed way more than she ought to. Ivy society was matriarchal. With some exceptions in the Elonta and Elanna royal line, the woman's surname was taken by her husband and children. But none of that actually mattered for Leah and Marcus. They already had the same last name—Elonto. Exactly five people in both worlds—human or Green Lands—shared that last name, one designated for royalty-adjacent misfits like them…

After the failed assassination attempt, Leah was offered a choice as to what she would be called. She wasn't fond of keeping her human-world alias—Edwards. It had all been a lie, and she'd wanted to leave it behind as she started a new life. She'd wanted nothing to do with her mom's family because of the way they'd treated Bomen, so she also turned down their surname—Remsgard. As her dad had been a prince, Leah was given the Elonto option.

Leah's shoulders slumped. Why was she in a dress shop letting someone try to talk her into this gosh-awful getup that she was going to pay way too much money on and feel guilty about, just to hate it?

"I'm going to have to think about it, but thanks."

With all the charm and sweetness of condescension coated in a bucket of sugar, the saleswoman addressed her. "No offense, honey, but your wedding is soon, and that baby bump isn't getting smaller."

Yep, that sealed the deal. "Then I'll pass, thanks."

Leah returned home and did some online searching. She found a website that offered beautiful bridesmaids dresses, including maternity options, and you could change the color to white. Happy to pay for rush shipping, she whipped out the card and let out a huge breath of relief.

***

Human–green-folk relations had become more complex in the last two decades as Seeder and Ivy societies made drastic changes, and their interactions with humans took on new purposes.

Admittedly, a lot of what green folk did in the human world was technically illegal. They all used fake identities to travel, obtain bank accounts, and study. But as long as it was done in the right spirit, keeping the Green Lands secret and safe, then those in the know overlooked it.

The marriage license would be a fake, but despite that, all human-world marriages were recognized as legal back in the Green Lands.

Leah's wedding dress arrived. It was a simple flowy design, and it made her smile. It fit just right around her stomach and chest, so she was grateful she'd ordered a size up.

They found a local pastor to perform the ceremony, but they needed a witness. It was awkward to confess they didn't have anyone. The pastor offered to have his wife attend. Leah and Marcus said they'd think about it.

Lying in bed, they snuggled up to each other, chatting about their day and making final decisions.

"How was your meeting with the nurse today?" Marcus asked.

"Pretty good." She threaded her fingers through his curly hair. "I definitely wish I'd started learning earlier."

If left untrained, she'd have to endure the birth much like unmedicated humans did, which was a terrifying thought. With her trained, it should go much smoother—quicker and minimally painful, fast to heal. But the training was complex. It was similar to how she'd heard Seeder flight was achieved, in that she'd have to shift her energy to the right places in her body to help the process along. It would help prevent injury and aid healing, all the while she'd try to keep her calm and focus on her chemical arts to balance things out.

Marcus smiled. "You'll do great."

She adjusted herself on the bed. "And what are your thoughts on the wedding witness?"

He softly grunted. "It's weird having someone witness who we don't actually know."

"I've been thinking about it, and there's another option that doesn't involve family… And they're *kind of* mutual."

"Yeah?"

Leah bit her lip. "What about seeing if Jake can make it?"

Marcus instantly lit up. "Really?"

She smiled as well. "Really. Why don't you message him and see if he wants to come? As long as he can keep a secret. And … you can enjoy a bachelor's night with him."

Marcus kissed her, then grabbed his phone from the bedside table. He typed up a message. After sending it, he gave Leah another smooch and cuddled back up. "But if we do a bachelor's night, what will *you* do?"

Jake and his girlfriend, who Leah had met in high school, were still together, but long distance, as she'd started to attend a university a few states away.

Leah breathed deeply, something that came with more effort these days. "I'll be happy here. I've been neglecting my journal with all the wedding and baby preparations."

Marcus wouldn't get drunk or have strippers; neither he nor Jake were like that. They'd probably play video games all night. "Are you sure?"

"My gift. Go have fun."

He eyed her skeptically. "We'll see what Jake says."

***

Jake responded soon enough and cleared his schedule. It didn't take much convincing for Marcus to agree to a bachelor's night since they hadn't seen each other in nearly a year.

And Leah really was fine hanging out at the apartment. Marcus came home shortly after midnight. He took a half day at work that Friday, and cleaned up, donning a sharp black suit. Leah wore a cute pink maternity dress she'd found, and Marcus carried her wedding dress in a garment bag.

It was a calm day in late April, and Leah's birthday. She'd always grown up celebrating her birthday in late November. That had been one of many lies told to her by her mother. The lie had been somewhat understandable, given Beata's paranoia about being found while in hiding. More than one of her aides had gone missing, and she'd always been afraid they had ratted on her, disclosing that she'd given birth in the human world.

Leah might have continued to celebrate on the November date if it had been *any* other day. Beata had been paranoid, but also too sentimental and guilt-ridden about her husband. She'd always celebrated Leah's birthday on *Soren's* birthday. The moment Leah had learned that, she'd chosen to celebrate on her true birthday.

It was a fitting day to be a bride. She celebrated another year of her life, and would soon bring new life into the world. This wedding would give her and Marcus a new start.

They met the pastor at the church, and Leah excused herself to get changed. Marcus lingered outside the door, and soon enough his voice became louder, joined by Jake's. Leah had only seen Jake once since she'd moved to the Green Lands. This would be fun for her too.

As the guys shot the breeze, Leah struggled to zip up the dress; it got caught on the fabric. Her vines could reach the zipper, but couldn't grasp it well enough to tug it free. She carefully cracked the door. "Marcus, I need your help," she muttered.

"Yeah, sure." He stepped up to the door. "But you said I couldn't see you yet."

She huffed. "Then close your eyes. It's not that hard to feel a zipper."

The door creaked as it widened, and his hands slipped inside the changing room. And then those hands roamed everywhere but the zipper. "I can't seem to find it."

"Stop it," she scolded.

"Ope, there it is. I'm usually much better blindfolded, aren't I?"

She blushed. "Stop it! We're in a *church*," she whispered.

"You never attended church a single time in this world," he whispered back, freeing the stuck zipper.

"So what? I know how to act in one…"

He softly chuckled, zipping it and kissing her on the neck.

"Thank you. I'll be out in a minute."

She straightened her dress and touched up her kissproof lipstick. Did she feel like a bride? Kinda? None of this was going the way she'd imagined growing up. But a smile still came to her lips, her anticipation building.

Leah took a deep breath and stepped out of the changing room for her big reveal, into the hallway where the guys chatted again.

She smiled brightly at Jake. "Hey!"

He did not smile. His jaw dropped, and his eyes widened, staring right at her baby bump. "*Wow*, Leah, you're… Wow!"

Rolling her eyes, she stood taller. "Pointing out how huge a massive pregnant bride is *isn't* the most polite thing to do."

Jake looked confused. "No. I just … didn't know you were!"

Placing her hands on her hips, she turned to Marcus. He stood there smirking. "You didn't tell him?!"

Marcus let out a goofy laugh. "I thought it would be more fun if it was a surprise!"

She lightly smacked his arm. "Not funny."

He kept laughing.

Jake recovered enough to pick up his jaw. "I mean, you look *great*, Leah."

"Mhmmm…"

"And it's *twins*," Marcus said.

Jake looked as confused as they had been about that announcement, and Marcus clarified that they weren't the first Bomen twins out there.

"Cool," Jake said. "I was wondering why you guys weren't having a big wedding back in the kingdom… So, this is why?"

Leah bit her lip. *No talk of back home. No guilt or spiraling.* "Nope. We just wanted it to be small, and to collude with our friend again. Like old times." She winked.

He gave her an ironic grin.

"We shouldn't keep the pastor waiting," Marcus said, offering his hand.

Leah took it, and they headed toward the room the pastor had designated for the ceremony.

"You do look breathtaking," Marcus whispered in her ear.

The ceremony was short. No pomp and circumstance. Just three friends and a stranger with authority to seal the deal. Leah held a bouquet, and they exchanged simple vows. She didn't cry, but she was at peace, a calmness settling into her soul. Marcus's smile was a mile wide.

They took a few pictures on their phones at the church and on the surrounding grounds. Everything was in bloom, and even if the spring here didn't hold quite the idyllic beauty it did in the Green Lands, this particular one couldn't be beat.

After Leah changed back into her more casual dress, the trio of friends went out for steak.

They gabbed and laughed. It wouldn't be everyone's idea of a successful wedding day, but it worked for them.

After occupying their table for far too long, the group said their goodbyes and parted ways.

Marcus had rented a car for the weekend, and he drove Leah to a resort forty-five minutes away.

It wasn't until they checked in and settled in that Leah fully relaxed, fully processed everything. A simple brand-new ring she'd bought for Marcus now gleamed on his finger as he carried in their things.

They were *married*. Man and wife. Woman and husband. Soon-to-be parents. Best friends.

Leah rested on the sofa, glancing out the sliding glass door to a balcony.

"I only have one regret about our wedding," Marcus said.

She frowned.

"We didn't get to dance. But we can do that now…" He pulled out his phone, selected some music, and extended his hands.

Smiling, she took them and hoisted herself up. She wrapped her arms around his neck and let him lead.

"Music," Marcus said. "I think I miss music most about the human world when I'm back home. Because you don't need a band over here to listen to it. And you don't have to hear me screeching out songs like a tree full of chatterbirds during mating season."

Leah chuckled as they swayed. "You're not *that* bad."

He beamed, sneaking a kiss. "How does it feel to be married?"

She drew lazy circles on his neck with her thumbs. How did it feel? They'd already been living together. Had already started a family together. People said it was only a piece of paper all the time. Leah used to think that way. But something special clicked into place for her in that moment, as he held her in his arms, her belly poking against his. He'd promised in his vows that he would always be by her side, and she believed it. They'd come so far, grown so much.

Her life had been an incomplete puzzle, all askew, a mess. She'd been fighting to line up the pieces, to match up the colors and patterns, and most of the time floundering.

There were still a lot of pieces left to sort, so much unknown about the future. But this day, this little step, was like snapping the last piece of the border into place. It gave her a secure framework. It gave her hope and happiness. And Marcus had always been that for her. Marcus was her home.

Her heart full, tears gathered in her eyes. "It feels great."

Chapter 30

THE NEWLYWEDS ENJOYED THE WEEKEND alone on their little getaway. It was hard to not acknowledge how blissfully silent it was at the resort. The absence of traffic, or neighbors with their movies and video games up too high, was stark.

They sipped smoothies their last morning there, sharing a wicker bench on the balcony, discussing preparations for the babies' arrival.

One baby was expensive. Two babies… Someday they'd find a way to pay Kaylah back.

Marcus's eyebrows knit as he sat pensive. "Did I ever apologize for getting you the wrong birth control tonic?"

She searched her memories. "I don't remember." They'd been in a pretty heated conversation when she'd told him.

"I am sorry. I mean, not that I'm sorry that we're having them, because I want them, but you know…"

She smiled softly. "I know." One of the babies kicked, and she moved his hand to feel it. He always ate that up.

"I promise I'll be more careful," he said. They hadn't brought any tonic with them, and as the tonics required ingredients only available in the Green Lands, they couldn't brew up their own even if they knew how to. Hormonal birth control wouldn't help either, as Ivy chemistry didn't align closely enough with that of humans. They'd have to use other methods of contraception while in the human world.

Like the dimmed energy over here, and the constant noise of electronics, ease and comfort of contraception was one more mental tally mark in Leah's mind as she processed where they were going with their lives. And the fact that she had to keep her vines hidden when in public sometimes brought back hurtful memories of her childhood and being forced to repress that side of herself.

Marcus broke her from her reverie. "We should peg down baby names. Or do you think we should wait until we see them?"

She slurped up the last of her smoothie, setting the glass down beside the bench. "I think one less unknown makes me less crazy. What are your thoughts?"

He shrugged.

Leah adjusted her seat. "I know Kaylah was joking in her text, and Ivies don't normally do middle names, but what would you think about giving them middle names? And having the girl's be Kaylah?"

Marcus smiled. "I'm okay with that." He rested a hand on her leg. "Any other suggestions?"

She chuckled. "I'm all out of names from decent people in *my* family, unless you want to include Eric." As soon as she said it, guilt weighed her down for so easily dismissing her mom. But Beata would never be a complimentary name for a child in the Green Lands. It was like a modern human naming their child Stalin or Putin.

"Mmm…" Marcus rocked his head back and forth. "No offense to Uncle Eric, but how would you feel about the boy's middle name being Guillen?"

Marcus respected his father *so* much. Guillen was kind. He had kind of implied that Leah wasn't equal to his son when he'd visited at the cottage, but she'd come to understand where he was coming from. His parents' marriage had been disastrous. He had also given Leah permission to not marry Marcus, and that was a bit awkward now that they'd tied the knot. But he'd given her permission no one else had. And he'd been the first to actually congratulate her on her pregnancy.

Leah rested her hand on Marcus's. "I think that's a great idea."

And then to decide on the first names… They considered other Ivy and human traditions. In the end, they agreed upon Aspen for the girl, Ash for the boy. It made Leah twice as excited to finally meet them.

Marcus carefully lifted Leah's shirt, exposing her stomach. He leaned down, pressing his lips to her skin, and then blew a massive raspberry.

Leah gasped, clenched, and pushed him off. "I swear you made them both just kick my bladder!"

He laughed. "Sorry."

She offered him a dirty look.

"I *am* sorry." His tone was all but apologetic as he lifted a hand to his heart. "But I've been neglecting giving you good luck. I think we're gonna have to do it three times a day until we meet them, to make sure everything goes smoothly."

She threw him a death glare. "You can give them luck once we meet them. I will continue to exercise my powers *without* your special brand of good luck, thank you very much."

He only smirked in response, and it took everything she had to not cave and kiss that smirk right off his face.

***

Seeder reproduction worked like clockwork; it was extremely predictable. Ivy pregnancies weren't on that level, but they were still far less risky and more predictable than those of humans.

Almost to the day, Leah went into labor around her eight-month mark. Olivia and her accompanying nurse were ready for her at a private birthing center.

She hadn't mastered the techniques the nurses had tried to teach her. The birth was painful and stressful, and involved a little swearing, a lot of sweat, and plenty of tears. Marcus gripped her hand tightly through it all, much calmer than she'd expected him to be.

Aspen and Ash were beautiful, their little cries music to Leah's ears. There weren't words to express their perfection and how much it meant to finally meet them.

As the nurses cleaned them up, Leah rested, taking slow breaths. Her Ivy energy and chemical powers surged within her as they tried to find a proper equilibrium again. Her stomach cramped as it set to work healing already. "If we ever do that again, I'm practicing those exercises from *day one*," she said.

"You'll want to have more kids?" Marcus asked sweetly, brushing aside a wisp of hair plastered to her forehead with sweat.

She stared at him. "Not the best time to make that decision."

He chuckled, kissing her cheek. "You were great, Mom."

And then she started to cry again. *Mom*. She was a mom.

They set little Aspen and Ash on Leah's chest, and her heart overflowed. They were *perfect*. They both had a full head of hair, and as expected, it was black like Leah's. They also had her and her mom's nose. Eye color could change a little with time as they grew, but for now, their eyes were light brown, and she hoped they'd stay that way. Leah's love for her own green eyes had been tainted by learning about the man she'd gotten them from.

Nursing the twins was intimidating, especially with two of them, but they sorted it out. She was grateful for that. They could have survived off formula, but it was expensive, and she planned to stay home. Plus, they didn't have any kittlefruit in the human world, the type of nourishment green folk used when babies over there couldn't nurse.

By nightfall, the couple returned to their apartment with two little swaddled ones in car seats. Leah rested, cuddling with the twins in bed while Marcus ordered them dinner. This had been such a massive hurdle in her life. From her puzzle box, it felt like a lot more than just two pieces clicking into place. It was more like an entire row.

She beamed as Ash made an adorable soft baby grunt in his sleep. With Marcus, this was her world. She'd never wanted to rule the kingdom, even if people misinterpreted the assassination attempt that way. She'd never been big on traveling, not when her mom had forced her to move so much growing up. She was a homebody. She wanted a place to call home, and people who wouldn't leave her, who she wouldn't have to leave. For once, she had that.

****

It took time to get their routine down as a family of four. Marcus couldn't take much time off if he wanted to keep his job, not as a newer employee with questionable work history, references, and legal paperwork.

Both Leah and Marcus gave their all, taking turns with shopping, cooking, and changing diapers. When she wasn't too exhausted and could make the time, Leah continued to work on her stories. The adventure in her fictional novels was enough for her. The truths in her memoir were hard to face, but also freeing, especially when she considered how it might change people's perspective of her.

On one of his days off, Marcus prepared dinner while the twins napped. Leah sat on the couch, scratching away at the plot of her adventure romance work in progress. Marcus kept encouraging her to continue. She definitely needed more opinions than his, but she enjoyed imagining herself as an author. She'd be crushed if other people read it and decided it was rubbish. But even then, she was willing to learn, to improve—as a writer and as a person.

In some ways, she'd corrupted Marcus, changing him from the shy, obedient, nerdy kid to a runaway, and one who was not shy in the bedroom. But he'd tamed her, too. She wasn't chasing the thrill with the next guy or party or shoplifting haul. She was a bookworm and a mother.

Marcus handed Leah a plate of taco salad, and she set her work aside. "I like what you did with the last chapter," he said, easing down next to her.

"Thanks." She smiled. "I've been doing some thinking… If we're serious about this being my thing, I want to publish the adventure romance books here, in the human world."

He raised an eyebrow. "That's … not going to go well. We should stick to Green Lands publishing, where it's, you know, legal…"

She sighed. The secrecy from humans was understandable. Imagine the uproar if the masses of humans discovered there was an alternate realm filled with botanical beings on their own planet? "I know… But it's fiction. People will think it's fake, like fairies and dragons and all that."

He eyed her, and she huffed. "Blah, blah, blah. Joint laws with Seeders, Ivies, and Bomen. I get it. But I could change the details. Instead of green folk in the Green Lands, they'll be … butterfly people in the … Blue Lands?"

Marcus laughed. "Butterfly people? Blue Lands?"

She pointed her fork at him. "Don't judge me. I'm sure most humans would think *we're* ridiculous."

Shrugging, Marcus dug into his salad.

"There's a wider audience in the human world, ya know? Instead of a few million potential readers, it's a few billion."

He crunched down on a piece of romaine. "If you do butterfly people, you could publish in both worlds."

She wrinkled her nose. That was true, but she also kind of didn't want people in the Green Lands to read those books. It felt weird to mingle her memoir and identity with something fun and playful. "We'll see." Maybe she'd use a pen name to separate them.

"What about those stories back at Kaylah's?" he asked. "The ones you wrote for Aspen and Ash?"

That brought another smile to her face. "I still want to get them made up. But I'd want them professionally illustrated." She cringed. "I don't want to give our kids nightmares."

"You should ask Saff."

Leah furrowed her brow. "Your mom and Kaylah's Seeder friend? I'm sure she's got enough on her plate."

He shrugged in reply.

Leah recalled a painting at Kaylah's estate. "Kaylah probably doesn't even know who painted it, and I don't know if they can do people, but there's a painting in her library I love. The colors are really soft. It's of daisies in a vase. I think I'd like the style if it were in watercolor."

Marcus choked on his salad and laughed. "Saff painted that."

Leah pursed her lips. "Fine. Point made."

***

Day after day, week after week, time passed, and they found their groove. Before Leah stopped meeting with Olivia for checkups, Olivia delivered congratulations from Marcus's family back in the Green Lands. No official announcements had been made. Olivia provided Leah and Marcus with two Boman jade tokens for Aspen and Ash so they could rift. And … to their discomfort, they discovered people were looking for the couple, here in the human world.

Had Marcus never gotten back together with Leah, he probably would have faded more into obscurity once there was a proper prince in the Ivy Kingdom to dote over, and now four princesses. But … Leah was gossip-worthy. They were a pair people kept tabs on. She'd been in hiding too long; they'd both been missing for far too long to go unnoticed. People had even stuck their noses in Marcus's family's business on this side of things, showing up at his grandparents' house, and that of Tobias and Camry.

As Leah healed physically and emotionally, she fought against the tug to go home, at least to the home Marcus had grown up in. *This* world had been her home. With the comforts of modern electronics, planes that could take you anywhere you needed, *light bulbs.*

But every day, she felt that subtle tug, that her time here was running out. She wasn't a Seeder; cut off from the energy of her ancestral realm, she wouldn't die like they did. But she *did* feel that lacking in her Ivy energy, every day.

Marcus, Aspen, and Ash wouldn't feel it nearly as much since they were Bomen with only wisps of Ivy energy. Aspen and Ash probably wouldn't even know the difference, since they'd never experienced the Green Lands. But could Leah really take them away from family, from their heritage? Just because she didn't like the attention over there?

No one had ever hunted for Leah when she was a child. They'd tried to hunt down her mom, but had eventually given up. They hadn't known about Leah until she'd revealed herself.

Now, she'd never be left alone. How long would it take for people to track them down? Would she and Marcus move to Argentina to run away? The thought of forcing her children into a life of hiding was nauseating.

So, she continued to write her memoir. Hopefully, someday it would make a difference.

And as she did so, Leah started to forgive herself. As she and Marcus grew into their parenthood and proceeded to focus on being better communicators, she started to see others' perspectives better, and began to forgive some of them too.

But she worried… Where would her relationship with her mom come out at the end of it all?

Chapter 31

ASPEN AND ASH WERE NEARLY five months old. Leah's manuscripts were getting close to completion. Marcus kept working construction, and he seemed to really enjoy it.

In the haze of a dream, Leah sat tall in a fancy dress purchased and fitted for her by the palace. She crossed her ankles as a proper lady ought to, wearing a perma-smile for the crowd. This meeting was taking place in Capital City, a gathering of mostly Bomen.

Leah tried not to sweat, tried not to show fear or panic. She was well-mannered, repentant—everything she should be to win over the people.

Queen Catrina, King Stephan, and other politicians and public servants took turns addressing the crowd. They shared plans for the future of Bomen, and more than one gestured to Leah, commenting how she'd come to realize the error of her ways. She was a shining example of how far people could come in accepting those born without powers. Leah tensed to not squirm, to keep that smile on her face as eyes rested on her.

Luckily, it hadn't been all about her, but it was an opportunity to show her off, to clear her name, to help her settle in.

As the rally came to a close, Leah and the others on the platform stood. She tried not to fidget, keeping that smile that told everyone she wasn't crazy or hateful.

To her surprise, a redheaded woman approached the platform, right in front of where Leah stood. She must have been an Ivy Boman, assuming the child she held in her arms was hers. The adorable little child had deep red splotches on its face and neck—the mark of a *Biman*. Less than a handful of Bimen existed in the Green Lands, the offspring of Ivy Boman mothers and Seeder Boman fathers.

Leah marveled at the child, at the miracle of unity it represented. She wished Marcus could have attended with her that day, her smile becoming more genuine.

And then the woman's gaze turned harsh, and she gave Leah a vulgar gesture. She stared Leah dead in the eye as Leah's heart faltered, as her smile faded. No, the woman hadn't wanted to talk. Hadn't wanted to give Leah a chance. She'd wanted to show her child and remind Leah that had her parents won the war, had things turned out according to their plans, this child would have been born into slavery, or more likely—wouldn't have existed at all.

Leah wanted to vomit. The child began to wail. Leah tried to open her mouth to say something, to reassure the woman she wasn't like her parents, didn't think that way, that she *loved* a Boman. But her mouth wouldn't budge.

The child continued to wail, louder and louder, as the woman simply turned and walked away.

Come back! I can explain everything!

Why is the crying getting louder?

Leah woke with a start, her heart racing. *What the… No, that's…* The crying was from one of hers. Either Aspen or Ash was crying.

She blew out a breath to collect herself, closing her eyes. The mind sucked when it played tricks like that. That rally *had* happened in real life. That interaction with the mother had happened.

It didn't matter. Hopefully, Leah's book would make a difference someday?

The bed was cold next to her, a dim light glowing through the open bedroom door. Marcus must have gotten up with one or both of the twins at some point.

Leah pulled back the covers and stumbled to the doorway. Marcus sat on the couch in his boxers, softly shushing Aspen. "No waking Mommy," he whispered. "Mommy needs sleep." His voice was groggy but gentle.

He lifted Aspen, sniffing her diaper. "Oh, man! What is Mom feeding you?!"

Leah watched while leaning against the doorframe.

"No more tacos for Mom, that's what I say, Stinky One," he cooed in the most adorable baby talk. Setting her next to him, Marcus grabbed a diaper and wipes, then proceeded to clean her up.

Leah held a hand to her heart, smiling wide as he took care of a now-calm Aspen. He continued to talk to her, animated and sweet.

Marcus was always like this with the twins. He'd been a great cousin to the prince and princesses. He was a great father.

And then Aspen giggled at his silliness. Her first giggle.

Leah turned to mush, her heart full, her smile gone. A thousand emotions flooded her, pouring out in the form of tears. Marcus was the type of dad she'd imagined she would have had as a little girl. The kind of dad she *wouldn't* have actually had if he'd lived—not with a monster like Soren.

With Marcus, she never once feared her children wouldn't be safe with him. Never once feared she'd have to choose between her kids and her husband.

That dream, that memory of the Boman mother… Even if it was the case that Bomen never came to accept Leah, they accepted Marcus. There was confusion about why Marcus would still be with Leah after what she'd done, but he was an insider they respected. And even if it hurt Leah to never be included in their circle, despite being a mother to Bomen, Marcus was a Boman and could help their kids where she lacked, where she was unwelcome or uncomfortable.

He deserved the world. He deserved to be happy.

Leah sniffled, wiping away tears. Marcus's gaze shot up to her. He only now realized he had an audience. "What's wrong?" Concern painted his face. "Are you okay?"

She nodded, sniffling again. "I'm fine."

"Do you want to talk?"

As she walked in, Aspen stirred once more.

Leah picked her up, supporting her with vines. "Might as well get a two-in-one diaper change and feeding." She sat back on the couch. "We all know you like Mom's *taco-flavored milk*." She gave Marcus a look.

He snickered. "You heard that, huh? I'm just saying, it might be the hot sauce…"

Leah rolled her eyes.

"Did you hear her giggle?" Marcus asked, wearing a broad smile.

Aspen latched on. "Yeah," Leah whispered. "It was cute."

He sweetly ran a finger up and down Leah's arm. "So, what's wrong? Why were you crying?"

They'd been happy tears. Mostly… "I…" She wanted to say it, but it was almost impossible to push out, and once she did, she couldn't take it back. She couldn't dangle that carrot in front of him and then take it back, not when he'd been so patient. "I think it's time to go home."

He studied her a moment, cautious. "Really?"

There was indeed hope in his voice. He'd been patient as she'd healed, as they'd worked to figure out what they'd needed as individuals, as a couple, as a family. But he had always wanted to be home, even if he'd never said so.

"Really." She explained her reasoning. She could continue working on her manuscripts anywhere. His family deserved to see him and meet the twins. And they couldn't hide forever.

"If you're sure, then I'm on board."

"I'm sure."

As she nursed and rocked Aspen back to sleep, they discussed their timeline and how they'd go about everything.

Long after Aspen drifted off, they continued to chat. Something nagged at Leah, her heart hurting as they discussed returning home.

And normally, she'd have buried that feeling, would have suppressed it until it probably came out in some unhealthy form of resentment. But they'd promised to be open and honest as a couple. And even though she knew it wasn't exactly right, she couldn't deny her feelings.

"When we get back … I know that…"

He'd explicitly declared during their big argument—before he'd left her—that she couldn't do what she wanted to right now.

"I know my mom can be a better person. And I know it's wrong, but I… Part of me wants her to be able to see the kids." Her mom hadn't been there to dress shop with her. To plan things. To help in the delivery room. Her mom had missed the most important moments of her life. And even though Leah recognized her mom's faults and shortcomings and sins, a part of her ached to have her in her life—the one constant she'd always known. And if her mom accepted her kids, maybe she'd finally recognize how twisted her prejudices were.

Marcus pressed his lips thin, looking down. He had to be angry, disappointed. "Let's talk about that."

***

The next day, after taking time to sleep on their decisions, they used their extra phone to text Kaylah. They didn't really know the state of things or how they'd be received when they arrived at the cave. This was going to be a *huge* move, and there were preparations to make.

A few days later, a text arrived from Kaylah.

<So excited to see you!!! Safe to head over. Give me forty-eight hours heads-up whenever you're ready, and I'll be there.>

She also provided a different number to text, that of a cell that would stay with a cave employee in the human world. They'd be dispatched to send for her.

Leah battled her nerves, but pushed forward. What they'd do with their belongings was the easiest decision to make. You couldn't rift with much other than what was stuffed in your pockets. Most big things they'd acquired were secondhand anyway, so they started to redonate them along with other items. It chipped a little at Leah's heart that they'd have to give up most of the clothes and toys they'd bought the kids. But they would never lack in the Green Lands. She picked out her favorite ones and donated the others to a women's and children's shelter.

They gave their apartment notice and cleared the place out. Marcus quit his job and collected his last paycheck. They took a rideshare to the city Marcus's family lived in, and rented a hotel room.

After their whirlwind of preparations, they texted the number Kaylah had given them, and quickly received a reply that they'd send for her.

Needing to keep their most important belongings compact, Leah had spent time at the library typing up her manuscripts and printing them in small print with narrow margins. They went to a drugstore and printed tons of photos of them, their wedding, and the kids.

Now, it was a matter of waiting the forty-eight hours, and visiting people in town. They met up with Jake for breakfast at a pancake place. It was his first time meeting the twins. Aspen made a mess by grabbing a syrup-covered pancake from Marcus's plate, and Ash cried for the last ten minutes. Parenthood had its perks. Since Jake would likely marry a human and be unable to have children with her, the twins' antics probably didn't serve as birth control, but still…

Despite the chaos with the kids, that was the visit she'd been looking forward to the most. The next was nerve-racking, and Leah considered having Marcus go without her, but she needed to get to a place where she could stand tall and endure scrutiny. Because scrutiny *would* come.

They each carried a car seat as they approached Tobias and Camry's house. Marcus squeezed Leah's free hand.

As Marcus rang the doorbell, Leah took a breath to bolster herself. *I can do this.*

Camry opened the door, all smiles. "Come in!" After the family of four entered, Camry lunged for hugs from Marcus and Leah, and Tobias emerged from the kitchen, hands in his pockets.

Leah prepared herself for embarrassment and resentment. They didn't know what the family had told Tobias and Camry about everything. All Leah knew was that she'd nearly died of mortification when Camry had come to visit her at the cottage, and that she already hadn't been one of Tobias's favorite people.

Marcus and Tobias exchanged a quick hug, and Tobias curtly nodded at Leah. "Leah."

That was basically what she'd gotten from him the past three years, so she could manage.

They sat and gabbed for a while, introducing the twins. They shared pictures and stories. It was a little weird talking about their wedding. Leah doubted she'd share pictures of her casual superpregnant wedding with many, but it was extra awkward since she'd ruined *their* wedding. But Camry asked, and they shared. They ordered food in, caught up on family gossip, human-world stuff, and just settled in.

It was uncomfortable, but bearable.

After another night in the hotel, they visited Marcus's grandparents. Leah firmly believed theirs would be one of the most uncomfortable relationships she had in her life. She'd apologized to them after the assassination attempt, and they'd forgiven her, but it was weird. Not tense like it was with Tobias, but … more uncomfortable than not. There was shared guilt there from the old war, and Leah's assassination attempt after having spent so much time in their home had only made it worse. Unlike with Kaylah, there was no dark humor about the debacle. Just a silent understanding that they'd all rather forget what had happened, would rather never speak of past mistakes in this group. And Leah could be content with that.

Samantha and Brad were happy to meet the twins as well. Who wouldn't be? They were freaking adorable. Leah couldn't help but smirk when Marcus's grandma commented on how grownup he looked. He really had matured a lot in the last year.

The next day was *the* day, the big day. They were both excited to see Kaylah, but nervous about stepping back into the public eye. They'd be recognized on sight.

Aspen lay asleep while Marcus paced the hotel room, burping Ash. "It'll be great," he coached. "We'll be fine." There might have even been a bit of an edge to *his* voice.

Leah stared at the pile of things on the bed in front of her. They had their pictures, her printed manuscripts, the jade tokens, and several other things. Pacifiers for the kids and a change of diapers, of course. The thing that claimed Leah's attention was Kaylah's ring. She turned it in her hand, examining it. They'd never had to use it. They weren't in the clear quite yet, but still… They'd never had to resort to using it in an emergency, and for that she was grateful. Kaylah had to be ready to be reunited with it.

And then there was the debit card. It was still in good shape. They'd used it far more than they'd wanted to, but not more than they'd needed to when things had gotten tight.

"Things will work out," she said.

Chapter 32

LEAH'S GUTS WERE A TWISTED mess of panic and anxiety as their rideshare rolled up to the 'nature preserve.' Somewhere in her traitorous mind where her Ivy energy resided, there was a yearning to return, like her body understood she was about to be flooded with Green Lands energy again, like a junkie with their favorite drug.

As it was early November, the nature around the fake preserve was lovely, at least to Leah. Fall had always been her favorite season, with the way trees sprinkled the world with varying shades and hues of red, yellow, gold, and brown, accented by sturdy evergreens. Leah halted before entering the building, to enjoy this last moment here. Eternal spring was nice, but mild seasons were hard to beat.

They couldn't take the car seats with them through a rift, and they didn't have cars over there, but they brought them inside, prepared to donate them to the cave for the next set of incoming parents to use on their arrival.

The solo employee at the decrepit nature preserve display did a double take, then gaped.

Yes, we're that couple. Yes, we've been missing for months, and people have been looking for us. Yes, these two children that look remarkably like me are indeed ours. Marcus and Leah gave them polite smiles as they passed. If the Green Lands had electricity, the employee would have likely already snapped a picture and scattered it on social media.

After winding through the hallways and back rooms to get to the cave opening, they finally arrived, having passed a few people, most of whom also eyed them.

Kaylah's text had been brief. They didn't really know what to do, but they assumed they should mention they were supposed to meet with her when approaching the customs employee. There would probably be a long list of paperwork to fill out for the twins since they didn't have Ivy Kingdom passports yet.

But they didn't have to get that far. Halfway across the room, a guard approached, nodding. "Mr. Elonto. Miss Elonto. Please follow me."

She wasn't about to correct him about it being Mrs. They'd almost pocketed their rings, but they were holding infants, so…

They'd specifically planned an early-morning arrival to hopefully avoid the employees who had been working the evening they'd arrived all those months ago.

Even then, as they neared that waiting room, the one where Leah had been detained, she felt sick. Emotionally, she was digging in her feet, clawing her way back. Marcus put a reassuring hand on her back, guiding her slowly forward.

It had been so traumatic, so violating when the previous guard had wrapped his vine around her, then threatened to have her strip-searched. But the place was small, and they probably didn't have a lot of meeting rooms like this here.

Leah's anxiety melted away once the guard opened the door and ushered them in. Kaylah *and* Eric greeted them, jumping up from the table they'd been waiting at.

Kaylah squealed, leaping to give Leah and Aspen a hug first. Eric more calmly strolled to Marcus and Ash, hugging them.

They spent a few minutes meeting the twins, gushing over their excitement to have Leah and Marcus home again. Eric assured them everything was ready for them at their estate, and that made Leah breathe easier, because they hadn't coordinated anything yet.

"Oh yeah, here," Leah said, digging Kaylah's royal ring from her pocket. "I don't want to have to keep track of it anymore."

Kaylah slipped it on her finger, smiling. "I knew it would be safe with you."

"Thank you."

Kaylah then showed Aspen some more attention, and she cooed. "For the record, I don't do diapers. I was traumatized enough the one time I changed Marcus's."

"Hey!"

Leah snickered. "Stinky, huh? Rachel and Guillen didn't pour hot sauce in his kittlefruit juice as a baby, did they?"

Marcus guffawed.

The inside joke lost on Kaylah, she looked a little alarmed. "I certainly hope not."

Kaylah explained they wouldn't need passports for the twins this trip, but they each already had one prepared for them back at the estate. They'd do a quick customs check and then rift back to the Green Lands. Kaylah hesitated in the last part of her delivery, albeit only slightly. "Just to prepare you, we won't be arriving at the cave by our estate. We'll be arriving at the palace's cave."

A tiny squeak of terror rose in Leah's throat. "Can't we settle in first?"

Kaylah locked eyes with her. "It's time."

***

The rifting process went smoothly. Leah and Marcus each carried an infant through a Seeder rift. To make sure Aspen and Ash had the necessary engravings touching their skin, Leah and Marcus held the jade stones in their little hands with them. No fuss, no muss. They were happy, relatively unfazed.

A familiar warmth of energy rushed into Leah as she filled her lungs on the other side of the rift. Even if the people here weren't fond of Leah, at least Mother Nature had nothing against her.

The guards at the reception cave made Leah uneasy, but she'd known they'd have to pay the piper eventually.

"Matron, Your Highness," a guard addressed Kaylah and Eric. "Please follow me."

This isn't a death march. It's going to be fine. Perfectly fine. She repeated that to herself with each crunch of twigs, leaves, and gravel underfoot as they marched through the woods and palace grounds.

Stepping inside the palace felt both nostalgic and foreign at the same time. Marcus tightly held her free hand as they walked.

After one long and one short set of staircases, they were taken to a waiting room. A couple of Catrina's nursemaids reached for the twins. "We can see to their needs."

It took everything Leah had to give up Aspen. Marcus's expression made it clear he wasn't excited to give up Ash, either.

"They'll be fine," Kaylah assured them. "Eric and I will stay here with them the entire time."

Leah allowed the nursemaid to take Aspen, then fidgeted with her hands. She wanted Kaylah to be there in Catrina's meeting with her, too. But Leah and Marcus were adults. They needed to rip off the bandage.

"Their Majesties are waiting," the guard said.

Leah and Marcus followed. She slipped her clammy hand back into his. She hadn't even noticed she'd extended a vine tendril and wrapped it around Marcus's wrist, binding them together, until he glanced down at their joined hands. He met her gaze. "We'll be okay. They just want to talk."

It was to be a private meeting. A *formal* private meeting. Upon entering the queen's office, Leah and Marcus curtsied and bowed, something they hadn't done in so long.

Queen Catrina and King Stephan sat together on an elegant settee. Catrina gestured to another opposite them. "Please take a seat."

The young couple followed directions, sitting thigh to thigh, arm to arm.

"We're glad you're home safe," Catrina said, all business. "And congratulations on your wedding and children."

"Thanks, Aunt Ca— er, Your … Majesty?" Marcus said.

Catrina sighed, softening a touch. "We're in private, and we're still your aunt and uncle."

Leah couldn't fathom ever addressing them as such, even as Marcus's wife, though the comment hadn't been aimed at her.

As Catrina eyed them both, Stephan spoke up. "We *are* glad you're back. And we look forward to meeting the twins…"

Leah smiled slightly at that.

"I didn't realize you were so unhappy here, Leah," Catrina said, letting the statement hang in the air.

"It wasn't that I was unhappy, or ungrateful, because I *am* grateful…" She dug a fingernail into her jeans. "I just didn't feel it was fair the way you expected me to follow stricter rules than any of your other subjects."

She and Marcus had done plenty of preparation for this discussion. Leah wasn't about to grovel, or apologize more than she needed to. But she was going to keep her temper in check, and use more 'I' statements. She was going to prove she'd grown since leaving.

"Most subjects don't live under our roof or have access to palace secrets," Catrina said. "And most of them don't date our nephew. You knew what you were getting into when you signed up for that."

Leah gritted her teeth, keeping silent, because she didn't have anything kind to say.

"I'm disappointed," Catrina continued. "In both of you."

Don't say anything. Don't say anything. Don't say anything.

"Respectfully, Your Majesty, I never asked to join your household, or to use your money. And I hoped that you allowing me to live and you taking me in meant you trusted me. But you never did. Not when you reacted that way about the passageways. I was *never* staging a coup, or trying to undermine you. I'm nothing like my parents." Her nostrils flared as she tried to keep her cool. "And I lost all respect for you—"

Marcus squeezed her hand in warning.

"You lost my respect when you fired Robyn. Maybe you don't know what it's like to be afraid of a pregnancy, but you didn't have to fire a servant when all she did was look the other way when I was panicking."

Leah could provide a laundry list of reasons as to why she'd acted the way she had, most of which were in her manuscript, but that wasn't the plan today. Today was about burying hatchets with the least pain possible.

Catrina waited a moment to respond. "No, I don't know what that feels like. I was raised with high expectations, so I know they're achievable. As for the passageways and security protocols… You're a mother now. I would hope you would do everything in your power to keep those children of yours safe."

In truth, Leah's understanding *had* changed, but it didn't all become rosy. They were still miles apart in their upbringing and temperaments, and always would be.

"As for Robyn, you were right."

What? Leah was dumbfounded. Was that the closest people got to an apology from a queen?

"I still stand by what I said."

Or not…

"For my children, for this palace, and for this kingdom's security, I *do* need staff who are unfailingly loyal, who do not disobey orders on a whim when a scared girl makes a plea."

She made it sound like Leah was a five-year-old.

"That said, I do believe in second chances, just like I gave you a second chance. I rehired Robyn the week after the two of you threw a tantrum and left."

Leah's eyes grew wide. "Really?"

Catrina's face was hard. "The two of you would have known that, had you deigned to accept my requests to visit."

No one expected a queen to chase down teenagers refusing to meet with her… Leah slumped a little on the settee. "Thank you, Your Majesty, for giving Robyn her job back."

"Are there any other objections you have about your queen and king?" Catrina asked. "Anything else we should know about?"

Stephan hadn't even been there the day Leah and Marcus had left; he hadn't been part of the drama. And did Leah have more to say? Absolutely. Was it wise and necessary? Absolutely not.

And that was the compromise she and Marcus had come to. Leah couldn't care less at this point if her relationship with the queen and king ever fully recovered. But Marcus still loved them. She didn't need to have their relationship in a place where they hugged. Leah didn't even like hugs from most people, and she wasn't the type to run after people until they liked her. She could be okay with civility, even if it was cold civility like she had with Tobias.

If they could sit at the same banquet table and exchange necessary small talk while Marcus still got to enjoy his family, then Leah could choke down her pride.

"That's all, Your Majesty," Leah answered.

Catrina switched her focus to Marcus.

"No, ma'am. I'm good."

They'd written letters of apology before leaving for the human world, so he'd already explained that the birth control tonic had been his mix-up, and that he hadn't told Leah how long he'd been holding on to her engagement ring.

Stephan rubbed the back of his neck. "And what are your plans moving forward?"

Leah let Marcus take it from there. He explained that they weren't sure yet. That he'd inquire about the possibility of returning to his internship, even though he'd been away for so many months. They planned to move in with Kaylah and Eric again until they could find a place of their own. Leah hoped to stay home with the twins. That part was a little more complicated, but he waited to address the book.

"And will you be needing to keep an allowance, Leah?" Catrina asked.

"No thank you, Your Majesty." She wouldn't be their ward anymore. She and Marcus agreed they *were* going to dip into Marcus's stipend again. That was his family's money allotted to him, and wealthy parents could do as they pleased with their investments. It would be helpful and necessary. But taking a payout from the queen's coffers didn't feel right anymore.

"Even after leaving the palace, you'll have access to escorts for security. We can add another allotment to ensure the children are safe."

That was kind of a tricky topic between Leah and Marcus. They didn't fully agree on this one. But Leah did want to publish in both worlds, and he might be busy with work, and they didn't always want to burden family with the twins if they needed help.

"I know it's not my place to ask, but… Well, I… Sometimes I feel like having escorts makes me *more* of a target. So, maybe if I go out on my own, I don't always need them, and maybe we could have a helper for the house instead?" She winced. "Obviously, the twins' safety is the priority, but…"

"I think we could manage to add an extra helper to your allotment without compromising your escorts," Stephan said. "Parenthood is hard, especially for new couples."

Leah tried not to cringe. It was true, but how many people were as lucky as them to have servants help them through those hard times? "Thank you."

"She's not currently trained as a nursemaid, but would you like to have Robyn assigned to your household?" Catrina asked.

Leah's jaw dropped. Was Catrina offering Robyn as a peace offering? Or as a way to get rid of a servant she still wasn't completely trusting of? Leah didn't care. "Yes, we'll take her. I don't care if she's trained."

Catrina cracked her first smile of the meeting. "Consider it done, whenever you're ready for her to start."

"Thanks," Marcus said.

Nervously rubbing the knee of her jeans, Leah knew she ought not to push her luck, but she couldn't help herself. "If we're picking which staff gets assigned, can I make another request? Can Wren be reassigned to my escort duty?"

Catrina cocked her head, curious. "Wren?"

"Yeah, he did a really good job when I was at the cottage." She'd love to see her old book buddy on a regular basis.

"What did he do a good job of?" Catrina furrowed her brow. "We didn't receive any reports about security threats during your time there."

Leah swallowed hard. There hadn't been. And she might have just opened her mouth and gotten him in trouble. Wren had undoubtedly crossed the line professionally, but Leah and her children likely wouldn't be here if it weren't for him. "When I say he did a good job, I mean overall, even before the cottage. He just … you know… I felt safe around him."

Marcus lovingly ran a thumb over the back of her hand. She'd confessed it all to him. He knew how much this man had done for her.

"We'd hope you feel safe with *any* of the staff, Leah," Stephan said. "But I'm sure we can arrange for this one to be reassigned as well."

Leah smiled, relieved.

Catrina's focus shifted to their hands. "Now about the wedding, the twins, and the announcements… This obviously got messy.

Nothing that happened here was ideal. But I suppose, despite the fact we've been combating rumors regarding your disappearance, your returning married and having delivered is in your favor."

It was a politician's job to weigh things like this, but it still rubbed Leah the wrong way to have her marriage and children discussed so clinically.

"I think the best course of action would be to do something a little like what your parents did with you and Tobias, Marcus."

That was actually what Marcus and Leah had been hoping for. It wouldn't be as grand, but it honestly wasn't all that different. It had been extremely controversial at the time of Rachel and Guillen's wedding for them to be married, and for them to adopt their boys. They'd done it all in private, only announcing it publicly when the time was right. When done properly, it gave the kingdom an opportunity to celebrate, from a subtle position of power at the palace. They'd told the kingdom 'we're an item,' with the comment section closed. It didn't mean everyone had liked it, but the deed had been done, and they weren't offering apologies for being who they were or for loving whom they would. Leah adored Rachel and Guillen's love story.

"We're on board," Marcus said.

"Very well. We'll discuss details. It would be good to do it soon, to get ahead of the rumor mill about your return. Perhaps with a ball at the palace?"

Leah smiled once more, happy about getting to dance with Marcus again in a formal dress. She might even fit in her old gowns—Ivies tended to bounce back pretty quickly from pregnancy.

Stephan drew a deep breath. "We do still believe it would be best to keep details a little fuzzy, or … perhaps altered, about the timeline. We can word the announcement so people will hopefully not pay attention to the order things happened in, but will only recognize that you wished for privacy, so you awayed to enjoy a private ceremony, and started your family."

It pained Leah to entertain that, just for the fact that it was all to help the royal family's image. But it *would* help Leah and Marcus's image to look tidy. There would be less judgment. And anything that deterred scrutiny toward them would benefit Aspen and Ash. "Sure," she forced herself to say.

Catrina smoothed her skirt. "Lovely. Then we're settled?"

Leah bit her lip. "Well, one more thing…"

Chapter 33

CATRINA AND STEPHAN WERE all ears.

"There's something I need your permission for," Leah said.

"She's amazing at it," Marcus said.

She gave his hand a little squeeze. She had this one. "I've been writing a book…" She wasn't going to address any of the fictional books right now. "A memoir. I want to publish it. And since there will obviously be mentions of the royal family, I know I need your permission."

"I don't know how comfortable we'd be with that," Catrina stated. Despite her queenly nature, her voice was gentle.

Leah caught herself biting her nails. She needed this and the hope it would provide. "It's mostly about me. About my parents and their secrets and what it was like for me growing up. And … why I was confused enough to try to hurt Kaylah. And maybe people would understand that I just want to be a good citizen, normal." She swallowed. "Please just consider it. I already have most of the first draft written. I want to do this for me, and Marcus, and the twins. They deserve this."

Stephan crossed his legs. "I'm assuming Marcus would be in this book?"

"Yes," Marcus answered. "And I support anything she writes in there. Good or bad. I've … made my mistakes, and she doesn't deserve to take the blame for them."

Nodding, Stephan turned his focus back to Leah. "And the palace family and staff?"

"Yes. I'll be fair, but honest. And I'll obviously make sure there aren't any unnecessary details or things that would compromise security." She hesitated. "I'm grateful you've tried with the rallies and announcements and stuff, but people still hate me. *You* get the rare death threat about me, but *I* get the stares and glares and comments on a daily basis. Maybe you're used to that, but I'm not. And I don't want my kids to have to live through that if there's anything I can do about it."

Catrina spoke again. "A book like that has the potential to make you a lot of money."

It wasn't like Leah hadn't thought of that. She was notorious, and people loved gossip. Even if they didn't go into it wanting to side with her, she had to take the chance she could win some people over. "I'm sure it will. And I'm not ashamed of that. If it means financial security for Marcus and me and the twins, then that's a bonus."

Leah cleared her throat. "And I don't want it published by the palace or backed in any way by you guys. I respect your opinions, and I'll follow your guidelines as I have to, but I don't want people thinking it's propaganda or lip service."

"If we said yes…" Catrina angled her head. "You should obtain written permission from those you share stories about."

"Not a problem." She *was* a little worried about that, including Rachel and Guillen and their parents, but she hoped they would understand the value, especially with Marcus on her side. "Do I … have to get permission from my mom?" She was obviously going to be front and center in Leah's memoir, like she had been in Leah's life.

Catrina pursed her lips. "As your mother and as a citizen, Beata has had her rights stripped from her for her crimes. You don't *ever* need permission from her for *anything*. Do you understand?" Her tone conveyed her distaste for Beata. Queen Catrina hadn't been victimized the same way Kaylah had, so she didn't loathe Soren and Beata as much, at least not openly. Maybe Leah read into it too much, but Catrina's tone almost sounded protective of Leah. "Write your story, Leah. All we ask is that you give us a chance to review it before letting outside eyes look it over."

Relief and hope washed over Leah. "Yes, Your Majesty."

***

After agreeing their main concerns had been addressed, the four of them adjourned to the waiting room, and Catrina and Stephan's kids joined the group. Marcus enjoyed introducing everyone to Aspen and Ash, and they got to meet the two new little princesses. It was heartwarming to watch as Marcus interacted with his young cousins.

"How was it?" Eric asked, now standing next to Leah as she lingered in the corner of the room.

She smiled. "It was fine."

"Hmm… 'Fine' as in 'not really fine' or 'fine' as in 'actually fine'?"

Leah grinned. "I like you, Eric."

He ran a hand through his blond hair. "Most people do." He squinted playfully. "I look innocent."

She let out a breathy chuckle.

"I'd say Aspen and Ash already have a couple of built-in playmates," he said.

Her eyes on the group, Leah nodded in agreement. "I guess you're right." Family trees were confusing, so Leah had to think about it a moment. Technically, Catrina's kids weren't cousins to Aspen and Ash. Aspen and Ash were to the princesses and prince what Leah was to Catrina—a cousin's child. Catrina's kids were grouped pretty close in age, and the youngest set of twins was just months older than Leah and Marcus's. Leah smiled more genuinely. She didn't want her kids to grow up pariahs like her, and even though she had a lot of hope with her memoir, she feared that down the road, her children would still grow up outcasts. But even if they were shunned by most, they had instant friends right here. She was grateful they'd managed to piece together civility with Catrina and Stephan, even if it was mostly for the sake of Marcus and the twins.

Leah studied Catrina as she crouched and listened to Prince Leon telling her something. Leah doubted she'd ever really see eye to eye with her. They were just too different. But she couldn't forget what Kaylah had said, that when they'd deliberated on the day of the assassination attempt, Catrina had been the first to open her arms to Leah, to invite her into her home. She couldn't overlook that kindness.

Leah had her rough edges, her painfully sharp moments. The stress she faced was small compared to what a ruler like Catrina endured on a daily basis. Leah had hated the pressure placed on her to be perfect. Had she expected Catrina to never make a mistake?

From the corner of her eye, Leah spotted Kaylah as she perched on a settee near the larger group. Kaylah gave her a reassuring smile, and then a wink.

***

Kaylah and Eric accompanied Leah, Marcus, and the twins as they entered the palace's rifting cave.

"Have one more stop in you before heading home?" Kaylah asked.

Leah grimaced.

"If not, I'm sure Rachel and Guillen would understand."

Marcus bounced Aspen, keeping his mouth closed.

"Sure. Let's go." It wasn't Leah's first choice, but she needed to push through that discomfort. Catrina's had been the visit she'd been fearing the most today anyway.

They gave the Seeder on duty the coordinates for the cave closest to Rachel and Guillen's home, and she opened a rift for Marcus and Aspen to go through first.

After their entire party had arrived and Marcus had tucked the twins' jade tokens into his pockets, they rented a pair of rickshaws to get to the house faster. Ash fell asleep on the ride, and Aspen looked pretty tired, too.

Leah was nervous. But also oddly excited as they got closer. It was hard to grasp her feelings. She didn't know how her and Marcus's apology letters to his parents had landed. And Leah didn't know if they'd forgiven her for slapping Marcus. She hoped they had, or that they could.

The more she'd reflected on her interactions with her now in-laws, the more Leah had made sense of how things had fallen apart during her time in the cottage. She had no beef with Guillen, and he didn't seem the type to hold grudges. And Rachel—Rachel was a protective mother, and a good mother. Leah had come to see why Marcus had pushed the two together after the pregnancy news came out. Leah could learn a lot from Rachel.

Society hadn't been prepared for a couple like Rachel and Guillen when they'd married, or even when they'd adopted Tobias and Marcus.

Despite that, they'd raised their boys in a loving home, and even with outside pressure on their blended family soon after the war ended, Tobias and Marcus had turned out relatively well. Leah's upbringing, on the other hand, hadn't done her many favors. She'd been a lying, thieving almost-murderer.

Marcus again rested a supportive hand on her back as they reached the front door. "I love you," he mouthed.

"You too," she returned.

Guillen opened the door with a smile, welcoming the group in. Leah and Marcus indicated with fingers to lips that the twins had both nodded off, so everyone was quiet.

Rachel stood from an armchair, shyly hugging herself.

Kaylah and Eric first exchanged hugs with Rachel and Guillen.

"Congratulations," Guillen said. "On your marriage." He nodded at the twins. "And on those two. Pretty exciting to have a rare set of Boman twins."

Marcus teemed with pride, giving his dad a side hug. "This is Aspen. Want to hold her?"

"Oh goodness," Guillen said softly as he carefully took Aspen from Marcus's arms.

"Congratulations, Leah," Rachel said, just above a whisper. She was acting as timidly as Leah was at the moment.

"Thank you. I'm sorry it was all … away. That family wasn't there."

Rachel had taken lives in the old war. She was as intimidating as anyone when she wanted to be. Leah had witnessed that heated rage only once, after the assassination attempt. But on a daily basis, Rachel was simply kind. She was tenderhearted, soft. No matter what Rachel would say, Leah would always know she had been hurt by missing their wedding and the births.

"It's okay, Leah." Rachel gave her a gentle smile. "You're your own family now, and I have to remember that. I didn't mean to step on your toes. I'm sorry."

Leah shook her head. "It's not your fault. And I'm *really* sorry I lost my temper with Marcus. That will *never* happen again." It was inevitable she'd lose her temper, but they both understood what she was getting at.

Rachel glanced at a smiling Marcus as he and Guillen chatted quietly over Aspen. She faced Leah and nodded.

"He's a great dad," Leah said. "He had great examples growing up."

"Thanks." Rachel blushed. She glanced down at Ash as he slept in Leah's arms. "Black hair like you."

"But they have brown eyes, like Marcus."

Technically, Leah had descended from a clan with mostly dominant traits. Without similarly dominant whisper rifter genes to compete with, like how Leah's dad had likely contributed to Leah's green eyes, Aspen and Ash's brown eyes had probably been inherited from Beata, not Marcus. Still, Leah was glad to have them look like their father in that way.

Rocking on her feet, still hugging herself, Rachel looked antsy.

"Do you want to hold him?"

"Yes!" Rachel swooped in, snatching Ash up and clutching him to her chest. "Oh my gosh," she whispered, positively lost in the moment. "Babies!"

Leah's heart warmed. A long time ago, Leah had asked Rachel how she was capable of allowing Leah into her life, given how much Leah's parents had traumatized her. Rachel had been frank with her, had told Leah that it *was* hard. But she'd wanted Marcus to be happy. More shyly, she'd confessed that it helped for her to think of her best friend, Kaylah, as Leah's mother, instead of the truth that Kaylah's brother Soren had been her father. It hadn't made as much sense to Leah back then. But she appreciated Kaylah's part in this more now, in helping them bridge a massive gap.

Rachel kissed Ash's head. "Leah, I will *never* forgive you for making me a grandmother so young. But I will *always* forgive you, because they're so *adorable.*"

After a few minutes, Kaylah and Eric excused themselves, letting Leah and Marcus know they were safe to take the nearest cave back to the estate whenever they were ready. Escorts would be left behind for them.

Eventually, Leah and Marcus sat on a sofa together, while Guillen and Rachel eased down onto armchairs next to each other, still holding the twins.

"Do you want to see pictures?" Leah offered. The palace staff had given them a bag they could unstuff their pockets into, so they'd be more comfortable, and their items safer.

"Of course!" Rachel answered.

As they talked about the wedding and birth and everything in between and after, Leah realized how much she'd miss having a cell phone with her for quick communication and for constant picture-taking. Rachel and Guillen had visited the human world often for family trips before she'd fully matured as a Seeder and become incapable of rifting over. Leah hoped she and Marcus would take the twins on plenty of adventures back there as well, and would definitely take the opportunity to snap pictures to bring back.

"So, do you plan to stay in-realm, then?" Rachel asked timidly.

Tobias had settled down in the human world for Camry, his human wife, leaving his little brother as the one to be there for his parents. Rachel would be devastated to have them both gone, even if they visited often. With how warm their relationship had been before the pregnancy drama, and how that was already rekindling, Leah wasn't afraid to spend time with her in-laws. They'd find healthy boundaries. "Yes. I might do some work in the human world on projects I'm working on, so I might travel often at some point, but we're planning on making things work here."

Rachel beamed. "That's great to hear. And projects in the human world?" She raised an eyebrow.

Leah wasn't ready to divulge anything about the books today, except perhaps… "It's a work in progress. But do you have your friend Saff's address in Seeder territory? I want to ask her about something."

Marcus quietly snickered, wearing a know-it-all grin about the painting in Kaylah's library. Leah gave him a dirty look.

By the end of their hours-long visit, they'd eaten a late lunch, Rachel had given Leah Saff's address so she could send her a letter inquiring about possibly painting for the twins' books, and the twins had woken, both needing diaper changes.

It was going to be hard to get used to cloth diapers, but at least they were covered already at the palace and at Grandma and Grandpa's place.

They stood at the doorway saying their last goodbyes before heading back to Kaylah and Eric's estate.

"And I mean it," Rachel said. "We don't want to step on toes, but we're happy to watch the kids if you need sitters, if you need breaks for date nights or anything."

Leah gave her a warm smile. She didn't trust many people enough to allow them to hold or watch her kids, but she had no doubt they'd be safe with Rachel and Guillen. And a date night with just her and Marcus sounded *amazing*. They hadn't had one since the twins were born because they hadn't had anyone in the human world they felt comfortable visiting and leaving them with. "I'm sure we'll take you up on that."

Chapter 34

IT WAS STILL LIGHT OUTSIDE by the time they reached the estate. The servants greeted Leah, Marcus, and the twins, fetching Kaylah and Eric.

"Good visit?" Kaylah asked.

"Yeah?" Marcus answered, half-question.

"Yes," Leah confirmed.

Kaylah smiled brightly. "Great. Let's show you some improvements around the house! We gremlin-proofed a bit."

"Are you *seriously* going to call them gremlins?" Marcus asked.

Kaylah clasped her hands in front of her, her posture, expression, and tone all exuding the authority of the queen she'd once been. "Yes, Marcus. As I've explained to your wife, *all* children are gremlins. I just happen to like some more than others. And I like these two." She grinned, holding up a finger. "But if you tell anyone outside of my household that I use that term, I will absolutely deny it. And I'll remind you there are no recording devices in this realm."

Eric shrugged. "Sorry, I just put up with her."

Kaylah's jaw dropped. "Ouch."

He chuckled. "C'mon, guys, let's go see the playroom."

While Leah and Marcus had been away in the human world, Kaylah and Eric had converted one of the smaller spaces downstairs into a kid-friendly room.

"No sharp corners or easily breakable things," Eric said. Wooden toys filled the room, as well as sewn plushies, bright colors, blankets, and a basket system for diapers.

"Wow," Leah whispered, dumbfounded. This was huge, given Kaylah and Eric had never wanted kids of their own. "Thank you. I'm sure they'll love it." She glanced at Marcus.

He raised his eyebrows. "Thank you. We're not sure how long we'll need to stay with you guys until we get a place of our own sorted."

Kaylah and Eric exchanged a look. "Take as long as you need," Eric said. "And it's really no bother. Even after you move out, we wouldn't hate it if you wanted to visit often, come for dinner now and then."

Leah smiled, but still felt a little guilty. "We'll try to keep them quiet. But … they *are* kids. Kids are messy and loud. We'll do our best."

Kaylah sighed. "We are well aware of how children work, Leah. We're happy to have you here. And you're *not* a burden."

Her cheeks warmed. "Okay."

"How about you two go check out the changes upstairs? Up in the adjoining room. We'll take care of these guys for a bit."

Excited, Leah and Marcus handed Aspen and Ash over and headed upstairs to their room. It looked identical to how they'd left it. Opening the adjoining guest-room door, however, gave them a big shock. More armoires lined the walls, probably holding Leah's gowns like they'd discussed before. But the big bed had been removed, replaced with two new cribs. Leah almost cried as Marcus held her from behind. It was going to be nice having more privacy with the kids in the other room, but also having the ability to open the door to hear if they cried during the night.

"What do you think, beautiful? Isn't it nice to be home?"

A calm smile graced her lips. The energy of the realm, having made amends with his family… This still wasn't her home, even if they had an extended invitation, but it was the closest to one she'd ever really had. "Yeah. It's nice to be home."

After a couple of hours catching up again downstairs, they ate dinner with Kaylah and Eric. A blanket had been laid in the dining room for Aspen and Ash to play and wiggle on.

"We're hoping you two have tomorrow free?" Kaylah said, slicing into a stuffed portabella mushroom.

"I was planning on rifting up north to ask about my internship. I doubt they actually held it for this long, but it would be good to check."

"Hmm… And after that?"

Marcus shrugged, glancing at Leah.

"That was the main priority. We should get clothes for the twins at the market."

"Oh," Kaylah said. "One of the dressers in the adjoining room upstairs is full of baby clothes. But if they're not to your taste, we could go to the market. I'd love to join you, if you want."

"We didn't even look in the dressers. I'm sure they're fine. Thanks again."

"Great. So, when Marcus returns, you're both free?"

"I suppose so," Marcus said. "What's up?"

Kaylah grinned. "A surprise. I think it's too late in the evening to plan on taking care of it today."

More surprises? "I'm sure we can make space in our schedule."

***

After finally getting the kids to bed, they quietly closed the door between the rooms. Only hints of colored light still danced on the horizon. Marcus lit the lamps in the room.

"Definitely one thing I'll miss," Leah said. "Electricity."

"Yeah… But it sounds like they're still hopeful about the static nettle research program."

"It's so peaceful, though," Leah said, perching on her side of the bed. "Listen." Not a single car drove in the vicinity. The train station was too far away to be heard. No loud TVs. "It's nice. I hope if they figure out how to get electricity working someday, that it doesn't change things too much over here."

"Agreed."

Leah sorted through the bag of things they'd brought from the human world. For now, she tucked most of it away in her bedside table drawer. Her gaze caught on a folded piece of paper in the drawer. "Huh…"

She pulled it out and unfolded it. "Oh."

"What's that?"

She swallowed. "It's … a distant memory." Part of her wanted to toss it, hide it away. It was something she would have done before leaving for the human world. But she'd changed. She'd grown. "Here. It was written for you."

Marcus came around the bed, standing in front of her. His face tensed into a frown as he read the letter she'd never sent him. It took him a while to read it; she'd been thorough.

Slowly, he folded it back up. "Wow," he whispered. "You really were going to leave me."

She frowned as well, taking the letter from his hands and setting it on the bedside table. "I would have come back, but I needed to get away to heal and sort things out." The letter had said as much. She'd come to realize during her time here that the *only* thing that would help was time away from this realm, whether with him or alone.

Leah took his hands in hers. "We're here now. That's what matters. That's very outdated."

He slid to his knees, kissing the palms of her hands, still frowning, hurt. "We lost time and memories that could have been shared. I'm glad I came back when I did."

"Well, you're stuck with me now. We'll have plenty more time and memories. And I'm glad you came back when you did, too, so I never had to send that letter."

He nodded pensively. She had figured he'd take it as a sign they'd done the right thing by leaving, and doing it together. She hadn't realized he'd take it this hard, hadn't meant to dredge up old hurt.

"I love you," she said.

A small smile quirked his lips. "I love you too."

"And you know…" She raised his hands to the bottom of her shirt. "The kids are sleeping. And I don't care what all those people out there say about you. I think you're pretty amazing."

He grinned, taking the bait. "Don't care what all those people out there say about *me*, huh? What exactly are they saying?"

She shrugged. "Oh, ya know. I've ignored them for so long, I've forgotten what they even say."

Sliding the first of several buttons on her shirt undone, he gazed into her eyes. "Do they say I'm handsome?"

"Nah. I'm sure that's not it." She couldn't resist digging her fingers into his curly locks.

He traveled to the next button. "Do they say I have the best wife?"

Leah chuckled. "They *definitely* don't say that."

"How about…" He unbuttoned two more. "Do they say I have two amazing kids who look just like their mother?"

"Psh. They wouldn't even know that yet."

He unbuttoned one more, leaving the last, top button done. "Well, I've never cared much what they think about me. So, I guess it doesn't matter." He snuck a kiss, stood, and turned to walk away.

She shot out her vines, wrapping them around his waist. "Don't you dare."

He laughed as she reeled him back onto the bed.

"You think you're so funny." She faced him.

Raising a hand to his chest, he smiled wide. "I'm the funny one in this relationship."

"Perhaps funny, but not smart. Because we both know something was a little less than ideal in the human world, when my energy and chemical powers were lower or off-balance. And if you were smart, you wouldn't have left this last button done up."

Without a word, he continued to smile, ever so slowly undoing it and gliding his hands down her bare sides. Her spine shivered.

In less than a minute, they were lips and hands, fast heartbeats and quick breaths. Only as he started sliding her pants off did she remember something crucial, and panicked.

"Wait!" That was the last thing her heart and body wanted to do, but she and Marcus hadn't stopped by a market. "We don't have birth control tonic. And I'm *not* ready to be pregnant again already."

He panted out a couple of breaths. "That's fine. We can do other things. Or…" He kissed the nape of her neck. "Or we can use the last of the protection we had in the human world. Which I just so happen to have tucked in my pocket."

"You are the best man I know." She crashed her lips back into his.

***

Only the crickets and the clouds knew how late it was as they faced each other under the sheets.

"There *are* perks to you being at full energy." He planted a kiss on her forehead.

She giggled. "Drop by the market for that tonic, and you'll remember how good it can *really* be."

"Everything with you is good," he replied sweetly.

She wore a contented smile. "Speaking of tasks tomorrow… What are you going to do if they don't give you your internship back?"

Marcus drew a breath. "I'm actually rethinking going tomorrow. Maybe I should wait until the palace announcement about us. Keep under the radar."

"Aren't you afraid of pushing your luck by waiting longer?"

He hesitated. "Would you be disappointed if I didn't go back to my internship?"

She frowned. "I'd feel guilty I lost it for you because we were gone so long."

"No," he replied softly. "I mean if I *chose* not to."

"But I thought you loved it."

"I did. I do. I think I do… I just… I didn't hate working with my hands on construction, though I can only imagine the disappointment my parents would have in that. I'd prefer to do something that makes a difference, but politics can suck at times. And then you and the kids… I don't want to be gone on long trips away from you. I want to support you in your writing and help with the kids. I guess I'm saying I don't know what I want to do anymore…"

Leah bit her lip, considering. For now, they had a roof over their heads, and he would start taking his family stipend payments again. "Your parents would be proud of you no matter what, and I would be too. But if you need time to explore your options, we can work around that. If you want to stay home more and watch the kids while I work on my books, I can get them published faster…"

"You're sure?"

She slid a hand to his heart. "Take your time. It's *your* turn to explore what you want to do."

***

After breakfast, Marcus traveled to the nearest market to purchase a few necessities, including two sets of wraps for baby-wearing. Kaylah and Eric said their surprise would take a bit of hiking, and that they'd set out on foot from their home.

For nearly an hour, the group chatted as they climbed around boulders and over downed logs, deep into the woods. Their grounds were expansive, and Leah had explored them, but not this far out, not in this direction.

It was heavenly to be able to use her vines freely again to help steady her over some of the more precarious spots. The trees suddenly thinned, opening to a wide clearing—and in the center lay a stone foundation.

"What's this?" Leah asked.

Kaylah kept quiet, giddy with anticipation as Eric retrieved a rolled-up paper from a storage box.

"Here." He handed it to Leah and Marcus.

They gave each other a glance and unrolled it together. "Blueprints for a building?"

"A home," Kaylah said. "*Your* home."

Leah was stunned speechless.

"We can't accept this," Marcus said.

"Yes, you can," Eric replied. "We've already partitioned the property. We'll have a main path cleared to meet our driveway so rides and walks will be much faster."

"No." Leah shook her head in disbelief. "This is too much."

"Like hell it is," Kaylah replied. "Eric and I worked our asses off for years getting this kingdom to a place of tolerance and peace. And you guys deserve it as much as anyone else."

"Yeah, but—" Leah started.

"No buts." Kaylah put her hands on her hips. "I never got to spoil my niece growing up. I never gave her Christmas presents or birthday presents, or baby shower gifts or a wedding gift. You can't tell us how to spend our money." She gestured to Marcus. "Rachel and Guillen got Tobias and Camry a cottage they barely ever visit for *their* wedding. If you don't like the location out here and you'd prefer to move somewhere in town, then consider this a vacation home away from the chaos and noise." She crossed her arms, not backing down. "Plus, you don't want to offend Rachel and Guillen, because they're planning on furnishing it for your wedding and baby gifts."

Marcus and Leah shared another glance.

"Can we, uh, talk about this a second, in private?" Marcus asked.

"We'll be right here."

He and Leah stepped a few yards away.

Leah struggled with guilt, but also yearned so badly for this. Not just a home. *Her* home. One of her own, like she'd never had. No moving. And quiet, peaceful, but still with decent access to a town, train, and rifting cave. "I want to say yes."

Marcus smiled. "Then let's say yes."

Leah wrinkled her nose. "Are you sure?"

"It's going to take a while for this place to be ready, but I could help build it. I'd love that." He changed hands supporting Ash against his chest. "And it might be fun for something my dad and I can do together when he has time off."

She considered, rubbing Aspen's back. "Even with bikes or rickshaws, it's not a five-minute trip to the market. There better be a big cellar, and a big garden." Her chemical powers were back to normal, so she wouldn't botch the garden anytime soon. "I bet your mom would love helping me get it started."

He smiled wider. "So…?"

Leah rocked her head side to side. "You know, we never *did* have sex out in the woods, and with the privacy out here—"

Marcus covered Ash's ears. "We'll take it!" he yelled to Kaylah and Eric in the distance.

Kaylah let out a celebratory whoop, and Leah laughed.

"I love you." She kissed Marcus.

"I love you too."

They returned to Kaylah and Eric, exchanging hugs, careful not to squish the kids strapped to Leah and Marcus. Leah stayed in Kaylah's arms just a touch longer. "Love you, Aunt Kaylah."

Chapter 35

SHE'D THOUGHT IT BEFORE, and she'd likely think it again, but *today* would be the new hardest day of Leah's life.

Aspen and Ash were back at Kaylah and Eric's place, watched by Robyn. She had kids of her own, so Leah didn't see a need for tons of formal training on how to take care of them.

Leah and Marcus walked hand in hand to the prison Beata served her life sentence in. Leah was already sweating and nauseous. She was seriously doubting whether she'd keep down her breakfast.

Marcus squeezed her hand. He hadn't seen Leah's mom since he and Leah had run away together to his brother's wedding in this realm over three years ago. He'd been on decent terms with Beata in the human world, but once he'd discovered who she really was, he'd never wanted to see her again.

Leah had never pushed it. She'd kept those parts of her life separated, compartmentalized. She couldn't blame Marcus, or any Boman, given her mom's history in the war, and her plans to further victimize Bomen.

Leah squeezed his hand back. He was all sorts of tense, but his presence there today was part support, part compromise. And she didn't think she could do it without him.

The guards welcomed them into the massive stone building. "Mrs. and Mr. Elonto." One nodded. "Congratulations."

"Thank you," Leah said. The palace announcement about their private wedding and Boman twins had just gone out, and word traveled fast, at least when it was the juicy kind.

The couple stayed in a waiting room while the guards fetched Beata for the meeting. Marcus paced the room while Leah sat, bouncing her knee and biting her fingernails.

A guard opened the door. "She's ready in room one."

Leah filled her lungs to capacity. *I can do this…*

Hands gripping each other, Leah and Marcus entered room one together. Beata smiled wide at Leah, but quickly dropped her expression at the sight of Marcus. She looked nervous. But she recovered, opening her arms to Leah.

Only then did Leah let go of Marcus's hand as she hugged her mom.

"I've been so worried," Beata breathed, holding Leah tight. "You said you'd be gone, but I didn't think it would be *this* long!" She stepped back, tucking Leah's hair behind her ears. "You're okay?"

Leah gave her a forced smile. "I'm great. Let's sit down."

Marcus had already sat at the round table in the small room. There would be no hugs between him and Beata, and everyone in the room was well aware of that.

"Marcus," Beata acknowledged as she took a seat, her wrists bound so her Ivy vines could cause no harm.

"Beata," he replied a little sharply.

Beata turned her focus back to Leah, not bothering to inquire why Marcus had joined her on this visit. "How was the human world? You didn't even tell me what university you got into, or what you're studying."

Leah blew out a breath. "That wasn't … completely true. I *was* in the human world for most of the time, but not in school. I needed a break from the realm."

"That bad?" Beata frowned.

"I mean, not everything was bad… It's a long story. But I'm in a good place, Mom." She held up her hand, showing her ring. "Marcus and I got married."

Beata took a moment to react. She couldn't be that surprised, not when Leah had outright told her to prepare for this eventuality when they'd last seen each other nearly a year ago. But Beata didn't deign to offer her congratulations. She turned to Marcus, giving him a little nod. "You *were* good for her in high school. She stopped stealing for you."

Marcus's jaw tensed. "Yes, I *was* good for her. I *am* good for her, and I will *continue* to be good for her." His tone dangerously rode the line of civility.

Leah rested a hand on his thigh under the table, giving it a gentle squeeze. Leah had been forced to sacrifice her pride to keep things civil with Catrina and Stephan upon their return. This time it was Marcus's turn to keep the peace. He deserved to tell Beata off however he wished, but that wasn't what they'd agreed upon for this particular visit.

"What was the wedding like?" Beata asked. "I assumed you would let me know before it happened…"

Leah stared at her wedding ring. She was a tiny bit mortified by her wedding pictures, with her ginormously pregnant, wearing a cheap dress in some random church in the human world. "It was beautiful and private. We did it in the human world while we were away. I'm sorry I didn't give you a heads-up. I … didn't think to bring pictures on this visit."

"Well, I'd love to see next time. Are you back to living in-realm now? You'll visit more regularly?"

Choking down the lump in her throat, Leah took a moment to respond. She didn't have that answer yet. Depending on how this visit went, she might make time for visits with her mom, or she may never see her again for the rest of her life. And that terrified her. "We'll have to see. I'm really busy right now. I have a job."

Beata smiled. "That's great! What are you doing?"

"And we're building a house."

"That's nice. What part of the kingdom? I assume you're staying in the kingdom?"

Leah's courage wavered, her hand shaky as she pulled a photo from her pocket, resting it in her lap. "Yeah. Staying in the kingdom. And honestly, a lot of time will be taken up with family. With … our kids."

Beata was rightfully confused. "Your what?"

Slipping the picture of Aspen and Ash onto the table, Leah tried to breathe regularly. "Marcus and I had twins."

Her mouth wide open, Beata slid her hand across the table, taking the photo. "You can't be serious." She stared at the picture of the two of them. "But they look like you." Her gaze shifted up in a subtle glare at Marcus, with a hint of 'you knocked up my daughter?!' in the mix. "That's why you were gone for so long?" She returned her focus to Leah.

"Yes."

Beata shook her head, studying the picture again. "I can't believe…" And the wheels churned, then it clicked. "Well, they're obviously not Marcus's. Sweetheart, I know the ins and outs of stunts, and they don't carry in multiples."

A low, rumbling exhale came from Marcus, a warning, or a sign that he and his balled fists were barely keeping back his absolute hatred for Beata.

Leah's heart broke. Not at Marcus's anger, but at her mother's continual use of the term 'stunt.' That was like 'weed' or 'leech'—terms that hadn't been commonplace since the old war, not with anyone civilized or tolerant.

"I'd like the picture, please," Marcus said, plenty of edge to his voice. He extended a hand. "The picture of *my* children."

Beata handed it to him.

"Mom, they *are* Bomen. They *are* Marcus's. There are actually a couple of other sets of Ivy Boman twins on record since I was born."

Beata furrowed her brow. "Oh…" It still didn't seem like she believed it, but that was the least of Leah's worries. "I guess they're old enough to have been confirmed as … what you say they are…"

"They're *Bomen*, Mom. Not stunts. Please stop calling them that. My children are *not* stunts. Neither is Marcus, or anyone else born without powers."

"Sorry," Beata muttered. "I'll try to do better." She studied Leah. "They're healthy? You're healthy? Were you okay?"

Leah nodded. "We're all fine. They're angels."

Beata smiled softly. "If they're yours, then I'm sure they're perfect. I'd love to meet them on your next visit."

Marcus's nostrils flared, and Leah's heart dropped into her gut.

"That's not going to happen," Leah said with as much confidence as she could muster. "I won't be bringing them."

Beata frowned. "I wouldn't *say*— I wouldn't *do*— I just want to meet them. I'd love them, because they're a piece of *you*."

Before they'd left the human world, Leah and Marcus had had a real heart-to-heart. She'd desperately wanted her mom to meet her kids, and Marcus had been adamantly opposed to it. Instead of fighting it out, they'd addressed it calmly, with an open mind.

The thing was, it didn't matter how much Beata repented of her actions and prejudices—she had committed crimes, she had planned heinous things. Bomen would never forget that.

And it didn't matter that Leah had never cared one way or the other that Marcus was a Boman, born without powers. But just because she wasn't a bigot didn't mean she'd understood his struggle. She had plenty of prejudices stacked against her personally, but she'd never been part of *that* marginalized group, and she wasn't necessarily the best advocate. She had to default to Marcus for that, trusting he knew best when it came to that aspect.

Leah wrung her hands in her lap. "No, Mom. You won't get to see them until they're old enough to understand who you are and what you've done. And then they can decide for themselves if they ever want you to be part of their lives."

Beata's eyes filled with tears. "I can be better. I promise. I can be better."

Leah still hoped with all her heart that her mom *could* be better, do better. But she and Marcus had agreed upon this ahead of time, and their decision was as immovable as the Outer Rim surrounding this realm.

They would not budge.

Yes, Beata still had to change, and she had, to some degree, already. She was civil with Marcus, making a tiny bit of effort in this meeting, but she still was cold toward him, and she still called him a stunt. But even *if* she had changed her tune without prompting, if she had turned a complete one-eighty and was now a saint, they wouldn't have budged on this.

Because children were not tools. Aspen and Ash were innocent and perfect, not born for the purpose of changing the minds of bigots. It wasn't Leah's responsibility to change her mother's mind, and it certainly wasn't her children's. Beata's story was tragic and pitiable, and her parentage had done her no favors morally. But the fact remained that she was a grown adult, and it was no one's job to fix her but her own.

Leah's children would *never* be tools. Not the way she'd been when her mother had conceived her as a manipulation against Leah's dad. She was breaking that cycle. She may *look* like a carbon copy of her mother, and they may have a lot in common, but Leah was *not* the same as Beata.

Aspen and Ash were not there to manipulate or educate, and even as tears moistened Leah's own eyes at witnessing her mother's devastation, that fire burned within her.

Leah could only imagine the hurt and horror and distrust it would earn her if her children eventually learned that she'd taken them to see their grandmother—a war criminal—when they were too young to consent.

To the entire realm, Beata was a villain. To Leah, the lines still blurred on a personal level. No one else had been protected by her the way Leah had been, even if she'd been somewhat negligent. No one else had loved Leah when she was younger. Beata would always be her mother, but she was selfish and toxic.

Leah's lip quivered. "No, Mom. That decision's final."

Beata continued to cry, her frown deepening. "Could I at least keep the picture? I'd love one with the three of... Well, with your family..."

Leah shook her head. She didn't imagine that would be much better for her kids. Leah's children were descendants of slaves, and she couldn't give her children's photo to someone who still believed slavery wasn't all that bad. Even if Beata considered this particular set of slave descendants somehow *alright* just because they were half-breeds of her daughter's.

Beata pursed her lips, staring at the table between them.

The silence was deafening, and it was time.

Leah rested her hand on Marcus's thigh again. "I need to talk to her alone, okay?"

He rubbed her hand. "Sure. I'll be right outside."

Chapter 36

THE DOOR CLICKED CLOSED behind Marcus. Beata wiped at her tears. "What's going on, sweetheart? Is he making you—"

Leah gritted her teeth. "Marcus isn't making me anything." He hadn't been there to strong-arm Leah. She'd agreed to everything she'd said, and she'd asked him to let her say it herself, but to be there for support if he could stomach it.

"But Eleana, twin stun— Twin Bomen? And not … letting me see my own grandchildren?"

"It's all true. And the decision is mine as much as it is Marcus's."

"I promise I'm trying here. And I'll do better."

"Good. Because I hope someday I can be proud of that change, and that they can see it in their hearts to forgive you."

Beata scrunched her eyes closed, shaking her head.

Leah looked at her, angry, hurting, and sad. This next part wasn't going to be any easier, but it was a different issue, more personal, and it hadn't felt right to have Marcus here for this one.

"About the job I mentioned." She rested her hands on the table. "It's more like, uh, a work in progress. I love books now."

Beata opened her eyes, gently smiling. "I'm happy you found a good hobby."

"I'm hoping to make it more than a hobby. I'm actually a writer now. I wrote some stories for the twins, and I'm hoping to have them illustrated and published." *Illustrated by a Seeder, who you also hate.*

A genuine look of pride graced Beata's face as she wiped away the rest of her tears. "That's great."

The adventure romance was being put on the back burner for now. The twins weren't getting any younger, and Leah was ready to get her personal story out into the world. Plus, Kaylah had mentioned reaching out to the author of the *Valeska's Adventures* series about seeing if they'd be willing to personally mentor Leah, and Leah was over the moon about that opportunity.

"I have another book that's almost finished that I need to tell you about." Leah sat straighter. "I'm not doing this lightly, but things haven't been easy. People hate me."

"And that's not fair."

"No, Mom. It's not. And the queens have tried to help, but I need to do this for me, okay?"

"Do what?"

Leah rubbed at a scratch in the wooden table. "I'll be publishing my story. My life story. I can't change the past. I can't change the way people look at me or think of me. But I *do* have the opportunity to change the narrative put out into the world about me, sharing my truth and allowing people a deeper look into who I am."

Beata was thoughtful. "I know it's been hard. If you think it would help…" Her eyes worked, her mind worked, and her fear became apparent. "What all are you going to tell them?"

"Everything that matters. I need people to know why I tried to kill Kaylah, why I lost hope that day. I need them to understand that I'm not like you." Saying the words tortured Leah, but she remained strong. "Because I'm not."

Beata's eyes filled with tears again. "I'm sorry I wasn't a better mother. It wasn't on purpose."

And … that made Leah start to cry, too. "But the fact is, you weren't better. And I've forgiven you for the past. Because you had crappy parents growing up, and times were different. But you let Cheryl hurt me. You lied to me about my dad and about *so* much."

"I'm sorry," Beata whispered, staring down at her hands. "Please don't do this. Please don't make people hate me more."

How selfish.

"You're serving a life sentence in prison. I'm sorry you'll be embarrassed, but I honestly don't know that people will care much about what's said about *you* in my book. But hopefully they'll better understand *me*. Because to them, Mom, you're a murderer, a hateful bigot, and a pawn. You *knew* my dad had Kaylah in the dungeons on your own wedding night, that he was torturing her, the rightful queen. You knew, and you did nothing." Leah sniffled, taking in a sharp breath. *And for me, Kaylah's done everything.* She almost uttered it, but it felt like too much. This wasn't about spite or revenge, and it wasn't for comparison or to make Beata feel worse.

"I'm telling you as a courtesy," Leah said. Her guts twisted. "I'm going to tell them what you did to my dad. That you got pregnant on purpose to trick him, and what it did to him."

Regret and ghosts of Beata's past flashed across her face. "I never meant to tell you that. It doesn't mean I didn't love you. I still love you, Eleana. I will *always* love you. No one else needs to know that about your conception. You said you wouldn't tell anyone."

Leah buried her face in her hands. "I know. But it's important to me. And I'm sorry if you've carried guilt over that all these years, that it might have been your fault you lost the war and my dad died, but most people nowadays are *happy* the war ended and are *happy* he died."

Beata sobbed. "I'm sorry! I didn't mean to! I didn't mean for any of this to happen!"

The door clicked open behind Leah. "We're fine," she answered. She didn't need Marcus or a guard checking in on them.

It softly closed.

As Beata gathered herself, Leah waited patiently, sopping up her own tears with a handkerchief she'd brought. "I'm not saying or doing this to be cruel or to punish you, but I'm going to do it. I'm telling the truth." She rubbed at that same scratch in the table. "Frankly, the guards might even like you more. I think people will like you more. Because of what happened, even if you didn't intend it."

Beata gave her a look of almost contempt, her eyes cold. "They will cheer me on because I got my own husband *killed*. You want me to be proud of that? Would you be proud of that if it were Marcus?"

That touched an unexpected nerve, and yet… "You want me to be happy? You say you love me, that you will *always* love me. If you do, and you do want me happy, then you'll understand that it's hell for me on a daily basis out there. I'm tired of being hated and misunderstood when it wasn't my fault. I want a better life, and I want a better life for my children. I'm not exploiting you. I'm allowing people to know the truth with hopes of a better future."

"I do want you to have a better life," Beata whispered.

"Then don't be mad at me for doing this." Leah pointed to herself. "Because I've had to live this, and I will continue to live this. And I plan to pass down a better legacy to my children than what I received."

Beata let out a shaky breath in resignation. "Then do what you have to."

Leah hadn't needed her permission, but her heart was lighter knowing she had it. "Thank you. I'll be honest and fair. I'll tell them the good too."

Something like an attempted smile twitched at Beata's lips.

Picking at her nails, Leah processed her thoughts. Tons more could be said, but how much of it was necessary? She'd said what she'd come to say. "Like I mentioned, I'm going to be busy. I'm a wife and a mother. We're building a home and starting a garden, and I'm writing books. I…" Guilt weighed her down, because it wasn't wholly the truth. "I'm going to be busy, and I don't know when I'll be able to see you next."

Leah was going to be swamped. A happy kind of swamped. But she needed time to process this visit, this day. And after she left this room, she wasn't sure when she'd next see her mom, or if her mom would want to see her after she'd had a chance to mull it over.

"Will you write me?" Beata asked.

"I don't want to make a promise I'm not sure I can keep."

"Can I still write you?" She was grasping at straws, and Leah couldn't blame her. Life in prison would be lonely.

"Yes. I'll be at Kaylah's. But I don't know how quickly I'll respond." And she wasn't sure when or if she'd be able to get herself to read any letters.

Leah stood, but she couldn't hug her. Not after all that. "I've got to go."

"I… I love you."

Swallowing, Leah acknowledged the truth. More than ever, she disliked her mom, and resented her, and was unforgiving. And in the most unreal way, the little girl who resided in her heart would always yearn for her mother. "I love you too." She turned and walked out the door.

"Eleana!" Beata pleaded.

She wanted her hug goodbye, not the vision of her daughter turning her back on her, but Leah was done giving. She was done baring her soul to her mother, and done ripping her mother's heart and hopes away from her.

In the hall, Marcus took Leah into his arms. And then sobs came from the other side of the door. Leah completely shattered in Marcus's grip.

A guard approached. "Are you alright, Mrs. Elonto? Were you harmed?"

"I'm fine," she croaked. "The visit's over."

He opened the door behind Leah. "Visit's over, Mrs. Remsgard. It's time to go back."

Even with the door closed behind him, Beata's screaming and crying was loud and clear. "No! Make her come back. I want to see my daughter! I want to talk to her. It can't end like this."

Leah whimpered, destroyed, burying her face in Marcus's neck. Should she go hug her mother? Should she give her more of her time? Leah had to choose herself in that moment, and doing so meant she needed to walk away for now.

The guard issued more orders, but Beata was nothing short of distraught. "I don't believe it!"

"Come on, let's get you out of here," Marcus whispered, pulling Leah away from the noise.

Soon, Leah filled an empty waiting room with sniffles and whimpers and tears. At this point, it might have been less painful to stab her mom in the heart.

"I'm proud of you," Marcus soothed. "I love you. It's going to be alright."

Cutting people out was hard. Choosing between people was hard. Setting healthy boundaries could be devastating.

After eons of calming her breathing, drying her tears, and gulping down water, Leah was numb and ready to see adorable faces that loved her unconditionally, and supportive family who were there for her no matter what.

They walked from the prison in silence for some time, Leah staring down at the picture of Aspen and Ash to remind her why she'd just done this.

"I really am proud of you, Leah," Marcus whispered, his arm around her waist.

Why did it have to hurt so much?

"You know, I got to thinking about how we talk about legacies," he continued. "Escaping our parents' legacies—yours *and* mine… But really, I feel like people mostly talk about legacies when they talk about people who have passed, and it's about good things they've contributed to the world."

So, my dad … and that would be nothing.

"And if Soren has a legacy, even if he never realized it or how it came about, that one good thing is you." Marcus leaned in, kissing her gently on the cheek. "And I wouldn't give you up for anything. Not for the realm, not for the world."

Epilogue

*** Four Years Later ***

LEAH RESTED IN HER ADIRONDACK CHAIR, watching the kids play with Grandma Rachel and Grandpa Guillen in the backyard. Marcus was in the front yard with Tobias, Camry, and the human girl they'd adopted through the foster care system.

Catrina approached Leah from behind, resting a hand on her shoulder. "We're taking off. Thanks so much for having us."

Leah smiled. "Thanks for coming!" She and Marcus were happy to host a large family picnic on their property, and glad to have Catrina and Stephan and their kids come all the way out there.

Things were monumentally better, in so many ways. Leah's relationship with Catrina and Stephan, for one. When she'd finished her life story and submitted it to them for approval, it had opened the door for more honest communication. She'd included the truth about them. How she'd been grateful for them welcoming her into their home. How they'd been kind and extremely helpful as she'd tried to find her bearings in her ancestral realm and powers. But she'd also shared, with as much tact as she could, how hard it had been for

"

her to follow strict rules, how hard the royal family had to fight to avoid any image of impropriety because of their sincerity to steer clear of past mistakes in the Elonta ruling family. They appreciated her candor and gratitude. There had been more sincere apologies from both sides once Leah had laid everything bare, and they were in a less heated, more casual meeting.

Catrina had even taken the opportunity to meet with Leah in private after that, and had shared more about her own life story. Leah had been sworn to secrecy about the matter since it was private information, but she and Catrina shared more than Leah could have imagined. Catrina and Guillen had endured rough childhoods, which Leah had already been told, but many dark secrets had been buried that the public wasn't privy to. If the Elonta family knew how to do something well, it was making and keeping secrets.

Leah and Catrina would still never be best friends, and that was fine. Catrina was born and raised to be a queen, an heir to the throne, a holder of the power of the Mother Vines. Leah's upbringing was far from that. But they always tried to meet in the middle now.

Stephan and Catrina gathered their children and said their final goodbyes. The backyard fell nearly silent without so many kids there.

"Mind if I join you?" Wren asked minutes later. "Their Majesties and Highnesses are off now."

Leah gestured to another chair. "Be my guest."

It had taken Wren a while to fully accept the casual atmosphere with which Leah and Marcus ran their household, but he didn't hesitate to join them now for a good chat when work allowed.

"Thanks for all of your hard work," Leah said.

He took a sip of watermelon juice. "Family visits are *always* fun days."

"Leah?" Robyn called from behind. "Oh, there you are." She straightened her dress once in view. "Is it still alright if I head out early? You don't need anything more for the little ones?"

"We'll be great, thanks. And don't forget to take the gift by the door." Robyn's oldest was celebrating another birthday this weekend.

"He'll love it. Thank you. I'll see you Monday."

After Robyn left, Leah and Wren chatted about security details for the rest of the weekend.

The house was completed, and the surrounding woods were always an escape from the crazy of life. Leah couldn't have picked a better location for their home if she'd tried. The property that Kaylah and Eric had partitioned off for Leah and Marcus was so beautiful, but also well protected from wandering eyes.

Kaylah and Eric had an outer gate on their lane that was always guarded, so for someone to sneak by would be an astounding feat already, and then they'd have to somehow get past the larger estate and the on-site security to continue on to Leah and Marcus's house. It was virtually impossible for lowly busybodies to invade their privacy.

Though, the busybodies and haters had lessened in their numbers eventually. The royal family's introduction of the married couple and their children had definitely helped. And Leah's book had made a significant difference. In their finances and in the way Leah was treated.

People nodded more, averted their gazes less. She'd actually had people approach her to sign her book, which had made her nervous because she hadn't practiced for that. People sometimes approached to thank her for sharing her story and for being a good example.

That didn't mean everyone loved her. No one was loved by everyone. No matter how kind a person was or how many mistakes they corrected, they would always be a villain in someone's story.

Leah wondered how much of a villain she was in her own mother's story. They still exchanged the occasional letter, but she hadn't found it in her to ever visit her mom in prison after setting the much-needed boundaries regarding Aspen and Ash. Maybe she was a coward, but any time she'd considered it, she imagined telling the twins that she was leaving them for a few hours to visit a woman who would have oppressed people like them. If it was between her twins and her mother, she would always choose her twins. If it was between Marcus and her mother, she would always choose Marcus.

The handsome devil himself stepped onto the patio, plopping on a seat next to Leah. "They're off. Tobias and Cam decided to take off too, but they'll be over first thing in the morning for breakfast."

Leah held out her hand, and he took it, resting it on his knee.

There wasn't a piece of her heart that didn't belong to him. He was a better husband than she ever could have hoped for. Shortly after her life story had been published, she'd sent a copy to her mom in prison. The letter she'd received in response had not been kind. Beata had essentially rescinded her permission to share anything about herself that she didn't want people to know, and she had accused Leah of using her. All because Leah hadn't visited her. Marcus had supported and consoled Leah. After Leah had responded with a strong letter of censure, setting limits and not apologizing, her mother had eventually written with an apology of her own. It may have been a desperate attempt to not lose Leah completely, but it kept things civil.

"The two of you are still planning on a human-world visit Monday?" Marcus asked.

"Yes, sir." Wren nodded.

"Yep," Leah said, kicking her feet up on a footstool. She still brought in decent income from sales of her life story, though that wouldn't last forever. There was a limited audience in the Green Lands, especially with the library systems being so popular. That book had never been about making money anyway. It had helped her heal, had helped her explain herself.

Marcus and Leah visited the human world a lot to get away and for outings with the twins. Leah also rifted over often to work with her agent on her romantic adventure stories, and Wren usually accompanied her for those trips. She was now publishing under a pen name in both the human world and the Green Lands realm. The stories were essentially the same, with obvious changes for those in the human world to follow laws green folk had about not disclosing their existence to humans. With Marcus's stipend from family investments, and Leah's income from publishing, they weren't stressed. And he'd had a chance to discover what his passion really was.

"Sounds good," Marcus replied, putting his feet up next to Leah's. "I'll have plenty of homework back here." He smiled as Aspen giggled at Guillen while they continued to play. Marcus had indeed been offered his internship again. He'd turned it down. Instead of going into public service full-time, he did volunteer work on the side like Rachel, Kaylah, and Eric did.

As much as he respected his dad and his profession, Marcus had gained the courage to pursue something he'd come to love. Not only had he worked tirelessly to help build this home, he'd made the twins a mini palace. Whereas Guillen had built his boys a nice sturdy tree house, Marcus had built the twins a miniature palace to play in, big enough for the adults to join them inside.

And right now, Ash was on the second floor, popping his little head up in a window and then ducking and running to the next one over. Leah couldn't believe how fast the twins were growing. They were like weeds, just not the … awkward derogatory nickname kind…

The playhouse they enjoyed right now was just a little thing for fun compared to what Marcus aspired to create. He was studying architecture and structural engineering while Leah worked on her books. He wanted to leave his mark on the world in a more physical way than his father. Unintentionally, his chosen path in architecture also helped their little family fade into private obscurity more than politics would have. It was a win-win.

Leah, Marcus, and Wren chatted a while longer. Like any other day in the Green Lands, it was warm, the breeze gentle, and songbirds whistled in distant treetops.

Wren eventually called it a night. Kaylah and Eric finally showed up, apologizing for arriving so late from a trip to the human world.

"I don't miss the crazy weather back there," Eric said. "Especially when it delays our flights to come home." They always made time to go on getaways together, and to visit his family.

They enjoyed some dessert, the twins with sticky fingers and trying to steal drinks from everyone's glasses. As it got dark, the older couples bid everyone good night, and Leah and Marcus prepared the twins for bed.

They loved being read stories by Mom and Dad from Mom's books at bedtime. That was the one thing Leah had decided to keep for herself. She and Saff had finished the children's books, and they'd had several professionally printed, but they hadn't put them out into the world. They were a passion project for Leah's kids, and for a few kids of close family and friends of either Leah or Saff. They were too close to Leah's heart to share with the world.

Once the twins were tucked in, Leah and Marcus returned outside, cuddling on a porch swing and staring at the dying embers of a fire pit.

"Today was fun," Marcus said, planting a kiss on Leah's cheek.

She couldn't hide a smile. It had been utter chaos. How could it not be, with that many people, that many kids? But she loved being able to host the gathering, being treated like an adult.

"It was," she said wistfully.

As they slowly swung, the realm became calm again. Crickets serenaded the couple, a frog in the distance accompanying them. As full darkness fell, bioluminescent moss on trees in the distance glowed softly.

Leah massaged Marcus's scalp, soaking in the moment. But she had news she couldn't wait any longer to share. "What would you say…" She drew a deep breath. "If I told you I was pregnant?"

"Really?" The level of excitement in his voice was beyond compare. The moonlight lit his face enough to show that excitement.

She beamed. "Really." This one they had planned for. He'd been ready for another one for some time, but she'd needed to mentally prepare herself. Her studies on maternal sickness were helping keep it at bay.

"Not joking?" he asked.

Laying a hand on his chest, she leaned in for a kiss. "I wouldn't joke about that."

He pressed his lips against hers and didn't hold back. They hadn't lost their spark, and she prayed they never would.

Eventually, they pulled themselves apart before the kiss turned into something that led to the bedroom. "What do you want to do about announcing it?" he asked. "About telling the family?"

She caressed his cheek. "I'm letting you decide this time."

"You're sure?"

Her heart beat wildly after that kiss, but her soul was at peace. He was a great father, a great husband. Along with Kaylah, he had helped her understand who she was, what powers she held. Had given her a home and family—what she'd never had growing up, what she'd always wanted and needed.

"Yes." She placed another kiss on his lips. His lips followed hers this time as she leaned back.

"I'm okay with whatever you decide. You mean everything to me." She still recalled what he'd told her when she'd needed it most. "I wouldn't give you up for anything. Not for the realm, not for the world."

~Don't forget to leave a review!~

On Amazon, Goodreads, StoryGraph, and/or anywhere else this book can be found.

Sign up for J. Houser's newsletter for publishing updates, promotions, and bonus content!

JHouserWrites.com

Also, connect with the author here:
On YouTube, TikTok, Facebook, and Instagram under:
JHouserWrites

Next up!

**Born without powers.
Easily forgotten.
Driven to change the
realm.**

Born into the Ivy royal family, Guillen knows what a childhood of privilege can look like. Born without powers, he becomes the shame of his family and the entire kingdom, the object of his mother's wrath.

As a teenager, he's forced to take the mark of a stunt—the cursed—and moves to one of the designated communities in the Ivy Kingdom where those born without powers work hard labor for the rest of their lives.

Only one relative consistently stays in touch—his younger cousin, the future queen. As they grow close, they exchange their discontent with the state of the kingdom, and with the never-ending war against the Seeders. Together they hatch a treasonous plan to start a revolution.

Nobody pays any notice to a weak stunt swept under the rug by the palace. He's not a soldier or politician—what harm could he possibly do?

More by J. Houser

The Green Lands Fantasy Coloring Book allows you to enjoy the magic & nature of the Green Lands realm, as featured in the *Seeder Wars* series!

The *Magic in the Match* series consists of standalone sweet fairy tale romances.

Grab a Trophy Reading Journal, available in both hardback and paperback, or select from a collection of lined and dotted notebooks designed by the author! Books and merch available at **JHouserWrites.com/shop**